Close to You

Christina Dodd

Close to You

DOUBLEDAY LARGE PRINT HOME LIBRARY EDITION

POCKET STAR BOOKS
New York London Toronto Sydney

This Large Print Edition, prepared especially for Doubleday Large Print Home Library, contains the complete, unabridged text of the original Publisher's Edition.

An *Original* Publication of POCKET BOOKS

 A Pocket Star Book published by POCKET BOOKS, a division of Simon & Schuster, Inc.
1230 Avenue of the Americas, New York, NY 10020

ISBN: 0-7394-5263-0

First Pocket Books printing April 2005

POCKET STAR BOOKS and colophon are registered trademarks of Simon & Schuster, Inc.

Cover design by Lisa Litwack
Cover image © Getty Images

Manufactured in the United States of America

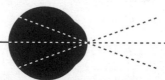

This Large Print Book carries the
Seal of Approval of N.A.V.H.

Prologue

Austin, Texas
Twenty-three years ago

Marilyn Montgomery sat in the straight-backed chair in the office of the adoption agency and stared at the door. This was the moment she'd been waiting for all her married life. She was going to hold a baby—her own baby—in her arms at last.

Skeeter sat shoulder to shoulder with her. God bless him, the big, gruff redneck knew her better than anyone else. Through fourteen years of marriage and innumerable fertility tests, he had been the rock on which she leaned, always joking, kind, and ultimately the most loving man she'd ever met.

Now, knowing exactly how excited she was, he took her hand and squeezed it.

She tried to smile at him, but her lips were trembling too much. What if the baby didn't like her? What if she, Marilyn, didn't know what to do? So much depended on this moment. So much . . .

She'd found the adoption agency in

a magazine, read the testimonials from parents who had been matched with the perfect child, sent letters to a few and received back glowing references. She'd filled out extensive questionnaires about her marriage to Skeeter (his real name was Stephen), their income (high), their educations (he'd graduated from Texas A&M, she from UT; Skeeter was a geologist for an oil company and she had a degree in psychology), and where they lived (in Indonesia, Saudi Arabia, Alaska, or wherever the oil company sent them).

Since this was a church-run adoption agency, she had been surprised there had been no questions about their religion. None of the other church agencies had been so easygoing. But perhaps this church was unusually tolerant—and really, she didn't care, because Pastor Wright had immediately called them with the happy news that he had found them a child. Not an infant, but that was all right. The photo showed a little girl, ten months old, with a faint wisp of hair across her scalp and wide, tearful blue eyes.

Best of all, Marilyn could take her right away. The church agency was satisfied with

Skeeter and Marilyn's references. The baby had been left on a church doorstep with a note pinned to her shirt telling nothing more than her name. Pastor Wright wasn't worried that Skeeter and Marilyn were scheduled to leave the country next week on a job. Pastor Wright pronounced the Montgomerys to be a perfect match with that adorable little girl.

Soon Marilyn would see her baby.

But the clock on the wall ticked so . . . incredibly . . . slowly. The afternoon was growing late, and she was growing too warm and incredibly worried.

"It's okay, honey." Skeeter's normal-sounding voice made Marilyn jump. "Pastor Wright said he'd be just a minute. He's going to get her from the nursery, and then we can have her. Take her home today and she's ours forever. After what we've been through with those other adoption agencies, that's a miracle, I'd say."

"Yes." Marilyn's ears strained to hear footsteps in the hall outside the closed door. Pastor Wright had explained the agency was in the process of moving into the small, previously empty strip mall; any sound had to be Pastor Wright. "He gave us all the paperwork, right? We have it, don't we?"

Skeeter patted his leather briefcase. "We've got her brand-new birth certificate right here, and copies of the adoption documents filed with the state of Texas."

"All right, then." Marilyn rubbed her damp palms on her trousers. "As long as they did a thorough search for the parents. Because I couldn't bear it if her natural parents came back and claimed her."

"Can't happen," Skeeter said easily. "What did he say her name was? Caitlin?"

He was making conversation, trying to ease Marilyn's tension, and she restrained her impulse to snap at him. "That's it."

"You going to change her name?"

Marilyn faced him, surprised. "I can't change her name! She's used to it."

"She isn't used to anything. She's only ten months old. Isn't she sort of like crude oil?"

This time, Marilyn managed a smile. "Like crude oil?"

"Yeah, a big gooey blob ready to be made into whatever we want?" He made a squishing motion with his hands.

"Skeeter, she's already got a personality. She's a person." Suspiciously, Marilyn asked,

"Didn't you read any of the baby books I gave you?"

"Naw." He stretched out his long legs and gave her the slow, gentle grin that had stolen her heart so long ago at the UT/A&M football game. "I figured I'd pick up this father stuff as I go along. My dad did. I came out all right." He squeezed her hand again. "Didn't I?"

"You're all right." She poked him in the ribs. "I guess."

"Damned straight!"

"Don't say 'damned.' " Marilyn never approved of his cursing, and now she had an excuse to stop it. "You can't swear anymore, Skeeter, or the baby will pick up your bad habits."

"Yes, ma'am," he said meekly. "So tell me what the baby's going to do."

"She'll be sitting up, probably walking with help, maybe be able to say a few words." Marilyn's attention returned to the door. "Certainly she'll know her name!"

"Caitlin." Skeeter mulled it over. "It's kinda pretty."

"It is." *What was taking Pastor Wright so long to bring her here?*

"But I'll call her Kate."

"Kate?" Marilyn turned to Skeeter in astonishment. "Why Kate?"

"I like Kate."

And she remembered his grandmother, the one she'd never met, had been named Kate. She remembered, too, that Skeeter wanted this baby as desperately as she did, and that he would be a wonderful father. "I guess that wouldn't confuse the baby too much."

They shared a smile.

The door opened.

Marilyn came to her feet.

Pastor Wright stood there, a man of thirty, tall, blond, and handsome, with striking blue eyes and a rugged profile. He was the kind of guy who could turn a woman's head.

Marilyn barely noticed him. All her attention was on the baby in the blue frilly dress in his arms. In Kate's picture, it hadn't been possible to see the fine grain of her skin—or the blotches caused by hours of crying. Her lower lip trembled, and her eyes filled with tears as she stared at them, more strangers in a life already torn asunder by abandonment.

Marilyn's heart went out to her. She opened her arms. "Oh, my sweet baby."

"Mumumumum." Caitlin launched herself at Marilyn.

At once Marilyn found herself engulfed in the scent of baby powder. Tiny hands closed around her neck and cheap diapers crackled on her arm.

"Mumumumum." The baby could talk.

She was calling Marilyn *Mum,* burying her head in Marilyn's neck and crying as if her heart was broken. As Marilyn cuddled the baby, she barely heard the men talking.

"Part of our policy is to give you a car seat and a diaper bag with the necessities." Pastor Wright looked annoyed, as if carrying the baby had been an ordeal.

"Don't need to worry about that." Skeeter accepted the diaper bag anyway. "Marilyn's brought everything little Kate will need."

"Kate?" For the first time, Pastor Wright looked interested. "Is that what you're going to call her?"

"Thought we would," Skeeter said laconically.

"Kate. Kate Montgomery." Pastor Wright thought about it, and nodded. "That's good."

"Glad you approve." Skeeter steadily watched Pastor Wright. "You want us to sign any more papers? Papers saying we got little Kate? Papers saying we'll let someone come and check up on her?"

"No, no." Pastor Wright waved his hand. "We're satisfied with your references, and I'm a good judge of character. Caitlin—Kate—will be fine with you. I'll walk you out." He shepherded them out and down the echoing hallway.

With both arms wrapped around her precious bundle, Marilyn walked toward the lobby. The baby stopped crying and rested her head on Marilyn's shoulder. Marilyn rubbed her cheek on the soft little head.

"I never asked," Skeeter said. "What kind of minister are you?"

"Congregational." For what seemed like the dozenth time, Pastor Wright asked, "You're going to take Kate out of the country next week?"

"If that's okay with you," Skeeter drawled.

Skeeter's hostile tone pierced Marilyn's contentment. She was surprised, and she was alarmed. What was wrong with Skeeter? He wasn't going to ruin everything now, was he? She was already in love with this baby. She *had* to keep this baby.

She rushed into speech. "We'll take the best care of her. I promise we won't take her anyplace dangerous or ever let her be harmed."

"That's good. I'm glad to hear it." Pastor Wright led them through the lobby and opened the door. The humid heat of a Texas summer rolled in to surround them. He shook hands with Skeeter, then looked at his watch. "Glad we could get this done. I'm running late for another appointment, so . . ."

"Of course." Marilyn watched as he disappeared down the empty hallway, and, in mild surprise, she complained, "He didn't even say good-bye to the baby."

"He doesn't seem to like children much." Skeeter gently slid his finger along little Kate's plump cheek. "Funny sort of a job for him, being a minister and heading up an adoption agency." Then he hurried ahead and opened the car door.

They'd parked in the shade and covered the baby seat with a blanket, but even so it was hot in the confined space, and little Kate gave a wail when Marilyn strapped her in. Marilyn could hardly stand it. In a pleading tone, she asked, "Do you suppose I could hold her in my lap just this once . . . ?"

"Nope. You know it's not safe." Skeeter opened Marilyn's door, took her arm, and helped her inside. "It's not far to home. She'll be okay." He hurried to the driver's side and started the engine.

As he backed out, the air-conditioning kicked in, the baby stopped crying, and Marilyn relaxed. Relaxed long enough to think about the way Skeeter had acted back there. Hostile and questioning, as if he didn't like what was happening. "What were you doing, talking to Pastor Wright like that?" She glared at him. "What's wrong with you?"

Skeeter didn't answer. He drove and stared straight ahead, his usually benign mouth a grim line.

Something was really wrong. "Stephen, what's wrong? Tell me. Is there something not right with Kate? Did you want a son?" In dread, she asked the question she most feared, "Have you changed your mind?"

"What? No! No, it's not that." He glanced at her and gave an unhappy shrug. "That building didn't look like any adoption agency was moving in. Pastor Wright doesn't like children. I don't know, honey bunch. I've got a bad feeling about this. That adoption seemed just a little too damned easy."

One

At twenty-four years of age, Kate Montgomery knew that a minimal hurricane packed winds of at least seventy-four miles per hour.

She knew that the clouds could put down five inches of rain an hour, generate dangerous lightning, and spin off violent tornadoes.

Most of all, she knew that a hurricane's greatest damage and loss of life came from the storm surge, a buildup of the seas that swept away homes, roads, and people who were stupid enough to think that a mere category one hurricane posed no threat and stayed in its path.

Which is why, as she waded into the surf at Galveston and turned to face the television camera, she felt like the biggest fool in Texas.

But someone had to be the sacrificial lamb, and as the cameraman had explained on the way down from Houston, it was always the youngest, prettiest newscaster who got the lousy assignments. Malik had made it clear that viewers liked to see girls with rain-wet hair buffeted by the wind. It was a lousy and indisputable broadcasting truth.

"What did *you* do to deserve this?" she had asked.

"It's the black man's fate to be oppressed," he had answered in mournful tones that didn't fool her at all.

"Plus you're the strongest cameraman at the station and the only one who can hold the camera in this weather." She had peered out the window of the news van at the strengthening storm.

"That, too." He drove them over the causeway and onto the fragile barrier island to join the other news crews as well as the hurricane thrill seekers who'd taken hotel rooms on the island to watch the storm.

Now she stood in the surf up to her ankles. The waves crashed behind her with far too much force and the camera lights showed a roil of foam that blew away with the wind. Her yellow slicker whipped around her legs. Her hood barely protected her from the slashing rain. And fervently she wished someone would tell her news director that if he lost a junior reporter, he would get in trouble.

Or maybe it didn't matter, because there were a hundred pretty young aspiring news reporters who would take her job and gladly wade into the storm-tossed surf for their chance at fame.

She'd worked hard for this chance, graduating from Vanderbilt in Nashville with a degree in political science and broadcasting. Her agent had sent out her résumé and her interview tape and finally he'd found her a job at this station in Houston. None of it had been easy, and she wasn't walking out of the water until they had the shot.

"Ready for the run-through?" she yelled at Malik.

He gave her the thumbs-up. From a safe distance, he lifted the camera onto his shoulder and pointed it at her.

"Three, two, one," she said into the microphone under her chin. Pitching her voice to be heard above the storm's roar, she said, "Here I am on Galveston Island, where once again nature's wrath has taken the beach hostage and transformed this usually placid vacation spot into—" Without warning, a rambunctious wave struck her behind her knees.

She stumbled forward.

Her heart lurched.

The sand shifted beneath her feet.

She flailed her arms like a madwoman and gave a high, girlish screech.

The storm surge rose to engulf her. She almost . . . almost . . . went down into the crashing surf.

She caught herself. The water subsided, sliding back and gathering strength to fling itself at the shore once more.

Minimal hurricane, indeed.

She staggered up onto the beach to see Malik grinning and still filming.

"You big jerk!" Sweat trickled down her back, and her hands trembled. "I could have died."

"No. Worst thing that could have happened was that you drowned the mike." He nodded, once again solemn. "Butch would have been really mad at you about that."

Her sense of humor caught up with her, and she laughed. "That'll go on the blooper reel."

"Oh, yeah, I always win the best of the bloopers award at the Christmas party. Try it again," Malik said, "and this time if a wave comes, I'll warn you."

In Austin, Texas, state senator George Oberlin walked into his dark-paneled, deer-head-decorated game room to find his wife sitting, staring fixedly at the television, apparently fascinated by the news.

"Is the hurricane coming on shore?" he asked without much interest. It wasn't a big hurricane, which meant there wouldn't be intense coverage in the national media. No use going down afterward and surveying the damage unless the nation was watching.

"It's her." Evelyn pointed with her skinny, beringed finger, and the ice cubes rattled in her drink glass.

"Who?" He glanced at his fifty-two-inch screen to see some silly reporter in a yellow slicker standing in the crashing waves, shouting her report against the howl of the wind. Mist coated the camera lens, and he squinted to see the woman's face. "Do we know her?"

"It's . . . it's Lana Prescott." Evelyn might not be slurring her words, but obviously she was already drunk, and it wasn't yet five-thirty.

"Jesus Christ, Evelyn, are you delusional? Lana Prescott's dead." Evelyn was going to prove a liability in his race for the U.S. Senate.

George's campaign manager didn't want him to talk divorce, but better now than later.

"Don't you see it? I tell you, it's Lana Prescott!" Evelyn's whole skinny body was shaking now, shaking as if she were old and palsied—and God knows the booze had been piling the years on her.

"Lana Prescott's been dead for twenty-three years." He knew that better than anyone.

"Yes, I know." Evelyn leaned back against the couch.

She didn't look at him. She didn't take her eyes off the television, and that alone kept him standing there. Normally she gazed at him whenever they were together, her big brown eyes pleading for attention like some kick-dog cocker spaniel's. It was her unusual behavior, and the sighting of a ghost, that made him wonder what was going on in her pickled little brain.

Then the cameraman pulled in for a close-up of the reporter.

A gust of wind swiped the yellow rain hood off the reporter's head.

A cloth came in front of the lens to wipe it clean.

And George saw what Evelyn saw.

Shoulder-length curly hair, black and wet, plastered around sweet features. Wide blue eyes surrounded by long dark lashes that blinked away the rain. A pale, fine-grained complexion and natural pink color on the soft, dimpled cheeks. A petite nose, and that smile . . . a man would bask in the warmth of that smile. He could kill for that smile.

Lana Prescott's smile.

He stepped closer to the television. He didn't remember to use his suave, strong speaking voice; and he heard the Texas country accent when he asked, "What's her name?"

"Kate Montgomery," Evelyn whispered.

"Kate Montgomery," he repeated, and he smiled. "Fancy that. Little Kate Montgomery."

Kate gave another report at ten, only this time the eye of the hurricane was passing overhead, and the relative calm gave her a chance to look professional, or at least less wind whipped. Then she and Malik made their way back to the hotel where all the reporters were staying, and with a cheery wave that indicated her continued good sportsmanship—she hoped—she made her way to her room.

She had sand between her teeth. She had sand on her scalp. She was cold and wet. She wanted a shower. A long, hot shower with lots of shampoo and soap.

But her cell phone on the end table was blinking. She glanced at the phone number recorded there, thinking it would be her mother; instead, it was her agent.

The message on her voice mail said, "No matter when you come in, call me."

Vik sounded calm as always, but he had never done business except during business hours, and she couldn't imagine what emergency required that she call right away.

Her mom . . . but no, that was silly. If something was wrong, Kate would be hearing from a totally different source. She was just nervous after what had happened to her dad.

But she carried the phone into the bath-room, and while she toed off her boots, she hit the talk button.

Vik picked up right away. Brief as always, he said, "I've had an offer for a job for you."

"What?" She wasn't looking for a job. She was looking for a shower. "At this hour?"

"Someone in Austin saw your hurricane report, and now Brad Hasselbeck at KTTV is offering you a position covering the capi-tol. He said they wanted to make an offer before another station grabbed you."

She blinked. "I could barely find a job in the first place. Now someone's worried about a bidding war?"

"Let's not tell him there is no bidding war. Let's take the job."

Everything about this was unlike Vik. The hour, the rush to accept . . . "Why? I just started the Houston job. You said it was a great starter position."

"It was. This is better."

"Better?" Leaning over the tub, she ran the water until it was warm. A shower. She desperately needed a shower. "How bet-ter?"

"Brad saw your coverage of the hurricane and said you looked great. He knows you've got political science and broadcasting degrees. He seems to think that makes you the perfect candidate to cover the capitol."

"How did he know all that?"

"I suppose he still had your résumé." She could hear the frown in Vik's voice. "The offer is good. Twice the money you're making now. You'll be in Austin, which you wanted in the first place."

"Yes, I wanted to be close to Mom, but—" The significance of what he said sank in. "Twice the money?"

"That's what I said. Twice the money."

"That seems too good to be true, and my dad always said if something seems too good to be true, it usually is." But she wanted to do more serious reporting than weather and parades, and the state capitol sounded challenging. Interesting.

Her dream job.

"I know. That's what I thought, but I've placed a client with him before, so I called her. She's gone on to a San Francisco station, so she hasn't worked with him for about a year, but she said Brad was good to work for, no perversions, totally dedicated to the business. If anything, he's a workaholic who doesn't have time for anything but the job. Apparently, he's almost manic about the job."

So Vik had done his best to ameliorate his doubts, and hers. "It's so tempting."

"It's more than tempting, it's perfect. In the city you want, in the position you want, for twice the money. Kate, if you turn this down, you'll be the biggest fool in Texas."

Two

With his beer belly, his receding hairline, and his small brown eyes, Brad Hasselbeck looked like the bad southern sheriff in a seventies movie. His windows looked out over West Austin's rolling streets. His office was decorated with an early Coca-Cola vending machine, videotapes, and seven televisions all showing something different. His hand hovered over the remote controls, his gaze flicked from screen to screen, and Kate had the impression he was keeping track of every one of them—and her.

But his smile was wide and welcoming, and he ground out his cigarette in his overflowing ashtray shaped like the state of Texas. "Miss Montgomery—"

"Please, call me Kate."

"We like to have a little decorum here at KTTV, so I'll call you Miss Montgomery. But you call me Brad." His West Texas accent removed any sting from the comment. "Welcome to KTTV. We're glad to have someone of your caliber. Have you been able to find your way around our great city?"

"Yes, I know Austin well." Kate knew the right answer to give. "My mother lives here, so you can send me wherever you need a reporter and I'll be able to find—"

"Good." He still wasn't looking directly at her. "You're probably living with your mama then."

"No, we live apart." How odd that he would think they'd live together!

His sharp glance darted to her, did a quick up and down, then returned to the screens. His gaze wasn't insulting or sexist, more analytical, as if he was weighing her, judging her . . . really observing her for the first time.

How strange. If he wanted her so much as a reporter, she would have thought he'd be done with his assessment. She hoped he hadn't changed his mind. "I rented a town house in a converted warehouse downtown."

"You should be safe enough."

"I would think so." What an odd comment, but then, Kate was beginning to think Brad was an odd man. "Mom wanted me to live with her, but—"

"Right. Right. You need your space, blah,

blah. Young, free, et cetera. We're going to have you work the capitol. The Senate is in special session, won't go on break until Thanksgiving or the governor declares they're done." Standing, Brad hefted his brown leather belt over his belly, and gestured through the wide windows into the newsroom where he could see each and every desk and each and every reporter— and Kate would bet he kept track of them, too. "I'm sending you over with Linda Nguyen so you can learn the ropes. Come on, I'll find her for you." With a gait like John Wayne's, he rolled out of his office.

She followed him down the hallway and wondered if anyone ever got to finish a sentence around Brad.

As they stepped into the newsroom, silence fell. Kate shot a smile around, but it wasn't returned. Not by anybody. Everyone, every single person in the newsroom, stared at her, flinty-eyed and hostile.

Her smile faltered.

She'd dressed carefully for her first day at work. Black pants, white shirt, midnight blue jacket, and everything cut without a hint of sexuality. Her heels made her legs look long and lifted her up enough to give her confidence when looking people in the eyes. Her makeup was subdued, her hair blown smooth and brushing her shoulders. She was the epitome of the perfect reporter. So why did they look at her as if she were a bug smashed on the windshield?

"This is Kate Montgomery, our new capitol reporter. You all make her welcome." Brad looked around, and his voice contained a threat as he added, "A good Austin welcome."

"Hi, Kate."

"Hey, Kate, good to have you in Austin."

"Good to meet you, Kate."

Each welcoming word was delivered in a monotone; the insincerity was palpable, and not even Brad's glare produced anything more than glances sidling away.

Kate didn't understand the enmity. Sure, this was a competitive business, but never had she felt so awkward.

"Here's your desk, your phone, your computer." Brad indicated a space beside the window. "You won't be here much. The happenings up at the capitol should keep you plenty busy."

"Good." Especially if the crew was always this surly.

"Linda, here's your trainee." He stopped by the desk of a young Asian woman and rapped on it with his knuckles. "Get Miss Montgomery out there, show her around. Introduce her to the right people."

"Sure, whatever you say." Petite, dark-eyed, with sleek black hair and the taut muscled body of a reporter whose job depended on her looks and her ability to chase criminals while wearing four-inch heels, Linda stacked papers, turned off her computer, and stood in one graceful motion.

"I say she better be up and running by next week." Kate jumped as Brad yelled, "Sonovabitch!" and pointed at the monitors clearly visible through the windows of his office. "Bomb scare at an elementary school!" He wheeled and headed for his office. "Roberts! Potter! Get in here!"

Two reporters slapped their work aside and hurried after him.

With his departure, the temperature in the newsroom dropped from cold to frigid.

"Come on, Miss Montgomery," Linda said.

"I've been waiting for you to get here, and now I'm late for a hearing."

As if it were Kate's fault!

Without a backward glance, Linda walked out to the elevator.

Everyone in the newsroom bustled with patently fake business, and they said not a word. If ever there was proof something was wrong, it was that, for newsrooms were never silent.

Determined to get to the bottom of the situation, Kate joined Linda at the elevator.

"You take your car; I'll take mine." Linda punched the call button. "Since you'll probably be leaving early." As if it would hurry the elevator, she punched the call button again.

"Why would I leave early?" Kate asked coolly.

"I can't imagine you want to hang around for the *real* work."

"You can't?" When Kate was in grade school, her mom had taught her how to deal with females untrained in the social graces.

"Look. Let's not pretend." Linda punched the button again, then looked surprised when the doors opened. "You're one of those girl reporters who make it on your looks, your expensive haircut, and your capped teeth." She stepped inside.

Kate followed, her indignation rising.

"I spent ten years covering blizzards in Chicago and debutante balls in North Carolina before I earned the right to cover the Texas state capitol." Linda jabbed the button for the ground floor, then punched the close-door button, then jabbed the ground-floor button again. "Now Brad creates a position for you so you can waltz in and take the glamour job. I don't know who you know, and I can't do anything about having to teach you the ropes." The elevator began its glide down to the ground floor. "But I don't have to like it, and I don't have to like you, and I don't have to pretend."

I don't know anyone. But what was the use of saying so? Linda wouldn't believe it. No one at the station would believe it.

"Are you going to run to Brad and tattle on me?" When the doors opened, Linda strode out of the elevator and turned to face Kate, her hands on her hips, a short, belligerent Vietnamese American with a righteous attitude and a blue silk suit that Kate coveted.

Kate's mother was a southern lady steeped in courtesy and elegance. Her father had been a man given to blunt honesty and plain speaking.

Kate was her mother's daughter—but at that moment her father's spirit took possession of her. "No, I'm not going to tattle on you. I'm going to go to the capitol and make contacts, and within two years everybody in Austin is going to know that I'm the best reporter who ever covered this beat."

Linda's jaw dropped.

"Anything you want to tell me? Like where to park or who to avoid because he's *your* contact? I'd hate to embarrass you, and I'd really hate to win by taking unfair advantage with my expensive haircut and capped teeth." Kate smiled, showing the sharp points of the teeth that had seen years of braces but no caps.

Linda's mouth snapped shut.

"By the way, if you like, I'll give you the name of my personal shopper." With another brilliant smile, Kate headed for her car, a sporty BMW coupe. As she sank into the leather seat and shut the door, she could imagine what Linda was thinking.

Rich, spoiled, untalented.

In the protected confines, Kate drew a long breath and pressed her cold hands to her hot cheeks. Damn! She'd pinned so many hopes on this job, worried about why she'd got it and what could go wrong, but this . . . this bitter personal resentment had never occurred to her. Sure, she'd come from a wealthy family and that had given her an advantage in being able to afford the tuition at any university she chose. But she'd worked hard to get into Vanderbilt, and studied hard to graduate at the top of her class. Sure, she knew people, but she hadn't tapped anyone to get a job, quite the opposite. And as for Brad creating a position for her—she didn't believe it. Why would he do that?

Set in the heart of Austin, the red granite of the capitol rose four stories and faced south at the end of Congress Avenue. The basement was connected to an underground mall to the north, which housed the Senate and legislative offices, and underground passages veered off to the state supreme court building and the buildings that housed various state agencies. The area was green with well-tended lawns and late-blooming flowers. Everything about the area was lovely and well planned—except the parking, which was a joke. The scramble for parking involved permits and assigned spaces and lots of asphalt striped with white lines. The few garages were reserved for visitors and legislators—even when the legislature wasn't in session. Kate followed Linda into a parking lot.

As Linda led Kate through the humid September heat toward the entrance to the underground mall, she said, "Usually, this time of year, there's not much going on, but the governor called a special session for school financing. Luckily for us the debates are heated and partisan." They headed down the stairway toward the Senate Finance Chamber. "The clerks and interns give us some of our best information. Don't step into an empty room with any of the senators unless you're prepared to fight for your virtue. Don't screw up." Linda's smile at the gentleman opening the door for them was at complete odds with her sharp tone. "Brad'll blame me."

"Remember, Miss Nguyen, after today we hardly have to see each other." The blast of air-conditioning took Kate's breath away. She walked quickly down the corridor, her long strides leaving Linda eating her dust.

Linda caught up with her in a hurry and steered her into the path of a short gray-haired man clad in a tan suit. "Representative Rimmer, this is our new reporter . . ." She pretended to forget Kate's name.

Kate stepped forward and shook his hand. "Representative Rimmer, I'm Kate Montgomery."

He heartily proclaimed, "How good to meet Miss Nguyen's replacement."

That did it. "I'm not her replacement." Kate could feel waves of heat coming off the fuming Linda. "She's showing me around."

"That's right, but Kate has a political science degree." Linda injected just enough scorn into her praise to turn it sour.

Pride whipped along Kate's nerves. *And a degree in broadcasting.* Again, a waste of time to defend herself. She would stand or fall according to her performance, not her qualifications. As a small crowd gathered, she widened her eyes in false innocence. "That's how I know the difference between the House and the Senate."

Representative Rimmer bellowed with laughter, a big laugh for such a short man.

"Very good." A gray-haired Hispanic woman listened to the exchange, then extended her hand to Kate. "We find education improves the coverage."

Kate recognized her at once. "Senator Martinez, I'm privileged to make your acquaintance." Kate meant it. The one female senator in the Texas capitol, Senator Martinez was a woman who had taken the seat on her husband's death and never relinquished it through twenty years of redistricting and partisan mayhem.

Senator Martinez took the time to chat with Kate. So did Senator Rimmer and two legislators who stopped by. It seemed reporters were important cogs in the wheels of government, especially young, single female reporters, and Kate worked hard to make a good first impression.

She glanced up once to see Linda standing on the periphery, smiling tightly, and when she did, another man caught her eye.

He was a good-looking man of fifty-something, his thick blond hair swept into a stiff Bill Clinton–style cut. His charismatic smile flashed, and for the briefest of moments, his blue eyes burned as he watched Kate.

She took a breath, startled by the heat of his gaze.

Then he smiled genially, and the impression of fire dissipated. He stepped forward, and the crowd parted to let him through.

Linda's voice contained a tone of respect when she said, "Senator Oberlin, this is the new reporter for KTTV, Kate Montgomery."

"Kate." His voice was deep, pleasant, without a trace of a Texas accent, and Kate guessed he'd taken the same kind of voice training reporters used. "How good to meet you." He shook her hand, and his touch lingered a second too long.

Oh. He was one of those. One of the guys who imagined his position made him attractive to women. Carefully she removed her fingers from his, and concentrated on the cool intellect he so skillfully displayed and the deference with which he was treated.

"I want you to have the chance to meet one of the most important people at the capitol." He extended his hand outside of the circle. "Mr. Duarte, come and meet our newest reporter."

Mr. Duarte hobbled forward. A name

badge on his uniform identified him as JANITOR. He looked frail, but he wasn't nearly as old as she first thought; pain, she suspected, caused the aging. He offered a warped, arthritic hand.

She took it carefully.

"Mr. Duarte is from Louisiana," Senator Oberlin said.

"I'm a Cajun," Mr. Duarte added proudly, his thick accent verifying his claim.

"And a Korean War veteran," Senator Oberlin continued. "Anything you want to know about the capitol and the politics, he can tell you."

"I'm pleased to meet you, Mr. Duarte. My dad was a Vietnam War vet."

His shrewd, blue eyes surveyed her. "You've lost him?"

"Five years ago, he died overseas." Her smile twisted. "He was an oilman." She heard a few people take a breath. They remembered, and she was sorry she'd let her empathy with Mr. Duarte lead to her confession.

"Your dad was the Stephen Montgomery who was captured and killed by terrorists?" Linda looked stunned—and dismayed.

"Yeah." Kate kept her gaze on Mr. Duarte. "But my mom lives here in Austin."

"That's good." Mr. Duarte's eyes warmed. "You stay close to your mama." He glanced around. "Guess I'd better get back to work. How about the rest of you all?"

A round of laughter followed his pointed comment, and the crowd drifted away.

Kate watched Mr. Duarte hobble off, then turned to Senator Oberlin. "Thank you for introducing me to him."

"He'll help you find your way around." Carefully, Senator Oberlin said, "I'm open to having you do a piece on me, too. Of course, any politician here would like to have a piece done on him or her. We're all publicity hounds."

"I'll remember that." He really was very handsome, very smooth. He might be interested in her, or he might just be the kind of man who easily created intimacy with people without seeking anything other than a vote.

"The committee meeting is starting on the hour." He glanced at his watch, then at Linda. "I'd love to see you in there. I'd really like public support for this measure."

"That's exactly where we're going," Linda

assured him with a smile. "Come on, Kate." Her smile disappeared as they walked down the corridor. In an undertone, she said, "Okay, now you know Senator Oberlin. He's fifty-six, from Hobart, a little town of ten thousand about a hundred miles south of here. He's been a senator for over twenty-five years. He keeps it quiet, but he has a lot of power. He married money, too." She glanced sideways at Kate. "He always swoops in and makes good with the re-porters."

"Lovely," Kate said sincerely. So she had imagined his interest.

"There's been maneuvering to get him nominated to the U.S. Senate, but he keeps saying he wants to stay in Texas."

"Hm." The wisdom about state politicians asserted that they stayed local only if they were hiding a scandal big enough to keep them out of a federal position.

Linda read her mind. "No scandals. I think he's got plans to make an announcement at the appropriate moment."

"All right." Kate glanced back to see him, trim and fit in an Armani suit.

He stood still, his hands on his hips under

the elegant cut of his suit coat, and watched them walk away.

And again she dismissed the stirring of unease. "I'll remember him."

Three

It was Wednesday. Kate had been on the job three days.

During the daylight hours, she smiled so much her lips felt frozen. At night, she studied everything about the special session: school funding, who was voting for what, what the teachers were saying, what the governor was saying. She discovered Linda wasn't particularly well liked at the capitol, not because she got the facts wrong, but because she got them right and gave them to the public without resorting to high-flown rhetoric.

Kate felt as if she'd stepped into a different world; she also felt as if she'd come home.

In the early afternoon she called for a cameraman, and Brad sent her Cathy Stone, a tall, broad-shouldered woman who wore a baseball cap and handled the camera with a careful efficiency. In Zen-like silence, she watched Kate line up her interviews in the capitol rotunda.

"What do you think you're doing?" Linda hurried toward them wearing the highest heels and the tightest skirt Kate had ever seen. "Where are you going with my cameraman? Why?"

"Legislator Howell says the Republicans had a secret meeting about changing the school district structure for the state." Kate directed Legislator Howell on where to stand while she asked him questions.

"It's a lie," Linda said automatically. With a glance at Legislator Howell, she corrected herself. "It's an exaggeration."

"Mr. Duarte sneaked me into the meeting. I've got photos. Now if you'll excuse me." Kate produced an insincere smile for Linda, then turned back to her task.

During each interview, she could feel the heat of Linda's glare between her shoulder blades until at last, when she had drawn every bit of information from her sources, she turned to glare back at Linda.

But Linda wasn't there. Instead, the inevitable crowd of people hoping to get on camera had gathered. There was a wide-eyed child and its mother, two Japanese gentlemen carrying briefcases, a thin young woman in a mechanical wheelchair, and slouching in the background was a tall man, Hispanic, about twenty-five years old. He wore dirty jeans that clung low on his lean hips. His black T-shirt had cutoff sleeves that displayed tanned skin, heavily muscled arms, and broad shoulders. He'd tied a gaudy purple-and-red silk jacket around his waist. His dark hair hung around his neck. He had a white scar that slashed across his brown cheek and a mustache, and his eyes . . . he had the most beautiful rich golden-brown eyes Kate had ever seen in her life. Beautiful—and cold. Cruel. They were narrowed on her now.

Twenty-five years old? No. She changed her estimate. Thirty, perhaps older, and tough. Frightening. Too old to be a gang leader. Drug dealer? No, that jacket was too bright for someone who wanted to remain in the shadows.

Then he smiled, a sharp slice of danger.

Her breath caught.

Without saying a word, he offered her sex. Without pretty words, without *any* words, he offered their two naked bodies intertwined in steamy passion.

And without words, she knew that sex with this—this brute would be a blast of heat, swiftly done, swiftly over. Satisfying. And when they were done, they would do it again. Something about the way he stood, the shape of his broad torso, the mocking lift of his smile, told her that he would be insatiable.

With him, she would be insatiable, too.

Her face flooded with heat. She wasn't that kind of woman. Strange men didn't appeal to her. She didn't understand raw sexuality. She was untouched by grand passion. Modest, disciplined . . . normal. So very, very normal.

She turned her shoulder to him and thanked everyone who had talked to her.

When she glanced back in his direction, he was gone.

But as she and Cathy walked toward the station truck to edit the tape, Cathy said, "Not that there weren't the usual quota of vidiots there, but that one guy—he stared at you. I'd keep an eye out over the next few days, and if he shows up again, I'd talk to the police."

"So it wasn't my imagination?" Kate knew it wasn't.

"Shit, no, and he looked like he can hold his own in a knife fight." Cathy looked down at Kate. "He scared the crap out of *me,* and you're a lot smaller."

"Then he officially scares me, too," Kate declared.

Linda was already in the station truck editing her piece, and Kate had to wait until it was almost too late to get hers done. But she did, and sent it to the station. Brad approved it so quickly Linda almost audibly gnashed her teeth, and Kate caught Cathy grinning. Then Kate went back inside the capitol, gave the live report, and went back to the station to watch as the e-mails flooded in.

Who's the new girl?

She looks stupid.

She looks smart.

She needs a makeover. May I suggest Luella's House of Beauty on the corner of Pine and Third?

Kate's first real day of reporting for the Austin station had been a success. She smiled at the tight-lipped crew at the station, then drifted home, knowing that she'd done a good job.

The next day, to celebrate, she watched everything go to hell in a handbasket.

In the morning, Senator Richardson

started a filibuster that ran thirteen hours. Linda, who obviously saw the handwriting on the wall, went home sick. The other reporters for the other stations drifted away as the day wore on, but then they had nothing to prove. Kate covered the whole, dreadful pile of stinking rhetoric, hoping for a breakthrough that no one else was there to catch, and when she finished she had not one viable moment of tape.

She staggered out of the capitol building at nine. Twilight was fading, the streetlights were on, and all she wanted was to go home and soak in a hot tub until her poor feet no longer resembled Barbie's feet in heels. She walked alone, but she wasn't fearful. She had lived in so many countries, gone to so many different schools, and made so many different friends, she was confident in almost every situation.

But when she got to her car, it was sitting crooked. It took a minute before she realized—she had a flat. And another minute before she realized—someone had slashed her tire.

She stood staring in disbelief at the rubbery shreds, and her mind, numbed by hours of oratory, leaped and twisted in sudden fear.

She was alone in the parking lot.

A man had watched her the day before, a Hispanic man with eyes so cold she had flinched from their cruelty and their sexuality. Kate was startled by the clarity with which she remembered him—the height, the sensuality, the menace.

Maybe he hadn't slit her tire with the express purpose of finding and raping her, or murdering her, but she wasn't taking any chances. In the gathering darkness, she pulled her cell phone from the inner pocket of her jacket.

While she dialed, she dug through her purse for her Mace. She was going to call the police, and if anyone tried to hurt her, she was going to spray the bastard right between the eyes.

"Miss Montgomery? Is something wrong?"

She turned too quickly, the Mace clutched in her upraised fingers.

"Whoa!" Senator Oberlin stopped five feet away, his hands upraised. "I didn't mean to startle you."

"No. You didn't. That is . . ." It *wasn't* the man with the cold eyes, yet in the twilight and the loneliness, the shape of him seemed menacing and overbearing.

Then, as he spoke, the illusion dissolved. "That's your car?" He *tsk*ed in disgust. "I've been telling the legislature we need some protection out here for our reporters, but nothing will happen. Those guys understand concealed weapons but not common sense."

Kate leaned a hand against the hood. Her imagination, usually so inactive, had transferred guilt to Senator Oberlin. Senator Oberlin, the man who had made her uncomfortable with his attentions and his touch that had lingered too long. "It would be better if there was a guard," she said.

"Since nine-eleven, the capitol has a contract with a private security company." He discarded his suit jacket and rolled up his sleeves. "They supply undercover guards who patrol the capitol. But they patrol only the buildings, and that leaves me out here to protect you. Now, Miss Montgomery, when I was a teenager, I worked in a gas station. I haven't changed a tire in about thirty years, but I bet I remember how."

Now her hand did go to her phone. "Senator, please, let me call a service to change it."

Faintly, she could see that his eyes twinkled. "I suppose you think I'm too old to use a jack."

"No, sir! That's not what I thought at all. You're in great shape." He was. She'd noted that. Not an ounce of fat around his belly, and his bare forearms were strongly muscled. "But you're dressed too well to be kneeling in a parking lot."

Opening the trunk, he extracted the jack and the tire. "Consider it a favor done with the express purpose of having you return the favor."

She must be really tired, for again the image of rape and murder rampaged through her mind, and Linda's warning—*Don't go into a hearing room with a senator unless you want to wrestle for your virtue*—rang in her mind.

"Someday I'll need some coverage for one of my bills." Kneeling beside her tire, he efficiently removed the nuts.

Relief filled her, then dismay. "Sir, I can't promise that," she said faintly.

"Then you can go out and get me a hamburger next time there's a filibuster." He wrestled the flat off and replaced it with the spare. He worked efficiently, spinning the wheel and tightening the nuts with the tire iron.

She relaxed. That Hispanic man yesterday had gotten under her skin. Everywhere she looked she saw trouble, even when none existed. "Wendy's or McDonald's?"

"I've got a better idea. My wife and I are giving a party next week. Perhaps you can come. September nineteenth. It's our anniversary, our twenty-fifth, and we're planning a big bash." He sounded genial, hospitable. He lowered the jack, threw the slashed tire into the trunk, and used his handkerchief to clean his fingers. "Bring a friend."

She couldn't think of a reason why not. Didn't see any harm in going to a party that would undoubtedly include other reporters and perhaps contacts that would help her. Plus, she really did owe him. She wouldn't have wanted to wait alone for the auto club to come out and change her tire. "I'd be delighted to attend. Thank you, Senator—for everything."

"I don't know, Mom." Kate cleared the dirty dishes off the carved Indonesian table in her mother's elegant high-rise town house. "In Houston, the station manager was a jerk and everyone else was nice. At KTTV, the station manager is fine, and all the reporters treat me like dirt."

"Is he cute?" her mother asked automatically. She had cooked one of her fabulous dinners to celebrate Kate's first week on the job, and now she let Kate do the cleanup while she sipped a small glass of port.

"Who?"

"The station manager."

"Brad? E-uw, no." Kate thought of the thick scent of tobacco that hung in the air around Brad, and reiterated, "E-uw."

"Too bad." Her mother reacted to Kate's single status like a bull to a red flag. "You need to have a social life."

"No, I need to find enough stories so that bitch Linda Nguyen has to be nice to me." Kate piled the silverware onto the plates with a little too much vigor.

"Don't say 'bitch.' If you're going to abuse the china, you can leave the dishes for the housekeeper tomorrow. And . . . wait . . . Linda Nguyen?" Mom was diverted. "I've seen her reports. I like her a lot."

"Well, she doesn't like *me.*" Kate handled the dishes with a little more care.

"You'll win her over." The two women shared a smile. A handsome woman of fifty-eight, Marilyn Montgomery was a slender, well-groomed brunette who kept herself in shape by working out at the gym and doing fund-raising for every charity that sent her an appeal. She was good at it, too, organizing parties ruthlessly and squeezing money out of corporations with finesse and charm. She served on the board for the Austin Symphony and as the chair-man of the Breadwinner's Shelter for Homeless Children.

Her mother had always believed in her. Her father had always believed in her. Believed she could do whatever she wanted, be whatever she wanted. That was the real reason Kate had to succeed. She wanted to fulfill their faith in her—and her own faith in herself. She might be an orphan. She might be the daughter of a frightened teenager or a prostitute. But she was strong. She would succeed. "If I don't win them over, I'll still do my job."

"Of course. You are your father's daughter."

It was the pain and tragedy of Skeeter Montgomery's death that had brought about the extremely close relationship between Kate and her mother. No two women could go through the agony of knowing the man they loved had been captured by terrorists, was perhaps being tortured, was perhaps being killed . . . When, after two months of waiting, his body had been found, it had almost been a relief to know for sure.

That was the worst part of all, that the confirmation of his death was a relief.

Since her father had been killed five years ago, her mother had been prone to anxiety. She had made a home for them in Nashville while Kate attended Vanderbilt. Kate had never admitted it, but having her mother keeping track of her so closely during her college years had felt restrictive. When Kate landed the job in Houston, her mother's decision to return to her hometown of Austin had come as a complete surprise. "You're going to be okay living by yourself now, won't you, honey?" her mother had asked. "You're not afraid anymore, are you?"

And Kate had realized that she *had* been

afraid . . . and that the time with her mother had healed her.

Her mom was the greatest, smartest person in the world.

"I'm my mother's daughter, too." Kate headed for the kitchen with the stack of dishes. "If you hadn't taught me how to break someone's kneecaps with a velvet stick, I wouldn't have done nearly so well this week. The capitol is everything I expected."

"Corrupt?" Mom followed, amused.

"And fascinating." The committee rooms with their seal of Texas at the head of the room, the broad staircases curving up and down, the official bustle of the Senate in session. "I've met so many people. Only a few even stand out. I did meet Senator Martinez. And Senator Oberlin. Do you know him?"

Her mom shook her head. "No, but government bores me. Is he important?"

"Linda says he has a lot of power."

"Is *he* cute?"

Kate rolled her eyes. "Old and married for twenty-five years."

"Oh." Mom subsided. "If you're not going to find yourself a nice boy, I'll have to do it for you. Dean Sanders is quite the catch. He's handsome. He's a lawyer with MacMillan and Anderson. He knows his way around Austin society."

"And?" Kate waited for the other shoe to drop.

"He's divorced, but his mother says that his wife caused the problems and that he's ready to date again."

"No. Please, no." Going to her mother, Kate wrapped her arms around her and gave her a hug. "Really, Mom. No. I don't want a guy who's getting over a divorce."

"But his mother says—"

"She's lying. You know she is."

"I suppose," her mom said irritably. "But he's a good man. He deserves someone like you."

"There's only one of me," Kate said with humor. "Not all the men can be lucky."

She left by nine—"Tomorrow's a workday, Mom." Darkness had fallen by the time she hurried to her car, which was parked in a visitor's space at the front of the building.

She heard a sound behind her. A hushed step, a brief brush of cloth against metal. She turned, expecting to see her mother hurrying after her with an extra helping of Cornish hen.

She saw no movement. A few parked cars, some nicely planted bushes, a few flowers . . .

A cat, perhaps. Or a squirrel. Something.

Still she scanned the sidewalk behind her.

There was nothing there. With a shrug, she got into her car and drove home.

That night, Kate's phone rang at two A.M. Barely awake, she fumbled for the receiver, her heart pounding in her throat.

Was it Mom? Had they gotten Mom, too?

When she picked it up, no one was there. The line was open, but no one spoke, no one breathed. She hung up and got out of bed.

Caller ID showed: "Private caller."

She dismissed the call as a mistake.

She got a drink of water and looked at herself in the mirror.

She hated this. One call in the middle of the night, and all the fear and anguish of her dad's kidnapping came rushing back. All the memories paraded through her mind. They were nightmares come to life, and no matter how hard she tried, nothing could erase them.

She went back to bed, and an hour later, she had just drifted back to sleep when her cell phone rang. She got up and looked at the phone, but she didn't answer this time. Again it read: "Private caller."

Coincidence, probably. A bad coincidence since both numbers were unlisted and un-published, but a coincidence nevertheless.

When her home phone rang again at five A.M., she let the answering machine pick it up. A low, growly, disguised voice said, "Leave, bitch."

And quietly hung up.

That day, to cover the dark circles under her eyes, Kate wore extra makeup.

Two nights later she left the capitol to discover a slap of whitewash on her car window.

In shaky letters, it spelled out, *Leave, bitch.*

Kate stared at the message. Her heart pounded in her throat. Her temples tightened with fear. She whipped around to check for onlookers, but none of the people who strolled past paid her any attention.

Yet she had to face the truth.

She had a stalker.

She just didn't know what to do about it.

She hadn't yet had the nerve to call the police. Despite Brad's assurances about her work—she'd scooped every other station in Austin on two more stories—there wasn't a doubt in her mind that every reporter at KTTV would love to see her fail. If she announced she had a stalker, she'd be regarded as a grandstander, and the laughter that went on behind her back would turn around to blare in her face. She couldn't bear to make things worse.

Yet Kate knew the facts. She knew that stalkers loved to target the "girl" reporters. Stalkers were unstable, and although hers hadn't done anything violent yet, the incidents were likely to escalate, possibly to serious crimes—to rape and murder.

More important, she was afraid all the time.

She suspected everyone.

The Hispanic man—he knew how to frighten a woman with a glance.

Senator Oberlin—something about him had made her uncomfortable right away, and he'd conveniently come to her rescue in the parking lot. Perhaps he'd arranged to have the tire slashed so he could approach her.

Linda—she was jealous and spiteful.

Brad, Cathy, everyone Kate met, every teenager who toured the capitol and recognized her as a broadcaster, every man who looked her over and flirted.

Even now, with the sun barely setting toward the west, she glanced behind her as she crossed the street behind the capitol complex. She had never been like this before, and she knew that, laughter or no laughter, mockery or no mockery, she had to contact the police. Now.

No job was worth dying for.

As she crossed the white line in the middle of the road, she heard a motor rev, tires screech. A gray car careened around the corner—straight toward her.

She dove toward the sidewalk. She landed hard. She rolled, frantic. Panic scraped her mind with sharp claws. *Get away! He's after you!*

But the car kept going. It wavered from one side of the street to another, out of control, almost overturning. Then it righted, and its tires threw up a pall of black smoke as it raced away.

Kate didn't know if she'd been hit or just landed hard. She didn't know if she could catch her breath. She sprawled on the sidewalk, one fingernail broken and bloody, her palms skinned, her pants torn at the knee. She blinked as black specks darkened her vision, and she fought back nausea.

"What the hell . . . ?"

Kate heard that sharp, impatient voice and lifted her head.

Linda knelt beside Kate, her dark eyes flashing with impatience. "What the hell just happened?"

"Someone tried to hit me." Crimson splattered the sidewalk beneath Kate's head. She touched her chin, and her fingers came away covered with blood.

"Don't be dramatic." Linda pulled out her cell phone. As she dialed 911, she said, "Whoever did it was probably drunk. I didn't get the license plate, but it was a gray Infiniti sedan, a G35, I think."

Pain was starting to seep through Kate's shock.

"I couldn't see the driver, the windows were tinted." Linda must have connected with the operator, for she said into the phone, "I need an ambulance on the corner of Fifteenth Street and San Jacinto. There's been a hit-and-run accident—"

"No." Kate shook her head heavily. "No. This was no accident."

Slowly Linda pulled the phone away from her ear. "What do you mean?"

"I've got a stalker." Kate finally admitted it aloud. "I'm being stalked."

Four

"Here's what we're going to do." In his office Monday morning, Brad rapidly typed an
e-mail with two short, pudgy index fingers.
"We're going to assign you to a story on
the premier bodyguard service in town.
Ramos Security provides security for the
capitol. Their bodyguards handle all the visiting honchos and escort the local society
ladies whenever they wear their big diamonds."

Kate stood before his desk and listened
and nodded. She had bandages on her
hands and knees and stitches closing the
cut on her chin. She wore a cream turtle-
neck sweater, a dark brown tweed knee-
length skirt, and a severely cut, matching
brown tweed jacket. The formality of the
outfit armored her with confidence, a confidence she usually sported in abundance. A
confidence that had been badly shaken.

Besides, the long sleeves and the dark
stockings covered her bruises. She sported
an especially large purple bruise on her hip

where she had apparently been hit by the car. "I'd like to know why I was the lucky one," she said bitterly.

"Now, don't you worry about this stalker picking you out of the litter of reporters. I've seen this happen before. These guys—and they're always guys—are weirdos who get fixated on a broadcaster—always a new young broadcaster—and start being annoying."

"Annoying?" She looked down at her bandaged hands.

"Yeah, this one's downright dangerous. But they're never too bright, so we catch 'em fast." He shot her a sharp glance. "Especially when the broadcaster is smart enough to recognize the problem and turn 'em in."

"I'd say I waited about one car incident too long."

"That's true, too." He hit send and leaned back in his seat. "If you'd said something a few days sooner, you wouldn't have been hit, and you would have been looking good enough to continue your reports. We're going to have to wait at least a week before we put you back on camera."

"I know. I'm sorry."

He grunted, obviously unhappy at the turn of events.

Kate gazed out at the newsroom where everyone was working on a real story, a breaking story. "Everyone's been kind, though." Interestingly enough, they had been. Evidently Linda's brisk dismissal of Kate's problems had been her way of expressing concern, for she had stuck with Kate through her time in the emergency room and her interview with the police, and Linda must have said the right stuff to the people at the television station, for everyone had seemed shocked, and a few of them actually offered Kate spontaneous expressions of sympathy.

"Yeah, they're good people." Brad lit a cigarette. "I'm going to have you follow the guy who owns the bodyguard service, Teague Ramos. You tail him through his week's activities, longer if it takes longer to catch this stalker"—obviously, Brad figured a week was plenty of time—"and get together enough information to do a piece on him and how he operates."

"When's it going to run?" Kate asked, always the reporter.

Brad shot her another sharp glance. "Two

minutes in the five o'clock time, and I'll give you six minutes on the Sunday-morning *Here's Austin* program."

"All right." Two minutes at five was okay, nothing like two minutes at the premier six and ten slots, but five was when all the human-interest stories ran, and doing a story on the owner of a bodyguard service was definitely human interest. The Sunday-morning show was a graveyard, nobody watched *Here's Austin,* a cheery local show that touted the state fair and discussed quilt making in detail. But if Kate was going to invest so much time in a story, the station had to do something to justify the outlay.

"This way," Brad continued, "when Teague goes to the capitol building to work, you can go with him, act like all you want is to complete your story on him. Any good leads"—he smacked his lips with satisfaction—"you can feed to Linda for on-camera."

Kate drew in a hard breath. Feed Linda the good stories?

"You have something you want to say?" Brad fixed his narrowed eyes on her.

"I'll do it," Kate said. Like she had a

choice. "But don't you think people at the capitol are going to notice I'm tailing some guy all day long?"

"Teague will make sure no one notices." Brad laughed. "You'll see. Don't worry, Teague's good at what he does. In fact, he's the damned best security guy I've ever seen, and I've seen a few. For years, I've tried to get him to let me do a piece on him. I'm surprised he agreed this time. It's going to slow him down. But with him on the job, this'll be over before you know it." Brad turned his attention to his seven television screens. "And you'll be back doing what I'm paying you for."

At that bitter little comment, Kate backed out of the office as quietly as possible. She knew she wasn't earning her exorbitant salary, and she didn't want Brad to start brooding about that. He didn't strike her as a man who threw money around without expecting a return on his investment.

A silence fell in the newsroom as she walked to her desk. Not the hostile silence she'd faced before, but more the concerned silence of people who didn't know what to say in an awkward situation. Kate knew that silence; she'd faced it many times after her dad died. Making sure her glance didn't light on anyone in particular, she shot a smile around, sat at her computer, and ran an Internet search on Ramos Security.

The address popped up; she scribbled it down then found it on MapQuest. But the search produced little information on either the firm or Teague Ramos. She found a few small photos of him in the society section, dressed in a tux and escorting tall, thin models to various fund-raisers. He didn't look like her impression of a bodyguard— she'd expected a bodybuilder with a shaved head and an impassive expression. Instead, he looked long-legged and trim, with broad shoulders and straight, shoulder-length dark hair tied back in a black ribbon. No one wore his hair that way anymore, but she saw why Ramos did. The severe style lent a stark frame to his vital face. His dark tanned skin stretched over strong bones that defined his cheeks, his chin, his nose. He smiled down at the woman on his arm, and the woman smiled back, her expression greedy and proud.

Kate wasn't surprised. He was the kind of man who, even in a photograph, exuded raw sexuality. If she had him, she would be proud, too. She stared at the photo, trying to make out more detail. He looked . . . familiar. She tried making the picture bigger, but all she got was a grainy blowup.

As she squinted at the photo, the reporter beside hissed the alert, "Brad's up!"

The reporters around her were suddenly very busy or leaping to their feet and bustling away. Brad burst into the newsroom, yelling at the top of his lungs: "Who the hell was supposed to cover that train derailment? Because the cars contain dangerous materials, and I haven't seen one piece of film on the evacuation!"

Snatching up the address, Kate left the newsroom in a hurry.

Ramos Security was located in a two-story bungalow in a restored neighborhood not far from the governor's mansion. The gingerbread that decorated the front porch had been freshly painted, the steps had been refurbished with new boards, and the front door had been given a rich, red stain. A small brass plaque read: *Ramos Security, Walk In,* so Kate turned the knob.

The door creaked when it opened, and the receptionist seated at a desk in the foyer raised her head and smiled. "Miss Montgomery? Come on in. Oh, dear." She frowned at the sight of Kate's injuries. "That bastard got you good, didn't he? Well, don't you worry, Mr. Ramos will catch him."

"Thank you"—Kate's gaze skidded over the name plaque on the desk—"Brenda." It was a little spooky to be recognized, but a reporter got used to it.

Brenda gestured toward an elegant beveled-glass door. "Mr. Ramos is expecting you."

Kate walked in and found herself in what used to be a parlor. The light filtered through the tall oaks in the yard and into the casement windows, and Kate stood still, waiting until her eyes adjusted to the dim light.

When they did, she approved of the room. Elegant, rich in color, it was the perfect update to a classic early-twentieth-century style. The walls had been painted with a dark green below the chair rail, a mellow gold above. Cherrywood blinds hung at the tall windows, and a burgundy Persian rug covered the gleaming hardwood floor. The desk was massive, carved cherrywood, and a man stood behind the desk—tall, lean, with broad shoulders that fit perfectly into the crisp white shirt and black Armani suit. Yet his back was to the sun, leaving his face in shadow . . . until he leaned over and turned on his desk lamp.

The light gave substance and detail to a man who had been only smoke and shadow. His face had a stark splendor and the pitilessness of an Aztec warrior. With a last name like Ramos, he was obviously Hispanic. And his build—tall, long-legged, long-armed—made her think he must be part Anglo as well. He had the powerful shoulders of an Olympic rower, and she supposed that beneath the clothes his biceps bulged. A white scar crossed his cheek, and his eyes were the most beautiful deep, rich golden-brown . . .

She gasped like a Victorian maiden. "You!"

This was the man who had watched her film her first piece for the station, the man in the sleeveless black T-shirt, the man she imagined had slit her tire.

"Me?" he mocked. It was obvious he knew very well what she meant. He sauntered around the desk toward her. "Have we met, Miss Montgomery? Do we know each other? Have you seen me somewhere and imagined that the grubby Mexican could be your stalker?"

Her spine stiffened as he deliberately stood too close to her, invading her space, making her want to back up. "I imagined the grubby Mexican was a drug dealer or a gang member." She looked him right in those beautiful brown eyes and asked crisply, "Isn't that what you wanted me to think, Mr. Ramos?"

He laughed, a brief bark of amusement. "You reassure me I look the part—but not that I'm doing my job."

"What do you mean?" He was taller than she had thought. Six-three to her five-seven, and standing this close, he gave off an electric atmosphere that shot from the fine hairs on the base of her neck down to her toes.

"When I hang around the capitol complex, I want people to glance at me, then look away for fear of catching my eye. No one wants someone who looks like me to ac-cost them because they were accidentally friendly. So I'm anonymous in plain sight."

He focused on her, his tone interrogating. "But you recognized me."

"I'm a reporter. I look at people's faces." She breathed carefully, making sure that her shirt—her breasts—didn't brush his coat.

"Most reporters don't give a damn about anyone's face but their own—on a television screen in front of thousands of people."

She didn't mind telling the truth. "I like that, too."

He smiled again, a slow stretch of amusement. "Honest and observant. That makes my work easier." He walked away.

She took a long breath and willed the goose bumps to subside.

"Please be seated, Miss Montgomery." He held a chair for her, the one in front of his desk.

"Thank you, Mr. Ramos." She sat.

He perched one hip on his desk, deliberately putting her on a subordinate level. "You don't seem like the kind of woman who would consent to a bodyguard."

But she was the kind of woman who recognized intimidation tactics—*his* intimidation tactics—when she saw them, and she knew how to counter them. She sat absolutely still—no fidgeting—looked him in the face, and told him the truth about that, too. "I'm a coward."

"Good. That's exactly the answer I want. People who are afraid are cautious." Still he smiled, inviting further confidences.

She chose her words carefully. "I'm sensible enough to know that when I've been threatened, I should seek help."

"And . . . ?"

How had he known there was an and? "My mother wouldn't hear of anything else."

"Because . . . ?"

"Mr. Ramos, you really have an obnoxious way of interviewing people." See how much he liked *that* honesty.

"Miss Montgomery, I'm not interviewing you. I'm interrogating you."

Honesty right back in her face.

"And if you'd tell me everything right now, you'd save me the trouble."

His voice was still lazy, his mouth still smiled, but he was intense and serious, and she recognized the truth in his statement. She inclined her head. "My mom's afraid . . . my dad was targeted and killed overseas by a powerful anti-American group."

"Where? How long ago?"

"In the Middle East, about five years ago." Almost exactly five years ago. Kate never forgot.

"Your father in particular?" Teague asked. "Why him?"

"He had a tendency to stick his nose into dangerous situations if he thought it was the right thing to do." Kate smiled, a wavering smile as she remembered the man she had loved so dearly. "He saw some orphans and widows who needed help. He helped them. Some people don't want Americans doing good because it messes up the image of the Great Satan."

"Your dad sounds like a great guy." Teague's voice was absolutely neutral and he arranged the crease in his pants as if he found it of great interest.

"He was." Kate felt defensive, and she didn't like it. She didn't understand it, either. Why didn't Teague believe her father was a great guy? Why would he think she was lying? "My mother's afraid there's a chance that the same group of terrorists has decided to eliminate his entire family."

Teague whistled, long and low. "Now, that's interesting. What do you think?"

"I think it's improbable."

"But not impossible."

"Nothing's impossible. I think it's more likely I've picked up a viewer who's proprietary or who doesn't like my perceived politics or the color of my skin."

"Any idea who?" Teague leaned forward, put his hands on the arms of her chair, and got so close to her face that his breath brushed her skin. "I'm open to any suggestion at all, no matter how ludicrous you might think it is."

She leaned forward that one extra inch so that their noses were almost touching. "Now that you're out as a suspect—no."

He didn't back off. He didn't move forward. He looked into her eyes, and again the hair on the back of her neck rose. She supposed this was his usual routine. She supposed this was how he dragged information out of any woman who came into his office for help. But this Teague Ramos guy had a presence such as she had never felt. Her breath grew short, and her eyes grew heavy. She thought he was going to kiss her . . . and she wanted him to kiss her.

Her thoughts tangled in her brain.

His lips looked soft.

She'd had blackened redfish for lunch.

His hands looked capable.

She should have popped a breath mint before she came in.

But how could she have known she'd be kissing a man today?

She bit her lower lip, and he watched as if entranced.

Then he straightened. "Right. The information Brad sent over said the car was an Infiniti."

"What?" Released from his spell, she felt oddly disoriented. "Oh, so you think the stalker is moderately well off."

"Or he rented an Infiniti. Or borrowed or stole one—although there are no reports of stolen Infinitis that week. Unfortunately, knowing the make of the car is not helpful."

"I missed the license-plate number." She touched her chin. "I was too busy bleeding."

"Too bad," he said, unimpressed. "But you'll let me know if you notice anything odd about anybody, or recall any incident where someone seemed a little off. Sometimes that's what it takes, for the victim to

remember a name or an episode that created an enemy."

Her temper flashed. "I'm not a victim."

"Make sure you keep it that way." He went
to his small refrigerator and pulled out two
bottles of water. He loosened the cap on
both. "Do you have any enemies?"

She wanted to say no, but she couldn't
help but recall the open animosity at KTTV.
"A whole station full of them." She took the
bottle he offered. "But I don't think the other
broadcasters would actually try to bump me
off."

"Calling them enemies seems dramatic.
Why don't they like you?"

"The usual reason. I'm prettier than they
are."

He paused, the bottle almost to his
mouth, and gave her a long, lingering pe-
rusal that started at her toes and went to the
top of her head, and he made sure he paid
plenty of attention to the good parts in between.

If she had had any doubt that this
man could sneak under the sheets with
any woman he wanted, the flush of heat
in her breasts and between her legs cured
that.

"You're prettier than all of them?" he asked. "I can hardly believe that. I've seen Linda Nguyen."

Before Kate could stop herself, she laughed out loud.

He watched her with satisfaction.

Then she realized he was a manipulator. He'd wanted to make her laugh, and he did. He'd wanted to make her aware of him as a man, and he had.

Lifting the bottle, he drank, and his strong throat moved as he swallowed. As he drained half the bottle, she observed each detail and told herself he was someone to guard against.

Standing, she wandered to the fireplace and peered at the beautiful old marble. She didn't want to meet his gaze.

"So let's recount the situation." As he got down to business, the change in him was startling. His voice grew crisp, so crisp she faced him, startled. His mocking smile had disappeared, the charm had vanished beneath a surface so hard bullets would bounce off it. "We could be dealing with possible terrorists, but that's not likely. Your fellow broadcasters are a possibility. This could be a friend, an acquaintance, or a

stranger who's watched you on television."
He ticked them off on his fingers. "Miss
Montgomery, think very carefully about who
it could be, because those are a lot of suspects."

"I'll think," she agreed, and rubbed her finger across the brass Buddha on the mantel.

"Now, here's the way we're going to play
it. You're going to be doing a piece on me,
so we'll be together all the time."

It wasn't a come-on, but a necessity. She
knew this. "If the stalker knows me, you're
going to make him back off."

"We'll spend each day at the capitol building. I'll work the surveillance, you can work
the politics, and my men and cameras can
observe you."

"That'll work. That'll keep Brad happy."
Briefly, she thought of the stories she would
hear, how she would have to pass them off
to Linda, and she winced.

"Keeping you off the air until your wounds
heal will help." Without an ounce of visible
sympathy, Teague studied her stitches. "If
the stalker is a viewer, the attacks are almost certainly related to your appearance
on television. If the attacks stop, we're
probably dealing with someone who only

knows you from the local news and who feels he's won by keeping you off the air."

"That's an advantage?" Austin had a population of 650,000.

"That cuts out a lot of immediate suspects." Teague rolled the bottle between his hands and smiled as if he knew something she didn't. "Do you have somewhere I can sleep at your apartment, or should I bring an air mattress?"

"Sleep?" Her mind leaped to the right conclusion, but she hadn't considered . . .

"I'm trying to keep you where the stalker can find you," Teague answered sensibly. "It's the only way we're going to get him to reveal himself."

"So I'm bait?" Kate liked this less and less.

"And I'm your bodyguard. I'll keep you safe." His charm returned, fully intact. "Trust me."

Not in a million years. "I've got a guest room. You can stay there. There's a lock on my bedroom door."

"I'll remember that." He smiled faintly.

Then she wished she hadn't said it. She had been trying to make it clear that she wasn't part of his fee. Somehow she thought he'd taken it as a challenge. But she hadn't meant it like that. She really hadn't, not even in her deepest, darkest, most hidden thoughts.

"Let's go to the capitol." He stood, walked across the room, and opened the door for her. "You drive your car; I'll follow. I want to see if I can spot anyone lurking and watching. We'll meet inside, I'll introduce you to my people, and we're set."

"All right."

In the foyer, Teague stopped at Brenda's desk. "Call me when you need me. Otherwise I'm going to be out on this job."

"Yes, sir. If you could sign these checks before you leave . . ."

Kate headed for the outer door.

"Kate, we need to clear up one last thing!" Teague said sharply. "You let me go out first." He caught her arm.

Pain shot through her. She flinched and gasped.

He let her go, steadied her with a hand at the base of her spine, and watched the expression on her face so very carefully. "Bruise?"

"Yes."

"Car?"

"Yes."

"Hurts?"

"Yes."

"Don't worry." Teague's eyes chilled to dark, unfathomable pools. "And don't doubt this—I'll get the son of a bitch."

Five

"I understand." Kate rubbed the sore spot on her arm. "Lead the way."

"And you trust me?" Teague held her in place with the heat of his touch and the strength of his gaze. "You know I'll get your stalker?"

"I trust you." She couldn't say more. Her throat hurt from tension. Her gaze clung to his. She wanted to cry, but that was silly.

"All right. If you're ever uneasy, let me know. I live upstairs here." He extracted his business card from his pocket. "That has my personal cell phone number. If I'm not with you, call me or come to find me, and I'll fix whatever's bothering you. You'll do that?"

"I promise."

With a brisk nod, he let her go.

While he signed his papers for Brenda, she said to Kate, "You can trust your life to this man. I did, and I've never been sorry."

Kate's tension eased. "You had a stalker?"

"I had an ex-husband. Nothing could convince him I wasn't his to smack around anymore. Not until Teague explained matters to him. He hasn't dared show his face since." Brenda's testimonial was fierce and loyal.

"Yeah, and now I get to check out every one of Brenda's damned stupid boyfriends before she goes out." Teague shook his head and kept signing.

"He thinks I run to type," Brenda informed Kate.

"A bad type." Teague walked past Kate and out the door.

"My life's no longer my own," Brenda complained, but Kate could see she wasn't serious. In a lower voice, she added, "Really, he is the best."

Kate joined him on the porch and found him looking up and down the street. He glanced at her Beemer. "That's your car? Very nice."

"Thank you. I like it. It has the smoothest five-speed I've ever handled, and it tracks around corners beautifully." *Oh, God, she sounded like a car salesman.*

"Give me your keys and I'll start it for you." He extended his hand.

"That's not necessary."

"Believe me, it is."

This grim guardian took the threats to her seriously. So seriously. He wouldn't let her stand near as he looked the car over, then started it. Stepping out, he waved her over and held the door while she stepped in. "Keep it locked while you drive. Don't worry, I'll be behind you."

Don't worry? She had a stalker, and the man who protected her from that stalker threatened her in a completely different way.

As she drove, she repeatedly glanced in her rearview mirror. Teague stayed a few cars back, and she watched the way he drove, without flash or daring yet with a cool efficiency that told her he could catch her if he deemed it necessary. Behind the tinting of his windshield he was nothing more than a dark shadow, yet she knew without a doubt he observed everyone around her.

She knew how to handle an aggressive man, or at least she knew as well as any woman. The trouble was—when she stood close to Teague, she didn't think of how brainless it would be to get involved with him. She didn't think at all; her reaction was visceral and instinctive, and that had to stop. She was known for her common sense. From somewhere, she needed to dredge some up.

Pulling into her usual lot, she parked, and briefcase in hand, she waited until Teague got out of his car before she unlocked the doors and joined him. "Did you see anything?"

"No." He looked her over with lascivious interest. "Damn it."

"Look, Mr. Ramos, professionals don't spend their time leering at each other," she said crisply.

"That's for sure." Gently taking her arm, he walked with her toward the capitol. "You haven't leered at me once since we left my office."

Her shoulders snapped back, and she glared.

"There's the sparkle back in your eyes. Are you still afraid you'll be attacked?" He asked as if he truly cared, and his interest was more disarming than his flirtation.

So she thought about it. Seriously considered the question. Doing something to thwart this stalker had given her a sense of control.

And while Teague was pushy and obnoxious, he also gave off an air of competence that reassured her. As much as she hated to admit it, if he lived with her, she would sleep well . . . or at least she would sleep without the fear of unexpected violence in the night.

"No, I feel better. You've reassured me. I'm not as afraid as I've been."

They entered the capitol building through the South Lobby.

"Let me show you the security office and introduce you to my people," he said.

"I really should go and see what's happening in the Senate Gallery. Today they're debating the Robin Hood bill. There'll be speakers from the rich school districts who stand to lose and speakers from the poor school districts who stand to gain and, of course, plenty of rhetoric from the Senate floor." She tried to slip around him.

Teague stopped her with an arm across her path. "It wasn't a request. If you're going to be here and not be with me every moment, my people need to meet you so they'll know who to keep an eye on."

She blinked at him in surprise, and in the soft, pouting lips and the baby-soft skin, Teague could see the indulged girl in her. She was used to getting her own way. In fact, this little prima donna was spoiled as hell.

"Come on, Kate, this won't take long," he

said, cajoling her the same way he cajoled all the overpaid, self-absorbed women he dated. "The Senate will survive without you for a few more minutes."

She gave in with a grace that surprised him. "Of course. After all, Linda is covering that story." With a laugh and a shrug, she walked with him toward his security center. "I'll be interviewing you. Do you mind?"

"If I minded, I wouldn't have agreed to it." In fact he'd agreed to it because she was the reporter in jeopardy. That first time he'd seen her, he'd liked her poise, her style, the crisp tone of her voice. He'd loitered in the crowd looking like everyone's idea of a gang leader and waited to meet her gaze. The blaze that ignited between them had surprised even him.

Now some bastard had stripped away some of her confidence.

Not a lot. It would take more than a stalker to wipe out the conditioning produced by money and security. In fact, if it were anyone else, he would have said this scare was just what she needed.

But he had liked her the way she was. He had wanted her the way she was.

Now, damn it, he wanted her more—and

she was a client. Teague needed to remember that. She was a client.

She pulled out her notebook and flipped it open. Pen in hand, she asked, "Where's your security center located?"

He put his hand over hers. "Some things we're not going to mention on television. Let's at least make the terrorists work for their information."

"Right." She put the notebook away and joined him in the elevator to the second floor. "Don't worry, keeping information back makes the piece even more intriguing to the public. When I'm done with you, you'll be a huge hit."

He looked down at her. It was on the tip of his tongue to tell her he didn't care one damned bit, but then she'd ask why he was doing this, and he wasn't about to admit he'd allowed his gonads to issue directives to his brain. Women, for some reason, didn't understand. "I direct security for the capitol. You're the capitol reporter. This'll be good for the company, so I put myself in your hands."

She smiled. She seemed to liked that. He supposed it gave her some sense of power over a life that had suddenly careened out of control.

To Teague, she looked an adolescent boy's version of Snow White, with pale skin, baby-soft cheeks, a plush, sensual, mouth, and black hair that curled around her face. She didn't flaunt her body, covering it in somber colors that played down her trim figure. Compared to the women he usually dated, expensive women who loved the challenge of dating a dangerous man, she was quiet, professional, and unassuming.

But Kate was nicely built, with breasts big enough to fit in the cup of his hands, a narrow waist, and hips that swayed when she walked. Her shapely legs made him long to see more. There was no art to her stride; she didn't make each movement an enticement, but just because she seemed unaware of the clean, smooth motion didn't mean it wasn't sexy.

"Here we are." He stopped in front of the reinforced metal door. With a hand on the electronic palm scanner, he identified himself, typed in a code, and the lock popped open. As they walked in, he announced, "I've brought a little excitement into your dull lives."

Four people faced them, three males and

a female, as well as a bank of monitors and blinking lights.

Kate walked in without hesitation. "How do you do? I'm Kate Montgomery from KTTV. I'm here to do a news report on your boss."

"Hey, hey, hey. The boss is going to be a star!" Chun was Teague's team leader from California, a single, handsome, twenty-eight-year-old Asian American who talked fast and liked to remind people he'd graduated summa cum laude from Stanford.

Teague liked to remind him his major had been art.

"I can hear the headline now. 'Super Security Keeps Senators Safe!'" Rolf was Teague's technology geek, a big blond German from North Dakota.

Big Bob was fifty-four, Texan to the bone, happily married with three kids and two grandkids, and he guffawed and offered up a high five.

"Nice alliteration, Rolf. You ought to look for work making up headlines."

Gemma was a petite beauty with beautiful black skin.

"There's a computer program for alliteration. I wrote it." Rolf grinned.

Gemma rolled her doe-like brown eyes.

The hilarity and teasing took Kate aback, but not Teague. In this business, grandstanding was ruthlessly mocked, and his people didn't stand in awe of him. He didn't usually want them to . . . although this outburst proved a little deference might be a good thing.

When the hubbub died down, Teague told Kate, "These so-called security experts rotate on and off duty. I'll introduce you to the people walking the corridors, too. If I'm not around and you suspect trouble while you're here, let any one of them know and they'll take care of you. Everybody is connected." He showed her the half-dozen earbuds and microphones hanging on hooks by the door. "Before anybody goes out, they hook up."

"Is it a walkie-talkie or a cell phone?"

"Walkie-talkie. We can cover a range of about two miles around the capitol. More than that, we turn to a cell phone." To his people, he said, "While Kate's busy filming me—and any of my people who manage to sound interesting—we're going to catch her stalker."

"Ooh, a television interview," Chun said.

"Ugh, a stalker," Big Bob said.

Trust Big Bob to get to the heart of the matter.

Teague stood off to the side and watched his people cluster around Kate. Three men, one woman, all trying to get interviewed . . . or just trying to get her attention.

"See, what we have here is the heart of the security system." Chun gestured at the computers and cameras. Chun did very well with women, and now he focused on Kate.

She seemed not to notice his interest. "So, Mr. Chun, you're saying that from this room, you can survey the whole capitol complex?"

"Pretty much," Chun said.

"Nope." Big Bob's slow West Texas drawl overrode Chun's assertive West Coast voice. "This gives the overview, but each wing has its own special cameras and its own special viewing room."

Kate's attention shifted to Big Bob, who was sitting in front of the monitors, his gaze moving from one to the other. "Is someone always working each room?"

"No . . ." Big Bob glanced at her, saw how intently she watched him, and his cheeks, already naturally rosy, flushed a dull red.

Teague wanted to laugh, except that Kate

smiled reassuringly at Big Bob. "Does someone check the rooms periodically?"

"Every fifteen minutes." The color in Big Bob's cheeks brightened.

She kindly pressed his shoulder.

Teague watched as she put his man at ease. She showed amazing poise as she drew out Big Bob about the positions of the cameras. She extracted details about the surveillance rooms.

While she took notes, Big Bob sidled up beside him. "Boss, Juanita called in sick."

"Did she?" Teague felt the familiar worry start grinding within him. "Did she say why?"

"She said it's just one of those difficult days. She has 'em, you know. Guess she's entitled."

"Yeah." Teague dialed Juanita's number, and when she didn't answer, he frowned. He left the message, "Call! You know me. I worry." And he did. Hell, he didn't know how to stop worrying about Juanita.

But right now he had to concentrate on the task of guarding Kate. He *would* care for her. He couldn't live with himself if someone under his protection was hurt . . . again.

Teague stepped forward. "I'll take Kate for

a personal tour. You can keep an eye on her through the monitors. That will be your duty when she's here. Remember that."

"It'll be a pleasure to observe Miss Montgomery," Chun declared with far too much enthusiasm.

With heightened color, Kate busied herself with placing the pad and pen in her big black bag.

Teague picked up his earbud, slipped his transmitter into his inside jacket pocket, and organized the wires so they were mostly out of sight. When he wore this, it looked as if he was talking on a cell phone.

He opened the door for Kate.

She waved and smiled as she exited. "Thank you all! I look forward to working with you." As Teague shut the heavy door, she said, "I recognize Gemma and Rolf. I've seen them around the complex, although I thought they must work for a senator or something."

"You have a good eye." She did. She impressed Teague with how much she absorbed. "If you ever decide to leave reporting, I'd hire you."

"Thank you." As they passed the south

exit onto Congress, she turned and headed toward the door.

"Where are we going?" he asked, taken by surprise.

"Starbucks. It's time for my double whipped frappuccino."

"Starbucks," Teague said in disgust. "There's coffee in my office."

"I want my frappuccino."

He supposed it wouldn't hurt to go outside. She was supposed to behave normally. Still he injected his tone with scorn. "A girly drink."

She grinned back at him. "I *am* a girl."

She certainly was.

A girl not so different from other girls, yet something about her drew him irresistibly. It wasn't just the way she looked. When he got close to her, she smelled . . . rich and wholesome. Most people would say there wasn't a smell that defined wholesome, but he knew better. Wholesome was the exact opposite of every smell in his boyhood. Nothing about the border town where he'd been raised had been wholesome. Nothing about the alleys and the rotting garbage and the humidity and the heat had been wholesome. So, he supposed, that made him the exact opposite of Kate Montgomery. She was wholesome, he was . . . not.

She came from money.

She'd probably gone to a finishing school.

She'd probably belonged to a sorority in college.

She probably had never done anything she needed to feel guilty about or heard a shrill voice from the past shrieking, *Hey, you little bastard . . .*

He needed to remember Kate was a client. Forgetting wouldn't bridge the huge damned distance between them, wouldn't give him anything more than temporary relief from a past that haunted him still.

Would haunt him . . . forever.

Autumn's first cold front was edging through Austin, sweeping away the stale humidity and replacing it with the first crisp hint of winter. Kate threw her arms out and took a long breath. "Isn't it gorgeous? I love winter in Texas."

"You've seen winters a few other places." He was making conversation, trying to draw her out and discover a clue about who might be after her. A former lover? An old friend? He was interested. Far too interested . . . far too enthralled with the glow of autumn's golden sunlight on her piquant features.

He automatically watched the people on the street, kept an eye out for the flash of sunlight on the metal of a firearm, and kept track of Kate.

"A lot of other places, most recently in Nashville." She made conversation easily. "We were there for the worst snow in years. No one knew how to drive in it. Everyone put their car in the ditch."

"We?" She was talking about that former lover he suspected.

"My mother and I." Kate mocked him with a smile. "Who else?"

"Your mother. Of course. Where's your mother now?"

"She lives here in Austin."

"So you're close." Way too close.

The world slipped into shades of gray, and in his head he heard that shrill voice. His mother's. *Teague, you little bastard, don't be so goddamned stupid. You're a stupid half-breed gringo, and if you get knifed, no one will care. I sure as hell won't.*

"We got that way after my dad's death." Kate smiled tightly.

"What? Oh, yeah." He needed to remember the circumstances that united Kate and her mom . . . they loved each other. Most mothers and their kids *did* love each other. "If we're going to catch your stalker, I'm going to need a list of where you go. The grocery store, the gym, parties, dates with your newest lover . . ."

"I don't date."

He didn't believe her. "Why not?"

"I haven't met anybody. I don't have any friends." She chuckled, a low, sexy purr of amusement. "How pathetic did that sound? I mean, the work keeps me busy, and I haven't had time to make friends here. In Austin. Yet."

"Tell me where you go on a typical day."

"The grocery store, the gym," she echoed Teague's speculation. "I'll give you a list. I go to my mom's." She brightened. "I've been invited to a party next Thursday night."

"Great!" That sounded promising. "Where?"

"Senator Oberlin invited me to his anniversary party."

"Senator . . . Oberlin?" Teague couldn't believe his own ugly luck, and he wanted to laugh. "Oh, that'll be a hell of a good time."

"What were you expecting?" A tinge of irritation colored Kate's voice. "Drugs and wild dancing?"

"We definitely won't get it there. George Oberlin's known for his high-class parties with all the right people saying all the right things." He entered Starbucks on Kate's heels.

"So you've never been to one before?" she asked in a snide tone.

"Only as a bodyguard."

"Oh." She didn't want to talk about it anymore.

Too bad.

The girl behind the counter called, "Hi, Kate. Want the usual?"

"Please," Kate said.

"I'll take a scone." Teague stood unsmiling. "And a coffee, black."

While the college-age kids got the order ready, he leaned against the case and fixed Kate with a cold gaze. "The right people have hellacious big diamonds they want guarded, and sometimes the females like to have a dangerous-looking guy following them around like some kind of Doberman on a chain. So yeah, I've been to quite a few society parties."

"You've certainly made me look forward to it!" Kate said brightly.

"I'll bet." He paid a fortune for the coffees, then headed for the table against the wall. He held the chair as Kate seated herself, then sat where he could see through the windows, observe whoever came in, identify any threat.

Kate took a sip of her silly, frivolous drink with the fervent dedication of someone who needed the caffeine. Pulling out her pad and pencil, she got down to business. "Tell me, Teague, how many employees do you have?"

"Eight full-time employees." He ate half the scone in two bites. "But I have another twenty-five employees under contract who I can call when I need them. Most of what I do is surveillance, so I can use anyone with a sharp eye and a keen sense of what constitutes trouble."

"Do you train them?" She took another sip.

"People who watch people are naturals. I test them. If they pick up on the right signals, I hire them, give them some pointers, and put them on the job. They love being paid for what they do spontaneously. The bodyguards are different. Ex-military, usually, with experience with weapons and hand to hand. I have the best." He made a proud testimonial and a bald statement of fact.

"How did you find them?"

"I was in the military with most of them." He saw her pen pause over her tablet. The silence stretched out long and thick. Most women—every woman he knew—would seize on the information to ask him personal questions.

Kate, who had every reason to ask, hesitated. Kate, whose task it was to probe his background, couldn't seem to get up the nerve to do her job.

And why? Oh, he knew. She had felt the same tug he did. She had refused it, but as she delved into his personal life, as she got to know him, she ran the risk of, not physical intimacy, but mental and emotional intimacy.

She was a woman. Women—his women, anyway—thrived on sex, but they fell in love with intimacy.

Kate would just as soon never have to see him again anyway.

He waited to see what she would do, and

he was both amused and surprised when she slid her cup across the table.

"Try it."

"On one condition." He pushed the scone toward her.

It was an impasse, two people involved in an ultra-civilized food fight. He didn't want to taste her frappuccino. She didn't want to taste his scone.

Fascinated, Kate watched as he lifted the cup and took a sip, his dark eyes daring her, challenging her.

She shifted in her seat. He made her uncomfortable.

But she could challenge him in return. She was a woman who had seen the world. She knew a few tricks herself.

Breaking a piece off the scone, she transported it to her lips in slow increments, sliding it into her mouth. "Do you like it?" she asked in a husky tone.

"Like it?" He never took his gaze off her lips.

"The frappuccino."

"I do." He pushed the cup back at her. "Have another drink—and ask me what you need to ask me. Or should I say—ask me what you dare to ask me."

She knew why he was so good at his job. He saw too much. He observed too acutely. She didn't want to ask him about his personal life. It brought a level of intimacy to their relationship when she wanted to remain professional . . . but if she was going to be professional, she had to stop responding to his challenges. "You were in the military. When did you join? What branch? How long were you in?"

"I joined when I was eighteen. I wanted to go to college eventually, but I lost my mother while I was in high school and goofed off too much to get scholarships. So I thought four years in the Marines, then college, then a job wearing a suit and carrying a briefcase." He laughed as if amused at his younger self. "I stayed in eight years. They put me in the Special Ops, trained me to be tough, and I found out I had a knack for leadership and organization. When I got out, I didn't want a briefcase. Five years ago, I opened the bodyguard business. Two years ago, I got the contract for security at the state capitol. And here we are."

"Right." His loquaciousness surprised her. She'd interviewed a lot of people, and while most were flattered and pleased at the chance to talk about themselves, Teague struck her as the type to be tight-lipped about his background. Of course he could be lying—she examined his face—but if he was, he was very good at it. "Where did you grow up?"

"In a little town on the border, on the wrong side of the tracks. My dad took off when I was little, never to be seen again, and we barely scraped by."

He seemed very easy with his misfortune. "Do you have family left?" she asked.

"No one."

"No one at all? Who do you eat Thanksgiving dinner with?"

"The people at the truck stop." His smile blazed forth. "They're lovely people."

"Yes." She chewed her lip. "I'm sure they are." If they weren't, he didn't want to talk about it, he made that very clear. "The bodyguard business is an unusual career choice. What sent you in that direction?"

"There was talk in the service about guys who did it and how well they got paid and how well they got treated for standing around and looking dangerous. After being in the Special Ops, I was ready for some easy money. But the job got damned boring damned quick, and I realized that a little organization could launch a big firm. There's never been as big a need for security as now, and the opportunities are there for a man who's willing to take chances."

"Does the paperwork take up all your time now, or do you still get into the field?"

"I'm the boss. I take only the jobs I want." He smiled another of those slow, heated smiles.

Of course. For a brief moment, she had felt normal, safe, unstalked. Because he was guarding her.

Reaching into the inner pocket of his jacket, he pulled out a vibrating cell phone. He glanced at the caller ID, said "Excuse me," to Kate, flipped open the phone, and in tones of great affection, said, "How are you, *querida*?"

He listened, and as Kate watched, his face changed from smiling to severe. He flicked a glance at her, and for all the interest he showed, she might be a stranger. All the intense consideration he had shown her he now fixed on his caller, and he said, "Of course I'll come at once." He listened again. "Don't be silly, you know there's nothing more important to me than you."

To whom was he speaking? Not a lover, surely. Not in that tone of firm cajolery. A family member? He claimed he had no one. Another case? Another stalker? Another female in jeopardy whom he could flatter and protect?

"Just let me get things wrapped up here, and I'll be right over." He hung up and stood, indicating the door.

She followed him, watched him as his gaze flicked out the windows toward the street. He might be distracted, but he still watched out for her safety.

"Kate, I'll take you back to the capitol and turn you over to my people." He led the way onto the street and toward the capitol. "I'll ask that you stay there until one of us can escort you home."

A sharp ache caught her. She looked around, seeing a threat in the laughing Senate pages who waited for a bus at the corner, in the tourist group that strolled the capitol grounds. Teague was leaving her, and she no longer felt safe in the city she knew and loved. "But I'm supposed to stay with you," she argued. "Report your life."

"It's a personal matter." He sounded perfectly polite, perfectly professional, and perfectly distant, keeping all his attention on the pedestrians and the cars that passed them.

"A *personal* matter?" She couldn't stop herself from asking. "This from the man who claims he eats Thanksgiving dinner at a truck stop?"

His lips twitched. His eyes warmed. "I lied. I eat Thanksgiving dinner with friends."

"Whew." She pretended to wipe her brow. "I was worried you were seriously maladjusted."

His brief amusement dissipated once more, and his voice had a bite and a bitterness she'd not heard from him. "Everything about my life is so normal I'm an advertisement for the American way." Using his headset, he spoke to his people and turned care of her over to them.

When he was done, she said persuasively, "Reporting on your personal matters would bring a dimension to you that the viewers would love."

"They can love me or not. It doesn't matter." He ushered her inside the great doors of the capitol. "You're under surveillance now. Run along and see if you can scare up some stories about the legislators. I'm sure they're fighting about something. Just don't go on TV, and don't leave the building alone. I'll try to be back before you want to go home."

She watched him walk out and wished fiercely for her life to go back to normal. She wanted to answer the phone and not worry about silence on the other end or worse, a voice saying, *Leave, bitch.* She wanted to walk down the street and not agonize that a car would swerve toward her.

She knew she would never feel secure again . . . except perhaps when Teague Ramos stood by her side.

And that troubled her almost more than the anxiety about her stalker.

Using his key, Teague Ramos entered a small apartment near the center of Austin, and shut the door behind him. He walked into the bedroom and up to the bed, leaned over, and kissed the woman reclining there. With all the love he was capable of expressing, he smiled into her brown eyes and said, *"Querida,* your call was the best thing that has happened to me all week."

Six

Troubled, Kate sat in her car in her parking space and stared through the windshield at the downtown lofts where she made her home. They were less than five years old, a remodeled five-story warehouse with large windows and a creaky freight elevator that should have been replaced but gave the place atmosphere. A Dumpster stood off to the side of parking area. Strips of green grass provided relief from the unrelenting concrete. Tall lights lit the parking lot, and security cameras pointed outward.

The area was still in transition from downtown slum to trendy apartments, but she'd liked it—before. It was fun, it was modern, it was in the old warehouse district—and she sat waiting, doors locked, while Teague parked his car in the guest slot and made his way to her side.

That was what he had instructed her to do. She gripped the blue leather steering wheel, the whorled pattern pressing into her palms.

Her worry came from the fact that she was more concerned about Teague's reaction if she disobeyed him than a possible stalker lurking in the shadows. In fact, she was more worried about the night ahead than she had ever been about anything in her life, and her stomach twisted in a knot of trepidation. How *stupid* to think about Teague instead of her safety.

Yet during the day, she had tailed him through his duties, taken notes on his activities, and listened to his deep voice as he explained procedure; his presence seemed to rub against her skin until she was chafed by the knowledge he would go home with her that night.

Then, worse, he had left her alone for four hours—four lousy hours!—and despite the knowledge that her safety was in capable hands, she'd been unable to concentrate on the job she loved. She had been waiting to hear his voice, wanting the security of his presence.

What a damned horrible situation to find herself in, disturbed by the man who was supposed to keep her safe.

When Teague rapped on the window beside her, she jumped. Jumped hard enough to shake the car, and when she turned to him, he smiled through the window, a slow, smooth, sexy smile.

He gestured for her to unlock the car.

He opened her door and slid his hand under her arm. "Which floor are you on?"

"Five." She eased her legs out, taking care not to flash him—her southern-raised mother had ensured that she knew how to get out of a low-slung car properly—but a quick glance into his eyes proved that no measure she took would be good enough to subdue his hunting instincts.

"How did you find this place?" He walked beside her, adjusting his gait to hers, a duffel bag in his hand. His gaze shifted between her and their surroundings.

"My mother's best friend's kid is the contractor, and when one of the owners got evicted, I got a deal on the place."

"Evicted. Why?" They entered the foyer, and Teague gazed around. The concrete floors and high ceilings were evidence of the building's warehouse beginnings, but the decorator had painted the walls in warm swirling oranges and lit the foyer with sconces of amber glass and bronze.

"Couldn't afford it. He was overextended."

For the next few days Teague was going to live with her. Unfortunately, he appealed to her. There was nothing she could do about it, but she didn't have to scratch that itch.

"Do you know his name?"

"No, but I suppose I could find out." Kate was an adult. Not a virgin. A woman with a strong mind and solid instincts.

"I'll find out."

Teague's tone jerked her to attention. The way he looked around, the way he walked one step behind her . . . she had forgotten, again, why he was here.

He had not. Flipping open his cell phone, he dialed a number and said, "Big Bob, find out who used to live at this address and see if we can talk to him. He sounds like a guy we could be interested in."

When Teague shut the phone, Kate asked, "Do you think he's the stalker?"

"It's possible. He could be angry that you're occupying his home."

The idea gave her the creeps, to think some guy might know her place better than she did. It also put a whole new complexion on Teague's presence here. She could almost imagine Teague struggling with an intruder, subduing him, tying him up, then turning to her, his chest heaving, sweat trickling down his brow, intent on claiming his prize. . . .

"Is that the only entrance to the building?" he asked.

"Huh?" Kate had to get a grip on her imagination. "No, there's a back entrance."

"Are there surveillance cameras there, too?"

"Yes." She foresaw the next question. "They all work. The homeowners' association pays Cleopatra's Security to keep an eye on the area."

Teague grunted, not happy, not unhappy. "They're dependable enough. I'll talk to them about getting the tapes." He grinned as he pushed the button for the elevator. "Your mom's best friend's kid, huh? Is he handsome?"

"*She's* very beautiful. Also good with a hammer." The broad warehouse-sized doors opened, and Kate stepped in the elevator. "Want me to introduce you?"

"No, I have enough on my hands right now." He followed close on her heels.

Kate almost retorted that she wasn't on his hands, but she caught herself. That was the kind of repartee that created more trouble than she could handle. Yet a tiny sliver of temptation slipped into her mind . . . if she succumbed to Teague's allure and slept with him, what harm would come of it? It wasn't as if she would fall in love.

She shot a sideways glance at Teague. He looked so good to her. She took a long breath. In the confined space of the elevator, he smelled good, too, like warm, clean skin and sandalwood.

The doors opened onto the hallway, also decorated in orange, amber, and bronze. If she hadn't been watching, his behavior would have gone unnoticed, so smoothly did he move. He stepped out, and his quick glance roamed each corner, noting the security cameras and the three closed doors that faced them. When he had ascertained the corridor was safe, he held the elevator for her, keeping it open so she could step out. He looked absolutely relaxed. But he wasn't. He was protecting her. At all times, he was protecting her.

Walking to her door, she inserted the key, stood aside—and swallowed as she watched him look the place over. Could there be a more attractive idea than to know he would defend her with his life?

The voice of good sense rang cold and clear in her head. *Because it's his job, Kate. Because almost all that machismo is invested in the successful pursuit of his work, and the little bit left over is satisfied with a quick tumble and an even quicker farewell.*

She hated that stupid voice in her head.

Teague prowled through the lower floor. The living room rose two stories. A huge rug covered the tile floor with splashes of color in an asymmetrical pattern. Decorated in the pure white and clear blue of the Grecian islands, the kitchen and dining room opened off the living room. Her copper pans hung from a rack on the ceiling, and a charm from Indonesia dangled from a chain.

He looked back at her. "See anything out of place?"

"No." From the door, everything looked blessedly normal and mostly tidy, thanks to her cleaning lady, who'd been in Friday.

A stairway curved up the wall and ended in the open loft. "What's up there?" he asked.

"My bedroom."

"Come on in. I'll look around. You can start dinner."

His assumptions scraped at her sensibilities. "What do you want on your pizza?"

His eyebrows shot up. "You don't look like a pizza kind of a girl."

"I'm a reporter. I live on pizza." She ate it a lot more than she wanted to, especially on the job.

"This isn't a typical reporter's place." He gestured toward the cream and brown leather furniture, the collection of African fertility gods.

"It is when there's a trust fund involved." She braced herself, waiting for sarcasm such as she'd heard in the newsroom, or perhaps more questions that insinuated she was stalked for her money, and that, of course, would be her fault.

Instead he said, "Everything."

"What?"

"I like everything on my pizza." He started up the stairs.

She watched him disappear into her bedroom. Somehow he'd gotten the last word.

She read the numbers for Papa Jerry's off the refrigerator magnet and ordered their large combination. Tensely she stared at the stairs and wondered what he thought of her bedroom, decorated sparsely in warm shades of amber, with matted and framed silk paintings from India on her wall.

Then she wondered why she cared.

Unfortunately, she knew why, and she knew she had to stop thinking about being with Teague, sleeping with Teague. When had she become one of those women who liked men who were destined to hurt them? Kate knew better than to yearn after a handsome jerk, yet here she was justifying to herself a night—or more—with Teague.

But what was she going to do with him? He was here for however long it took to find her stalker. She had a spare bedroom off the dining room, but there were still hours until bedtime, and here he was invading her personal space. She put place mats on the marble-topped kitchen table, then took them off again and carried them into the living room. Her coffee table was the same green marble, the couch was deeply cushioned and comfortable, and most important, her television covered the facing wall. Usually she kept it tuned to KTTV, but she had the biggest cable package with every sports channel imaginable. That would keep Teague entertained, and they'd never have to say a single word to each other.

Thoughtfully she considered the seating arrangements. They could both face the television if they sat on the couch, but bumping shoulders would lead to a full-frontal naked encounter on the couch—there went her imagination again!—and if she was going to remain upright, she needed to strategize.

She put one place mat in front of the chair at a ninety-degree angle to the couch.

She'd sit there.

She placed forks and napkins, then hesitated over the bottles in her refrigerator, wondering if he'd want a Bud rather than one of her designer beers.

With a mental shrug, she decided he'd take what he got, popped the tops on two Blue Moose ales, and headed for the living room.

"Nice place," he said as he came down the stairs.

She handed him the bottle. "The previous owner had it like this, and I like it."

"So you didn't change a thing?"

"The furniture. I painted the wall behind the TV cream. The rug is mine. I thought we'd eat in here." She gestured him toward the couch. "Watch some football." She flipped through the channels until she found a matchup between the Texans and the Cowboys. She turned the sound way down, then placed the remote on her place mat.

"Sounds good." But he headed for her bookshelves. "What do you read?"

The question was as innocuous as conversation from a curious date. She knew it. She knew she was overreacting. Yet . . . why did he want to know? She didn't need him poking his nose in what she read, how she decorated, who she was. "Mystery. Romance. Science fiction. Fantasy."

"Romance?" Of course he picked up on *that.* "Why would you read romance?"

"Because the only alternative is guys like you," she answered crisply.

Throwing back his head, he laughed. "Romance is for sissies. For people who are afraid to face up to real life."

He was teasing. She didn't have a doubt about that. But she couldn't resist rising to the bait. "I'm a reporter. I face real life every day. I know what real life is . . . did you like the latest James Bond movie?"

"You don't know anything about real life." Teague spoke quickly, lightly. He grinned as

if he were joking, yet he sounded all too serious to Kate.

"So tell me, Mr. Worldly, what's real life all
about?" The doorbell rang, and she headed
over to grab the pizza.

He caught her wrist as she reached for the
doorknob. "Real life does *not* include answering the door without looking first."

"I know that." She pulled her wrist away,
and he let her go . . . after a good long moment.

She retreated to the coffee table and
fussed with placing the forks perfectly on
the center of the napkins.

He looked through the peephole. Apparently satisfied, he opened the door, collected the pizza, paid the guy, and brought
it to the coffee table. He smiled at the place
mats, the napkins, the forks. "Nice."

What was it about Teague that sent her
into a tizzy? In less than twelve hours, he
had managed to make her more sexually
aware than any other man, and he'd done it
just by existing. It was almost frightening,
the way her body responded to him.

"First down," she said. "The Texans will
lose this one for sure."

"No, they're looking good today. I'll bet they win."

"Bet?" The Texans hadn't done anything this season. Of course, neither had the Cowboys, but they were ahead by twenty-one points in the third. "To win?"

Teague nodded.

"How much?"

"Ten?"

He reached across the table to shake.

She took his hand. He had a good handshake, firm but not aggressive.

"So how'd you learn so much about football?" he asked.

"My dad was a sports fiend." She smiled in fond memory. "He held me on his knee when I was a year old and explained the difference between a balk and a bunt. Before I was three, I could recite the names of all the quarterbacks in the NFC. When I was eleven, I broke my shin playing soccer and ended a really promising career as a goalie. Dad was crushed. Mom was relieved."

"So you're really going to hate it when you lose this bet?" he asked.

Her competitive spirit took a leap. "I'm not going to lose."

"Yeah?" He indicated the screen.

The Texans made a field goal.

"That's a long way from winning," she informed him. She took a bite of pizza, and the flavors burst on her tongue. Pepperoni, tomatoes, tangy cheeses, mushroom, onions, peppers, and underlying it all the masterful flavor of garlic. This pizza wasn't made for romance, and maybe that was why she'd ordered it. Because if she didn't take measures to counter her attraction to Teague, she'd fall in bed with him because he—she froze—because he was a man she could love.

She stared blindly, the pizza forgotten, the game forgotten. If she weren't careful, if she didn't take evasive action, this man would be the one who could break her heart.

My God. Twelve hours. In twelve hours, she'd come to *this?*

"Were you suddenly stricken by the horrified realization you were eating with your hands?" Teague's teasing voice broke through her reverie.

She realized she sat with a slice of pizza halfway to her open mouth. She put the pizza on her plate. She looked at him, his eyebrow raised quizzically, his dark, handsome face an allure she couldn't resist. "Do you believe in fate?"

Teague's other eyebrow winged upward. "Of course. I'm Hispanic. I'm Aztec. Fate writes her name on my soul."

"You're not all Hispanic and Aztec."

"No. My father was as Anglo as apple pie." Teague smiled, an easy smile. "But I don't remember him. Do *you* believe in fate?"

"Gosh, no." The action on the screen caught her attention, and she frowned at the instant replay. The Texans had scored. A touchdown, and they'd made the extra point. "My parents are Methodists."

"That would, of course, preclude any other belief system."

"Now who's being sarcastic?"

"Another score!" he said.

For a moment, she felt pleased that he'd acknowledged her wit. Then she realized he referred to the game. "What do you mean? The Texans just made a touchdown."

"The Cowboys turned over the ball on the first play, and the Texans took it on home. Again." The Texans were suddenly down by only four points, and they had a full quarter to play.

"I've never seen evidence of fate." Al-though when it came to this game, she was starting to wonder.

"Have you seen evidence of God?"

"Yes," she said truculently.

"Evidence you could prove without a doubt?" He laughed at her expression.

"You're cynical. You don't believe in God or fate. Why not?"

He took a pull of beer. "Every turning point in my life has come because I *chose* change. *I* made the decision to join the Marines. *I* made the decision to become a bodyguard. I've never had fate stick out her foot and trip me up."

"Me, either." She hoped that was true, al-though when Teague sat across from her wafting pheromones her way, she wasn't so sure.

An image flashed across the screen, an image she recognized. She frowned and came to an abrupt and nasty realization. "This game is a rerun!"

"Yeah, last year's preseason matchup be-tween the Cowboys and the Texans." He grinned as he watched her realize that he'd conned her. "Want me to tell you how it turns out?"

"Like I couldn't figure that out." The phone rang, and Kate rose to answer while glaring at the television. She should have known, but she'd been so distracted by Teague she hadn't even noticed this was a rerun. Now she was out ten bucks. Man, she hated to lose.

She hit the speaker on the phone, said, "Hello!" in a surly tone.

"Dear, what's wrong?"

"Mom! How are you?" Kate picked up the receiver and spoke quickly, breathlessly. *Guilty!* She might as well have shouted it to her mother. *I'm guilty! I couldn't prove the existence of God, I didn't notice I was watching last year's football game, and I'm considering sleeping with a guy for no good reason except that he makes me smoke, and I don't mean with a cigarette.*

"I'm fine, but are you? You sound frightened, Kate." Her mom's voice lowered to a whisper. "Is someone there with you? Is it the stalker? Should I call the police?"

"No! I mean, don't call the police!" Of all the things Kate didn't want, that was number one on the list. "The bodyguard is here with me. I'm safe."

Kate could almost hear her mother's mind

processing the information. "The body-guard? He's staying with you? Is *he* cute?"

Don't go there, Mom! "What do you mean?"

"I mean every time I ask if someone's cute, you tell me he's fat or he's old or he smells." Mom sounded sharp and impatient. "Is this guy fat or old or smelly?"

Kate looked across the large room at Teague, tough, muscular, young, and . . . Kate lowered her voice to a mere whisper. "He does smell."

Her mother huffed in disgust.

"Sort of exotic and masculine. Animal. I think it might be pure distilled sex."

Teague lifted his head, and for a moment Kate feared he'd somehow heard her.

But no, he looked down again.

She breathed a sigh of relief.

"This sounds promising," Mom said. "So is he cute?"

"Cute is the last word I would use to describe him."

Her mother knew Kate too well. "Handsome? Virile? Irresistible?"

"All those things, and absolutely unavailable."

"You mean he's married?" Mom sounded horrified.

"No. He's most definitely not that."

"So he's gay." Mom sounded satisfied with her deduction.

Kate burst into startled laughter. "N-no," she sputtered. "Absolutely not." Nothing could be more ludicrous.

Teague got up from the couch, collected the plates, put them in the dishwasher. Was he trying to convince Kate he was domesticated? Because it wasn't going to work.

Kate lowered her voice. "I mean he doesn't want to get involved."

"Show me a man who does," Mom said.

"Does what?" Kate asked absently. Teague looked really *good* being domestic.

"Want to get involved. If he's not married, he's available, he's catchable." Her mother spoke with the absolute confidence of a woman who knew her wiles. "You can have him dangling after you in no time."

"No." *Bad idea. Don't tempt me!* "I can't."

"Why not? You're pretty and smart."

Kate turned her back on Teague and talked toward the wall, her voice dipping ever lower. "Some men don't like smart."

"Dear, the trick is not to let them know."

Mom sounded as confident as any southern lady when faced with a recalcitrant man.

"It's a little late. Besides, I don't want a man like that. I want a man who appreciates me as I am."

"Dear, if you don't want this man, just say so. It's not as if I would urge you to grab the first man who doesn't stink." She sounded exasperated.

"It's not that, it's . . ." A masculine hand appeared from behind her, offering a snifter with brandy. She stared at the fingers, at the broad palm and the dark hair that sprinkled the knuckles and the back of the hand. His wrists were thick with muscle.

"Dear?"

"I gotta go, Mom." Kate took the drink, trying too hard not to touch his fingers. "He's serving me a drink."

"Good. You could use a night life."

"I'm stuck at home with a bodyguard."

"Who doesn't stink," Mom said cheerfully. "I don't know whether to hope he catches the stalker right away or hope you have to spend some time together. Bye, now!"

Kate stared at the telephone and listened to the buzz of the dial tone, then reluctantly turned to Teague, sure she'd have to explain something she had no desire to ex-plain.

Instead he said, "You're supposed to be following my routine. Observing my week. I work out every day. Do you have a problem with gyms?" He raised a mocking brow. "Do they not smell right?"

She pretended she didn't know what he meant. "I have a gym, too, right around the corner. Does that work for you?"

"Sounds good." He wasn't the sort of man who caviled at the necessity of working to remain physically fit. It was his job, and he would run or ride a bike or beat a bag with-out complaint.

The trouble was, when she thought of his doing those things, she noticed a marked increase in the temperature in the room. She considered the brandy. "I think I might need a bottle of water."

"Great." His cell phone sang a tinny rendi-tion of *Carmen.* "Get me one, too."

All right. He'd cleaned the kitchen. He'd fixed her a brandy. She could get him a bot-tle of water without any loss of womanhood.

She fetched two plastic bottles from the refrigerator and brought one back to him.

He took it with an absent nod. "That was

fast," he said into the phone, then he went to the window and looked out. "Doesn't like to have people check up on him, huh?"

"Who?" she asked.

He hung up and strode to the door. "The guy who just walked in the front door of the building, the former owner of your home, one Winston Porter. When Big Bob called him a little while ago, Winston threw one hell of a tantrum. Threatened you. Said he'd come by to teach you a lesson for sticking your nose into his business."

"My God. Then he's the stalker?"

"Maybe."

Someone pounded at the door, and her heart jolted. The bruises she'd been dismissing suddenly ached with renewed fervor, and she had a flash of that car bearing down on her.

She must have looked sick because Teague said soothingly, "I'd feel better if you got out of the way. Go into the bedroom or the bathroom."

"Shouldn't we call the police?"

"That would be great. Go and call them." Taking her arm, he escorted her toward the downstairs bedroom. "And stay in there until I call you."

She stared at the door he shut in her face, then dove for the phone. What if this guy had a gun?

Her hand trembled as she dialed 911, and while she reported an intruder she listened for action in the other room.

She could hear the murmur of men's voices in the living room. They sounded civil. They sounded unruffled.

The operator promised to send a squad car.

Kate's initial alarm dwindled. She began to feel foolish and cowardly for hiding in the bedroom.

The minutes ticked by, and she convinced herself she should take a peek. Taking a breath, she opened the door a crack.

The two men stood in the entry facing each other. At once she realized their low tones were a camouflage for at least one flaring temper.

Winston was tall, probably six feet six, young—and livid. He wore a tailored Armani suit and a starched white shirt with the collar open. He had a five-o'clock shadow on his square jaw. His big fists opened and closed as he spoke, and he towered over Teague like a man who was used to winning fights. "Who do you think you are? You've no right to harass me. So I've a few problems. Who doesn't drink too much and do the occasional line?" His British accent strengthened, and his voice rose with every word.

In stark contrast, Teague sounded cool and decisive. "We just called you and asked a few questions."

"Do you know how many people are calling me? I'm sick of it. Sick of all the vultures swarming around as if I were a carcass to be picked clean."

Kate realized Winston was drunk or high.

She wanted to call 911 again, to urge them to hurry. Her finger twitched on the numbers.

"I'll pay you when I get the money," Winston shouted. "I told you that before."

"We haven't talked before." Teague stood absolutely still, his gaze fixed on Winston's hand.

"This is my house. My place." Winston threw his arm out and knocked a vase off Kate's side table. It shattered on the hardwood floor.

The sound, the violence in her private sanctuary, made her flinch.

Something altered in Teague's stance.

He was no longer waiting. He was antici-pating. Prepared to finish the scene.

"She's changed it," Winston raged on. "That bitch has changed it."

"It's her place now." Sounding cocky and smug, Teague thrust his face into Winston's. "You're a loser. Now everybody knows it."

Winston sprang at Teague like a runaway dump truck.

Teague stepped aside and grasped Winston's wrist. In a smooth, swift motion, he sent the younger man crashing to the floor, then, planting his foot on Winston's spine, he twisted the man's wrist up and be-hind his back.

Kate gasped, the first noise she'd made, then covered her mouth to catch back the sound.

Teague's gaze flashed to the door where she stood, and for a moment she stared into the stark, soulless eyes of a predator.

Seven

Teague pulled on his weight-lifting gloves and flexed his fingers.

As far across the gym from him as she could be, Kate worked out in her kickboxing class. He could see her through the glass that separated the two rooms. She lifted her leg and her foot smacked the bag again and again. She wore a sleeveless blue T-shirt and matching blue bicycle shorts, and she scowled with effort. Right now, she didn't remember he was alive.

Or rather, she didn't want to remember.

Last night, with one damned, unguarded look, he'd frightened her into wariness.

And for what? That Winston guy might be strung out on drugs, but he had a great alibi—he had been in jail for the last week for DUI and possession, and he'd posted bail only two days before. So he was no longer a suspect.

Teague adjusted the weight on the tricep machine and began a slow, steady lift.

Teague had frightened people before with

his rage. The first time he'd done it, he had been fifteen. His mother had been drunk. From the time he was a kid, he'd carried the marks of her belt on his back. In the past, she had slapped him hard enough to cut his face with her cheap rings. This time, she'd come at him, fingernails bared, and she'd opened his cheek with her claws.

This time, as the blood trickled off his chin, he'd had it.

He'd grabbed her hands: that's all, just grabbed them, and *looked* at her.

And she'd gone from a shrieking witch to a blubbering mass of nerves.

She'd never physically attacked him again.

He hadn't understood what had happened that day, but slowly it had dawned on him that he had power in his gaze. Every once in a while in the service, when he lost his temper, people drew away from him, and when he was fighting . . . well, when the violence swept him, he'd more than once seen a soldier on the other side flee in terror.

Rolf had called him a berserker, a Viking invincible in the rage of battle.

Teague had laughed and pointed out that not a drop of Viking blood flowed through his veins. But . . . who knew? He sure as hell didn't.

Only Juanita had never been afraid of him. Only Juanita had ever loved him.

And look what he'd done to her.

The muscles at the back of Teague's arms screamed, and he winced as he lowered the weights. He'd better pay attention to what he was doing—he couldn't afford a torn tendon now. He had to care for Kate.

Well, not *care* for her, but make sure she was safe.

He moved to the next machine and set up for the bicep curl.

Last night, Kate had been polite to the police when they'd shown up to arrest Winston. She had given them a precise report on the whole scene and signed an autograph for one cop's daughter. She'd shown Teague his bedroom, offered him towels, extra blankets, and any toiletries he might have forgotten, and with a civilized smile paid him his ten-dollar winnings.

But the sexual tension that had hovered in the air between them had vanished, and when he'd touched her elbow she'd shied away from him as if he were a demon. Not that he minded her being a little in awe of him, but if danger threatened, he needed her to run toward him, not away from him.

And, in all reality, his ego was smarting. What had she told her mother on the phone last night? That he smelled like pure distilled sex.

His gaze flashed toward the window where Kate punched at the air.

Now . . . now she couldn't bear for him to touch her. He had to lull her fears and talk to her, touch her, without having her flinch as if he were the damned devil.

Yet why was he surprised at her reaction? He knew who he was. What he'd done.

The gray shadows of the past enveloped him, and he heard his mother's voice, shrill and contemptuous: *Goddamn it, Teague, you little bastard, you can't take that kid to a gang fight. Don't be so goddamned stupid. You're a stupid half-breed gringo and if you get knifed, no one will care. I sure as hell won't. But that kid—*

Teague cut off the voice. He didn't have to listen to her anymore. She was dead. His mother was dead. The past was set. No matter how hard he wished or fought, he couldn't change a thing.

He was waiting outside the door when the

kickboxing class let out. He could see Kate inside, milling around in the midst of the other women, waiting to get through. She smiled and chatted, stripped off her gloves, gulped from her bottle of water, used her towel to wipe at her forehead.

The first women out the door stopped short at the sight of him, then kept going, and each in turn gave him an intimate smile.

He smiled back. Every one of those women confirmed that his black sleeveless workout shirt and shorts worked wonders on the female libido, and that fit his plans exactly. He would demonstrate what a teddy bear he was, make Kate a little jealous, and get back in contact with her.

The hitch in the lineup caused women to bump and push. When he directed a smile at Kate, elbows jabbed her from every direction. The jostling made her roll her eyes, then crisply say, "Teague, I've got to shower and get ready. If you want to work out for a little longer . . ."

"No." He stepped in front of her, and she stopped so fast everybody behind her plowed into her and knocked her right into his chest.

She pushed away so fast the contact was as quick as a brand.

"Actually, I'm going to take you back in there"—he nodded at the workout room—"and give you some pointers on punching."

"What?" Kate cocked her head as if she'd developed difficulty with her hearing.

"You punch like a sissy. You need to put your body behind it. Let me show you." He started to take her arm to lead her back.

She slithered away through the crowd. "What's wrong with punching like a sissy?"

He gave her a look, one that plainly told her what he thought of her inanity.

One of the other women, an older gal who'd made her appreciation of his assets quite clear, asked, "Can you really teach us how to punch? That idiot Steve used to lead the class, and he never taught us how to do the moves right."

This was perfect. A large crowd would give Teague the chance to get back in touch with Kate without her feeling threatened. Yet in that brief moment of contact, the scent of Kate—sweaty, pungent, womanly—made him want her again. None of the other women here, and there were more attractive women, interested him at all.

Life was a bitch.

"What happened to Steve?" Teague herded them all back into the workout room.

"He flaked out about a month ago. Now one of us always leads the class." The woman pursed her lips. "Badly."

"Bobbie Jo, I think I do a nice job of leading this class!" one of the women objected.

"Nice and sissy," Bobbie Jo retorted. "C'mon, girls, let's learn how to kick the crap out of a mugger." She moved closer to Teague. "That *is* what you're going to teach us, isn't it?"

"Yes, ma'am. I'm Teague Ramos, and I specialize in kicking the crap out of muggers." Teague took his place in front of the milling women. "All right, fall in!"

They laughed, but they assembled in rough lines and looked at him expectantly.

Amazing how those military commands worked on civilians.

Kate hung back in the middle of the group, eyeing him cautiously. Of course. She had seen the beast, she was still scared, and Kate Montgomery didn't scare easily.

Sometimes during the rare and long

nights he spent alone, the question haunted him: Was he a beast? With a look, he panicked toughened warriors. He'd killed men—men who needed killing—and never dreamed of their corpses. The only thing that had ever haunted him was his memory of the streets, the odors, the high-pitched laughter . . . the helplessness. Especially the helplessness. He hated the memory of being little, of bigger people, teachers, guidance counselors, his *madre,* shoving him around, laughing at his aspirations, stripping him of dignity.

He hated the memory of what had happened to him, and he hated to think of it happening to Kate. To any of these ladies with their gold chains, their perfect workout clothes and their well-applied cosmetics. He was going to enjoy teaching them.

"First of all," he said, "you women don't have the muscle mass to carry off a punch or a kick unless you put your weight behind it. So don't punch with your arms, punch with your shoulder. See?" He demonstrated a punch that propelled his shoulder forward. "That gives you more momentum. Give that a try." He walked among them, adjusting their stances, grasping their wrists and showing them how to lead with their body.

Kate followed his instructions exactly, watched herself in the mirror, and practiced with a concentration that boded ill for any potential attacker.

That figured. She was soft, privileged, but he hadn't a doubt that something drove her to be the best, always. And he knew, for he saw it in her eyes, how very much she disliked having to look at everyone as a potential stalker.

He didn't like it, either. He didn't like having to casually question all the trainers at her gym, and feeling murderous when one of them made an admiring comment about Kate. He didn't like noticing little details like how short she trimmed her fingernails and her fascination with the local news—all of the local news—and how many hours she could watch it.

When this job was done, he could screw her, of course, and not give her a thought when he was done, but somehow . . . her allure felt different. Less trivial. More intense. A man with his background had no future with a woman like Kate. Didn't want one . . . but damn, he hated that he had no chance.

He was already committed, bound to a past that could never be corrected.

He strolled back to the front of the class. "Where should you hit someone with this kind of blow?"

"In a dark alley?" Bobbie Jo asked.

"Very funny." He flashed her a grin.

Kate marveled at how well he handled the class—and how cleverly he had maneuvered her. He wanted to teach her the basics of self-defense, so he inveigled his way into her group. Every one of the ladies was anxious to please him, worked hard for him—but none of them had ever looked into his eyes and seen the darkness that lurked there. That single glimpse into the bleakness of his soul terrified her. This man's outward appearance seemed so . . . normal.

Who was she kidding? He was definitely not normal. He was extraordinary. Every talent, every charm, every confidence seemed to reside within him. Yet within him no emotion seemed to flourish: no love, no hate, no empathy, no desperation, no happiness, no . . . nothing. If there was a hell, he personified it.

"Kate." His voice jerked her from her reverie. "Come up here and help demonstrate. Don't be shy."

Kate, who hadn't been shy since she was two and a half, glared venomously at him.

Then Bobbie Jo planted a hand in the middle of her back and gave her a shove.

Kate stumbled forward and kept going. What was the use of resisting? This time, he was going to win the battle. He simply wasn't going to win them all.

When she stood before him, she waited tensely. It didn't matter that yesterday he'd comforted her with his mere presence. Last night she'd looked into his eyes, and today when he touched her, she would feel the chill of his emptiness.

But he confounded her by being businesslike and efficient, and when he took her hand, his touch was impersonal and almost . . . well . . . normal.

He spread her fingers and showed them to the group. "Here's the problem with bones, especially delicate bones like this. They break. You've got to make a good fist, thumb here"—he manipulated the thumb across the outside of her fingers—"use the weight of your shoulder. The two best places to punch are the nose—noses break even more easily than fingers—and in the throat. The lips are okay, but splitting a lip isn't going to bring a grown man down. The eye—I'd stick those fingers out and gouge."

"Ohh." One of the ladies, a soft, gentle woman, put her hand to her stomach.

"No." He focused all his attention on her. "Don't get sick. Get mad. What's your name?"

"I'm Sandra." She squirmed, obviously embarrassed.

"Look at me." He gestured at himself, gestured at Kate. "I outweigh Kate by seventy-five pounds, and you might not have noticed, but I'm a guy."

The women chuckled.

"Guys like to watch boxing. They like to watch football. They like to fight, and some of them like to kill. I grew up in a rough neighborhood. I've seen fights between gangs for no more reason than someone wanted to prove his machismo. I've seen kids, little girls, crippled by stray gunshots, heard the wail of the ambulance, smelled blood." He wasn't pulling any punches now. His face was set and gray; his eyes were empty and cold.

He made Kate shiver.

"A soft-looking woman wears a target on her back." He paced before the class with a tread as soft as any predator's. "I can't promise that this stuff I teach you will save your life—if some guy is determined enough, he's going to take you down—but I can promise you'll make any son of a bitch who attacks you run and yell. Don't be afraid to hurt a man who hurts you. Maybe you'll make him run away and leave you to live another day with your husband or your kids or whomever you love."

All over the room, heads were nodding. Even Sandra, soft, gentle Sandra, had a determined expression on her face.

His intensity and honesty amazed Kate. In less than ten minutes, he'd changed a bunch of suburban housewives and career women into warriors. With a simple, powerful description of his experiences, he'd made them aware as they had never been aware before.

He returned to a brisk, instructional tone. "Stay away from the bony parts of the face like the cheeks and the chin. Now." He turned to Kate again. "About kicking. Kate, where are you going to kick someone?"

She gave him a significant look. "In the groin."

The room exploded with laughter and a release of tension.

He waited until the hilarity had faded. "Where else?"

She studied him, looked him over thoroughly. "Your knees."

"Right." He turned back to the class. "Any joint is vulnerable, and I like the knee for a couple of reasons. You can bring a strong man down with a well-placed blow that knocks his knee sideways or backward. Your attacker's hands aren't in the vicinity, so he can't grab your foot."

"Want me to practice on you?" Kate offered.

The women were laughing now, and she played to the crowd.

"You're too kind," he mocked. "Now let's talk about your kicking technique—which is none too good. Aim your knee at your target," he said.

"You mean the foot," she answered.

"No, the knee," he corrected. "The knee determines where the foot is going to go and where the kick is going to land."

That made sense, and she nodded.

"Then you turn your hip and snap the foot in one smooth motion." He demonstrated, then indicated Kate should try, also. He moved with her as she kicked, adjusting her forward, giving her more power. As she kicked, he told the class, "If you're wearing flat shoes, and I hope you will be, use the ball of your foot. You'll devastate him. If you're wearing high heels"—he grinned— "put the heel through his foot. A heel is a great weapon." He let go of Kate easily. "But that's a different technique altogether."

Kate aimed her gaze at the mirror and repeated the move until she had it perfect. She was surprised at how much more in control it made her feel to know how to defend herself. She hadn't really felt that way since her dad's death. For that peace of mind, she was grateful to Teague.

Teague. He stood with his hands on his hips and watched Bobbie Jo kick. She had her jaw locked and her eyes narrowed, and she didn't let him go until he pronounced her lethal.

Bobbie Jo asked, "Teague, could you come and talk to my knitting group? We have a wife whose husband beat her up.

Twice. We could use someone who'll tell us how to protect ourselves."

Teague chuckled, a long, low laugh that raised goose bumps on Kate's skin. With a kindness she never suspected of him, he said, "Yeah. I'd be glad to do it. Tell me the night and the time. By the way, did you know you can do a lot of damage with those knitting needles?"

As Kate watched him, she thought that perhaps he did have a soul somewhere inside that glorious shell. Perhaps it was only wrapped in layers of indifference cultivated by seeing too much pain and hearing too many cries.

It was an intriguing proposition: Could a woman bring life back to a man who was determined never to allow emotion to touch him?

Eight

"She's walking. She's walking. . . ."

"C'mon, baby, turn around, let me see a little of that ass."

"Whoaaa. There she goes."

Teague paused just inside the security center. The guys were gathered around one of the monitors, ignoring their duty and making the kinds of sounds a construction crew would make when a fine-looking woman walked by.

Teague didn't really care. It happened occasionally—guys would be guys, and surveillance was a tedious job that involved watching innocent people and trying to decide if they could be guilty. He required only that his men refrain when the women he employed were around, and that they made damned good and sure someone was keeping an eye on security while they ogled the goods.

"That is one fine piece of—"

Teague lazily shut the door with a click. "Is this something that requires my attention?"

The comments and the laughter died, leaving his men looking abashed enough to rouse Teague's curiosity. He pushed his way into the crowd—and saw *her.*

There, on the monitor, Kate walked.

She wore a skirt, a clingy pink skirt with a ruffled hem that flirted with her knees and drew a man's gaze up toward her fine and rounded rear . . . which she had apparently encased in one of the smallest thongs on the face of the earth.

At least he hoped she wore a thong. He sure didn't see any sign of one. But a girl like her never went without underwear.

Did she?

For all intents and purposes, she was bare-assed beneath that skirt. That set his imagination on fire.

"Look, Boss." Big Bob pointed to the screen. "Juanita's stopping her."

"Hell." Teague watched as Juanita introduced herself.

Juanita had never let that wheelchair slow her down. With her short brown hair and her comfortable wardrobe, she patrolled the corridors of the capitol, listening to conversations, looking innocent, batting her big brown eyes at the compassionate who helped her and bugging the people who tried to ignore her.

"Juanita must have heard rumors about you and Miss Montgomery," Big Bob said. "That Juanita—she's the best on the floor. Nothing escapes her attention."

"Yeah." Teague loosened his tie. "I know." Right now he wished there were things that *did* escape her.

Kate took Juanita's hand, smiled, and made conversation.

Why couldn't life be easy? Why did everything have to get jumbled up in love and guilt and sex and . . . well, sex was okay. Sex was *great.* But the rest of those lousy emotions left a man stumbling around in the dark trying to figure out what to do to make his women happy, and wondering why seeing Juanita and Kate together made him feel this weird combination of horror and delight.

"They're going in opposite directions!"

"Good." Because now Teague could concentrate on Kate and that skirt and those panties or lack thereof.

Okay, she'd been wearing that outfit this morning when they'd left her loft, but it was raining, the first cool rain of a Texas autumn, and she'd donned a raincoat. When they got to the capitol, she'd gone off to find a cameraman—whenever she found one taking a break, she had been filming bits for the piece about him.

God. He tugged at his tie. What was wrong with him? He couldn't take his gaze off her or her austere tan shirt, which looked like a reporter's on-camera garb, or the tall crisscrossed sandals that added inches to her long, sleek legs.

Senator Oberlin noticed. Teague watched as he lingered at the corner of the corridor, waiting to intercept Kate, then faked surprise and pleasure at running into her. Too bad it made Teague murderously angry to see the senator slide his arm around her shoulders and hug her like a paternal uncle when in fact he took the occasion to try for a peek down her blouse. Teague was pleased when Kate had the good sense to slide out from under Oberlin's arm, make her excuses, and continue on her way.

Oberlin stood and watched her go.

"I've got to give it to him—the old guy has good taste." Chun sat glued to the monitor, his nose only inches away from the screen.

"That is one fine pair of legs, and they are connected to one fine—"

Teague had him by the collar and up against the wall before Chun could gasp for air. "What were you saying?"

"Shit. Sir. I forgot you were here." Chun's eyes bulged. "I didn't mean to be disrespectful, sir. I would never stare at your woman."

Teague smacked him against the wall again. "She's not my woman, but she is a client." He looked around at the other men who stood sheepish and embarrassed. "While you're enjoying her various body parts, gentlemen, I hope you're also watching for suspicious behavior."

"Yes, sir, we are!" Big Bob saluted as if Teague were his commanding officer. "No suspects close, sir! You don't need to worry about us keeping an eye on her, sir! We're doing our damnedest, sir!"

Teague loosened his grip on Chun's shirt. "All right, fine, get back to work. Miss Montgomery's not the only job we have here."

"Yeah, but she's the most fun to watch." Big Bob smiled slyly. "Course, we can't blame you for wanting to do the watching yourself. If she were mine, I'd beat up guys who looked at her, too."

"She's not mine, and I'm not beating anyone up over her," Teague said testily.

Chun made a choking sound and rubbed his throat.

"I didn't hurt you!" As eyebrows rose throughout the room, Teague's ire shot up. "I don't pay you guys to hang around in here. Go find the bad guys."

"Yes, sir."

"Yes, Teague."

He heard murmurs and saw smirks as everyone sidled past him, and when he turned to glare at Big Bob, Big Bob pointed to the monitor and said, "I have to watch her for the next hour. That *is* my job."

"Right." Teague shut the door on the closet and headed down toward the East Wing, ground floor. He had business with Miss No Underpants.

He and Kate had settled into an odd sort of truce. He lived in her house, took his turn ordering takeout, did his own laundry, argued about who should have control of the TV remote. The first two days, she'd looked at him warily a lot, as if expecting him to give her *the look* and send her fleeing again.

But he'd been careful to keep it light and normal—even though, for him, it was not normal to spend time in a woman's apartment and not in her bed.

But he didn't tell her that. He didn't kiss her, he touched her only casually—although he made sure he did touch her frequently—and he got his reward. She had relaxed back into letting him take care of her, and he had concentrated on keeping it spontaneous and breezy so he could keep her safe from a stalker. He seemed to have succeeded, and, weirdly enough, he sort of liked living with her . . . even without sex.

Not that he wanted his guys to know that.

He glowered for a moment, thinking of when she blew off his nuts by winning an argument about the education bills in the Senate. He never had been a good loser, although he wasn't stupid enough to think he won that one. But a moment later a crooked little smile curled the edge of his mouth. Maybe for Kate he could become a good loser. She could argue him right into the sheets.

After hearing his qualifications in security, Kate's gym had let him take over the kick-boxing class. Every morning he worked with the ladies on their self-defense skills—and he liked them. He'd never really dealt with American women in their natural habitat. He'd seen them on the streets in Brownsville. He'd guarded them when they were wearing their best diamonds. He'd dated them when they wanted to walk on the wild side. But he'd never hung around long enough to hear them brag about their kids, complain about their husbands and their jobs, tell each other how good they looked with that extra ten pounds. They were really nice people, and Kate fit right in.

In fact, Kate fit right in everywhere. She had the gift of adapting, making herself welcome wherever she went, empathizing in a way that made everyone like her. Even Linda Nguyen seemed to tolerate her, and Linda had a personality like an Uzi.

He turned the corner and caught sight of Kate.

So while he'd been playing house with her, apparently he'd convinced her he was as harmless as a fixed old tomcat because here she was, prancing around the corridors of the Texas Capitol with no panties. "Kate!"

She turned at the sound of his voice and

smiled. Smiled as if she were pleased to see him.

He was damned pleased to see her, too. Too damned pleased, and still way too re- lieved that she didn't sidle away. "Come with me."

She hurried to his side and followed him to the smallest surveillance closet. In a low voice, she questioned, "Did you see some- thing?"

"I sure did."

"About the stalker? So this is over?"

He stopped before the door and looked at her in exasperation.

She stood with her hand on her chest as if she were relieved. Glad their time together was over.

"Hardly that." With his key card, he opened the lock.

His men would see them go in. They'd know what he was doing. They'd laugh and nudge each other.

Teague didn't care. Someday he would, but right now he needed to know what Kate wore under her skirt. Everything about Kate called to him, and he needed to see, to taste, to know. . . .

In a fury at his own lack of control, and in a frenzy of desire, he gestured her inside.

There, monitors gazed out on hallways and computers hummed, and she walked from one to another, her hand flexing on her briefcase.

He shut the door behind him, the definite *thunk* of a reinforced door against a metal frame.

She turned to watch him, her head tilted as if sensing something of his turbulence. Yet her eyes were puzzled. She didn't understand the cause of his mood.

He stood, back against the door, his chest rising and falling as he stared at her . . . and lusted.

Three nights ago she had seen the killer in him.

Today she obviously saw a different sort of beast, for she flushed. Her gaze dropped. He saw her and realized that this was the moment that proved whether he had frightened her beyond all possibility of desire. This was the ultimate proof—would she let him touch her intimately? Would she trust him not to hurt her?

A hesitant smile trembled on her lips. When she lifted her gaze once more, her eyes were heavy, slumberous. "Is it news you have for me? Or something . . . else?"

She wasn't afraid. She wanted him, too.

He advanced so quickly she didn't have time to retreat. Didn't have a place to retreat. He pushed her against the bare wall, pressed her there with his body against hers. Taking her face in his hands, he kissed her. Penetrated her mouth at once, without taking the time to soften her with gentle touches of his lips and murmured words of admiration.

He didn't understand himself. With her, he lost all finesse, becoming a primitive, overcome with lust and half mad with need.

Maybe that was what the guys had seen in him.

But Kate answered him as if she felt the same madness. Her mouth opened beneath his. She grasped his head, sliding her hands into his hair and holding him still as he held her. And they kissed. God, how they kissed! His tongue ravaged her mouth, and she sucked on it so passionately he thought she must want to be taken as fiercely as he wanted to take.

Like a narcotic, the taste of her filled his senses, making him want more. She smelled of soap and amber and lavender, clean, warm, and expensive. He nibbled on her lower lip, slid his tongue along the smooth ridges of her teeth. With his eyes closed, he sampled the skin on her cheeks and her eyelids, and as he smoothed his lips over her brow, his hands glided down to her shoulders and settled on her breasts.

He loved boobs, all shapes, all sizes, on any woman and every woman.

But Kate's boobs . . . as he cupped them, weighed them, those two lovely round globes, he found them more magnificent than any he'd ever held. She wore a bra . . . why the hell did she wear a bra when she wore tiny panties, or none at all?

But he didn't pretend to understand women, and certainly not this woman with her intelligence and her wit.

She leaned her head against the wall, distracting him with the sleek length of her throat.

He nuzzled the softest place, sinking his teeth in the skin over her vein.

Her intake of breath vibrated through him, and he pressed his hips against her, trying to relieve the pressure in his loins.

Nothing could do that except to have her.

She moaned as if he'd brought her to ecstasy. Her lips were softly open. Her eyes
were closed. She looked like a woman in
the throes of climax.

The sound, the scent, the view drove him
to satisfy the curiosity that had brought him
in here.

Gently, so gently, he cupped her buttocks.
The material slipped smoothly beneath his
grasp. So soft. So feminine. "Am I hurting
you?" His voice was a husky rasp.

"No." Her eyes opened. She pierced him
with glorious blue desire. "No, you're not
hurting me at all."

He could be gentle. He could be . . . hers.

Once again he kissed her.

Or tasted her, she wasn't sure which. It
was an investigation, a questioning, as if he
wanted to know . . . all kinds of things. Like
whether she wanted to kiss him back, and
how their bodies meshed together, and if
the two of them could remain vertical when
the biggest magnet in the world was trying
to knock them off their feet and into bed.

The answers were yes, nicely, and God
she hoped so.

Because as their bodies melded together,
and adjusted, and melded again, and as

their lips touched, and turned, and touched again, she wanted nothing so much as to push him onto the floor, rip off his clothes, and screw him silly. The offer he'd silently made the first time she'd seen him—to pull her into a maelstrom of sex and show her pleasure until she reeled from delight—sprang to life in a blaze so hot she felt singed, wicked, glorious.

My God. As if she didn't have enough complications in her life, this one had to come up now.

Vaguely she was aware of the pun, for what had come up was pressed tightly to her belly, and when she rolled her hips against it, Teague pulled her up onto her toes. His fingers explored her. They found the waistband of her thong.

And he gave a husky laugh. It sounded as if he were speaking to himself when he said, "Wouldn't you know it?"

"Know what?" Languorously, she watched him from beneath lids that felt too heavy to lift.

"That you would always be a lady." He caught her chin in his hands. His voice was a husky murmur. "When you want me, when you're ready to submit to me, all you have to do is leave your panties off. And tell me, darling, let me know what you've done. When you tell me, I'll be yours for as long as you want me."

He had always been a handsome man, but now, with his lips damp and his smile flashing, he wore the face of a lover.

Yet he was ruthless.

She was still catching her breath when he delivered the ultimatum. The kind of ultimatum that required working brain cells, but in fact Teague and his magic kisses had ruined every cognitive function.

She stared at him and tried to think, but her reaction was more instinct than intellect.

It didn't matter that Teague looked as if he would fit in her life. That was an illusion.

It didn't matter that she suffered an infatuation so acute it felt like love.

He was dangerous.

She knew it in her bones, just as she knew he wanted her. She'd seen it in his face. She knew, too, that if she gave in, landed in his bed, found ecstasy in his touch, she would be the one hurt when he walked away.

And he would walk away. He was the kind of man who left every woman, every time.

Without moving, he watched Kate. He saw

the moment she decided against him, and he said, "You're probably right. I was unprofessional. We should never have touched. Catching your stalker is a job, and I don't screw my clients. But we would be so good together." His voice dropped to a heated whisper. "So good together."

All too aware of the cameras and the eyes that were fixed on her from every angle, Kate walked down the corridor. Her face was hot, her fingers trembled, but she managed to maintain her dignity right up to the time she entered the ladies' restroom.

Thank God it was empty, for her knees buckled, and she used the sink for support.

The woman she saw in the mirror had swollen lips, rosy cheeks, a febrile sparkle in the eyes. This woman looked as if she perched on the edge of orgasm. And perhaps she did.

It had been only a kiss. Or two.

From Teague Ramos.

She moaned softly.

Her relationships had been with middle-class and upper-class white guys because those were the guys she knew, the guys with whom she had stuff in common. Backgrounds, schooling, religion. She didn't have a single thing in common with Teague Ramos.

She looked at herself again, wet a pad of paper towels, and blotted her face.

His expensive clothes fit him perfectly, and he wore them as if he'd been born to them. His voice was deep, cool, and smooth, like blended whiskey over ice, and he used words with precision. His hands . . . his hands were a seduction: broad-palmed, long-fingered, nails smoothed and clean. The kind of hands a woman imagined giving ecstasy with each intimate touch.

The water did nothing to cool her thoughts. In fact, she was surprised steam hadn't fogged the mirror. She wished it had. She wished she didn't have to look at herself and know . . . know she would have jumped his bones right there in the surveillance closet without any attention to comfort, birth control, or safety.

She had obviously lost her mind.

Teague hadn't been born to the wealth or the privilege or the accent or the cleanliness. When he wished, he looked like a thug, and he did such a good enough job of it that he had fooled her.

Because at one point in his life, that was who he had been.

And that was the problem, wasn't it? None of the men Kate had slept with—none of the men Kate had ever known—knew how to be bad. None of them gave off waves of sexuality so intoxicating a woman wanted to breathe it in and forget everything she'd ever known, because what he would show her would be better, more . . . fulfilling. If she slept with Teague, she would never find satisfaction with another man.

Suddenly, violently, she threw the paper towels into the garbage.

Sure, she was being stalked. But tonight she was going to Senator Oberlin's anniversary party. Everyone in Austin would know she reported the news. They would feed her information or try to keep her from the truth. She had to be at her sharpest. She didn't need the kind of conflict she felt with Teague. She needed to carry on confidently, to show the world, all its skeptics, and, most important, Teague Ramos, that she was a reporter on the brink of success.

And success would not come by hyper-

ventilating about Teague, no matter how attractive and irresistible he might be.

Action must be taken.

Pulling out her cell phone, she punched in
her mother's number, and when her mom
answered, Kate said, "I need a date for
tonight. Do you think Dean Sanders is
busy?"

Nine

Kate dabbed Jo Malone amber and lavender eau de cologne in each of her pulse spots, and lightly misted her hair. She clipped her bangs back with a gold spangled barrette and applied her cosmetics with great care and a mind to the drama of evening. She donned a strapless bra and matching panties she had purchased only that day. Made of thin rose silk, the bra contained her breasts and gave them a smooth line, while the panties were a thong so brief it was ludicrous to wear it. . . .

But she would. She would.

Tonight was, after all, Senator Oberlin's party and the first time Teague would be seeing her dressed in anything except workout clothes and the basic reporter's outfit—a shirt that looked good on film, and anything at all on the bottom.

That was what got her in trouble today. Teague had seemed to appreciate her frilly pink skirt a little more than she had expected.

Sure, she knew she looked good in it, and maybe she had worn it to provoke him, but in her wildest dreams she couldn't have imagined those kisses in the surveillance closet.

At the memory, she found herself standing in the middle of her bedroom, eyes closed, hand pressed to her heart, trying to contain her breathing.

Teague had been ruthless in giving her pleasure and she'd been insatiable in seeking it, and nothing like that had ever before happened in her life. She hadn't imagined she could respond with such desire, without embarrassment, without a thought to the consequences.

But she had done the right thing. She had dodged the bullet. She was going to this party with a date, putting Teague firmly in his place as her bodyguard.

With quick, nervous motions she put her diamond studs in her ears. Of course, she hadn't told Teague yet. . . .

The fact that she was considering doing as he instructed, and leaving her thong off . . . well, that showed how severely he'd influenced her. And not for the better, either. All the way through college she'd been known as the girl who exuded common sense and responsibility. She'd been the one to whom her friends came to sing their sad songs about the guy who'd done them wrong. Now some weird combination of hormones and abstinence had produced a personality she scarcely recognized as her own. As she slithered into her simple ankle-length red shantung silk sheath, she hung on to sanity by a thread.

She would *not* go out there with nothing beneath her gown.

She slipped on her short-heeled gold strappy sandals, picked up her Mary Francis purse, and looked in the mirror.

The silk skimmed her figure, clinging at her breasts and hips. Slit on both sides up to the knee, when she walked it drifted away from her calves to tease a man's interest. With its all-over coverage yet its hint of mystery, this was the kind of gown of which her mother approved. Kate looked good— even wearing her panties.

With a satisfied smile at her reflection, she walked out of her room and down the stairs—then stopped short.

If she looked good, Teague looked fabulous. He stood there in a European-cut black suit that fit his narrow body and broad shoulders so well it could only have been designer made and expertly tailored. His starched white shirt gleamed, his red tie spoke of power and assurance. He was easily the most handsome man she'd ever met, and in that garb, he raised her internal temperature to that of a blast furnace.

When he saw her, his face went still. His golden eyes widened, then narrowed. He looked as if he wanted to spring on her.

She could have sworn he stopped breathing—God knows she did.

She didn't know what she would have said, what blunder she would have made, if not for the ringing of the doorbell.

She jumped.

Teague looked at the door, and as if he knew what she'd done, he asked, "Who do you suppose that is?"

"My date." She winced at the bright, nervous tone of her voice.

"Ah." Teague considered her, and he saw right through the sophisticated veneer down to the woman grappling with her own sexuality—and her unwelcome attraction to him. "Then I'd better let him in, hadn't I?"

"I'll do it." She started for the foyer, then stopped. "I guess you *should* do that."

"It would be better."

She watched him walk away and wished she'd thought this out a little more thoroughly. Teague was answering the door like a father. Not a disapproving father; his face revealed no expression. But he was not who Dean Sanders expected to see.

Dean Sanders was tall, blond, blue-eyed, and looked, in some indefinable way, like a lawyer. "Hello?" He ducked back and looked at the name over the doorbell. "I thought . . . that is . . . I was looking for Kate Montgomery?"

Kate went forward to rescue poor Dean. "I'm here."

Teague moved aside to make room for her in the doorway.

"This is Teague Ramos, my bodyguard." She placed her hand on Teague's arm as if that would prove he was harmless.

He didn't move. Didn't flinch. Might as well have been the wall for all the reaction he showed.

"Your . . . bodyguard?" Dean blinked as if his contact lenses were too tight.

"I see your mother didn't fill you in on the

details," Kate said. Teague might have been the sun—she didn't dare stare directly at him for fear he'd burn her with his glare. "Come in and we'll tell you all about it."

"We?" Dean looked from one to the other again.

What a slip of the tongue. Freud would be proud! "I thought you'd be interested in how a bodyguard does his job. Most guys are fascinated. Come on in while I get my wrap."

"Yeah." With open enthusiasm, Dean stuck out his hand to Teague. "Dean Sanders—glad to meet you. What are you guarding Kate against?"

Kate went to collect her purse while Teague filled Dean in on her stalker and the measures they were taking to thwart him. Teague sounded neutral, a professional doing his job.

That was good. She wanted him to be disinterested. Or rather—she wanted to be uninterested in him. She loitered by her closet, listening as Teague said, "I know I can trust you to keep quiet about the stalking. We're trying to lure the stalker in, and that won't happen if a spotlight suddenly shines on the case."

"Heavens, yes, I understand completely! Thank you for taking me into your confidence. I assure you, I won't betray it, or her." Dean sounded wrenchingly sincere.

A pang of guilt clutched at Kate. She was using Dean as a screen between Teague and her. She didn't have one iota of interest in him, but apparently he was already interested in her.

This was a disaster.

"I drive Kate when she goes out at night," Teague said. "I know it puts a real crimp on your date, but those are the rules."

The rules? Since when?

"Do you want to ride along with us?" Teague continued his impassive bodyguard act.

"Oh." Dean chewed his lip. "That would be awkward."

"She's got a small Beemer," Teague informed him.

"And uncomfortable. This one time, why don't I follow you?" Dean sounded like a good soldier.

She returned, pretending that she hadn't overheard a word.

"Kate, I know I'm being gauche, but I'm almost glad this happened to you. I've been admiring you on the news, bothering Mother to fix me up with you, and I'll bet the only reason you consented to this evening was because you were going crazy being confined under tight security!" Dean said winningly.

Kate stared at him. Realized that he was a decent-looking man. Realized he was probably a nice guy. Knew for sure the two of them had a lot in common. And she wished he were anywhere but here. "I'm flattered," she said. "But Teague has made my situation quite bearable."

"I can see that." Dean beamed at him. "You're right, he's a remarkable guy. I don't normally expect a chaperon on my dates, but I sure understand this time."

"Yeah." For the first time, she gathered the nerve to look at Teague.

He stood straight, shoulders back. His black hair had been tied back from his face. His golden eyes never blinked as they watched her, and she fell into his gaze, helpless to stem the tide of desire and insight that united them. The atmosphere grew heated and smoky. He spoke not a word, but she had never seen anyone say nothing with such eloquence.

Dean seemed to notice nothing out of the ordinary. He straightened his tie and asked, "Ready?"

"Just a minute." Her voice did *not* sound normal; rather, it sounded as if she were speaking into a fog. "I forgot something."

Going back up to her bedroom, she removed her thong.

George checked his watch. Where was she? All the other guests had arrived, but not the guest for whom he had given this party.

Kate Montgomery still hadn't put in an appearance.

He and Evelyn stood in their elegant foyer in their sleek, modern home and ignored the other room in which sixty-five very influential people sipped champagne and chatted. A five-piece ensemble played light jazz, the kind that sounded hip but was still recognizable as a melody. George had spent a great deal on a new focal point over the fireplace—an original oil painting by Gilford Blumfield—because Kate was a well-brought-up young lady who appreciated fine art. Everything was as he'd planned. Everything was perfect.

She *had* to come. Kate had said she would come.

Evelyn tugged at the sleeve of his tuxedo. "Shouldn't we go in?"

George had forgotten she was there. He jumped, and he almost swore at her, almost let loose the string of profanity his daddy had used when he put his fist through the wall and cursed his poverty.

Yet Senator George Oberlin did not swear. Swearing was bad for his image as a righteous, law-abiding, churchgoing man. And more than anything, the memory of those profane words told George he needed to gain control.

Kate Montgomery didn't want a man who cussed like a stupid truck driver.

"We'll go in in a minute." George's heart soared with hope as their very proper British butler opened the door. "This might be . . . ahh. There she is."

Kate Montgomery had arrived, with a face like her mother's, but younger, firmer, not quite so kind and not at all trusting. She wore red silk. She moved like a living seduction and—he frowned—it looked as if she wore nothing beneath her gown.

That was not appropriate. When she was his, she'd have to change.

Beside him, he heard Evelyn gasp.

"Kate." He started forward, his hand outstretched to grasp the woman whom fate had returned to him.

And Teague Ramos stepped to her side.

George froze. He couldn't believe his eyes. His head pounded. Teague Ramos. Here, in his house, with Kate Montgomery. It wasn't *possible.*

"Senator Oberlin." Kate smiled up at him without a hint of personal awareness. "Thank you for inviting me to your anniversary party. May I introduce Teague Ramos?"

George stared at the man who towered over him by three inches, who was twenty years younger and had a well-deserved reputation for heartlessness. Ramos slept with beautiful women and never cared when they fell in love with him. He kept his own secrets and everyone else's. When he gave his word, he never went back on it. And he was almost, *almost,* as dangerous as George himself.

Then another man walked up. Blond, tall,

with an easy smile and a confident stride that shouted he'd attended the best schools and had the finest background. George recognized him. Dean Sanders, a lawyer with a good firm, a man with political ambitions that would no doubt be fulfilled. "Good to see you, Senator Oberlin." His handshake was firm and confident. "I hope you don't mind me dropping in, especially since I'm escorting the most beautiful woman here."

Ramos stepped back.

"Yes, of course!" George didn't have to feign confusion when he asked, "So Miss Montgomery has two escorts tonight?"

"Teague is the man I'm currently doing a story on." Kate's hand wasn't on Ramos's arm. She didn't smile at him as if they were lovers.

But . . . currently doing a story on? Maybe, but sexual tension steamed between them. Any fool could sense it, and George was no fool.

Or maybe he was, for standing here greeting the ghost of his lost love and discovering that history had repeated itself.

But right now, no matter how much he wished to, he couldn't have Ramos taken out and beat up. His stylish home in Austin's most prestigious district was full of guests elegant, influential, wealthy guests. Dressed in tuxedos and designer dresses, they mingled and gossiped, and they did not need to gossip about him . . . and Kate. So with a little too much heartiness, he shook Ramos's hand. "I'm constantly surprised at what a small world this is." To Kate, he said, "I'm the one who recommended Ramos's firm for the job at the great Texas Capitol."

"Really?" His eyes inscrutable, Ramos returned the handshake. "I had no idea."

Actually George's point had been: *He's a minority and a veteran. It'll look good to the public.*

"Welcome to my home. All . . . three . . . of you. I'm so glad you're settling in here in Austin, Kate." George half turned his back on Ramos and looked between Kate and Dean. "How long have you two been dating?"

"This is our first date," Kate said.

"But hopefully not our last," Dean added.

She smiled at him. "I'm sure our mothers can arrange something."

Dean laughed and hugged her shoulders. "I've got your number now."

George didn't give a crap if that white-bread lawyer escorted Kate anywhere. Sanders was the kind of guy women married—upright, honorable, and boring. No threat to George at all. *Ramos* was the man who could sucker a woman into a hot affair, the kind that branded her for life and left her longing for the wild side.

But reading Ramos's narrow-eyed stare, George would say the Mexican didn't like the camaraderie between Sanders and Kate one bit.

Good. George could build on that. "So, Dean, Kate, your mothers know each other. You two have a lot in common."

"It's amazing we never met before." Dean didn't seem to notice when Kate slipped out from under his embrace. "I've only lived in Austin, but she has family here. My sister attended Vanderbilt, too, and they were members of the same sorority. And we're members of the same health club!"

"Delightful." George was talking about that sneer on Ramos's face, not Dean and Kate's acquaintance.

Evelyn touched his sleeve, recalling him to his duty. So he introduced their guests to the quivering pile of sagging skin and trembling bones that was his life's mate. "This is my wife, Evelyn, my love and the reason I'm blessed enough to be able to give this anniversary party." Turning to Evelyn, he saw the glazed shock on her face as she gazed at Kate, and he squeezed her hand warningly—and hard.

"Wel-welcome," she stammered. "Mr. . . . Mr. Ramos. Mr. Sanders."

"Call me Dean," Sanders said heartily.

"Yes. Thank you, Dean. I will." Evelyn transferred her attention to Kate. "You . . . here. Welcome, Miss Montgomery." As if she were in a daze, she raised her hand and stroked Kate's cheek with her fingertips. "I've been watching you on the television. It's amazing how much you look like your mother. Like—" George's elbow made contact with her ribs. She broke off with a gasp, and the words rushed out on a single breath. "Thank you for coming to our anniversary party."

Their anniversary wasn't for four months, but no one knew that except George and Evelyn. A lot of glittering presents had made their appearance, despite the invitation's *No gifts, please,* and he didn't want to have to explain that his wife was an alcoholic and didn't remember the date of their anniversary. Especially not with reporters around. He glanced in at Linda Nguyen from KTTV and Maxwell Estevez from KTRQ. They had a tendency to check on every little slipup, and it wasn't that hard to discover the true date of their marriage.

Although—George transferred his attention to Brad Hasselbeck—he had insurance there. Brad Hasselbeck badly wanted to stay on George's good side, and he did as he was told when he was told. Right now, George was happy with Brad for moving so swiftly to bring Kate to the station.

Brad had better hope George stayed happy.

"Your twenty-fifth anniversary!" Kate said. "How wonderful to be married for so long. Congratulations, Mrs. Oberlin."

For so long? George and Evelyn had been married thirty-two years, ever since he'd realized the unattractive eighteen-year-old's family owned land and wealth in Hobart County and had convinced her to elope. He'd told Kate twenty-five years because he thought it made him sound younger, but to a girl Kate's age, even that was too much. He should have said . . . it didn't matter what he should have said.

She was young. He was more mature. Women her age married men his age all the time.

"Your silver anniversary. That's great!" Dean smiled widely and turned to Kate. "My parents just celebrated their thirty-fifth."

"Incredible," Kate murmured.

Her gaze was on that Mexican Ramos, who took Evelyn's trembling hand and bowed over it. "Twenty-five years is indeed a reason for celebration. Congratulations, Mrs. Oberlin." He glanced at George. "You, too, Senator."

Evelyn's southern belle persona had taken a battering over the years, but she donned a gracious smile and gestured toward the doors that opened into the gallery. "Won't you go on in and join the other guests? Ah, Freddy"—the butler made his appearance—"please find Miss Montgomery, Mr. Sanders, and Mr. Ramos some champagne."

As Freddy escorted Ramos, Sanders, and Kate into the gallery, Evelyn sagged as if her knees had given way. It was funny how much she feared her husband. George had never laid a hand on her, but somewhere along the line she'd slowly turned into this trembling bowl of Jell-O—Jell-O mixed liberally with vodka.

"Stand up." George grabbed her arm. "Smile. You knew she was coming."

"I didn't . . . I didn't know." Evelyn sounded as if she were dying. "You didn't tell me."

He'd had the butler handle the invitations, and George *hadn't* told her, but he didn't let that change his answer. "Yes, I did. You must have been drunk. Again."

"You *didn't* tell me." She jerked her arm away, and it must have hurt because he'd been pinching it hard. "I would have remembered *that.* You didn't." Turning her back on him, she unsteadily walked away.

"Evelyn," he called in his coldest, most deadly tone.

She stopped. She didn't turn, but she stopped, a slender figure dressed in pristine white velvet.

"Remember—no drinking tonight." He made sure his voice reached her and only her. "Or I'll make you sorry."

Turning, she stared at him, her eyes glowing with anguish. "I'm already going to burn in hell. I warn you, George, I'm not going to let you get away with this again."

George laughed with genuine amusement. "Oh, my darling, I'm trembling with fear." As if *she* could ever hurt *him.*

Then he realized—she hadn't been so careful about her voice. People had heard her. They *stared.* Then they looked away, and a few of the braver or more ignorant souls tittered.

Kate was deep in conversation with Dean, and she seemed not to notice, but Ramos turned his head and listened, and in his stillness it seemed he was weighing each word.

George burned with fury. He'd worked too hard to be a part of this society to be disgraced by his alcoholic, psychotic wife. He smiled a brave, pained smile, willing to sacrifice his image as a happily married man. After all, he wouldn't be married to Evelyn for much longer. He'd already discussed divorce with his lawyer and, more important, with his campaign manager.

Moving into the great room, he took a glass of water; he wanted his abstinence to be noted. He smiled, spoke, worked his way through his guests toward Kate. He wanted to talk to her, to step between her and Ramos and see if he was imagining that sexual attraction between them.

He wasn't. He knew what he felt, what he saw. But he had to be sure.

It didn't matter that Kate had a date who never left her side. Ramos watched Kate as if she were a diamond and he a thief, and that comparison was more apt than George cared to consider.

Spying his chance for information, George moved unnoticed to Brad Hasselbeck's side. "An interesting couple—Teague Ramos and your new reporter."

Brad jumped as if George had discovered his guiltiest secret—which, by coincidence, George had. George had a tendency to find out people's secrets. He found it made them malleable and easily influenced, and in the case of a police chief, a fellow legislator, or the head of a television station, that kind of influence was worth its weight in gold.

"Senator Oberlin! I didn't hear you." Brad assayed a weak smile. "Lovely party. Lots of potential news stories here."

"Go and do your worst." George waved an expansive hand. "Maybe you could give me a little information about Kate Montgomery."

Brad swallowed audibly. "Sir?"

"How did she come to meet Ramos?" George smiled, all teeth and fangs.

"Kate?" Brad glanced at his reporter. "I thought she was dating that Dean Sayers."

"Sanders." George dismissed Sanders without a qualm. "But she arrived with Ramos in tow, too. Why?"

"She . . . oh, it's not what you think." Brad chuckled.

George didn't join him.

Brad got serious in a hurry. "What I'm trying to say is—she's got a stalker. Ramos is her bodyguard."

"A stalker." George's gaze drilled into Brad's. "What do you mean, a stalker?"

"Did you see the, um, cut on her chin? She's got bruises all over. She's had her tire slashed and some more vandalism, and someone in a car tried to run her over." Perspiration beaded on Brad's forehead. "Yes, sir, it's definitely a stalker."

George backed Brad toward the corner beside the floor-to-ceiling fireplace. "And you didn't inform me?" After the strings he'd pulled to get her hired?

"I got her the best bodyguard in town, sir, and gave them a reason to be together. She's doing a story on him." Brad beamed with anticipation. "It's a great trade-off."

"I don't want a trade-off, I want her to be safe."

"Ramos doesn't lose clients, sir."

"Right." Ramos didn't. George knew that.

"And I've got a responsibility to the stockholders of KTTV to make a profit."

Brad was right there, too. He wouldn't do George any good if he got fired. "All right. Keep me updated. I want to know who this scum is."

"The one who's stalking Kate?" Brad sounded smart, smug, almost as if he were laughing at George.

With venial intent, George stared at Brad.

Brad stopped smiling. "Yes, sir. The one who's stalking Kate."

George caught Ramos watching the scene with amusement, pity . . . and interest. George didn't need Ramos sticking his nose into his business. Ramos had a reputation for being inquisitive and thorough, and maybe he wanted to bang Kate, but that didn't lessen George's interest in her. Quite the opposite. This was his chance. His last chance.

Things were going to be different this time.

Ten

Teague stood against the wall, watching the action at the party, and thought that Oberlin must be the biggest fish in the pond.

The police chief was there. So was the county sheriff. So were Texas Supreme Court judges.

Senators gathered in the corner and spoke in whispers.

Worst of all, Dean Sanders was headed his way, champagne glass in hand, a hearty smile on his lips.

Teague muffled a groan. Okay. So Kate was afraid of the passion between them. So she'd brought in a decoy. But did it have to be open-faced, genial, unsuspecting Dean Sanders with his upper-crust Texas background, his position in a posh law firm, and his weekend job providing free legal assistance to female immigrants who were being abused by their husbands? Teague should have hated him, but it was impossible to hate Dean. Teague could see meeting him for a beer at the sports bar and watching a game. Dean was one of those rare, genuinely nice guys.

"Hey, Teague, you're looking dry. Do you want a drink?" Dean waved his champagne glass.

"No, thanks. Not while I'm working."

"Oh. Right. Right." Dean glanced around guiltily. "I forgot. You're working."

"Yes." Teague folded his arms behind his back, doing a good imitation of hired muscle.

"I shouldn't drink, either. I've got to drive home." Dean put his half-filled glass onto a passing tray. "Do you think Kate could ride with me?"

Drive Kate home? Not a chance. "I'd prefer if she rode with me." The expression on Dean's face made Teague add, "But we'll follow you to your house first."

Dean squared his shoulders. "Do you really not care if Kate dates someone else?"

"Kate Montgomery is a job." Teague's gaze sought her in the crowd, and when he didn't find her, he moved until she was visible. He'd always been able to protect the client and at the same time take care of himself and his social life. But here, with Kate, the only social life that interested him was one *with* Kate. She moved like a red silk flame, and, if he didn't know better, he would say she wore no underwear beneath the gown. He did know better. Damn it. That spangle in her dark curly hair caught the light and sparkled almost as brightly as her blue eyes, and those diamonds in her ears called attention to her long neck . . . and that made him want to kiss her right under the jaw and work his way downward. . . .

She seemed oblivious to him.

"She really is great, but she's not paying much attention to me." Dean quickly added, "Not that I'm complaining, but usually a first date involves a little more face-to-face time."

So she was oblivious to Dean, too.

Yet jealousy clawed at Teague's gut. She smiled with shy eagerness, talked with genuine interest, shone with inner beauty. He wanted all that eagerness, that interest, that beauty focused on him.

"She's doing the groundwork that might pan out into a story." And why the hell was Teague comforting Kate's date?

"Of course she is. I should have realized that." Dean took a glass of Perrier and sipped it. "And what do I know about dating, anyway? This is the first date I've been on in ten years, since I met my wife. But I'm over her now. I'm ready for a woman like Kate."

It said wonders for Teague's control that he managed not to kick the shit out of Dean, and that only because Dean *so* wasn't ready for a woman like Kate. She'd ride over the top of him, and Dean would count himself privileged to be part of the asphalt.

"Hey, Ramos." Brad Hasselbeck strolled up, clutching a bourbon and Coke and reeking of cigarettes smoked on the terrace. Keeping an eye cocked at Dean, he asked, "How's the story going? Is Kate getting close to"—he glanced at Dean, and his voice dropped significantly—"wrapping it up?"

"Her date *knows* about the stalker, Hasselbeck."

"I won't tell a soul." Dean placed his hand on his heart.

"Okay, then." Hasselbeck shrugged. "When *are* you wrapping this investigation up, Ramos?"

"Shouldn't you be asking about Kate's safety instead?" Teague turned cold eyes on the news director.

Hasselbeck exploded with exasperation. "My God, is everybody obsessed with Kate's safety? I've got a job to do, and it isn't easy explaining to my bosses in Florida that the new girl I hired is off-line and unusable because she's got stitches in her chin."

Teague took his arm. Said, "Excuse us," to Dean. Moved to a quiet corner and asked, "Who else is interested?" The question wasn't idle. He wanted to know who was asking about Kate, and why.

"Everybody knows she's the new reporter," Hasselbeck said. "They like her news stories. They want to know how she got hurt. All I've done all evening long is answer questions about Kate Montgomery."

"I'm trying to find her stalker so she can go back to work, and you're not a lot of help." Teague's gaze sought Kate as she spoke with the socialite Winona Acevedo, who was laughing animatedly and gazing— oh, hell, they were both gazing at him.

Normally he wouldn't care if his former lover met the woman he was trying to get in the sack, but right now he wanted to walk over, grab Kate by the wrist, and drag her away.

"What about the story?" Hasselbeck asked.

"She's been taking notes and filming for the last three days. I'd say she has enough for ten stories. But what do I know?"

"That's right." Hasselbeck brightened. "There's one thing you don't know anything about, and that's television news."

"Too true." It didn't matter that he hadn't got her in bed. He shouldn't want her right now while she was his client and danger stalked her. He needed to get this job done, to get away from Kate before she could entangle him any further in her web. "I'd say if we haven't flushed out the stalker by tomorrow, we should let her run the story and see if the attacks are related to the broadcasts."

"Good." Hasselbeck beamed. "Unless there's a disaster that requires coverage, I'm blocking you in for Friday. Let's get this thing done."

"Yes." Teague looked across the room at Kate.

She seemed to feel his gaze on her, and she met his eyes. Her lashes drooped. She smiled with such implicit invitation, Teague took a step before he realized it.

Stopping himself, he repeated after Hasselbeck, "Yes, let's get this thing done."

He needed to concentrate on business. He needed to remember where he came from. What he'd done. The gray shadows of the past started to envelop him, and for the first time in his life, he encouraged them . . .

In his mind, his mother's voice started: *Goddamn it, Teague, you little bastard . . .*

Then Kate did something Teague never could have anticipated. She slid her palm down her hip, smoothing the red silk until the thin material was taut against her skin.

Heat flashed through him, burning all the old memories away.

"Hey, look." Hasselbeck waved his drink toward the door. "Governor Grant!"

"What?" Teague stared at Kate, tried to catch his breath.

"Man, you got to give it to Oberlin," Hasselbeck said enthusiastically. "He gives a party, and they all come."

"Um-hm." Teague wasn't paying attention as the governor of Texas, his wife, and his whole entourage swept in the door.

Kate looked . . . it looked as if . . . but no. That was impossible. She would never do as he had demanded. She would never leave off her thong.

She would sure as hell never tell him in the middle of a party when he could do nothing about it. That would be too cruel a revenge for his ultimatum.

Her eyelids fluttered up; she looked at him with the sultry invitation of a temptress. And she mouthed: No panties.

This time nothing could keep him from her side. Date or no date, Teague did not leave her alone for the remainder of the long, boring evening.

"With Evelyn at his side, George has proved to be an exemplary senator, leading Texas through difficult waters to our current prosperity." Governor Grant stood on the bandstand with George and Evelyn at his side. "But not only politics has benefited from George and Evelyn's union. Evelyn has made the education of the state's youngest and poorest citizens her objective, and with George's fund-raising assistance, she has started the L'il Texans' Pre-School Program, benefiting underprivileged children throughout the state."

George smiled his best genial smile and pretended as if he gave a crap what the pompous windbag of a governor had to say. He didn't. He wanted everyone to go home. He had planned this party as a chance to chat with Kate, to take her on a tour of his home, to show off his art and his gentility. The evening he had planned as a triumphal kickoff to his marital campaign had become a stultifying nightmare.

"Here now to present the Oberlins with a plaque commemorating their accomplishments is the chairman of L'il Texans, Carol Murphy!" The governor stepped away to allow Carol to heft herself up on the stage.

"Senator Oberlin, because of your belief in our solution to a serious problem in the state and your willingness to use your connections to raise money as well as contribute generously yourself, and because of Mrs. Oberlin's personal hands-on approach to early childhood education, we'd like to present. . . ."

Carol finally wound down and presented the plaque. George and Evelyn posed with her for the photos, then George indicated that everyone should quiet down. "I was proud to be the man who escorted Evelyn to the prom twenty-five years ago, and I'm more proud now to know her compassion and caring. Let's all toast my wonderful wife, Evelyn Oberlin!" He lifted his glass and saw the tears sparkling on her eyelashes.

Because she really did believe in education for poor kids, and she really was grateful he helped raise the money for the program. Why wouldn't he? It looked damned good to the public.

Governor Grant lifted his glass. "To the Oberlins—may they enjoy another twenty-five years of wedded bliss!"

Everyone at the party raised their glasses and drank, then applauded politely as Governor Grant descended the bandstand and made his way through the crowd, shaking hands and making political hay. If George had needed proof of his own importance, here it was—the most popular governor in a dozen years courting his favor. He hoped Kate noticed.

But damn Ramos. He had that expression on his face, the one a guy got when he was blindsided by lust. George usually liked to see that expression on other men, because men could be led by their peckers and blackmailed by their affairs. But he didn't like to see a Mexican looking at his sweet Kate that way.

In fact, his sweet little Kate seemed to be trying to get away from Ramos. She'd walk away, and Ramos would follow like a junk-yard dog. She circulated among the legisla-tors, held a conversation with Senator Martinez . . . but while Ramos spoke to the models who flocked to his side, he didn't flirt, and he never let Kate out of his sight. Never. It was enough to make George lose his temper—and that had happened only once before.

Only once before.

"Senator." Governor Grant shook his hand. "Congratulations. The wife and I are off to another social gathering. Thank you for your hospitality."

George accepted other congratulations on his long marriage. He smiled so much that when he got done with this evening, he would be a candidate for an Academy Award, and all the while he was hating Teague Ramos and lusting after Kate Mont-gomery.

"Excuse me, sir." The butler's smooth, En-glish tones intruded on George's obsession.

"Jason Urbano is here. I showed him to your office."

"Urbano?" George moved to the foyer for privacy. "Here now?"

"He says he wants to negotiate." Freddy was impassive.

"Urbano . . ." George reflected on the man he'd taken such care to blackmail and use. "Tell him I'll see him."

"Yes, sir." Freddy bowed and retreated.

George had had Freddy for more than a year now. Freddy had claimed on his application that he was seventy years old, although George thought he looked more like eighty. George didn't care. Freddy came with impeccable references; he had an English accent, a bald head, nineteenth-century ideas of the proper way to run a household, and the authority to enforce his requirements. Furthermore, he provided George with such a facade of respectability all of Austin envied him, and George considered the exorbitant salary he paid the man a fair exchange for the status Freddy brought.

George ordered another round of champagne—champagne had a way of making guests ignore the disappearance of the host—and headed for his study. Entering the room, he shut the door behind him. "Urbano, good to see you. Thanks for responding to my invitation."

Urbano lifted his head.

George laughed aloud at his savage expression. Sobering, he said sternly, "I assume you showed up at my party with important news, or you wouldn't be here."

Urbano was large, broad-shouldered, about forty-five, and a former hockey player. His nostrils flared. His brows lowered.

It was like holding a slathering pit bull by a chain, and watching him choke himself on the iron collar around his neck. The sense of power George got from holding that chain couldn't be duplicated. "Well?" he prodded.

"Yeah. I've got news. Zack Givens's oldest daughter just turned eight, and she's having some kind of"—Urbano's fingers made quotation marks in the air—"*identity crisis. So I spoke to Hope.*"

"Dear little Hope." The oldest Prescott daughter, the one who had been a thorn in George's side since the day she'd married Zack Givens. She had been sixteen when her parents were killed. She'd seen her eight-year-old sister Pepper sent to a foster home. She'd seen her foster brother Gabriel returned to Texas state custody. And she'd cried when her baby sister Caitlin had been taken from her.

George should have guessed Hope would be a problem, but he had thought—naively, he now knew—that sending her to the far end of the country, to Boston where everything was alien, where she had no money, no family, no high school diploma, would neutralize her.

Nothing stopped that bitch. She had overcome every obstacle to marry a Givens, and not just any Givens. Zack Givens, the son and grandson of New England industrialists. She had made a shrewd move, trading her preacher daughter's virtue to a man who could help her find her siblings. George didn't know what magic she hid between her legs, but she'd kept Givens in such thrall he'd pursued her family as diligently as if it had been his own.

She'd found Gabriel right away, but she'd had no luck with the other two.

Of course not. Pepper had been rebellious and wild, and ugly to boot. George had sent her to Seattle, the far opposite corner of the country, and eventually she'd disappeared from the face of the earth.

George hoped she was dead. That would serve Hope right.

Hope had tried to trace her siblings through the records in the courthouse, but a fire had conveniently destroyed them.

She'd tried sending investigators to Hobart to talk to the people who remembered the Prescotts. But George had a grip on the town, and no one dared cross him. No one would talk. Most of them didn't even know what had really happened.

Actually, none of them knew for sure, not even Evelyn.

But Hope knew too much.

If she went public with her suspicions . . . well, no amount of influence and bribery could cover up all his actions.

He had been trying to figure out what he could do to divert their attention when they made a mistake. They sent Jason Urbano to do some underground investigation of him.

George had so many connections he'd caught on to Urbano's snooping almost at once, and he had hired an investigator to look into Urbano's past.

George still held Urbano's dossier under

lock and key as one of the most precious documents in the world, equal in worth to the original copies of the Guttenberg Bible and the United States Constitution.

It turned out Urbano had been the legal counsel for Givens Industries since he'd graduated from law school. He was a good friend of Zack Givens, and Givens had a thing about loyalty. If he discovered Urbano had been skimming money out of the companies for almost as long as he'd been working there, Givens would have him strung up by his short neck. Added to that, Urbano had enjoyed a number of indiscretions, and his wife not only had a great prenup but an explosive temper. Of course, she didn't vent her anger in public, but when a man had enough money, influence, and the right investigator working for him, he could get all the information he needed.

Which was just as well, because George had suffered from the Boston Connection long enough.

George fixed Urbano with a cold eye. "So tell me what Hope said about her daughter's identity crisis."

"She said they're taking Lana to Europe—"

"Lana?" George swayed. "The kid's name is Lana?"

"Yes. Why?"

George poured himself a straight shot of whiskey, and downed it in one swallow. Hope's mother's name had been Lana. "So they're taking her to Europe?"

"Hope insisted that Zack go, too." Urbano's voice dropped to a low tone, as if he feared someone would hear. "Zack is leaving the company in my hands."

"So this is it." Slowly, George turned on Urbano.

"Yeah, this is it." Urbano swallowed and tugged at his tie. "With hints placed in the proper ears and a little judicious juggling of the books, I can topple the Givens empire."

"When I give you the word," George coldly reminded him. "You do nothing until I give you the word."

The clock struck midnight. The noise at the party hit an inebriated high and stayed there. The guests danced and laughed.

After a final survey, Teague decided none of these people were Kate's stalker. As they drank, they all became less interested in her and more interested in themselves. They were, after all, politicians.

Beside him, Kate held his arm and took off one shoe, then the other. She stood on the cool marble next to him in her bare feet. "Nice," she sighed.

Her scent rose in subtle wafts from her hair.

He leaned close and inhaled, and imagined that scent mingling with his as they made love. The warmth of her hand seeped through his coat sleeve, and he visualized her heat against his, her eyes closed in bliss as he slipped into her welcoming body.

He leaned close to Kate's ear and spoke, and despite the cacophony around them, he knew she heard every word. "Let's get out of here. Let's go someplace where we can be alone."

And as he had imagined, she followed him without protest.

Eleven

Jason Urbano moved through his hotel room, discarding his coat, loosening his tie. He rubbed his eyes as if he were exhausted by his confrontation with Oberlin. With a curse, he pulled his cell phone out of the pocket, and dialed his wife. "Hi, honey," he crooned, his frown the exact opposite of his tone. "How are the kids?" He rolled his eyes as he pretended to listen. Then he said, "Yeah, everything went well. I should come home pretty soon. Yeah, honey, really. Nothing's wrong. Everything's great!"

If he did say so himself, he gave a masterful performance as the lying husband for the camera hidden behind the mirror. The camera he theoretically didn't know anything about.

Oberlin had great power, and no one could stop him when he wanted to place an observation camera in a hotel room. On the other hand, nothing could stop Zack Givens when he decided to sabotage Oberlin's efforts.

Stepping out of the lens, Jason kept talking, the kind of soothing nonsense a cheating man would give his stupid little wife.

Luckily for Jason, he wasn't really talking to her. The line was closed; he popped open his laptop, logged onto the cordless connection, and waited until he saw Gabriel's face on the monitor. Gabriel was in the next room tapping into Oberlin's system with the expertise of a man who had learned his business with revenge in mind; Gabriel was the Prescotts' foster son.

Gabriel inserted a tape that fed pretaped video and audio into the camera behind the mirror, then gave Jason a silent thumbs-up. The picture Oberlin now saw was of Jason, pacing back across the room, cell phone pressed to his ear. The sound he heard was Jason talking to his wife.

In reality, Jason pulled up the program that gave him a live video connection to Zack's study in the Givens mansion in Cambridge, Massachusetts.

Zack's face came on first. Jason's wife said Zack was too handsome for his own good, and God knew Jason agreed. With black hair now threaded with silver and piercing dark eyes, Zack sent shivers of fear down the spine of every employee in Givens Industries . . . except some of them who had discovered he had developed a kind streak after sixteen years of marriage to Hope. "How did it go?" he asked tersely.

"He went for it," Jason said.

Hope's face moved into sight beside Zack's. She had recently added blond highlights to her brown hair, and a new chin-length cut accented her cheekbones and almost made a man forget the intelligence in her beautiful blue eyes.

Zack hated the cut.

Hope told him to get used to it—she respected his opinion, but not about feminine hairstyles. Jason had known her for sixteen years, and he still grinned whenever he saw Zack and Hope together—the conservative, self-contained executive and the liberal, strong-willed artist.

"How could he be so stupid as to believe you would betray Zack after all these years?" Hope asked incredulously.

"Because we've been very careful to set up a false trail of previous betrayals for Jason, both personal and professional," Zack reminded her.

"And because that's the kind of man

George Oberlin is, so of course that's the kind of man he expects to find wherever he looks." The voice of Pepper Graham, Hope's younger sister, echoed across the connection, and she moved into camera range.

Her long black hair hung in waves around her face, and her smile reached her green eyes. She was much more street-savvy than Hope, much more inclined to recognize and accept the dark side of human nature.

Not surprising, since at the age of eight she'd been separated from her siblings and sent to live in foster homes. Although she never talked about that time, Jason got the feeling some of the homes had been cruel and Pepper's existence had been lonely. By the time Hope had found her, twenty-three-year-old Pepper had seen far too much of the grim side of life.

Now, eight years later, she lived on a ranch in Idaho with her husband, Dan Graham, their three children, a thousand head of cattle, and a highly successful mail-order-catalog gardening business. Urban-bred Jason considered that his idea of hell, but Pepper looked happy. Very happy.

When the family had been together brainstorming ways to twist Oberlin's ass into a pretzel, it was Pepper who came up with the plan they pursued.

Jason admired Pepper a lot.

"In your estimation, does Oberlin realize that if he's successful in bringing down Givens Industries, it will be a collapse as damaging to the country and to the investors as the Enron debacle?" Jason knew Zack wanted to be very, very clear on this matter, because for Zack, the idea that someone could so betray their country and its people was an anathema.

"If I were you, I'd check to see if he's bought competitors' stock," Jason advised.

"You already know the answer, Zack," Pepper said. "Oberlin is a thief—and worse."

Everyone shared a moment of silence. They were so close to their goal of righting the wrong that had been committed long ago.

Twenty-three years ago, Bennett Prescott had been the minister of a church in Hobart, Texas. He and his wife, Lana, had disappeared and were found dead, their car a wreck, apparently on their way to Mexico, apparently abandoning their children.

Within days the church board discovered the treasury had disappeared with them. The Prescotts were declared criminals, and their children, three daughters and one foster son, disappeared from Hobart. Over the years, Hope, Pepper, and Gabriel had suffered, but eventually they had been reunited.

Yet their baby sister, Caitlin, had disappeared. No one knew where. Despite the best efforts of the reunited Prescott siblings, no trace of her had been uncovered.

It had all come down to one man. George Oberlin had been on the church board when Bennett and Lana Prescott had disappeared. Not long after, George Oberlin had begun his run for the Texas State Senate with a formidable campaign chest, and although he had documented donors, a brief Givens investigation proved he had lied about his financial backers. In fact, his father-in-law, a crusty rancher with fire in his eyes, swore a blue streak at the mention of Oberlin's name.

Yet according to the campaign documents, he had provided Oberlin half his campaign funds.

Griswald, the Givens family butler, Gabriel,

and Jason had proved that George Oberlin had stolen the church treasury and been the driving force in separating the children.

They suspected he had had the courthouse burned down to destroy their records. And he had a way of commanding the silence of everyone in Hobart.

The focus for Zack and Hope, for Dan and Pepper, and for Gabriel, was finding the last child, Caitlin.

But the search always ended at George Oberlin, and George Oberlin would not cooperate, for to do so would be to admit culpability.

So with the help of Jason, Givens Industry chief legal counsel, they had put together a scheme brilliant in its simplicity. They had tricked Oberlin into thinking he could blackmail Jason, get him to do his bidding, and bring down Givens Industry. Oberlin was motivated to do it. Somehow he had to hide his wickedness. If he didn't, he would never be able to run for the U.S. Senate.

Like any man who let greed and evil rule his life, Oberlin couldn't see beyond the obvious. He didn't realize that not only could he manipulate, but he could be manipulated, and blackmailed, and destroyed.

When they had him trapped, they would offer a deal—provide them with Caitlin's whereabouts, or face a scandal big enough to destroy his chance at winning national office.

"I so wish we could send him to prison," Hope muttered.

Jason laughed bitterly. "The man's an octopus. He's got tentacles everywhere. There're plenty of people who'd like to see him brought down, but they don't have the guts to face the consequences of helping us."

"We couldn't find a judge in Texas to convict him," Zack said.

"But, darling, if we can find out that Caitlin's alive and that she's happy, that would put our minds at rest." Pepper rubbed Hope's back.

Jason saw the glow of commitment light Hope's face. "And if we could be reunited with her . . ." Hope swallowed.

This family had waited so long to be whole. Too long. Jason almost couldn't stand to see the agony of their uncertainty.

While the women struggled with their emotions, Gabriel's face flashed across their screens. "Two minutes," he warned.

"We've got to finish up," Zack said.

"I wish we could be there!" Pepper exploded. "I hate staying here in Boston while you guys do all the work."

Hope swallowed back her tears. "If we did that and Oberlin saw us, recognized us—"

"I know," Pepper said bitterly. "It would ruin all our plans."

"We'll fly down when we get ready to close the trap," Zack promised. "Not too much longer."

"One minute," Gabriel warned.

"One last question—how is Griswald holding up?" Hope asked.

"Freddy?" Jason shook his head dolefully. "Freddy Griswald? Poor old Freddy?"

"I told Zack this project was too much of a strain on him." Hope sat straight up. "The man is almost ninety years old!"

Zack, who obviously recognized the expression on Jason's face from their years in college, asked patiently, "What's wrong?"

"He told me he now realizes he wasted his life being a butler," Jason said.

"Really?" Zack lifted his eyebrows. "And why is that?"

"He says he should have been a spy." Jason grinned. "He said he would have saved England a lot of trouble in World War II."

Zack and Pepper burst into laughter.

Hope's expression went through various perambulations before it settled on disgust. "All right," she said grudgingly. "So he's having the time of his life. Can you blame me for worrying about an old man?"

"We expect nothing less, darling." Zack hugged her shoulders, and, after a moment of stiffness, she laid her head on his chest.

Before Jason could make kissy noises—juvenile, he knew, but so necessary when two men had known each other so long—the video went dead.

Gabriel had cut the transmission with Boston.

As Jason got ready for bed under the watchful eyes of Senator George Oberlin's flunkies, he managed to look worried, but when he shut off the light, nothing could stop his grin.

Griswald was right. This sort of vigilante justice was fun, especially if it succeeded in reuniting the Prescott family at last.

And Jason cherished a secret dream, because although everyone knew the truth, no one talked about it. Yet the unalterable fact was—someone had murdered Bennett and Lana Prescott, and that person needed to be brought to justice.

George Oberlin should be brought to justice.

Twelve

That is one damned clumsy kiss.

It was two in the morning. Teague sat parked in front of Dean's house with the headlights fixed right on Dean and Kate while Dean tried to get more than a peck on the cheek out of his date.

Teague was not in the mood to see Dean Sanders put his hands on Kate and discover for himself what she hid beneath her skirt.

God. *Nothing. She had nothing on under there.*

Teague put his hand on the door, ready to leap out and pull her free of Dean's embrace.

But Kate pushed herself away, gestured toward Teague, and shook her head.

"Good girl," Teague whispered. He watched as she walked carefully back to the car. He opened the door for her and watched her slip inside. "Did you make another date?" he asked roughly.

"Let's go home." She slid her hands down

her thighs as if smoothing the wrinkles out of the fragile silk of her dress.

Yet Teague couldn't tear his gaze away. "You know, for such a prissy girl, you're good at torment." Jamming the gearshift into first, he roared away from the curb. The dark streets whipped past them. *"Did* you make another date?"

"No. Slow down. We don't want the police to stop us."

"I know them all." But he eased off the gas and made his way sedately to Kate's loft. Because he *didn't* want the police to stop them. He didn't want to take the time to prove he was sober. He didn't want to show his ID and explain what he was doing with Kate. He just wanted to get to Kate's home, into Kate's bed, and sate himself with her body.

He pulled the car into her marked parking place. He surveyed the well-lit sidewalks, the small patches of grass, the meager planter beside the door. His gaze lingered on the Dumpster, the only place where anyone could hide. But nothing moved. For the moment, they were safe.

Yet while Kate's safety remained of paramount importance to him, his own safety meant nothing. He didn't care about professional ethics. Beyond all sense, he had to have her.

The faint light painted Kate in shadow like a classic drawing created in the dusk. Her large eyes watched him, but he couldn't discern her expression. Trepidation? Excitement? Triumph? He didn't know. He couldn't guess. He only knew she'd been teasing him all night with the motion of her sleek, clean body, her knowing laughter, the rich scent of her lavender perfume. She embodied every dream he'd never allowed himself to have . . . and she had agreed to his terms. She had offered herself to him.

He had been holding himself in check for hours. Now, with a deep groan, he reached across from his seat to hers. He pulled her into his arms. The console with its emergency brake was between them; he didn't care. He didn't care about the discomfort of their positions. He had to touch her.

He cradled her neck in his hands. Her heart beat rapidly against his fingertips, her breath hurried through her lips. He kissed her and she kissed him back, giving everything, keeping nothing.

She was pliant, leaning into him, her

hands tangled in his hair, her fingers palpitating with some inner rhythm he recognized as akin to his own. Her tongue pulsed in his mouth; she was aggressive and yielding at the same time.

The slow, wet kiss tested the limits of his endurance. He'd watched her all night. When he had discovered she was nude beneath her gown, each step she took became torture for him. He had imagined touching the silk of her gown and the more intriguing silk of her bare shoulders, imagined sliding one slender strap down and freeing a taut breast.

Now with his eyes half closed, he smoothed his palm across her back. His fingertips skated across her shoulder blades. He moved along each vertebra, worshipping the strong muscles and sinews of her back. With each touch, an anguish of anticipation shot through him.

And her, for she broke away. Her voice was breathless, husky, dangerous. "Are we going to have sex in here? Because if we are, I get the top. That gearshift would be murder." She was laughing, yet she was serious, too.

"Do you want to have sex in the car?" His

mouth watered as he imagined immediate payback after the hours of torture.

"I don't know . . . I don't know if I can wait any longer."

Her admission allowed him to take a long breath. She wanted him as much as he wanted her. She was as desperate as he was, and that . . . that gave him the power to break free of the enchantment that bound him.

"Come on," he said roughly. "We've got to go in. I want to make love to you all night long. I can't do that here."

And it wasn't safe. Her stalker was still at large. Since Teague had come on the job, there had been no contact at all. That made him hypervigilant. Before he lay down with Kate, he needed to be somewhere protected by locks and alarms. For once he slid into the depths of her body, he would be blind and deaf to every threat.

All his life, oblivion had beckoned. He had challenged death, taunted death, not caring whether the darkness took him or not. But now . . . he wanted to live with a fierceness that burned his soul. He had to have this chance with Kate. He had to taste her once before he died.

And then, if he was lucky, he would taste her again.

Once more he surveyed the parking lot. Nothing had changed. Nothing had moved.

"Come on," he said again, and started to open the door.

She grabbed his lapel, jerked him back, and kissed him. My God, how she kissed him! Her tongue separated his lips, took his mouth with a thunderstorm of brilliant, superheated lightning. For too many long seconds, the only thing in the world that existed was Kate Montgomery and the way she branded him with need and lust.

Pulling away, he leaped from the car. The weight of sexual desire was so heavy he almost staggered as he moved quickly to her side to help her out.

She let him assist her, sliding her legs from the car and standing in one graceful exercise.

She strode toward her building and didn't look back, appearing regal and cool. Yet he knew the grip of excitement carried her along. As he watched her the reality hit him—he was going to press her into the mattress and take her, and when they were done . . . his whole life would be different.

He didn't want that change, knew it would result in anguish for him, but damn it, he couldn't resist her.

He hurried to catch up with her, herding her with his hand in the middle of her back. She leaned into him, surrendering to him as completely as he surrendered to her. Her breathing, her warmth, her beauty overwhelmed him.

Yet . . . his instincts could never be completely subdued. As they passed the Dumpster, he went on alert.

A blur of motion drew his gaze to the right.

A blade flashed in the dim light.

Someone rushed at them. At Kate.

This was it. Her stalker.

Sexual frustration transformed into rage.

Teague shoved Kate out of the way. He whirled and met her attacker, knocking the knife away, taking the oncoming body down with all the finesse of a linebacker.

At once he registered the thin, fine bones of a woman. He couldn't halt his rush, but he didn't twist and break her wrist as he had intended. He only held her as they bounced on the grass.

She screamed, a thin, high-pitched sound of terror that was cut off as his weight momentarily crushed her. She smelled of fine perfume, velvet, and vodka. He flipped her on her stomach, arms behind her back.

"Who is it?" Kate demanded from beside him. Then, "Mrs. Oberlin!"

Yes, of course. He held pathetic, tearful Evelyn Oberlin. The senator's wife began weeping violently, tears pouring out of her as if a dam had broken. "I'm s-s-sorry." Her teeth were chattering. She shuddered in great convulsions. "I'm s-so sorry."

"Me, too, lady." Grimly, Teague ran his hand down her body, looking for more weapons. She had none. He found nothing more than a fine silk bag hung on a string around her neck.

Taking it off, he handed it to Kate. "What's in there?"

Kate glanced inside. "Pills. A lot of pills."

"Yeah." This lady was so skinny she was on the verge of starvation. She shook like she had the DTs, and he would bet if they checked her medical records, she'd been in a dry-out facility more than once.

"I d-didn't mean t-to hurt you." With her free hand, Mrs. Oberlin clawed at Kate. "I just . . . I just didn't want him to kill you again."

Teague exchanged a significant glance with Kate. This lady was an alcoholic drug addict, and crackers to boot.

"So you tried to hit her with your car?" he demanded.

"A few b-bruises are better than dying!" Mrs. Oberlin managed to make that sound like good sense.

"Good Lord," Kate blankly said to Teague. "I didn't think she'd really done *that.*"

"Did you see the knife?" Teague asked. "That wasn't a bouquet she was holding."

"You don't understand." Mrs. Oberlin's tears dried. Her voice rose to a shriek. She struggled to get up.

Teague wouldn't release her wrist.

"What doesn't Teague understand?" Without a care for her expensive, sexy dress, Kate knelt beside Mrs. Oberlin. "Tell me."

"Kate, this is no time for a goddamn interview." Teague was so furious he could scarcely speak. He wanted to crush Mrs. Oberlin into the dirt for threatening Kate. If she hadn't been a woman, hadn't been impaired, he would have. As it was, he could scarcely contain his rage. "Call the cops."

"In a minute." Kate stayed on the grass, her voice so kind Mrs. Oberlin stopped fighting and pressed her head to the grass. "What doesn't Teague understand?"

"He was going to kill you again. He did it before." Mrs. Oberlin enunciated each word with painful clarity. "I wanted to chase you away, that's all, because otherwise he was going to kill you again."

"Damn it, Kate!" Teague fumbled in his jacket for his cell phone.

"You're not the only one, you know." Mrs. Oberlin kept her gaze fixed on Kate.

Softhearted Kate, who listened as if she could make sense of that mumbo jumbo.

Teague dialed 911 and instructed the operator to send a squad car *now.*

"Mrs. Blackthorn realized it first. Before I did, even. She thought . . ." Mrs. Oberlin panted as if she were hyperventilating. Then she pulled herself together. "The old woman thought she was invincible, so when I came home, she was at the . . . at the . . . at the . . ."

"Take a breath." Kate stroked Mrs. Oberlin's hair back and waited while she did as she was told. Then she prompted, "Where was Mrs. Blackthorn?"

"At the bottom of the stairs. Her skinny neck was broken. They said . . . the sheriff said . . . he said she smelled like whiskey, that she was a secret tippler. But she wasn't. Then when I said so, the sheriff said"—Mrs. Oberlin stopped, groaned as if she were recalling some great pain—"he said maybe I pushed her. But I didn't! I wasn't home!"

"I believe you," Kate said soothingly.

Teague couldn't decide if Mrs. Oberlin knew something or had a marvelous imagination. Then he decided he didn't care. This damned crazy Evelyn Oberlin had interrupted his night with Kate.

"Then he said he wasn't there when she died." Mrs. Oberlin looked around as if she were afraid someone would get her, and she whispered, "But he was."

"Senator Oberlin?" Kate questioned.

Mrs. Oberlin screamed so suddenly Kate jumped back. "Of course, Senator Oberlin!"

Teague tightened his grip.

Mrs. Oberlin struggled briefly, then subsided.

As if she'd never exploded in excitement, Mrs. Oberlin said, "Then . . . then . . . then I started to be afraid . . . and I knew it was my fault."

"What was your fault?" Kate signaled to Teague to let the old lady up.

He refused with an emphatic shake of the head. He'd seen cases like this before. People so berserk and strung out on drugs they could rise from frailty to attack and tear and maim. This old lady admitted to stalking Kate—for Kate's own good, of course. Now she was blaming her husband—who Teague knew to be a pompous ass, but without a whiff of scandal attached to his name—for her problems, and babbling about how she had prevented him from killing Kate again.

"That he killed you. I should have known." Mrs. Oberlin closed her eyes as if she were in agony. "I should have told them, but I love him." She started blubbering again, and her words were so slurred Teague had to struggle to understand her. "I love him so much. So I try not to think about it, but the ghosts are always there, staring at me, their flesh all ragged and their eyes . . . their eyes . . . their eyes empty . . . Lana, I'm sorry. Please . . . I'm so sorry."

Mrs. Oberlin gazed into thin air as if she saw a ghost now, stared so fixedly the hair rose on the back of Teague's head.

He couldn't help looking, also. Nothing was there.

Kate looked, too, and shook her head.

Spooky.

In the distance, he heard the wail of sirens.

"He's going to kill me. He hates it when I . . . when I . . ." Mrs. Oberlin started to convulse beneath him, and at last Teague let her go.

Bleakly, he and Kate watched her vomit in the grass.

"Go upstairs." He didn't look at her. "Put on some jeans, make some coffee—the cops will want it. I'll take care of her."

"What's going to happen?" Kate whispered.

"She's going to a hospital to dry out. There'll be a big scandal. Oberlin's going to let it die down; then he'll divorce her." All of Teague's latent cynicism came out. "She's a liability to his position."

"She thinks he's a murderer." Kate watched her with sorrowful eyes. "Do you think . . . ?"

"Damn it, Kate, she thinks he killed *you.* She's been stalking you *for your own good.*" Teague didn't want to touch Kate right now, but he had to take her hand. It trembled in his, and her fingers felt like ice. "Honey, she is so crazy, and he is so fastidious. I don't know why she fixated on you, but she's hallucinating. You saw her do it. She thought she saw a ghost standing right there." He pointed. "You know she did. Go upstairs. Make yourself comfortable, and settle yourself in for a long siege because the police are going to want to question you for quite a while."

"Okay." Kate lingered still, and she sounded guilty and torn when she said, "I have to call Brad. This is a tragedy, but it's a story, too. He'll break me into tiny pieces if I don't."

"Do what you have to do."

She heard the tone in his voice, saw the way he half turned away. "This is the end, isn't it?"

He didn't pretend. "Yeah. It's a good thing this happened, because you and me together . . . that's stupid."

"I don't think it's stupid."

"We've got nothing in common."

"Since when did you become the voice of reason?" she asked bitterly. He tried to reply, say something else superficial and soothing, but she slashed the sounds with her hand. "You and me would be the best thing that ever happened."

Now he pretended he didn't know what she meant. "Obviously, the reports are over-rated. I'm not *that* good in bed."

Because she wasn't talking about sex. She was talking about the ties that bound them, and how making love would cement those ties.

"Yeah. Sure." She tugged her hand away from his.

He held it for a second too long. "Go call your mother. Tell her you're all right." Then he let her go. He watched her walk away, then turned his attention to the wailing police cars as they swung into the parking lot.

She'd be happier. He'd be happier.

It was better this way.

Softly, he heard Mrs. Oberlin say, "Lana, I'm so sorry. I'm so, so sorry."

"Get me the car." George Oberlin put the phone down gently, oh so gently, and turned to Freddy. "I've got to go."

"Yes, sir." As George tried to shrug his way into his discarded dinner jacket, Freddy caught the collar and assisted. "I hope it's not an emergency, sir."

"Don't be ridiculous," George said angrily. "Why else would I go out at this hour?"

It was two-thirty in the morning. The anniversary guests were all gone. The caterers were still cleaning up and carrying dishes to their vans. Servants wiped up wine spills and moved closer so they could listen.

And George was livid. That stupid bitch he'd married had really done it now.

"Is there anything I can do to assist you, sir?" Freddy asked.

George wanted to snap at him. But he had a reputation for being calm in a crisis. It was a distinction that had served him well when it came to public appearances. "No, thank you, Freddy. This is something I have to do for myself. I'll let you know if I require aid."

He headed for the door, and somehow Freddy got there before him to open it, a courtesy that annoyed George so much he could scarcely breathe.

Then Freddy followed George down to the car and opened that door for him, too, and that almost sent George over the edge.

But it wasn't really Freddy who aggravated George. It was Evelyn. According to

the cops, she'd tried to attack Kate Montgomery with a knife. Worse than that, it
wasn't the first time she'd attacked Kate.
Kate had been in fear for her life. She had
had a stalker, and Teague Ramos had been
her bodyguard. . . .

George bent to enter the car, then slowly
straightened.

Of course. Now that they'd caught her
stalker, now that they'd caught Evelyn, Kate
would be done with Ramos.

"Senator?" Freddy hovered beside the
door, uncertain what to do as George stared
into space. "Did you forget something?"

"No. Instruct the chauffeur to take me to
the police station, and hurry. My wife"—
George managed to pretend to choke up as
he loudly leaked the information he wanted
the whole city to know—"has been arrested
for violent behavior, alcohol and drug possession. I'm going to have to do something
about her again, and I'll tell you, Freddy"—
he put his hand heavily on the butler's
shoulder—"this just breaks my heart."

"Yes, Senator, I can see how it would."
Freddy stood stiffly beneath George's
touch.

George risked a glance around. The servants crowded the porch. The caterers were standing beside their vans with their mouths open.

He seated himself in the car. Freddy shut the door. As the chauffeur drove away, George smiled a secret smile.

"I'm here at Ramos Security, where Teague Ramos, the man who keeps the Texas Capitol safe, directs his operation." Less than twenty-four hours later, Kate looked at the camera, then turned to Teague. "Mr. Ramos, with the experience of a Marine veteran and the expertise of a former Special Ops, does this assignment meet the challenges you've set yourself in your life?"

Teague met her eyes, but she saw no emotion there. No interest, no regret. It was as if they had never kissed, never lusted for each other. "Guarding the Texas Capitol is the kind of job security men dream of."

Kate signaled Cathy to turn off the camera, and the station tape took over. With the help of the editor at KTTV, Kate had put Teague's piece together. She put together a longer piece for the Sunday-morning show. For all intents and purposes, when this interview was over, she would be done with Teague.

While they waited for the film to finish, Teague joked with Cathy and talked with his secretary, Brenda, who watched the proceedings with awe.

This two-minute piece seemed to last forever as Kate stood beside Teague and pretended she didn't mind that she had explicitly offered herself to him—and that he had managed to resist her.

Humiliation burned in her, and she was afraid it showed in the heat of her cheeks. But she still had those stitches on her chin, so between those and the carefully applied foundation, most of the viewers wouldn't notice anything was amiss with her state of mind.

Yet she could eventually deal with humiliation. She wasn't sure if she could bear the knowledge that she would never know the ecstasy of being one with Teague. Watching him walk away would have been hell; never having him was worse.

She got the signal to start filming again. Looking into the camera, she finished the piece. "Teague Ramos is one of a rare breed, the man who stands between us, the common citizens of the United States, and anarchy. So next time you tour the Texas Capitol, smile and wave at the security cameras. The people behind them protect us every day."

The red light on the camera blinked off.

Kate unhooked her microphone from her jacket. She turned to Teague to help him, but he removed his microphone and handed it over before she could touch him.

"Thank you, Kate, for putting together such a great report." Teague offered his hand. "I'm sure this will make me a celebrity."

"A position to which I know you've always aspired."

They didn't shake. They looked at their joined hands.

Then Kate broke away.

Kate left Teague's office . . . for the last time.

Thirteen

With one ear, Kate listened to the anchor-man on the ten o'clock news while at the same time she considered how pitiful her social life must be that she was cleaning her apartment on a Friday night. God knew she could have had a date. Dean Sanders had called repeatedly.

But she didn't want him. She wanted Teague, that rat. She hadn't seen him in three weeks, not since the five o'clock news where she had wrapped his story and he'd broken her heart.

She'd spotted his people at the capitol. They smiled at her, waved at her, spoke to her.

But he had used his stupid monitors to avoid her, as if that would make her stop craving him.

Or maybe—she brightened—maybe he avoided her because if he saw her, he wouldn't be able to resist sweeping her away and taking her to some isolated desert island with waving palms. He'd take her in

his arms and do all the things she'd imagined rather than backing off just because
he'd been interrupted by someone wanting
to kill her. . . .

Poor Mrs. Oberlin. She'd been sent to a
place where she could recover from her
"nervous breakdown." Senator Oberlin had
stopped Kate in the corridors of the capitol
and apologized for the ordeal his wife had
put her through. He had made excuses for
Evelyn, the kind of excuses that made
Kate's heart bleed. To all appearances, he
adored his wife, yet she'd seen the tension
between them at the party.

And why had there been no mention in the
press about the incident at the dumpster?

When Kate had asked Brad that question,
he'd shrugged and said senators' wives
were always having problems. When she'd
told him problems were different when they
involved possible attempted murder, Brad
had informed her she didn't understand
and, as punishment, made her cover the social beat for a week.

She didn't ask Senator Oberlin. She knew
that he wouldn't want to publicize his wife's
sad, scandalous behavior.

But more than that, it didn't matter that

she'd seen Mrs. Oberlin vomiting in the grass, that she'd witnessed the little sack of pills and smelled the booze. The things Evelyn had said strengthened Kate's sense that Oberlin was not to be trusted.

Kate fought her skittish agitation every day as George Oberlin sought her out. He gave her hints about what was happening in the Senate and about the bills, so many that she took the lead in the competition to break the most stories at KTTV and made Linda Nguyen hate her again.

Kate should have been ecstatic to achieve her goal so swiftly, and she would have . . . if it weren't for the lingering agony of Teague's rejection.

Now, recognizing the name spoken by the anchorman, Kate's head jerked around.

". . . found Mrs. Oberlin at the bottom of the stairs. Medical examiners declared her dead of a broken neck. They'll investigate to see if alcohol or drugs are involved. Mrs. Oberlin had just returned from her fourth visit to an exclusive rehab center." With that damning phrase, the anchorman turned to the meteorologist. "So, Marissa. What's this rumor I hear about strong thundershowers this evening?"

Kate stood in front of the television, hands loose, eyes wide.

Mrs. Oberlin was dead? Dead from falling down the stairs? The police were investigating possible alcohol abuse?

"Dear Lord." Picking up her jacket, Kate walked out of her house into the rain, and headed for Teague's place.

Teague heard the doorbell ring. Without looking out, he knew who it was. He'd seen the news report. He knew why she was here.

But before he left his study, he checked the front-porch camera. There she stood, Kate Montgomery, scowling up at the lens.

So with the switch at the top of the stairs, he cleared the lock.

She opened the door and walked into his home. She looked up at him.

He looked down at her.

Outside, lightning flashed, and, after a pause, thunder rumbled.

"It's coming closer," she said.

She meant the storm.

Or did she?

He hadn't seen her for three whole weeks.

But even dressed in worn jeans, a white T-shirt, and a silly pink pair of flip-flops, she was beautiful. Raindrops sparkled in her dark hair like diamonds in the night sky. Her face . . . he'd seen her face in his dreams, but his dreams hadn't conjured up the sweet curve of her cheek, the stubborn angle of her chin, the way she looked so alive, so vital. . . .

Without saying a word, she slipped off her water-stained jacket and hung it on the newel post. She shook her head. Raindrops flew, and her hair bounced to unruly life. Placing her hand on the banister, she started up the stairs.

There was an inevitability about this meeting. He'd spent three weeks avoiding her, yet it had never occurred to him their time together was over. She had asked him if he believed in fate. Well, he did, and as he watched her walk toward him, he recognized that this was confirmation.

"I take it you saw the news," he said.

"Did *he* kill her?" Kate's sensual mouth trembled, and her blue eyes were large and grieved.

"I don't know." He could scarcely suppress his disgust with himself. He had lis-

tened to Mrs. Oberlin's alcohol- and drug-
induced babbling, and because he was angry, because she had made a fool of him,
because she had threatened Kate, he had
assumed she was delusional. He had investigated her accusations against her husband, but Oberlin was guilty of no more
than a parking ticket—and he'd paid it.
Teague had looked through the Austin social register for the Blackthorns, found the
family, and contacted them to ask questions
about a family member who had fallen
down the stairs. They had acted as if he
was crazy. Worse, the cops had no record
of any such accident.

So Teague had decided nothing Mrs.
Oberlin said was true. He wasn't usually so
careless. But then, he wasn't usually so . . .
emotional. Entrapped and fighting entrap-
ment. "But I'm willing to bet she didn't fall
by accident. She either killed herself, or he
killed her."

Kate reached the top of the stairs, stood
beside him, extended her hand.

He took it, and he experienced a sense of
relief, as if she'd just placed a bandage over
his wounded heart.

Just as they had moments before they

parted, they looked at their entwined fingers. There was a symbolism here, a sense of coming full circle.

And now they were going to take another step into an abyss that he could not comprehend.

"Come on back. My living quarters are up here." With her hand still in his—now that he had touched her, he couldn't release her—he led her toward his study.

The stairway was painted white, decorated with framed black-and-white photos of women dressed in Edwardian splendor and men posed stiffly with their collars starched high. The way to his private quarters was different: soft, warm golds and reds.

She followed him inside his study and looked around, and he knew what she thought.

This wasn't the place she would have envisioned for him.

He used the kitchen downstairs, but for the most part, he lived on the second floor, away from his paperwork and his office. He'd torn down the wall between the two biggest bedrooms, remodeled the attached bathroom, and lined the study with bookshelves. He had decorated with a big overstuffed chair and an ottoman, a long comfortable couch, and a huge pillow chair in front of the entertainment center. He'd had the hardwood floors refinished with a rich burgundy stain and covered them with a couple of Oriental rugs that glowed with jewel tones. He enjoyed his collection of knickknacks from foreign countries—a camel saddle and a collection of silk paintings from India.

He'd noticed she had a similar collection in her bedroom. He wondered if she would notice, and knew that she would.

The heavy gold drapes kept out the night. The place was a cave where he could read, where he could watch television, and where he could brood—something he'd done quite a bit lately.

"Make yourself at home." He gestured toward the couch and headed toward the bathroom.

Shutting the door behind him, he leaned his hands against the counter and stared at himself in the mirror. Dark, desperate eyes gazed back at him. He recognized this Teague. This was the Teague he'd been as a teenager, frustrated, angry that life was not fair, determined to grab all he could regardless of the cost.

He had hoped never to see those eyes again.

Yet *she* had come.

Outside, the lightning flashed, and the thunder grumbled.

He'd had everything under control. He'd thought he'd never see Kate again, and if he did, so what? He'd have another model on his arm. He'd have a dozen women in his bed. He would smile at Kate without interest, view her as a momentary aberration caused by too much refinement forced on a ghetto boy. Never mind that it had been three weeks since he'd seen her and during that time he hadn't gone on a single date. Never mind that he found himself remembering her in the dark hours of the night where before only demons of his former life had visited. He had just needed a little time, although time for *what* he dared not asked himself.

Now she was here. She'd recognized her danger, and she'd come running to him. Come into his lair, come seeking his help, as if she knew no other man could care for her as he did.

She was right. God help him, she was right.

Stiffly, he stood upright. With the slow motions of a man who bowed to fate when it wrapped him in its coils, he did the things a guy does to make himself ready—for anything.

Kate scanned the bookshelf, and what she saw there surprised her not at all. Teague read paperback thrillers and war stories, manly books that manly men read— except in Teague's case, he understood what he was reading. He wasn't some armchair quarterback; he'd played the position and coached, too. She touched the ruined spines. He read them hard, and, from the looks of his favorites, he read them repeatedly.

She glanced at the muted television. Jay Leno shook hands with his excited audience and settled into his monologue.

She still couldn't comprehend the news she'd heard tonight. *Mrs. Oberlin had fallen down the stairs.*

Had she overreacted by coming here?

How was it remotely possible that Senator Oberlin had killed his wife . . . and other people, too?

And if it was true . . . why had she come

running to Teague? *Why did he make her feel so safe?*

Teague's voice in the doorway made her jump. "If you find my sanity on those shelves, let me know."

She tried not to smile with pleasure at seeing his tall figure, his broad shoulders, his golden eyes. His dark hair was damp and tousled. He wore dark blue jeans and a blue T-shirt that stretched across his pectorals and over his biceps. He might have known she was coming, for he had dressed in a manner guaranteed to make her knees go weak. His feet were bare . . . she was a pushover for a man with bare feet.

Why did he make her feel so safe?

Because she knew, without a doubt, that he could keep her safe.

"Have you lost your sanity?" she asked.

Inside, behind the protection of his drapes, she could barely see the flash of the lightning.

But the thunder rumbled and growled.

No measure they took could completely keep out the approaching storm.

"Possibly. At least I'm feeling a little off balance—aren't you?"

Kate's brief flurry of euphoria faded. "That poor woman."

"Yes, and I'd like to keep people from saying that about you." He went to the small refrigerator built into the bookshelves. "Would you like a drink?"

"Yes. Chardonnay if you have it."

"Not chardonnay." He pulled a bottle of champagne out of the refrigerator.

Special occasion? But she swallowed the question. She didn't dare ask what he was thinking. She was here, in his quarters, bound to him by danger again. The atmosphere between them was thick with sexual frustration. At least . . . *she* suffered sexual frustration. None of her needs had faded in the three weeks of thinking of him. Now, just being with him heated her with excitement.

He popped the cork and poured two tall flutes full of golden bubbling liquid. He paced across the room toward her, and pressed the glass into her hand.

The flute was cool.

His gaze was hot.

"How is it?"

While he watched, she lifted the glass to her lips and took a sip. "It's . . . wonderful."

"Yes." He clinked his glass to hers,

watched her take another sip, took a sip himself. "Wonderful."

She smiled into the slowly rising bubbles. He made the act of serving champagne seem like foreplay.

"Why is Senator Oberlin interested in you?" He shot the question at her.

She recognized the tactics. Relax the victim, then knock the truth out of her. She'd done it herself, so she refused to let him shake her. "The usual, I guess."

"Sex?"

"Yes." She remembered the flat tire. She had thought it was the stalker—but maybe not. Maybe Senator Oberlin had arranged a convenient chance to rescue her. "Yes. Definitely."

"Mrs. Oberlin said he'd killed you before."

"I know." Kate smiled painfully. "That's why I thought . . . that's why I didn't look into any of that stuff she said."

"That was my job. I failed."

"I'm a reporter. *I* failed." Kate looked him in the eyes, her mouth straight and grim, and insisted on taking the blame.

Regardless of danger, she sought out her stories. The truth of the matter was, if she had to, she'd step back into the raging Gulf of Mexico during a hurricane. It *was* her job, and now she would pay for not following up as she should have. Evelyn Oberlin had paid, too. "Mrs. Oberlin was so crazy that night. I thought she was always crazy."

"Certainly a little crazy. Just maybe not as crazy as we thought." Teague's regret was palpable. He indicated the easy chair.

She sat down.

Jay Leno was flashing headlines on the television, mugging for the camera, faking sincerity.

Pulling up the ottoman, Teague sat beside her. As if he couldn't resist touching her, he stroked the skin on the back of her hand with his little finger. "Are you close to your family?"

"Yes." She sneaked a glance at him.

"Do you have any unsolved murders in your family?" He watched the screen without amusement, without seeming to see it. "Any skeletons lurking in the familial closet?"

"Not that I know of." She took a hasty swallow of her champagne, then a longer swallow, savoring the bubbles and the bite.

"Do you resemble your long-lost aunt Gertrude Blackstone?"

"Who? Oh, you mean *Blackthorn.* Mrs. Oberlin called her Mrs. Blackthorn. The other person whom Senator Oberlin . . . pushed down the stairs." Kate seldom felt awkward about her background, but she did now. "I may resemble someone. I don't know. I'm adopted."

"Really?" Teague seemed remarkably unimpressed.

Poker face, she thought. He couldn't fool her. He was interested. Very interested.

"What do you know of your blood relatives?" he asked.

"Nothing. I . . . nothing. I'm not even positive about the exact date of my birth."

His head turned slowly to her. His golden gaze raked her features. "Isn't that unusual in this day and age? Don't most people know at least a little about their birth parents?"

"I've never checked the stats. I only know my parents got me when I was ten months old, or thereabouts, and they were wonderful parents."

"You didn't try to trace your background?"

"When I was a teenager, I wanted to run away from home because I was so ill treated." She grimaced wryly as she remembered her melodramatics. "There's nothing there. It's a dead end. Everything about my adoption records has vanished due to clerical error."

She watched with painful fascination as Teague sipped his champagne. His long fingers caressed the flute. How could she concentrate on a possible murder when Teague sat within touching distance? She recognized a scent and leaned closer to sniff it. Herbal shampoo and warm, clean skin—

He turned on her so quickly, he caught her with her nose close to his shoulder. "Do you see Oberlin?"

"See him?" She straightened indignantly. "Like—date him?"

"No, I mean—at the capitol. Do you run into him a lot?"

"Yes." It was embarrassing to admit it. "All the time. It's almost like he's . . ."

"Stalking you?"

"Yes. Damn it." She hated to say the words. "Stalking me."

Teague lifted his brows.

"Well, really," she said in disgust. "Two stalkers in two months? Most people never even have one in a lifetime."

"Yet I watched him in the monitors. He waited for you."

"No. Gross." She didn't want to believe it. She didn't want this whole thing to start up again. And this time, to know her stalker, to suspect he had killed his wife . . . "Why me?"

"Good question. Why you? That's what we'll have to find out." He caressed her cheek with his finger. "Okay, look. I don't believe in coincidence, and there are far too many here for my comfort. You've got a problem. You're in danger. I'm not your bodyguard anymore, but I'm not leaving you alone again."

"What will we tell people when they ask why we're together?" Kate's question hovered in the air above them like a challenge, and thunder roared through the super-charged air.

Teague finished his champagne in slow, long swallows. He put down his glass. He took hers and placed it beside his. "We'll tell them the truth." His hand encircled her wrist. "We'll tell them we're lovers."

Fourteen

Her heart seemed to strike the inside of her ribs, then settled into a roaring beat. This was the moment she'd imagined, dreamed of, wished for, and now it came at her unanticipated and unexpected.

"Did you think that you could cross the threshold of my home and escape unscathed?" Teague's whisper was rough. "I've waited longer for you than for any woman in my life, and now by God I will have you."

She could scarcely breathe, but when he tugged on her wrist, she followed him.

They walked through the door into Teague's bedroom. He flipped a switch, and a bedside lamp flicked on, revealing a golden den dominated by a huge rosewood bed with tall square posts. In this room, the air conditioner hummed, the atmosphere was civilized. Yet outside, the storm swept across Austin, sending torrents of rain over the hills, using hail to slash the autumn leaves off the trees. The old-fashioned casement windows rattled in the wind, and beyond the rosewood blinds the panorama of lightning created mad black-and-white still lifes of the branches against a violent sky.

Some of that wildness and ferocity came with Teague and Kate into the bedroom.

They brought it themselves. They carried it within them.

He shut the door behind them. He turned the key as if he feared intruders when, in fact, they were alone in the house.

So maybe it was her escape he intended to thwart.

She touched the side of his face, stroking her fingertips over the hollow of his cheek and down his determined jaw. She didn't want to escape. She was frightened—what woman wouldn't be when she stood on the precipice of a cliff?—but she wasn't going to run.

Catching her hand, he pressed a kiss on her palm. The scent of him filled her lungs, a scent she would always associate with Teague—clean, warm skin with the faintest hint of sandalwood. *Pure distilled sex.*

The silence between them weighed as little as silk yet bound them as tightly, and he watched her with brooding intensity as though seeking . . . something.

A sign of willingness?

She slid her other hand up his arm to his shoulder, opening her body to him.

He looked down at her, at her jeans, her T-shirt, her flip-flops, and his expression was no less hungry than when she'd worn an evening gown and heels. He flattered her. He frightened her. He personified everything that was dominant in a man, and he left her in no doubt—he wanted to dominate her.

Yet he moved with care, urging her back against the door, pressing himself against her so that every inch of her knew every inch of him. He rubbed the faint pink scar on her chin where the stitches had been. "Bruises all healed?"

"I'm fine," she whispered. "Fine . . . all over."

Heat blazed from him, turning her to liquid gold. Her breasts grew taut. She could no longer support herself, but she didn't need to; he held her upright with his weight.

Leaning down, he kissed her mouth, her cheeks, closing her eyes with his touch. Without sight to distract her, she experienced each breath as it left his lungs, savored each touch of his lips. She imagined his eyes were shut, too, as he explored her ears, her chin, her throat, and then made his way back to her mouth and kissed her . . . kissed her.

He tasted her with elusive sips that made her seek him. She wanted more than his gentleness. She wanted his fire.

Her body stirred restlessly. She slid her fingers along the nape of his neck and into his hair. Catching his lower lip between her teeth, she nipped at him.

He froze, his body stiff, as if her daring goaded him to the precipice beside her. In that second of stillness, she felt the thumping of his heart against her chest, each long breath as he dragged air into his lungs . . . his erection thrust tight against her belly.

"Love me," she whispered. Softly she pressed her mouth to his. Deftly she slipped her tongue between his lips.

Her small provocation created desire that exploded between them . . . but no, that was the boom of thunder. Lightning slashed the sky, over and over, as the storm raged overhead and passion raged between them.

He thrust his tongue into her mouth, coercing pleasure on her, taking pleasure for himself. The taste of him burst through her senses, Teague and . . . and mint? Toothpaste? He'd been drinking coffee when she came. When had he brushed his teeth?

As soon as she got here.

He'd excused himself, gone into the bathroom, and done what people do when they know they are going to have sex.

She wanted to protest, to say it wasn't fair, but he held her head, slid his thumbs under her chin, and insisted she give him her full attention. Insisted with his tongue and his teeth and his lips. Insisted with the pulse of his hips against hers.

He overwhelmed her until she had no thought except to meld with him. She wanted to be *here,* back against the wall. She wanted to wrap her legs around him and have him push into her until they moved together in a primitive dance.

But Teague seemed to want nothing more than to immerse them in the kiss. His tongue stroked her lips, her teeth, and sang a song of heedless, endless obsession.

She struggled to answer him in kind, but he imposed his will on her, and she was too mad with delight and desire to fight.

Fight? Hell, why should she fight when this moment, this *now* was the greatest passion she'd ever experienced?

When he lifted his head from hers, she was drunk with need, giddy with lust. When she blindly tried to walk toward the bed, he stopped her with his hands on her shoulders.

"Wait. I want this first." He slipped his hands under her T-shirt, rested his palms flat against her belly, and smiled into her eyes. It wasn't a happy smile, or even a triumphant smile. In that curve of his lips she saw torment unleashed and need denied. "I've dreamed of this," he told her. "I have obsessed about this."

"You're not happy with your dreams?"

"No."

"Or your admission?"

"No."

"Then you should take your revenge," she whispered, staring boldly into his beautiful dark eyes.

He sucked in his breath, and the flame in his gaze turned savage. "You're either extremely brave or exceedingly foolish."

"Or else I trust you." She imitated him, tugging his T-shirt from under his waistband

and placing her palms flat on his belly. "I trust you."

Once again she saw into the dark soul of a predator. But this time, it was she he was hunting, and this time, there was nothing cold in his regard. He wanted her with a fire that scorched a brand on her heart and burned everywhere they touched. The loneliness she saw there made her want to weep, and burned her clear down to her bones.

She wasn't afraid. He would change her. After tonight, she would never be the same. But he wouldn't hurt her. Not physically. Not ever.

His hands moved beneath her shirt to the back clasp of her bra and popped it open. Grasping one strap, he slid it beneath the sleeve, down her arm, and off her hand. As smoothly as a magician—or a man with far too much experience—he brought her bra through the other sleeve and off.

He dropped it to the floor. With fierce, golden eyes, he stared at her breasts flattened by the tight T-shirt, at the nipples poking through the thin white material.

Color rose in his face, and she thought his

need would compel him to take her breasts in his hands, in his mouth. In anticipation, her nipples hardened to painful points, and her hands clenched into fists against his skin. She stifled a whimper.

But he didn't touch her. Not there. Instead he loosened the button on her jeans and dragged down her zipper. The metal rasp sounded loud in the silent room. She might as well have been nude before a tribunal that passed judgment and rendered punishment, for still he said nothing. Still he didn't touch her.

But she wasn't confined by whatever constraint he had placed on himself. She loosened her fists. She let her hands roam up to brush his male nipples, then down to follow the arrow of hair that pointed at his fly. She struggled to loosen his belt—no guy had ever held himself back long enough to let her undress him, so she had no experience. The button was easier—his jeans were loose as if he'd lost weight in the last few weeks. And when she unzipped his pants, she let her knuckles rub against his erection.

He flinched.

"Did I hurt you?" she whispered.

"Yes, damn you. You hurt me."

"Maybe that's because you're so aroused that each caress is agony, and waiting for the next caress is greater agony," she whispered huskily, letting her fingers shape him, watching the shifting emotions on his face. "Each pulse of blood in your veins is another moment of need. The air in your lungs burns like fire because nothing can complete you except being inside . . . me."

He moved so swiftly that before she could say another word, do another thing, his hand slid into the front of her jeans and cupped her.

She was swollen, tight, needy . . . orgasm swamped her, engulfed her senses with the swiftness of a flash flood. The desire that had clawed within her for so many nights took her, swept her legs out from under her, drowned her in a burst of ardor so powerful colors burst beneath her eyelids and her lungs burned from lack of air. The uproar was everything she wanted . . . and nothing at all.

It wasn't enough, could never be enough, and she thrust herself against his hand, trying to extend the sensation.

He laughed, low and exhilarated, and

withdrew his hand. "Are you satisfied already, darling? Can you go away now and know you've had all the satisfaction you can find with me?"

"No." Was he threatening to leave her like this? "God, no."

"Or is that just the hors d'oeuvre that leaves you hungry for the full meal?" His dark eyes sparked with gold. He was taunting her, making her want more, making her admit all.

"Please." She sucked air into lungs. "I want everything. I want *you.*"

He nodded, that pained smile tilting his lips, and shoved her jeans down to her ankles.

The cool sluice of air-conditioning against her skin brought a semblance of sense, and as he swung her into his arms, she opened her eyes.

The flip-flops, the jeans dropped off her feet, leaving her in a T-shirt and her tiniest panties—she'd been wearing mouth-watering underwear every day for no reason except that she prayed she might, *might* find herself almost naked in Teague's arms.

She hoped he didn't realize what had

been going on in her mind. She certainly hadn't fooled herself.

He opened the blinds, placed her on the mattress, then stepped back and gazed at her sprawled on his bed. Oh, when he looked at her like that, as if she were a jewel he would possess and keep forever, she could scarcely breathe for hope and . . . love.

Love.

What madness had possessed her to fall in love with a man so dangerous that he dealt death with his bare hands and handled weapons with frightening proficiency? He'd said the words when he sent her away that last night—they had nothing in common.

Except for similar humor and lively curiosity. And they could live together; that was important. She could tease him into trying new foods, and strive ineffectually to work out at his pace . . . and bask in his gaze as he watched her. He made her feel safe, and she made him feel at home. They weren't alike, yet . . . they were. Their minds worked in similar ways, and she loved him with a sharp, hot passion she'd never imagined.

He pulled his shirt off and she saw again

the rippling muscles of his stomach, the toned shoulders, the broad chest, and the smooth, bronze skin. At the gym, he'd been posing. Now he had no thought of letting her admire him. He was concerned with nothing more than undressing, and as rapidly as possible. He dropped his pants and underwear into a heap at his feet, and her breath locked desperately in her chest.

His narrow hips were made to fit between her legs, his muscled thighs would move him in an endless rhythm . . . but his cock would never fit inside her. Either the two other guys she'd slept with were puny, or Teague was overendowed and just plain scary.

"It's all right." He must have had to soothe other women at other times, for he put one knee on the bed beside her and with his palm he petted her arm. Catching her hand, he lifted it to his lips and kissed the back of her fingers, then turned it and kissed her wrist. His lips lingered over her pulse. "You were meant for me, and I will make this so good for you you'll"—he smiled a buccaneer's smile, as if he knew he was politically incorrect but was unable to resist—"you'll beg me to take you."

Yes. Politically incorrect . . . and probably true.

Her gaze skimmed him as he rose above her on the bed.

Definitely true. Her body prepared itself for another one of those bone-wracking orgasms, and he had done nothing except undress and smile.

"Do you know why I haven't taken off your shirt and panties?" With his thumb, he circled one nipple, but he looked into her eyes.

No. Her lips moved, but no sound came out.

"I want to draw this out as long as possible. I want this to be as hot and sweet as your coffee. I want to steal your mind away"—bending down, he spoke against her lips—"for so long that when you think of love, you think of me."

"Of love?" Had he read her mind?

"No two people will ever make love like we do."

Making love. Oh. Of course.

She closed her eyes against his heated gaze, not wanting him to read her thoughts or the reckless longing in her soul. A man like him bestowed boundless pleasure. He did not love. She would do well to remember that.

He cupped her breasts, holding them as if he relished their weight. Now his lips encircled one T-shirted nipple, and he suckled strongly, bringing her into his mouth with a skill that made her heels dig into the mattress and her back arch. When he relented, he blew on the damp cotton, and the cool breeze felt like sin personified. When he stripped off the shirt, he inhaled long and slow, and she found herself peeking beneath her lids.

As he gazed at her breasts, his stony expression revealed nothing. Then his gaze shifted to hers, and she saw it—a fierce exultation that made her feel proud and threatened at the same time. If he gave in to that savagery, she would be ravaged like a pirate's captive.

Worse, she would like it.

Outside the storm clamored, wanting to sweep everything from its path.

Inside, he caught her breasts in his hands and tasted them, one after the other, his wet mouth against her bare skin, until the storm within her gathered strength and she cried out and tried to get away.

He didn't let her. He held her trapped in his arms, doing with her as he wished, sucking, nibbling, kissing, and when he had finished he pushed his knee between her legs and settled himself there. Catching her thighs in his hands, he opened her widely. His weight pressed her into the mattress, holding her down, keeping her helpless . . . except for her hands, which selfishly roamed his torso.

Selfish, because she touched him not to please him, but to please herself.

She didn't know whether to struggle or to submit, but she knew one thing for sure. "For this to work, I have to be naked, too." Her thong still formed a barrier between them.

The head of his penis probed at her, finding the right place, pressing against the nest between her thighs.

"Not yet." His voice was a husky taunt. "I want you insane with need. That way when I push my way into you, you'll be damp and open, and each time I pull out, your body will cling to me, reluctant to give me up. . . ."

Not yet? His every word made the knifepoint of need twist tighter within her.

He knew it, too. Every move he made,

every word he spoke was deliberate, chosen to fan her desire. His domination made her want to submit to him; he wanted more than submission. He wanted mad impatience, desperate fever.

He probed her again, a firm imprint that stretched the cloth over her clitoris and made her squirm against him, trying to get as close as possible. Trying to lure him inside.

She no longer cared that he was too big for her. She would put up with any amount of discomfort to mate with Teague . . . but in the dim recesses of her mind she realized there would be no discomfort, because Teague would do just as he promised. As he threatened. He wouldn't take her until she was so crazed with passion she would be soft and pliant to his touch . . . until the moment when climax made her spasm around him.

This wasn't the sex with Teague she had imagined. She'd thought it would be fast and hot. Instead, he lingered and probed until frustrated tears trickled down her cheeks. She couldn't squirm away; his grip on her legs held her in place, and his weight controlled her every movement.

He kissed her, lingering kisses of such pleasure she wandered through sensual passages of dark delight. He kissed the hollow of her throat, the swell of her breasts, the soft delicacy of her inner elbow. His penis touched her again and again, and when her body reached and stretched toward climax, he pulled away.

She groaned in an agony of frustration. Time submerged beneath the tide of passion. She lost all awareness of the minutes passing, becoming quarter hours, half hours. . . .

"Please," she chanted without even realizing she spoke. She stroked his shoulders, his arms, his chest, his back, loving the sleek stretch of skin over each well-defined muscle. "Please, Teague. You're *hurting* me."

"How am I hurting you, my darling?" He released her legs, slid his palms up her thighs, and caressed between her legs with his thumb. He brought her to the brink again, so close that she trembled and lost the power of speech. Then he pulled back, a beast who specialized in sexual torment.

"Come into me." She wrapped him in her embrace and tugged at his hips. "How can you wait so long? Don't you really want me?"

"Really want you?" He laughed, short and bitter. "I've been up nights wanting you. I've walked the floors. I've imagined how each moment was going to be." He drew back. Hooking his fingers in the waistband of her panties, he pulled them down and tossed them aside. "You're not going to rush me now. I'm going to make this last forever."

It sounded like a vow that a woman in love could relish. Sighing, she stroked his face. "Forever."

He didn't flinch from the word. Instead his lips curled in a smile—not a pleasant smile, an almost cynical smile—but before she could question him, he reached up and turned off the lamp.

At once the storm, subdued by light, possessed the room. Lightning ripped the darkness, stripping his face of softness, illuminating his dark soul. The thunder roared triumphantly, and it seemed that Teague commanded the elements as he commanded her. Certainly he gloried in the violence; as he donned a condom, his teeth gleamed and his amber eyes sparked with lightning.

Yet the ferocity of the storm did not possess him; he touched her softly, repeatedly, finding the place where he would enter. His finger slid just inside and rimmed her, and through the anticipation that possessed her, she realized he had prepared her with lubricant.

So he had anticipated the difference in their sizes. As he promised with words and smiles and glances, he would make this good for her.

Then he pressed inside.

The tug against her flesh confirmed her suspicions. He was . . . so big. He stretched her. She whimpered on the verge of discomfort. But as he had vowed, she wanted him too much to draw back. First the lubricant eased his way, then the wonder of at last being united with Teague Ramos swept her. Her body softened, grew damper.

When he slid back, she moved her hips, trying to capture him inside.

Yet he left her . . . left her bereft and empty.

When he slid back inside, the fullness

soothed her desperation . . . and incited every brash instinct.

She tightened her legs, nipped at his chest. . . .

The small pain made him groan and thrust.

Then he caught himself, stopped himself.

She groaned, too.

He looked down at her. She looked up at him.

The lightning beat at them like a strobe. The thunder growled and roared like a living beast.

And finally, Teague thrust all the way inside her.

The sense of being *taken* swept all rational thought aside. He set a rhythm that made her arch and twist beneath him, seeking the primal pleasure this magnificent creature had promised in the way he walked, in every glance and every touch. She was full; she had no room for loneliness or pain or memories. He commanded her body, her mind, her emotions . . . her soul.

He held her down, controlling her motions, whispering husky encouragement in her ear, and all the time he filled her, and filled her again until she was aching with a desire made more frantic as it was denied.

She clutched at his shoulders, moaning softly, almost insensate with need.

"Don't be frightened." He nuzzled her lips with his.

His breath fanned her skin.

"I'm not frightened," she managed to gasp. She wasn't. She was part of the lightning and the thunder, part of the glory of the storm . . . part of him.

Burying her nose in his chest, she took a long breath of the heat and the scent of Teague, and as she exhaled her body, deprived for too long, found its release.

Outside, nature battered the world with noise and light.

Inside, Kate screamed with ecstasy and climax. Sex with Teague was erotic and sensual, so filled with power it overwhelmed her five senses and gave her something more. She held him with her arms and her legs, arched beneath him, demanded with action and sound and yearning.

He gave her everything she required, and at the height of her orgasm, he gave up all restraint and with a shout, he joined her. His hips thrust in the rhythm of life, providing everything he had promised her—every morsel of pleasure, every long moment of rapture, and an intimacy that fused them into one—one being, one spirit.

While outside the storm faded to a whimper . . . and gathered strength to strike again.

Teague looked down at Kate, her eyes closed as the last remnants of climax swept her. Perspiration beaded her forehead. Her chest heaved, and her body trembled.

And he realized he had been right. He had taken her. He had controlled her. He'd spilled his seed in her.

It wasn't enough. It would never be enough. Not with Kate.

This was why he hadn't had sex with her before, because this act wasn't sex, it was something more, something beyond his ken.

Then she opened her eyes and looked at him, and that slow, warm, sensual smile stretched her lips. "Tell me, why didn't we do that before?"

Every sensible thought disappeared from his brain, and he forgot fear, forgot trepida-

tion, forgot everything in the need to con-
quer her again.

He kissed her, savoring the freshness of
her breath, the warm twist of her tongue
against his.

My God, he would almost be satisfied just
to kiss her.

Almost.

He stroked her breasts, marveling at the
pink blush that rose beneath her pale skin,
and the way her nipples turned from a
relaxed peach to a puckered raspberry.
She watched him from beneath lids that
drooped, and a satisfied smile played
across her lips.

He'd satisfied her.

Why was he not completely satisfied?
Why did he need to take her again so soon?
When had he become a glutton for this one
woman?

What did it mean?

He was sure she was in trouble. Really big
trouble with George Oberlin.

Usually Teague could smell menace,
sense it in his bones. He had an intuition
about the bad guys, and what he sensed
was a dangerous man's disquiet with his
own deeds.

So why hadn't he been aware of the threat caused by Oberlin?

There could be only one explanation. Oberlin had no conscience, no thought of right and wrong, no thought of anything beyond his own wishes. He had murdered before, murdered more than once, and he had never been caught. Somehow, he had covered up the evidence.

If he wanted Kate, he would use every weapon in his considerable arsenal—respectability, money, influence—to remove Teague and take her as his own. And if she refused . . . would he kill her, too?

"What are you thinking?" Kate smoothed the hair across Teague's forehead. "You're frowning."

"I'm wondering if I can borrow a friend's jet."

"Why?" She smiled as if she read his mind.

"I have a place in Mexico with a private beach. There's a hut. It's not big and it's not pretty, and the cockroaches are as big as mice, but—"

"What are we waiting for?" She sat up—bare, unself-conscious, and beautiful. "I have the weekend off. Let's go."

Damn. She *could* read his mind. "Not so fast." He tumbled her onto her back. He'd dreamed of her dark hair spread across his pillow and her blue eyes sparkling up at him. Now he held her between his hands and discovered just having her here wasn't enough. He required more.

Fate. She was his fate. He'd tried to avoid her, and it, and Fate had laughed at him. Now he was bound to Kate by sexual desire and by . . . no. Not by love. He'd seen love at its worst—at home when another son of a bitch battered his mother, in the service when a Dear John letter arrived and destroyed a man from the inside out.

He himself had suffered for love. Suffered . . . but not enough. His torment could never be enough.

If Teague knew how to love, if he'd ever learned, he would love Kate. But he was too scarred by the events of that fateful day to learn now.

For if by some chance he did learn, he knew how love must end.

With death and pain and wounds that never healed.

So he pretended to himself that he'd never thought the word. Outside, the storm stirred again. The lightning and thunder began anew, and he grinned down at her. "Before we do anything else, I need to kiss you . . . all over."

Her eyes grew large and, for a moment, uncertain. Then she took a long breath. That ever-present spark of desire sprang to life between them. She stretched, a long, slow, sensuous provocation. "If you do that, it could take all night long."

"It's too stormy to fly anyway." He bent to her again. "We'll go in the morning."

Fifteen

"*Senator,* I'm sorry to bother you in your time of grief, but two FBI agents have arrived and are waiting in the foyer." Freddy stood in the doorway of George's study.

"The FBI?" With great deliberation, George put down his glass of single malt scotch. The steady motion gave him time to calm that instinctive reaction of horror. No one had seen him coerce Evelyn into taking the pills and chasing them down with booze, but it *was* possible someone had seen him help Evelyn down those stairs. . . .

But even if someone had, the FBI wouldn't follow up on the case. That would be the jurisdiction of the Austin police, and on George's forceful suggestion they'd done their investigation *quickly* and come up with exactly the right findings—Evelyn's death had been an accident, possibly suicide, caused by a dependence on tranquilizers and alcohol. "What do they want?"

"I questioned them, but they showed me their credentials and claimed they had to speak only with you." Freddy was dressed in black, as befitted a butler in a house in mourning for its mistress. He'd had to calm the maid who'd found Evelyn's body at the bottom of the stairs; she had thrown a shrieking fit that brought everyone running and provided George a great audience for his shock and anguish. Freddy proved his efficiency when he ordered the house draped with black crepe—excessive, yes, but it looked good to observers—organized an immediate funeral that had gone off with great success today, and screened the steady stream of visitors who came to express their condolences, allowing in only the most distinguished as well as those likely to be impressed by George's profound grief.

Yes, in these last couple of days, Freddy had truly proved his worth.

Yet it was Sunday afternoon, and George had not heard one word from Kate Montgomery. The other reporters had dropped by, but not Kate. And when he'd gently asked Linda Nguyen if Kate would arrive soon, she stared at him with those fierce black Asian eyes and said, "I don't know,

Senator. Contrary to popular belief, I'm not on Kate watch this week."

That skinny bitch would never get another quote from him.

Still, maybe Kate was out of town. If she didn't know about his travails, she couldn't offer her condolences.

"Senator?" Freddy said. "I did try and send them away, but they were quite insistent."

"The FBI agents. Yes. Of course I'll see them. Just . . . stall them. Give me a minute to tidy myself." George waited until Freddy left, then buttoned his shirt, rolled down his sleeves, retied his tie, shrugged into his jacket. He always found it best to present a powerful facade to any agency whose members might otherwise forget his importance.

Freddy tapped on the door, then opened it, and as the two FBI agents entered, he admonished, "Senator Oberlin suffered the loss of his wife in a tragic accident only two days ago. Please be brief."

"We know."

"We'll get right to the point."

At the sound of their high, gentle voices, George could scarcely believe his luck. The FBI had sent not one, but *two* female agents. They were both young—of course, there weren't that many females in the FBI, they hadn't been welcome for very long— and no matter how much the ladies tried to harden their hearts, he was sure they couldn't help but sympathize with so recent a widower.

But why the hell were they here? What *were* they after?

The taller, less attractive girl offered her hand and her credentials. "I'm Agent Rhonda de Lascaux, and this is Agent Johanna Umansky."

The petite, bouncing blonde held out her credentials, too.

As he shook hands, he looked over their badges. He'd seen a few in his time, and these looked genuine, right down to the bad photos.

"I believe you know Mr. Howell in the Austin office," Johanna said. "Silvester Howell sent us."

"Please sit down." George waved them toward chairs before his desk.

"We're sorry to disturb you at such a difficult time," the plain one said, "but we have a report we need to clear."

"Yes, of course, whatever needs to be

done, but . . . I can't imagine . . . but of course, I'm tired, not sleeping well . . . what can I do for you?" He thought he did a good imitation of a bereaved and bewildered husband. So he was surprised when the women nodded without expression and without expressing their condolences.

What a couple of bitches.

He seated himself in the desk chair, using the power of his position to impress them.

Johanna flipped open a Palm Pilot, consulted it, then flipped it closed. "Senator Oberlin, do you know a Mrs. Cunningham of Hobart, Texas?"

He tensed, sat forward. What had Gloria Cunningham done now?

"I did know her, and her husband, too. Years ago, I worked with her on my church board." He tried to act interested, but distant, as if her name meant little to him. "Has something happened to her?"

"She died." The little blonde pronounced the news of Gloria's demise without a qualm. "Of cancer."

"I'm sorry to hear that," he said, while his brain buzzed with speculation.

Gloria never knew anything, never showed a sign of wanting to look beyond the obvious.

Never indicated anything other than an undying fury toward Bennet and Lana Prescott and their kids. The minister and his family had been poorer than Gloria, but even though Gloria's husband was a doctor, the Prescotts had been more important in the community. She'd never forgiven them for that. Worse, her daughter Melissa had never been as talented as Hope Prescott, and Melissa had suffered the position of second fiddle with ill grace. Gloria had been thrilled when the Prescotts disappeared, and she'd watched with tight-lipped satisfaction as the family was broken apart and the children sent away.

She sure had never asked what happened to them. So why were FBI agents informing him of her death?

"She was sixty at the time of her death, at M. D. Anderson Cancer Center in Houston." Rhonda consulted her Palm Pilot, too. "Before she died, she wished to make a confession, which she did—to her minister and then to the police. That confession concerns you, Senator Oberlin." Rhonda pointedly looked over the rims of her glasses. "Would you know what that was about?"

"No. I'm sorry." He spread out his hands and with pleasure noted they were steady.

"While I visit Hobart periodically—it is my district, and I keep a home there—I'm afraid we didn't have—that is, my wife and I— didn't have much in common with the Cunninghams." George liked the way he included Evelyn in the conversation, as if he still couldn't believe she was dead.

"Mrs. Cunningham claims that, twenty-three years ago, after your minister and his wife were killed"—Johanna glanced at her Palm Pilot—"a Mr. and Mrs. Prescott, you organized a situation that thwarted the assignment of their children to one family, choosing instead to separate them."

"Why would I have had anything to do with the placement of those children?" Folding his hands on his desk, he leaned forward and radiated indignation. "I had barely started my run for the Texas Senate, and, contrary to popular belief, it's a grueling ordeal to get elected. I believe someone else handled the adoptions." He rubbed his forehead as if he couldn't quite remember. "Some pastor from a church outside of town . . . a Pastor John Wagner? Wilson? No, it was Wright. Pastor Wright."

Johanna used her stylus to record the information.

"Where is Pastor Wright now?" Rhonda asked.

"I have no idea. I'll tell you, I talked to the pastor about the Prescott kids, put the situation in his capable hands, and left town to campaign." Which was such a lie, because Pastor Wright's name may have appeared on any official documents, but he never existed as anything other than a name. It was George who had made damned good and sure those kids were scattered like dust on the wind. Somehow he'd known they would cause him trouble.

It was a good thing he was about to bring Givens Industries tumbling to the ground, because if Hope Prescott Givens heard about Mrs. Cunningham and her inconvenient repentance and confession, she would never let up until . . . she met the same fate as her parents.

"So you maintain there's no validity to Mrs. Cunningham's assertion?" Johanna asked.

"None whatsoever." He was safe in making the claim. There weren't that many people in Hobart who had known what was going on, he'd made sure of that. And many of those people who'd known weren't alive today. He'd made sure of that, too.

Yes, some of the congregation had tried to stick their noses in to find out what was happening with the Prescotts and their children, but they'd been of no consequence. Poor parishioners, most of them, easily controlled with a threat or a bribe. One way or another, he'd shut them down, and, by the time he was done, he'd held Hobart and its population in his hand. "Why are you investigating an adoption from so many years ago? Do you always pay this much attention to the ravings of an obviously very sick woman?"

"We pay attention to whatever the federal government instructs us to pay attention to. So, yes." Rhonda recorded a note into her Palm Pilot. "Senator Oberlin, Mrs. Cunningham told us she suspected foul play in the burning of the county courthouse, and since important city, state, and federal documents were destroyed and the fire was listed as suspicious, we listened to her accusations with interest."

"The fire was listed as suspicious?" It most certainly hadn't been. He'd made sure of that. "I understood it was faulty wiring in the attic."

Both Rhonda and Johanna lifted their interested gazes to his at the same time.

At once he saw his mistake. He should have pretended ignorance of the fire and its cause.

"Is there anything else?" he asked crisply. "Anything that Mrs. Cunningham said that actually incriminated me for anything, or is this all speculation?"

In unison, both women shut their Palm Pilots.

They came to their feet.

"We're sorry to have disturbed you, Senator," Rhonda said.

He stood also, feeling relaxed and a little expansive. "Not a problem. I know you have to do your duty." He herded them toward the door.

"Actually, Mrs. Cunningham's story is so fantastic, we probably wouldn't have come to you." Johanna stopped at the door.

"Except for the strange coincidence." Rhonda smiled sweetly at him.

"The strange coincidence?" he asked.

"Come on, Rhonda, we don't want to disturb Senator Oberlin with this." Johanna tugged at Rhonda's arm.

"We got an anonymous report of a dreadful similarity to the manner in which Mrs. Oberlin died." Rhonda's brow knit in perplexity. "A tragic similarity, really."

At the words *anonymous report,* a chill ran up George's spine. "I don't understand."

"It's the kind of thing that makes law enforcement officials sit up and take notice," Rhonda explained. "You see, Senator, it's unusual for anyone ever to fall down the stairs and break her neck, and it's happened twice in your home while you were in the vicinity. Once in Hobart. Once in Austin. A strange coincidence. A dreadful similarity. Don't you agree, Senator?"

Freddy showed the FBI agents out.

From the study, he heard the crash of porcelain. It appeared Senator Oberlin had lost his vaunted control on his temper. How dreadful. It appeared that the pressure was beginning to take its toll.

Freddy Griswald smiled.

Kate walked up the steps onto the porch of Teague's little hut on the Mexican beach. What was taking him so long? The sea-

borne wind ruffled her hair and breathed romance across the sands, and she wanted
Teague with her.

The sound of his voice made her stop.
Who was he talking to? They were alone
here, as isolated as it was possible for two
people to be . . .

"*Querida,* you are too smart for me. But I
won't tell you anything about that. Some
things are not to be discussed." He
laughed, and he sounded so . . . at ease.
Affectionate. "I won't tell you that, either.
Now I have to go, but I'll talk to you tomorrow night when I get back. We'll have dinner
this week, yes?"

He was on the phone! Why? With a
woman, obviously, but who?

"You're busy all week? I can't believe
you're blowing me off!" He laughed again.
"All right, I'll see you Monday. *Adios.*"

Kate stepped into the doorway, watched
him shut his phone, and wondered why, in a
day of sunshine and laughter and sex, he
had felt the need to call . . . someone. "I
can't believe you have cell service here."

"Satellite service," he said briefly, and
stowed the phone in his duffel bag. "I was
just checking in."

Coming in from the bright sun, she couldn't see him well, but she recognized brooding when she saw it, and he was brooding. "Checking in with your people?"

"Yeah. My people."

"Is everything all right in Austin?"

"Everything's under control." He tilted his chair back against the wall. He surveyed her. His lips lifted. "Do you know, with the sun behind you, I can see right through that pareu? It looks like you have a rainbow between your legs."

She looked down at herself, at the wispy, bright wrap tied around her waist and the matching one-piece bathing suit that covered all the essential parts of her body . . . and yet displayed them with admirable subtlety.

Then she looked back up at him. He was barefoot, bare-chested, a pair of worn jeans slung low across his narrow hips. In the day and a half since they'd arrived at his beach hut in a broken-down Jeep, he'd tanned a beautiful toasty brown. With his dark hair loose around his neck and his incipient beard shadowing his chin, he looked like a pirate—a pirate who gazed lasciviously at her.

There was nothing subtle about Teague.

Subtlety, she decided, was overrated. Instant desire sprang to life, which was absurd, because they'd spent the entire time here making love—on the bed, in the sand . . . they'd even tried it in the water and decided that that was impossible. So they'd done it on the beach again.

They both had tans in unusual places.

But she'd heard his conversation, and it hadn't been with one of his employees. It was personal, like the conversation in Starbucks, and important, or he wouldn't have dared the satellite rates. But she didn't care if he had a personal life. It was the fact he lied about it that bothered her.

He rose, an unhurried, leisurely stretch of bone and muscle. "Don't worry, Kate. Trust me to take care of you."

"I do. But—"

"The call had nothing to do with you." He took a measured step toward her, his eyes warm with humor and . . . desire.

How well she recognized that desire. Her heart took a large thump, then settled into a racing beat. She took a slow step back. "Are you stalking me?"

"What do you think?" He moved forward

again, his footfall soft on the creaking floor-boards.

"I think you're trying to distract me." She backed across the porch until the post met her back.

Still he moved forward, his pace casual. "Is it working?"

The man knew he could catch her. She knew it, too, but the instinct to escape was too strong to resist. She inched along the railing. "Seems to be." As soon as she reached the steps, she turned and dove onto the beach.

She heard his foot thump on the porch.

She ran toward the bay, her heels sinking into the sand with each step. This was silly. She had nowhere to go. The beach was a small crescent of brilliant white along a sparkling azure bay bounded by rocks on either side and jungle behind. The town with its tiny airstrip was five miles away on a rut-ted dirt road, and the rusty old Jeep that provided their transportation was not only slow but required hotwiring to get it started.

Yet she raced along, laughing, the wind cooling her hot face. The pareu tied around her waist loosened and fluttered away.

"I'm gaining on you," he shouted.

She increased her speed. She heard his footsteps behind her.

Then, just as it seemed her heart would burst with anticipation, his arm circled around her waist.

He took her down on the sand, rolling her beneath him. He caught her wrists. She fought, but he anchored her hands above her head. This was play, the kind of marvelous, free, glorious play she'd not indulged in since her childhood. Yet with him on top of her, she felt anything but childish.

He looked down at her laughing face. "Now you have to pay the fine."

"No, I don't." She tried to wiggle out from beneath him.

He thrust his knee between hers, anchoring her in place. "Don't you want to know what the fine is?"

"No. Because you need to pay my fine." Breathlessly she laughed at his expression. "You knocked me down."

"Aren't you the spirited one?" He leered like a villain in an old play and flexed the muscles in his chest. "But you have no chance against my superior strength."

"Oh, yeah? Watch this." Lifting her head, she caught his lower lip lightly between her teeth. Resting her head in the sand, she used her tongue to insinuate herself into his mouth.

He tasted like happiness, like juicy mangoes, and like lust.

She deepened the kiss, loving his slight hesitancy, then his yielding as he let her suck at his tongue and give him hers.

He had a tendency to overwhelm her. He always wanted to be in command. He dominated in a way that sent her spiraling out of control, yet sometimes she liked the freedom of being on top, of controlling the rhythm and the speed. He didn't seem to know how to let her, and that surprised her.

With a reputation like his, she would have expected he would be familiar with every delicate nuance of sex.

She comforted herself with the thought that he would learn, and enjoyed the heaviness of his body on hers. He made her lose her mind with joy, and that, she knew, was a rare and wonderful gift.

So now she kissed him with the scent of warm man skin and soft salty breeze in her nostrils. When at last she let him go, he lifted his head. "See? My fine for tackling me is the same as your fine for catching me."

"Not quite the same." He stared down at her with narrowed eyes.

She thought she detected a trace of that brooding again, as if he were a man on the brink of some great revelation.

Yet the button on his jeans poked into her belly, and beneath his fly, she felt the heat and hardness of him—a promise for the future.

"What did you have in mind?" She rolled her hips invitingly.

"Snorkeling."

"Oh." At once the bubble of her joy deflated.

"Come on. You'll like it, I promise." Standing, he extended his hand and pulled her onto her feet.

"But what about . . . ?" She reached for the bulge in his jeans.

He deftly caught her wrist and led her toward the pile of snorkeling equipment in the shade of a palm tree. "You promised you would try this."

"I didn't mean it." She'd been all over the world and managed to keep her head above water. Now, she had agreed to try swimming over a coral reef populated with sharks. She had lost her mind, if not her claustrophobic distaste for being unable to breathe.

No, worse, he'd screwed her brains out.

"We'll snorkel only in the bay. It's dead calm today. The waves aren't high. See?" He slipped his arm around her and pointed out at the water, which lapped almost at their feet. "Kate, look out there. Isn't it beautiful?"

She viewed her lover with suspicion. "You said it was dead calm, which means there should be a total lack of waves. Yet I can still see the Gulf churning away. And why do they call it *dead* calm? The mere term sounds ominous to me."

He ignored her nonsense as he ignored her protests. "The waves won't splash in your snorkel, and you know how clear the water is. I'll be right there with you. You'll see corals and bright fish." He smiled, his teeth flashing white in his tanned face. "I know a place where the manta rays swim. Wouldn't you like to see manta rays?"

She buried her feet in the warm sand, looked down at them, and said sulkily,

"That's why I watch National Geographic specials."

He chuckled as if she were joking. "Have I told you how much I like your bathing suit?"

"No." The purple, blue, red, yellow, orange, and green striped her body in paint-splashed slopes. "Mostly you haven't wanted me to wear it."

"I do like what's under it better." If he was trying to distract her from her fear, he was doing quite a lovely job. His hands smoothed up her thighs and over her bottom. "I will take absolutely perfect care of you. So come on. Let me help you on with your swim fins."

As he knelt before her, she wondered how he had managed to talk her into this madness.

Standing, he discarded his jeans, leaving him clad only in his suit.

Ah. That's right. He'd lured her from good sense by wearing the smallest pair of black spandex swimming trunks she'd ever had the good fortune to see. For the chance to lean her body against his, she would do anything, no matter how stupid.

"I wouldn't let you do this if I didn't have absolute confidence in your abilities to swim," he soothed. "I've never before met anyone who only does the sidestroke, but you're very strong."

"You're chatting me up." *And seducing me, too.*

"I am?" He tried to look innocent, which was ridiculous because he could never look anything but dangerous.

"Trying to make me forget my fear. I learned that trick in broadcasting: When the person you're interviewing is nervous, talk to him and don't tell him when you start filming."

"I don't have a camera on me." Standing, he spread his hands and let her scrutinize his body. "See?"

"I see." What she saw distracted her more than words ever could. Which accounted for how Teague got her into the water.

They flew back that night and spent the night at Teague's place because they couldn't stand to be apart.

Monday morning, Teague held Kate in his arms and said, "Tonight we'll go get your clothes. You can stay here with me until we get this situation with Oberlin settled."

She hesitated. Stay with Teague? Live with him? But she loved her home. And—a pang of guilt shot through her—what was she going to tell her mother? Mom wanted Kate involved. She wanted her bound in holy matrimony. She sure as hell didn't want her living in sin with no chance of marriage and no prospect for grandchildren.

Seeing Kate's indecision, Teague moved to sweep away her objections. "I could move back in with you, but he knows where you live—and I've got better security."

"I know." Kate surrendered. "All right. I'll stay here . . . for a while."

Teague took that victory and built on it. "Avoid Oberlin today. Do everything you can to stay away from the bastard."

She rather enjoyed the idea of turning over the problem of Senator Oberlin to Teague. Idly, she decided her inaction was a combination of two things: the incredible revulsion she felt knowing a man like Oberlin was interested in her, and Teague's lovemaking, which had rendered her soft and mushy—and deeply, dreadfully, terribly in love.

Stupidly in love.

Sixteen

All day Monday, Teague sat in the main security room in the capitol as his on-duty staff—Chun, Big Bob, and Gemma—came and went. He researched Oberlin on the Internet, watched as Kate cooperated with his order, and reflected with grim satisfaction that he had her under control.

If only he held the same influence over George Oberlin.

Oberlin wandered the corridors searching for Kate. He questioned her coworkers. He made calls to her television station. He saw one female who, from the back, looked like Kate, and he primped. He caught her arm. And when she furiously turned on him and cursed, his face turned dark red and his fist rose.

Truth to tell, Teague wanted him to hit her. Teague would have made sure the female got rescued right away, and a public mistake like that, backed up by videotape Teague would provide, would be hard to hide.

In the service, Teague had known how to deal with enemy soldiers. In the security business, he knew how to prosecute criminals. But a senator? A senator who had committed murder? Multiple murders? Who had gotten away with it?

And Teague was bitterly aware of his own vulnerability. He was half Hispanic, half Anglo, with no family, no influence, a house with a mortgage, and an outstanding loan taken to expand his business.

But he'd damn well better figure out some way to protect Kate pretty soon, because as Oberlin failed to find her, he grew more and more agitated.

By late afternoon, Big Bob leaned over Teague's shoulder, gazed at the monitor, and asked, "What's up with Senator Oberlin? He looks like he rubbed honey on his ass, then sat on a mound of fire ants."

It was time to bring his people in on the situation, so Teague faced them. "He's making Kate Montgomery uncomfortable, and she asked me for help in ducking him."

"I thought you didn't care what happened to Kate Montgomery." Big Bob hooked his thumbs in his belt loops, rocked on his heels, and grinned. "You said once we caught her stalker, she was no big deal."

"I'm no longer sure," Teague said softly, "that we caught the right stalker."

His pronouncement smashed through the room like a gunshot.

His people stared at him, wide-eyed.

"Are you accusing Oberlin?" Chun asked incredulously.

"You are shittin' us, Teague." Big Bob pointed at the monitor where Oberlin stood, arms crossed, a thunderous expression on his face. "That man is a white, God-fearing, influential son of a bitch, and if he's chasing Miss Kate Montgomery you're better off letting her handle it, or he'll cancel our security contract so fast it'll make your head spin."

Big Bob had captured almost every ounce of Teague's attention. A few ounces remained to watch the monitors as Oberlin started walking again. "Now why do you say it like that? I had heard Oberlin had a reputation for being a power dealer, but fair and honorable."

"He does. *Here,*" Big Bob said. "But my aunt lives in his county two little towns and a hopscotch over from Hobart, where he's from, and there he's *not* known for being such a good guy. She says a long time ago there were some pretty nasty rumors making their rounds about Oberlin, and they've never quite gone away."

Teague had never seen Big Bob so emphatic. "What kind of rumors?"

"The kind of rumors that suggest it doesn't do to stand in his way, or he'll run over you with a filled cement truck, then back over you just to make sure he's done the job." Big Bob looked as solemn as a funeral.

Teague realized Oberlin was on a collision course with Kate, and he spoke into the microphone. "Juanita, do you see Kate Montgomery talking to Mr. Duarte the janitor?"

On the monitor, he saw Juanita nod her head.

"Yes? Go instruct her she needs to head east, leave the building, and circle around to enter underground. That's right. Thanks, Juanita." Turning back to Big Bob, Teague asked, "Why didn't you ever tell me this before?"

"Didn't matter before," Big Bob said. "You weren't trying to go crossways of him before!"

"So we're going to let him run over Kate

Montgomery with a cement truck to save our own asses?" Teague asked.

It was interesting to watch his people struggle with the dilemma—save their jobs or do the right thing? But Teague hadn't hired Big Bob or Chun or Gemma because they did things the easy way. He'd hired them for their integrity, and they didn't disappoint now.

"Sleazy bastard," Chun muttered, his gaze on Oberlin.

"He always gave me the creeps." Gemma shivered.

"Well, hell." Fondly, Big Bob patted his stomach. "I was eating too well anyway."

"I knew I could depend on you all." Standing, Teague started toward the door.

"You taking Kate home at night, boss?" Chun asked in sly amusement.

Teague stopped.

"Sure he is." Gemma chuckled. "He's making sure she's safe *night* and *day.*"

"What's wrong with that?" Teague snapped.

"Nothing." Big Bob rocked on his heels again. He grinned again. "Nothing at all. But if I were you, boss, I'd be careful, or you could end up driving that sleek little sports car permanently."

Teague snapped the door shut on their hilarity.

He was the quintessential bachelor. He had nothing beyond good sex to give to a woman. Some women—good women, women like Kate—eventually craved things like love and intimacy. Craved a *relationship.*

When he was a kid, on the occasions when he'd tried to show affection, his mother had used a coarse laugh or a sharp slap to drive home the fact that his hugs and his tender words repulsed her. He couldn't try for a loving bond with Kate—if she laughed at him, whatever bit of soul he had left would wither and he would be nothing but emptiness and anguish.

No, damn it. Big Bob was wrong. There was no way he and Kate could last.

When Kate wanted more than he was willing to give, he would make it clear she needed to respect his space and back off.

Regrettably, she picked that moment to walk around the corner from the Senate Chambers. Worse, she smiled as if she were happy to see him.

The woman knew no shame.

He did not return her smile. "C'mon." Grabbing her hand, he headed for the cars.

She giggled. Giggled!

Had he really thought he had her under control? She was leading him by the nose—or rather, by the dick.

An early norther had blown into Austin, dropping the temperature twenty degrees in less than an hour. The cold cut right through his suit.

Kate crossed her arms over her chest and lowered her head against the stiff breeze as they walked to her car.

But he didn't pull her close.

If what he'd seen of Oberlin on the monitor proved anything, it was that they were dealing with a full-blown obsession. Too bad it had taken Mrs. Oberlin's death to sharpen Teague's perceptions. Mrs. Oberlin's *murder.*

What a damn mess.

Teague glanced sideways at Kate.

She caught his look and smiled at him.

He couldn't help it. He smiled back as if he hadn't a care in the world.

He hoped no one blabbed to Oberlin that Teague and Kate were leaving together. No telling what the senator would do. Go ballistic, Teague guessed. It would be better if they left separately, but Teague couldn't take a chance that Oberlin would find her.

And Teague needed her now, now. . . .

She offered him her car keys.

Teague opened Kate's door. He started her engine, and when it caught with no problem, he jumped out and stuffed her in. "Drive to my house."

"I thought we were going to my place so I could pack." She looked up at him, her wide eyes fluttering with astonishment. As if she didn't know *exactly* what he wanted.

"Later." He slammed her door and leaned his palm against the cool metal of her car. He was a turmoil of worry and lust and aggression and love . . . no. He already knew that.

Not love.

He followed her through the streets of Austin. He was the only one following her, he made sure of that, and when they got to his house, he ushered her inside with his hand on her back. It was as if the idyllic weekend of making love and swimming and talking had never happened. He was desperate with need. He had to have her. Had to have her *now.*

At the sight of Brenda ensconced at her desk, they both stopped short.

"Hello, Teague, Kate, how's it going?" Brenda asked cheerfully.

"Working late?" Kate sounded only mildly interested in the answer.

Teague wanted to snarl at her. He had a boner she could hang her coat on, and she wanted to chat with his secretary.

"I planned to catch up on my paper-work"—Brenda caught Teague's killing glance—"tomorrow." Standing, she shuffled pages into neat piles. "So I'll see you tomor-row morning. Or, um, not. Good night!" She grabbed her jacket off the rack and headed out into the windy evening.

Kate leaned against the wall. With a half smile, she watched as Teague set the lock and the alarm.

Then, with a ferocity that took him by sur-prise, she wrapped herself around him and kissed him. She was reckless with passion, greedy with desire. Her arms held him, one leg wrapped around him, and for a long mo-ment he let her take charge.

Then he remembered—when the time

came, when she began to demand intimacy, he planned to give her up. To drive her away.

Picking her up, he carried her into the living room. He lowered her onto the rug and made fast and furious love while the formal nineteenth-century black-and-white photos looked on.

And Kate stayed with him. She matched his speed, his wildness. Without self-consciousness, she cried her pleasure aloud, and for a moment, one moment, he forgot that he had to dominate her and he just . . . lived. Lived as he had never lived before.

Afterward he lay sprawled on the rug, staring at the cove molding, his chest heaving as he tried to regain his breath. His composure.

Himself.

Rolling over, Kate raised herself on one elbow and looked down at Teague. "It's time we went to visit my mother."

Teague tensed, but he didn't open his eyes. "Why?"

"Because this thing with Senator Oberlin may have something to do with my birth parents, and Mom might know something."

Kate was right about that. But that wasn't all. She had something else on her mind.

"And we're involved," she continued. "She'll want to meet you."

Exactly the reason he didn't want to meet Mrs. Montgomery. He had never made the acquaintance of the mother of any female he was screwing, and he didn't want to do so now. "How's she going to find out we're involved?" A logical question.

Kate gave him a logical answer, while at the same time adjusting herself so her boobs rested on his chest. "We're going to tell everyone we're involved to cover our investigation of Senator Oberlin. Remember? Mom's well liked and well connected. If I don't tell her, someone else will." Kate stroked his ribs with her index finger. "I love my mother. I don't want to hurt her."

He grunted and wished Kate's nipples weren't poking into his skin. He could muster better resistance when his mind was not clouded by lust.

"You understand. You had a mother and you loved her. You miss her."

"No," he said without politeness or frills.

Goddamn it, Teague, you little bastard. Don't be so goddamned stupid. You're a goddamned stupid half-breed gringo and if you get knifed, no one will care. I sure as hell won't. But that kid—

"Teague, why do you look like that?" Kate smoothed her hand over his breastbone, over the place where his heart beat erratically.

Teague, you little bastard, you can't take that kid to a gang fight. If you get knifed, no one will care. I sure as hell won't. But that kid is only fourteen. She's your cousin! If something happens to her—

"My poor baby." Kate sounded absolutely sincere. "I knew you said you had lost your father when you were very young, but I thought . . . I thought you and your mother were close. What happened between you?"

If Kate thought sleeping with him gave her the right to pry into his private life, to ask questions and reel in the truth, to pity him, she had another think coming.

But that kid is only fourteen. She's your cousin, for shit's sake.

Teague stared at Kate with narrowed eyes. Kate was a reporter. She'd covered crimes, hurricanes, Senate hearings. But she didn't have a clue how the real world worked. He would bet that, if asked, she'd say that people were basically good, and that made him want to howl with laughter. Or howl with impotent fury. For when he remembered his mother . . . grabbing Kate's hand, he pressed it against his chest. With an adroitness that had, all these years, kept his secrets safe, he said, "All right, I'll go visit your mother, but you have to make it worth my while."

Kate's other hand slid down his hip and caressed the bare, hairless place where his stomach met his hip. Near enough to target zero to make his heart jump, yet far enough away to make him yearn. Her smile glowed as warm and intoxicating as tequila. "Why, Mr. Ramos, what did you have in mind?"

"Mom, you home?" Kate tossed her key on the table in the foyer.

"In here, dear," Mom called back. "In the sewing room."

Teague looked out of place, which surprised Kate, for he had been all that was suave at Senator Oberlin's party, and all that was businesslike at the capitol. Now he shifted uneasily, as if ready to bolt.

Taking his hand, she led him into the bedroom that doubled as her mother's sewing room.

The place was a sea of cream-colored raw silk and tiebacks made of gold cord. The elaborate sewing machine sat under the window, where it would catch the light. In the middle of the chaos sat her mother before the long table, a pair of shears in her hand and two pins in her mouth.

"Yipes," Teague said under his breath.

Kate grinned. She was used to her mom's projects, but how she took them from chaos to finished product was still a mystery to Kate.

To Teague, this must seem like the impossible.

"What is it this time?" Kate inquired.

Mom took the pins out of her mouth and stuck them in the pin cushion on her wrist. "I'm making drapes for Aunt Carol's bedroom, and I declare, this silk she picked is possessed of the devil."

"More likely the devil is in the sewing machine." Kate leaned on the doorframe and smiled at her mother. Despite her mother's best efforts to teach her, Kate had never learned to sew. Every time she tried, the thread broke or bunched on the back of the material or mysterious spots of oil appeared along the seam. The whole experience left Kate disgusted with the process—but when she looked at Teague, she burst into laughter.

If she was disgusted, he was panicked. His amber eyes were wide, his jaw clenched.

Kate thought she'd better introduce him before he fled. Putting a steadying hand on his arm, she said, "Mom, this is Teague Ramos, my former bodyguard and new boyfriend. He's not afraid of anything, but I think he's met his match with your sewing room. Can you quit for a while and have tea with us?" Kate asked.

"Why, yes, dear, I'd be delighted to chat with your Mr. Ramos." Mom rose and gently shifted lengths of material to the side until she'd cleared a path. She stepped out of the room, her gaze fixed on Teague.

If anything, Teague looked more panicked, and Kate would have sworn he broke out in a sweat.

This was fun.

Mom stopped right before him, crowding him as surely as he had crowded Kate the first time they met. "Mr. Ramos." She offered her hand. "It's a pleasure to meet you at last. I've heard so much about you!"

"From . . . Kate?" He took her mother's hand as if she were fragile, which she most definitely was not.

"No, most of the gossip came from my friends. It was not the kind of gossip to ease a mother's mind." She smiled with a sweet southern-belle smile. "Teague—may I call you Teague?"

"Yes, ma'am, please do." Like a mouse trying to escape the claws of a circling hawk, he stood motionless.

"Let me be absolutely clear. You had better be good to my little girl, or I'll use my biggest carving knife to remove your family jewels."

"Mom!" At Teague's expression of affronted astonishment, Kate laughed. "Mom, Teague's been wonderful to me."

"Exactly as he should be. Now, Teague"—Mom slipped her hand through his arm and led him toward the kitchen—"you look like a man who knows the value of a well-made loaf of bread. Come and tell me what you think of my newest experiment for Christmas."

Kate followed them, grinning so wide

she thought her face would split. Of course, she hadn't *known* that her mother would threaten Teague, but it didn't *surprise* her. Teague had a reputation as a lady's man, and Mom was a churchgoing Methodist, most definitely *not* the kind of woman who approved of casual sex, and certainly not if her daughter was the one participating in the act.

"It's a hearty wheat bread swirled with cinnamon, cream cheese, pecans, and dates." Mom sat Teague down on one of her stools at the breakfast bar.

Kate enjoyed seeing them together: her slender, poised mother with her beautiful, kind brown eyes, and her handsome lover with the thin veneer of civilization that barely covered his rough edges.

Mom bustled over to the loaf of bread cooling on the rack. She picked up her wickedly long bread knife.

Teague flinched.

Kate's mother must have been watching. "This isn't my carving knife." She showed him the serrated edge. "You'd have to stand very still for me to use it. This"—she pulled the long, wide, shining blade from its holder on the counter—"is my carving knife. Impressive, hm?"

"Mom." Kate collapsed on one of the kitchen stools at the breakfast bar. "You sound like Daddy!"

"I don't want Teague to think we're a couple of helpless ladies," her mother said.

"I don't think that at all," Teague said drily.

Kate experienced an odd frisson of worry. With the exception of certain social climbers and men who kicked dogs and small children, everybody liked her mother. Yet Teague held himself apart from the cloud of cheerful kindness that permeated her mother's house. It seemed he dared not relax or he would betray himself.

And Kate suspected he blamed her for his discomfort.

Kate didn't understand it, and she didn't like it; as they spoke, she watched the two people she loved—and she struggled to understand them.

Her mother cut two slices, placed each on a paper napkin, and passed them across the counter. "Tell me, when did you two start dating?"

Kate slid her stool over beside Teague's and pressed her knee to his.

He slid a glance sideways, and in his eyes she saw a glimpse of that bleakness in his soul. Yet this time she saw more than emptiness; she saw a flash of pain-driven loneliness.

Then he took a bite of the bread and, just like a man, lost interest in everything but the food. "This is wonderful!" For a minute, just a minute, he seemed to forget whatever bee was in his bonnet and allowed himself to *like* her mother.

"Thank you," her mother said. "Where are you from, Teague?"

Oops. Of course, Mom would have to interrogate him in a proper motherly manner and ask the questions that Kate, as a reporter, had barely dared.

"I'm from Brownsville, on the Mexican border." He gave up the information grudgingly.

"Who are your parents?" Mom poured him a tall glass of milk and passed it over.

He drank before answering. "My mother is dead. She wasn't married. My father abandoned her before I was born."

Kate took a swift, indrawn breath. She hadn't realized he would lie to her. "But you said your dad took off when you were little."

"I applied a little spin." The harsh set of his face grew grimmer.

Kate didn't understand him tonight. He was abrasive, almost belligerent—and he was hurting her. He had to know he was hurting her. "So now you've decided my *mother* needs to know the truth."

"I'd say he decided *you* needed to know the truth." Mom tried to press her hand to his. "I'm sorry. It sounds as if you had a rough childhood."

He withdrew from her touch, rejecting her sympathy. "Someone like me isn't fit to touch your daughter."

"Teague, I'm sitting right here and not liking your attitude," Kate said furiously.

His gaze never left her mother. He didn't even acknowledge Kate's presence.

"I don't think there's any man who's worthy to touch my daughter." Her mother smiled a terrible smile. "Yet I find myself insulted that you consider me such a snob."

"The sins of the father are visited on the son. So I hear." Teague's smile was equally unpleasant. "I *am* a bastard."

"I'm a religious woman, Teague, and I concentrate on the part of doing unto others. I don't pick on children because of the foolish acts their parents committed." Mom's smile returned to normal. "Do you have any family left?"

"No. No family. No one."

"Which explains why you and Kate have so much in common. She's adopted, you know. Our families have always treated her as their own, but I suspect in her heart she felt the difference." Mom held out her hand to Kate.

Kate took it and held it. Mom's family, and her Daddy's family had been Kate's family, but she couldn't deny that occasionally the desire had stirred in her to meet her own flesh and blood. But she had spoken of it to her mother only during her turbulent teenage years, for it had been a child's desire, made up of fairy tales and melodrama.

"Let me go get the photo album." Mom took Teague's hand, too, before he could move it, and pressed it between her fingers. "You'll want to see Kate's baby pictures."

As her mother bustled out of the kitchen, Kate sighed. "I'm afraid you'll have to look at them and *ooh* and *ahh.*" She wondered if he would stay for that ordeal.

"I can do that." As if he couldn't help himself, he let his gaze slide over her, heating her from the inside out. "I'll bet you were a beautiful baby."

"Another something we have in common."

"I wouldn't know." He sat up too straight. He spoke too stiffly. "I don't have any baby pictures."

Truth spilled from him, and her heart ached for the hostility he showed. Yet hostility was better than that dark oblivion she had once glimpsed in him, so she asked, "Do you have your school pictures? Starting with a cute little five-year-old boy with big golden eyes and dark, dark hair, with two teeth missing in the front?"

At her enthusiastic description, his forbidding expression cracked slightly, and he smiled. "That's a pretty close description."

"And then a photo every year until you graduated from high school?"

"Once I got into junior high, I usually skipped picture day." As if impelled to test the limits of her tolerance, he said, "I do have one from when I was fifteen, with my ear cut half off and my nose broken. I wanted to have that day memorialized."

Her mother appeared in the doorway, and, from the way she viewed him through narrowed eyes, it was obvious she had heard

Teague's confession. "I can see how you would do that," she said, putting the album down on the counter in front of Teague and opening it.

"Excuse me." Kate slid off her stool. "While you two laugh at my pictures, I'm going to call the station to see what they know about events at the capitol. Stuff was happening this afternoon, and I couldn't stand still long enough to find out what was going on."

When she looked back, Mom was sitting on the stool Kate had abandoned and saying, "This is when Kate was two and a half. She sang in the children's choir at Christmas. That was the year she discovered it was fun to stand in front of a crowd and have them admire her. She's liked being center stage ever since."

Seventeen

Where was Kate? George had looked for her all day long. He knew she had been in the capitol. When he asked, people said things like, "Yes, I just talked to her," or "You just missed her. She said she had to go to the ladies' room." And, "Dear Lord, Oberlin, what are you doing here? You just buried your wife. You should be home."

"The vote's coming up," George kept saying. "Evelyn wouldn't have wanted me to shirk my duty. She cared deeply for the welfare of children. She would have wanted me to vote on school funding." At seven o'clock that night, almost everyone who was anyone had left the capitol building, and George stood in the empty rotunda, his chest heaving in frustration.

Was Kate avoiding him? He couldn't believe she was avoiding him. She hadn't even come to pay her condolences to him. She was supposed to feel *sorry* for him.

Both his campaign manager and his lawyer had called about Evelyn's accident.

Been nervous about her death. Asked George if he had told anyone else he had been considering divorce. George could truthfully assure them that he hadn't.

He'd made it very clear to his lawyer that if a rumor started about his intention to divorce Evelyn, he would know whom to blame. He'd done the same with his campaign manager.

He was not a man who left such matters to chance. He didn't like to be surprised.

The visit from the FBI agents had surprised him.

At the back of George's mind, worry plagued him like a hangover. Someone had sent in an anonymous tip about Mrs. Blackthorn. Her accident had been twenty years ago and miles away, but someone still remembered—and suspected the truth.

Who?

Before she died, Gloria could have told the FBI of her suspicions, but she had kicked the bucket before she could make the connection between Evelyn's death and Blackthorn's. Had Dr. Cunningham finally worked up the nerve to be suspicious? No, because although the good doctor was a cowardly little weasel, he was also a smart man, and he knew if he started slinging accusations, George would nail his ass to the wall.

He smiled at the thought, his first genuine smile of the day. His whole life right now was rife with potential.

He was going to make so much money in the crash of Givens Industries he would be one of the wealthiest men in the United States. His wallet twitched when he thought how close he was to cashing in the deal. With that financial backing, he could skip the U.S. Senate altogether and go right to the presidency.

And Kate would like to be his first lady.

Not a first lady like that domineering bitch of Clinton's, but a real first lady like Jackie Kennedy, the kind that everybody envied for her poise and good taste.

But first Kate had to learn some manners.

She hadn't sought him out. She hadn't sent a note. He'd received no flowers from her. When they were married, he would teach her better manners.

He'd teach them. He'd show her. He'd push the school-funding vote through tomorrow. She was a reporter. She'd be there with bells on.

"Senator Oberlin, what are you doing here?" Mr. Duarte shuffled over, dragging his mop and his wheeled bucket after him. "It's late."

"Have you seen Kate Montgomery?" George had lost any ability to dissemble. "Is she still here?"

"Ah, Senator, I feel so pitiful for you. You just lost your wife, and that young lady is off with her boyfriend. But you stop fretting about her. I know you took her under your wing when nobody else would help her fly, and God will bless you for your kindness, but the little bird is winging her way skyward right now."

George heard only one word. "Boyfriend?" He gaped and whispered, "What boy-friend?"

"That nice young man, the one who does security here." Duarte smacked his lips as he thought. "I can't quite amember his name . . ."

"Ramos? Teague Ramos?"

"That's him." Duarte nodded, his brown eyes rheumy. "He's a nice young feller, and I've seen enough to recognize a man in love."

"In . . . love." George felt sick. Then,

swiftly, he recovered. *"He's* in love." Of course he was in love with Kate.

"Yes, sir, Senator," Duarte said with the enthusiasm of a born romantic. "That boy's in love. And you know what? She's in love, too. He's in love. She's in love." Duarte's singsong voice went on and on. "They're in lu-ove."

Another betrayal.

A betrayal that cut as deep as the first one.

Duarte's foolish, wrinkled face swam before George's eyes, and it was all George could do to remember the security cameras and not choke the old man. George hadn't been this angry since he . . . since he had killed the minister and his wife with his own hands.

While Duarte was still talking, George walked away. He strode out of the capitol, toward the phone, toward his car, toward revenge.

At the corner, he picked up a public phone. He inserted fifty cents and, with careful fingers, dialed the number that would put him in touch with Jason Urbano in Boston.

When Urbano's voice answered, George

said, "Remember that task I set for you to do? I want you to do it *now.*"

"Senator? Senator Oberlin? Please don't make me do this." Urbano's voice shook like a little girl's.

"Do it, or you know what will happen." George usually prided himself on sounding upbeat while he delivered his threats. This time, such a performance was beyond him, and his voice crackled with irritation.

"All right. For everything to be done right, it's going to take two days. Day after tomorrow, Givens Industries will be nothing but rubble." Urbano took a deep, painful breath. "But you promise you'll cover for me? When the Feds investigate the collapse, you'll make sure they don't press charges?"

"Yes. I'll save your ass. Now—do it!" George hung up and stood, chest heaving, his hand still on the receiver. His knees shook so hard he could hardly stand. His eyes felt swollen with rage. The voice he'd heard coming from his mouth had been his father's.

Was George Oberlin losing his mind?

He took a breath and again started walking toward his car. No, not him.

He had everything in hand.

Yet all the while, rage bubbled in his veins and Duarte's words echoed in his mind.

That boy's in love . . . She's in love, too . . . He's in love . . . She's in love. They're in lu-ove.

Kate did not understand the forces she had unleashed.

After she hung up her mother's phone, Kate sat looking at it. The call to KTTV had set her on edge. She felt funny, not being in the midst of things. She had settled into her position as political reporter: digging out stories, sniffing the air for upcoming events. She *liked* her job.

She understood why Teague wanted her to avoid Oberlin. It would be stupid, considering what they believed of him, to take the chance of running into him. My God, they feared he was an obsessive-compulsive murderer who had fixated on her.

But she had never turned tail and run away from a situation before. Never had she avoided her profession because she was afraid. And now after only a few hours away from the action, she feared she had lost her edge.

Silly, really. Politics moved at the speed of glacial crawl. Nothing would happen this week, and by next week Teague would . . . would do what? This situation with Oberlin was more frightening than anything she'd faced since the terrorists had kidnapped her father. She felt just as helpless, and she itched to take control.

She believed in Teague. She believed he was the best security man in the country—but what could he do? This was big. This was huge. This was more than either of them had ever faced, and they needed to face it together. Somehow, they needed to draw strength from each other. . . . Kate found herself smiling foolishly into the air. She was madly in love with a man who had bristled with antagonism when her mother asked about his family.

Maybe it was her mom's knife threat that had caused his hostility.

Hastily, Kate rose and headed back into the kitchen.

Her mother was busy with a kettle, a china pot shaped like Dumbo, and a canister of loose tea.

Kate leaned against the counter. "Nice teapot, Mom."

"Aunt Carol brought it to me from Disneyland." She held it up and looked into its amiable, gray face. "May I say, it does look like her."

Kate laughed because she couldn't help herself, and turned to Teague. "Aunt Carol has a round tummy, big ears, and a big nose"—she bent an admonishing glance at Mom—"and my mother has a biting sense of humor when she chooses."

"Yes, I'm going to hell for that. By the way, I hope the reason you two are seeing each other isn't because someone else is stalking Kate." Her mother considered them with that cool, penetrating gaze that used to have the effect of making Kate sit up straight and study her math.

She caught Kate by surprise. Kate's gaze dropped.

"Oh, dear." Mom sat heavily on a stool. "I wanted to hear you were dating."

"We *are* dating," Kate said.

"I wanted to hear you were involved."

"We are involved."

"I wanted to hear you were engaged."

Teague intervened before Kate had to tangle with that. "About the stalking—there are a few coincidences that make us uneasy."

"Coincidences." Mom turned that mother-look on him. "Tell me all about them."

"Are you sure you don't know Senator George Oberlin?" Kate asked.

Mom thought for a moment. "I'm sure. But I do remember you decided *Mrs.* Oberlin was your stalker." She looked from Teague to Kate and back again. "Wasn't she?"

"Yes, she actually was. The trouble is, Evelyn Oberlin died in a fall last Friday." Teague observed Mom as acutely as she had observed him earlier.

"My God!" Mom covered her mouth. "How?"

"She was drunk," Teague said. "She fell down the stairs in her house."

"I'm sorry to hear that, but if she was drunk . . ." Her brow furrowed in puzzlement.

"She was drunk the night I caught her behind the Dumpster at Kate's apartment, too." Teague's mouth flattened grimly. "She babbled about Kate, about how she was stalking her to chase her away and keep her safe."

"She was crazy." The kettle started whistling, and Mom poured the boiling water into the pot.

"But how crazy?" Kate asked. "While she was talking, she apologized to Lana. Do we know a Lana?"

"No." But her mother looked cautious.

"She said Kate looked like her mother." Teague watched her mother.

Mom's naturally rosy complexion turned pale.

"She said Kate needed to leave before *he* killed her *again.*" Teague ruthlessly pressed Mom for information. "I'll feel a lot more peace of mind if you tell me you know more about Kate's adoption than she does."

Mom's eyes shifted away as if she were guilty. Lifting the pot, she poured tea in a cup. "It's not ready yet," she said, and dumped the liquid down the drain.

Kate's reporter instincts came alive and honed in. "I wondered, Mom, if Senator Oberlin had anything to do with my adoption."

"No. No, it was a church adoption." Her mother spoke with absolute certainty.

"Which church?" Teague asked smoothly. "Where can we find Kate's records?"

"The adoption agency is out of business."

"But her records must be somewhere," Teague insisted.

"When we went back . . . it was two years before we came back to the States. Business kept us away." Mom poured tea again, and this time she was satisfied for she filled the three cups and passed them out with a container of sweetener. "By the time we came back, the adoption agency was gone."

"But adoption agencies don't disappear." Kate leaned toward her mother. This was important. Her mother had to know more than this.

"This one did," Mom said sharply.

"But you must have tried to find them, to get Kate's records," Teague said.

"We did, but we couldn't find them." Mom's voice grew higher, louder. "And as I said to my husband, Kate had been left on the church step. What kind of records could the agency have had?"

Teague started to say something, but Kate squeezed his thigh. Hard. He fell silent.

Mom's gaze dropped to Kate's hand, then she looked back at them. "I have a birth certificate that the state made up for her. The birth date is approximate. The place of birth is left blank. And I have her adoption papers. But why is this important?"

"We wonder if the reason Senator Oberlin's wife stalked me, if the reason she died in a fall, has something to do with my other family. My blood relatives."

"How could . . . how could they have found you?" Mom's voice wavered.

"We don't know that that's it. Maybe Oberlin periodically picks out some girl to be infatuated with," Teague said.

"And kill?" Mom grasped Kate's shoulder. "You can't go back to that capitol to go to work. You need to stay away from that man!"

"Mom, I have to work. Teague's helping me avoid the senator." Kate glared meaningfully at Teague. "Aren't you?"

"Mrs. Montgomery is right," he answered. "It would make me feel better if you stayed away from work for a couple of days."

"A couple of days?" The opportunistic jerk had sided with her mother!

"The legislators are dragging their feet about the school funding vote. What can happen in a couple of days?" he asked in his most soothing tone.

"I've already been off because of the stalker." Kate was exasperated with both of them. "If I ask for a couple more days off, Brad will fire me. You know he will."

Mom took her hand. "Please, darling. Do it for me. If that Oberlin has killed before—"

Teague interrupted. "We don't know that that's his intention. This may be a special case because from what Evelyn Oberlin said, Kate strongly resembles someone. Maybe someone in Kate's biological family."

"Darling, you have to be careful." Mom's lips trembled. "Promise me you won't go to work this week."

Kate surrendered. How could she not in the face of her mother's deep and honest distress. "All right. I'll stay home." She flashed a dirty look at Teague. "But I won't like it."

"Better unhappy than six feet under." Teague stood and brought Kate to her feet with him. "I promise I'll keep her safe, but please, Mrs. Montgomery, if you remember anything we should know, give one of us a call." He placed his business card on the counter. "Kate's life may hang in the balance."

Eighteen

"Where were you yesterday?" Wednesday morning, as the elevator ascended toward the newsroom, Linda grabbed Kate's arm and glared into her eyes. "After two months of wrangling, the Senate votes on the school funding, and you're nowhere in sight? Brad yelled at me for letting a story get away, then he yelled at me because I didn't know where you were!"

"I'm sorry." Kate removed Linda's claws from her arm. Kate *was* sorry. She'd been chasing news stories ever since she'd got to Austin, and they'd all been building toward one big story, the school-funding vote. And she'd missed it because she'd done as Teague had instructed her—she'd stayed home to avoid Oberlin. For one lousy day!

"Everybody, and I mean *everybody,* seems to think that I should keep track of you. Brad, Cathy, Oberlin—they all ask me where you are, and they all act as if I'm delinquent if I don't know. Well, let me tell you, Kate

Montgomery"—as the doors opened, Linda's voice rose to a crescendo—"I don't care what you're doing as long as you do your job!"

Ducking her head, Kate scurried into the newsroom. It felt very much like her first day when no one liked her because they thought she had got her post through influence and money. She could see the criticism in every gaze, and she realized that was exactly what they thought. The spoiled rich girl had got tired of doing her job and screwed up when they needed her most.

She would have to start from ground-zero building her reputation again, and this time it would take a lot longer.

"Miss Montgomery!" Brad bellowed from his office. "If you would come in here, please!"

She dragged herself in, a dunce expecting punishment.

"I'm pleased and proud that you could drag your poor, wretched female body in today." He paced his office, his belly rolling over his belt in an undulating wave. "After months and months of wrangling, we have the school-funding vote, and you call in sick."

"Last week, I broke the best stories," Kate said. It was a feeble argument. Last week was dead and gone. A reporter was only worth the news she discovered today; this week, she had avoided Oberlin and, thus, the news.

"Linda said she saw you and Teague Ramos out having a cozy dinner last night! Damn it, Miss Montgomery, I want my reporters out there chasing stories, not canoodling with the goddamn security men."

Kate almost drowned in embarrassment. Of *course* Linda had seen Kate and Teague together, and of *course* she had run right to Brad with the information. Linda had a nose for sniffing out the stories no one wanted known, and she was mad at Kate.

"Yes, sir. It won't happen again, sir." No explanation existed that Brad would accept. Certainly not that Kate was being stalked— again—by a prominent senator. She knew the skepticism that would greet that announcement.

And Brad wouldn't care even if it was true. Kate was a reporter. Even in a hurricane, she was supposed to wade into the Gulf. Even if she faced death or, at the very least,

PMS, she was supposed to get the story. If she had to look George Oberlin in the eye and pretend she knew nothing about his past and his crimes and his weird obsession, she would do it. "I'll be on top of things today."

"You'd better be." Brad pulled his belt up over his belly as he glared at her. "Or I'll damned well know the reason why."

"Look at him." Teague pointed to the monitor in the security center in the capitol and spoke to nobody in particular. "Every time he sees Kate, he preens like a bird."

Big Bob leaned over the monitor. "A tough, burly, old hawk."

"He keeps luring her in with stories." That son of a bitch Oberlin was doing some sort of weird political courtship dance designed to lure his chosen mate to his nest, and Teague could barely stand it. He knew Kate was in trouble at the station for missing the big news yesterday, but did she have to be so *driven?* As a reporter, Kate was doing okay; why couldn't she be satisfied with that?

"Boss, I can hear your teeth grinding," Rolf said.

"She has to know Oberlin is lying in wait for her. She understands what a psychopath he is. But for the love of her job, she keeps stepping right into danger's way."

"I wouldn't say it was exactly *dangerous,*" Gemma pointed out. "She's not leaving the capitol complex, and he's not going to do anything to her here."

Teague whipped around and glared at her, then turned back to his surveillance.

Kate had dressed for the part. Today she wore a tight black skirt, a black leather jacket, a red silk shirt, and such tall spike heels she stood absolutely upright and walked with this jiggle . . . no man in the capitol would be able to resist giving her an interview if she wanted one.

Hell, Teague would give her another interview if she wanted.

But today she didn't want to talk to him. She wanted to talk to Oberlin and the other important newsmakers, and that bit the big one.

In a soothing tone, Gemma said, "Teague, it's time for Kate's coffee fix. She's alone right now. No Oberlin for miles. Why don't you take her to Starbucks?"

"I can't. I need to stay here until I figure out what Oberlin's been up to all these years." Teague indicated the computer he would be using for research—if Kate would cooperate and behave and stop distracting him.

"I can investigate Oberlin." Rolf cracked his knuckles as if he couldn't wait to get into the game. *"I'll* find out what he's been hiding."

Teague considered Rolf. Rolf was a genius at computers, and he was right—he could dig deep enough to find out what Oberlin was hiding. "All right." Teague stood. "I'll go down on the floor. But if I run into Oberlin—"

"You're going to nod politely and not tip your hand," Big Bob said sternly.

"Yeah." Teague picked up an earbud with microphone attached, stuck the battery pack in his pocket, and headed for the door. "But I'm not going to like it."

He headed off to intercept Kate and found her walking toward him down the corridor in the South Wing of the capitol.

For the first time since they'd started

sleeping together, she did not look pleased to see Teague.

Well, too damned bad.

"So." He stopped in her path. He stood with arms crossed over his chest. "Do you want to go for a frappuccino?"

"No. It's a little chilly for a frappuccino. But I would like a latte. Thank you for asking." She had a snarky expression on her face, as if he'd issued a challenge.

He hadn't. He had simply asked her for a coffee. Teague didn't understand women. He never would. "All right. Come on."

They walked out of the capitol and toward Starbucks.

"I saw you interview a lot of people. So you had a good day?" Teague realized he sounded as if he was sniping at her.

"Not good. No. Since I'm on everyone's shit list for abandoning them yesterday, I've had the privilege today of chasing follow-up stories." Kate's clipped voice grated on his nerves.

"It is hardly my fault that I asked you to avoid trouble."

"I didn't say it was."

To any onlooker, it was clear that they were at odds. She kept her briefcase, stuffed with papers, close to her chest, her arms folded over it. He strode with his hands free—when he was outside, he always walked this way, so he would be ready for attack—yet everything about his gait felt foreign, as if he weren't comfortable in his own skin. They walked stiffly, with a designated distance between them.

"You can't blame me for being concerned when he looks at you as if you were his last chance at salvation," Teague burst out.

"His last chance at salvation?" She rubbed her forehead as if it hurt, and she sounded fretful like a child faced with something she couldn't comprehend. "That is exactly right. He is so . . . he's so normal when other people are around, but when we're alone, he seems to think I understand him. I offered my condolences on the death of his wife—"

"For God's sake, why did you do that?" Teague asked.

"Because that's what you do when you see someone after the death of their spouse." She spoke in that irritated, logical tone a woman used when she thought a man was being unreasonable. "I was *trying* to act *normally.*"

"All right. Don't get fussed about nothing." Teague took a breath. "What did he say when you offered your condolences?"

"He said I was his Jackie Kennedy. What does that mean?"

"It means he's already picked out his second wife, and you're it." The Starbucks was still a block ahead. The outside of the capitol complex was quiet; a cold front had settled in, and the breeze nipped at Teague's nose.

Three guys in suits waited between them and the hot latte.

Three really big guys.

"And he plans to run for president."

"That's grim." Even from a distance, Teague could see these were not regular suit-wearing guys. They were muscle. They loitered on the curb as if they were waiting for someone.

Teague's menace meter hit the red zone.

Kate? Did they have instructions to kidnap Kate? That would indicate a level of weirdness he hadn't previously considered from Oberlin, but with his wife's death, his sanity seemed to be slipping.

Or was it Kate's appearance in his life that had sent him over the edge?

Kate came for coffee at the same time every day, so it would be easy to schedule a pickup. . . . In a low voice, Teague instructed, "Go back to the capitol."

"Why?" She spun to face him on the sidewalk. "Because you don't want to discuss this situation with me? You know, I'm not only a reporter, I'm personally involved, and I need to know what you know about Oberlin."

"I know you're a reporter." The three muscle guys were still standing there, trying to look as if they were waiting for a cab. Teague's tension escalated. "You hang your job over my head all the time. I'm trying to protect you, but you insist on being out in public talking to crazies when it would be a lot easier to protect you if you'd just stay home." Damn! He had said too much.

"Stay . . . home?"

For the first time ever, Teague saw Kate almost incoherent.

Unfortunately, it didn't last.

"What home would that be? Mine? Yours? Should I wear pearls and dust while I'm cooking your dinner and waiting for you to arrive?" She dropped her briefcase, and it hit the ground with a good, solid thud. "C'mon, Teague, get a grip. We're not married. I've got a job, you've got a job—is yours more important than mine?"

"Yes." The guys abandoned their casual stance and headed toward Teague and Kate. "Right now it is." Turning away, he spoke softly into the microphone. "We have a situation out here, Congress Avenue, half a block from Starbucks." He turned back to her. "Now would you go back to the capitol, please?"

"Yes. Oh, yes. I most certainly will go back to the capitol." Her eyes shot blue sparks. "Where I will work. Where I will do interviews with senators and assorted other crazies." She poked her finger in his chest. "And you had better learn to deal with that." Picking up her briefcase, she strode away.

Thank God. He had thought she'd never leave.

Turning, Teague fixed his gaze on the guy in the lead and moved to intercept. With a nod but no smile, he asked, "How's it going?"

As they swerved to close in on him, he realized he had made a fatal mistake.

Kate wasn't their target.
He was.

Kate strode up Congress toward the main entrance to the capitol.

What a dreadful man. How could she ever have imagined herself in love with him? He complained about her job. He complained about the way she behaved. He invited her to Starbucks, then sent her back without an explanation. . . .

We have a situation out here, Congress Avenue, half a block from Starbucks.

She stopped. A situation? What did he mean by a situation? Why . . . ? Enlightenment burst into her mind. Those men . . . Teague . . . he was in trouble!

Wheeling around, she ran back up the street.

But she couldn't see Teague. He had disappeared. And she couldn't run. She could barely walk in these preposterous Jimmy Choo stilettos. Stopping, she took them off. She dropped one on the sidewalk, kept the other one in her hand. She remembered what Teague had said: *A heel is a great weapon.* She sprinted down the street.

Where was he? Where . . . ? Her head swiveled as she searched. Her nylons shredded on the concrete. She took her cell phone out of her jacket to call the police.

How far could they have taken him? Had they shoved him into a van, taken him away to be murdered? She'd never see him again except for . . . except for photos of his mutilated body. . . .

"Come on, come on, come on, come on," she muttered as she ran. Her heart hit her rib cage. She felt sick with anxiety. "Where are you?"

In an alley beside a Dumpster, some garbage cans, and a pile of trash, she saw a flash of movement. She raced toward it, saw a coil of bodies.

Four guys. It was them. Foolish to be relieved, but she was. She had found Teague.

She called 911. Gasped, "A mugging in the alley at Congress and Tenth." Stuck the cell back in her jacket.

She heard the smack of flesh against flesh. One man flew out, propelled by a well-aimed kick. He hit the trash pile in an explosion of junk.

Kate leaped over the top of him, screaming at the top of her lungs.

Two men crouched over some poor sucker on the ground.

Teague. They were beating the crap out of Teague.

Lifting her shoe, she smacked one thug in the back of the neck. Blood spurted.

He swung around.

With both hands on her briefcase, she swung and hit him in the face.

He tumbled sideways.

The briefcase went flying. She screamed again, long and loud. Somebody would hear. Somebody would come to help.

The other guy, the one crouched over Teague, sprang at her—and in seconds, Teague changed from prone to a charging bull.

Teague tackled him. They went tumbling across the alley.

And the first mugger, the guy in the trash, came at them. Ignored her, and came after Teague.

Grabbing a full, heavy garbage can, she slung it at him. She couldn't get the weight far off the ground, but when it hit him in the shins, the collision knocked his feet out from under him. He flew over the top. Landed flat on his face.

The impact twisted the handle from her fingers, taking skin, taking flesh, twisting her shoulder half out of its socket.

She swung around, seeking trouble, seeking Teague. . . .

And realized more people were running at her, yelling. For one moment, she tried desperately to think how she would defend Teague.

Then she realized these were Teague's people. Gemma, Rolf, Chun, all looking reassuringly competent—and furious. They went into action and within seconds the muggers were subdued.

Kate heard sirens. Saw flashing red and blue lights and police cars.

Teague staggered to his feet.

Teague was safe.

They were safe.

Her feet hurt. Her hands hurt. Her chest heaved with exertion and residual panic. The papers from her briefcase were scattered across the alley. Her shoe was . . . she didn't know where her shoe was.

Police in uniforms swarmed the yard.

Kate looked through the pack to Teague.

Teague stood, hands open and hanging at his sides, looking back at her. Blood oozed from his swollen lips. He had a bruise rapidly closing one eye, and she could hear him wheezing from across the yard.

She had never seen anything as beautiful in her life.

He started toward her.

She started toward him.

They met in the middle.

And Teague said, "Why didn't you run away? Why did you come back? You're no self-defense expert. Are *you* crazy, too?"

She stared, open-mouthed, and hated him as much as she loved him. "You're welcome, asshole."

Turning on her bare foot, she walked toward one of the police officers to give her report.

Nineteen

That evening, in the light and warmth of Teague's kitchen, Kate pulled an orange Popsicle from the freezer and handed it to him. "Here. This'll bring down the swelling."

With the care of a man in pain, he stuck it in his mouth. The expression on his face wavered between agony and relief. "That's good. That's better." He sat perfectly upright at the table, his cracked ribs wrapped to relieve the torture of breathing. "Who taught you that?"

"My mom." Kate paced between the freezer with its multiple, reusable ice bags, the blender with its milk shakes and smoothies, and the sink where she peeled fruit. The acid stung the cuts in her hands— a nurse at the hospital had cleaned the rust out of Kate's palms while Kate waited for Teague to get X-rayed and stitched.

"And how did your mom know?"

"Because she's a mom." What an insensitive thing to say. Savagely Kate stuck the waste down the disposal. He'd had a mom, too, only his mom hadn't cared enough to give him Popsicles when he hurt himself. So Kate supposed she was sorry. She certainly knew she should be.

But he'd lied to her about his background. He'd lied, and now she doubted his truths. "Dad and I used to play catch, and in the beginning I usually caught with my face. I got better."

"I can see that. Your face looks great." Teague tried to smile, tried to be conciliatory. Blood oozed from his battered lips.

Yeah, well, the soles of Kate's feet were raw from running on concrete, gravel, and garbage, and her left big toe had a slice deep enough to require hydrogen peroxide, a butterfly bandage, and a tetanus shot.

Her aches did not improve her mood. "Don't smile," she told him callously. "Smiling doesn't make *you* look better."

"What's wrong?" He put down his Popsicle. He caught her hand, kissed the scraped skin. "You're upset."

"Who wouldn't be upset when her boyfriend gets beaten up?" She freed her hand. "Your eye looks like hell." It did. He had stitches just below his eyebrow, and the doctor said he'd been lucky the socket hadn't been broken. "Let me get you another ice bag."

"I can do it." He stood, but he didn't get in her way. "You're upset with *me.*"

She hesitated. But what difference did it make? She didn't want him touching her. She might as well tell him. "I'm not *upset* with you. I'm *mad* at you."

He knew she was mad. She could see by the expression on his face. Well. The man would have to be stupid not to know he'd screwed up, and Teague Ramos was anything but stupid.

She mashed the blue ice bag until the insides were pliable, wrapped it in a dish towel, and handed it to him.

"Look, I'm sorry about your shoes," he said. "I'll buy you some new ones."

She was wrong. He *was* stupid. "I paid four hundred dollars for them in New York."

Before he had looked battered. Now he looked ill. "I've never understood how women can justify paying that much for a silly pair of—"

She had to stop him before she made his other eye swell. "What? I can't quite hear you. You're muttering."

"I *said* I'm sorry I spouted off about your

career." Sinking down in the chair again, he carefully applied the ice to his eye. "I don't know where that came from. Out of the fifties, I guess. I didn't really mean it."

"Yes, you did. I don't know any man who wouldn't prefer to be the center of the universe. You're used to being the hottest stuff around. When you tell people about your job, you're the center of attention, and you don't like it when I am." She could see he hated hearing the truth. Good. "But I can deal with that. The trouble is, your complaining about my ambition is the tip of the iceberg. When we were walking to Starbucks, why didn't you tell me you suspected those guys were thugs?"

He lowered the ice bag to look at her with his one good eye and the almost-swollen-shut bad eye. "Because I thought they might be working on instructions to kidnap you."

Kidnap. The word sent chills down her spine.

Her father had been kidnapped. He'd been tortured. He'd been murdered. She didn't want to end up like that.

But that wasn't the point here, and she wouldn't let Teague distract her. "So you ordered me inside the capitol, no explanation, when if you'd said, 'Kate, those are bad guys, go away,' I would have run."

"No, you wouldn't have." He snorted in disbelief. "I know you. You would have done just what you did and jumped into the middle of a fight."

"If you were going to insist on facing them, then yes, I would have hung around with my high heels until the cavalry came."

"You're not trained to fight."

"I'd say I did a pretty good job. In fact"— she surveyed him critically—"I look a lot better than you."

He reared back in the chair and snapped, "They overwhelmed me."

She could see she'd wounded his macho vanity, and that gave her a great deal of pleasure. "You needed help, and you got it—from me." However, it was obvious she could wait until hell froze over before he thanked her. "If you had told me the truth, at least I would have known what was going on. I would have been prepared instead of caught by surprise. I wouldn't have felt like"—oh, no, her voice wavered—"like some worthless bimbo on your arm." Like every other useless woman he'd ever dated. Like one of the crowd.

"There are worse things to be." He put the bag back on his eye, as if the discussion was closed.

"Than a bimbo?" Outrage lifted Kate out of her momentary weepiness. "No, there aren't!"

"You could be dead!"

"They weren't going to kill *me.* They were going to kill *you."* She stuck her finger in his face. "You *yelled* at me for not letting them kill you."

"I'm supposed to be protecting you."

He seemed to suffer from male-onset deafness, so she repeated herself. "You yelled at me for not letting them kill you."

He repeated *himself.* "I'm supposed to be protecting you."

Apparently she was mistaken. It wasn't male-onset deafness. It was male-onset idiocy. "This is too much. I've learned my lesson. I let love sweep me off my feet and out of any good sense I ever learned, but today showed me my mistake. First I get yelled at by Brad for not doing my job. Then I have to talk to that creep Oberlin three times." She showed Teague three fingers. "Then you shout at me because I didn't run away screaming like one of those dim-bulb girls you usually sleep with. Fine. I'm going to do what I do best. I'm going to find the story on Oberlin, expose him for one murder and God knows how many more, and then get my life back to normal."

"Normal? Get your life back to normal?" With controlled force, he threw the ice bag into the sink. "Do you know how stupid that sounds? Your life won't be back to normal! You'll be dead like Evelyn Oberlin. Like Lana Whoever it was he killed. Like the other people he possibly took out. We haven't said it yet, but do you realize we're talking about a serial killer? One with money and power and who kills without remorse?"

"A serial killer who appears to be after *you.*" That shut him up—for about five seconds.

"I'm not the target. He wants me out of the way so he can get to you."

"My incredibly brilliant analytical mind already figured that out. Unfortunately, it doesn't matter whether you're the real target, you'll be just as dead." Today Oberlin had made her skin crawl. The way he'd looked at her, the way he'd made excuses to touch her . . . she hadn't told Teague, but Oberlin had said things. Things that sounded innocuous, but weren't.

Kate, from the first minute I saw you, I knew you were the one woman who could help me through my wife's death.

But Senator, when we first met, your wife wasn't dead.

He laughed genially. Oh, Kate, you're smart—and pretty, too. I have to take care of you. After all, you're my own special reporter.

She couldn't tell Teague that stuff. He'd go ballistic, try to put her in an ivory tower and rush himself into harm's way to get to Oberlin. She was flattered that Teague thought enough of her to be so concerned—actually, more than flattered, she was plunging more deeply in love than ever—but she couldn't let him protect her at the expense of his own life.

She'd already lost her father to torment and death. She couldn't lose Teague, too. She couldn't bear that.

"I'm a damned good reporter," she said, "and I'm going to do what I do best. I'll do my research, get my facts—"

"I've got a man doing that. Rolf's been researching him on the Internet, and Oberlin's clean as a whistle."

"That's impossible. There's no *way* a senator couldn't have people who hate him." The red fog of rage and fear cleared a little, and her brain started clicking through the facts. "The Democrats, the Republicans, the conservatives, the liberals—somebody hates him."

"Apparently no one is allowed to express an adverse public opinion."

She whistled in amazement. "That's fascinating. I'll have to go to the source."

"What are you talking about?" He enunciated each word.

"I'll have to go to Hobart." Mentally, she was rubbing her hands together. She was going to search out some hidden thing that desperately needed to be revealed. *This* was a story.

"No." Teague shook his head as if he knew the right thing to do. "No, you do not have to go to Hobart."

"Don't be silly. That's where Oberlin's from. That's where Mrs. Oberlin was from. They have to have family there."

"Unless he killed them all."

"Don't exaggerate. My God, you act as if I

would rush in, announce I'm investigating Senator Oberlin and his previous murders, and allow his local goons to take me out." She tried to control her exasperation, tried to talk sense to a man who had none. "Hobart is just a town, Teague, a little town of about five thousand with four stoplights and the county rodeo grounds outside the city limits."

"You've already investigated the place," he said, obviously aghast. "When did you do that?"

"As soon as I realized Senator Oberlin was after me. I called the city council for the stats."

"No." Teague slapped his palm on the table. "You're not going."

"No? Are you telling me *no?*" Kate itched to slap her palm, too—against his bruised, superior, smart-aleck face. "You're not my boss. You're not my husband. You're just my lover, and you've proved very conclusively today that there are big differences in how we view our relationship."

"There are big differences in how we view the *world.* You had money that protected you. You had parents who sheltered you. You're a privileged woman. You think that good triumphs and evil is punished, but that's absolute bullshit. I've been all over with the Marines, and evil triumphs all the time."

"Is that who you think I am?" How could he have lived with her, talked to her, been with her, and still be so wrong? "Some fairy-tale princess who sees good in everyone? Some child to be protected from life?"

"With this plan to chase after Oberlin, you've proved that's who you are."

"And you've proved you don't know me at all." With his opinions and his words, he was stomping her into the ground, making her less than she knew herself to be. In a low voice, she said, "I've lived in countries where women are valued less than horses, where unwanted babies are exposed to the elements to die. I've seen children starve, their bellies swollen, their bones protruding; and we couldn't feed them fast enough to save them. I've seen women torn by gang rape and villages destroyed by war." The images paraded across her mind. "And yes, when I was a child my parents protected me, but they wanted me to know the world I lived in. They wanted me to be the kind of person who called other members of the human race my brothers and sisters. So when I was old enough, I saw it all. My dad and mom and I worked in refugee camps. We worked in hospitals. We *helped*."

She must have looked like she was about to go nuclear, because he started backpedaling with all his might. "All right. I was mistaken. You've seen the world. I simply meant—"

"I recognize brutality. I recognize senseless death." She didn't give a damn what he meant. "Do you know that when my father died, the government advised my mother and me not to look at the body? His murder had been too brutal." She lowered her voice to a whisper because if she didn't, she knew she would scream. Scream in agony like she'd screamed before. "So the men who had done that to him . . . sent us photos through the Internet. Sent us photos of . . . the torture. Sent us photos of . . . Dad's mutilated body."

"My God, Kate . . ." Teague started toward her, his expression horrified.

She backed up. She hadn't realized it, but she was crying. Tears dripped off her face. Her throat hurt from holding back the sobs. "You've never had anyone you cared for, so you never lost anyone . . . you loved." Her voice broke and, desolate, she hugged herself. "I have, so don't tell me . . . that I'm weak and you're strong, that you can face the demons . . . and I can't, because you haven't . . . passed the greatest test of all. You haven't died of a broken heart . . . and awoken the next day to die again."

She made a dash for the stairway, but he caught up with her before she cleared the kitchen door. He wrapped her in his arms and held her. She tried to escape, but she couldn't bring herself to punch him in his ribs, and her own consideration made her weep harder.

She *was* a well-brought-up, privileged woman, and right now she wanted to be a callous bitch.

"I'm sorry. I didn't know. I mean, I knew, but not that you . . . You're a brave woman." He kept one arm around her and, with the other, stroked her hair.

Just what she didn't need now. Compassion. What a lousy, cheap ploy on his part to make her like him again.

"When the kidnappers first sent those photos to my mother and me, they were in my mind all the time." She trembled in

Teague's arms. "Everywhere I looked, all day and all night, I saw blood and gore. I couldn't stop thinking about him. He raised me. He loved me. He taught me sports, confidence, humor. He taught me to do the right thing. And he had been tortured." She took a painful breath. "They flayed him. All I could think was that he died in agony. Mom said the memories would fade." Kate shook her head, the truth too big and raw to wrap her mind around. "But she was in agony, too. I heard her crying at night."

Teague rubbed his hand up and down her back.

"She was right, though. The memories eventually faded. I see them every once in a while—at night in my dreams and in the daytime when I cover a child abuse case or a five-car pileup." Kate's heart ached. She recognized the sensation. She had spent the months following her father's death, suffering this exact feeling.

Now the fight with Teague had dredged them up again, and she was hurting once more. "I h-hate you."

She was lying.

It wasn't Teague she hated. It was the memories.

"I know. You should. I'm a jerk." He walked her toward a kitchen chair. He sat and drew her into his lap and lightly hugged her until she stopped weeping. "As soon as we get Oberlin taken care of, you should wipe your feet on me and walk away."

"I w-will." Too bad the idea made her feel worse when she already felt like hell. Crying did that to her.

She knew she *looked* like hell. Crying always did that, too.

Teague didn't seem to notice. He was staring at her as if she were the most beautiful creature he'd ever seen.

No fair.

"I shouldn't have said that stuff. But you want to know stuff about me? Bad stuff?" He kissed her forehead. "I'll tell you. I envy you your parents. It's not a nice envy, either, it's a bone-deep, ugly jealousy that you have something I've never had and never will have." He was making her feel sympathy for him.

She didn't want to. "I need a Kleenex."

"My mother despised me." He handed her a kitchen towel off the table. "My father abandoned her before he knew she was expecting. Her father threw her out when he discovered she was pregnant. Her brother barely tolerated her. She had a chip on her shoulder the size of a Volkswagen. From the day I was born she hated me and the burden I placed on her."

She stared at the towel, then shrugged and wiped her eyes. "You never gave me a hint about that. Have you ever told me the whole truth about anything?"

"I'm telling you now. Do you want to hear it or not?"

Of course she did. She wanted any little crumb of knowledge she could gather about Teague. She closed her eyes, but another tear seeped out. She didn't want to love like this. It hurt too much.

"Tell me," she said.

"My mother used to say, 'You think you're so smart. You think you can be more than scum in the gutter. More than me. You are what you are, one of the bastards of the biggest bastard of all, and you'll die here like the rest of us.' "

Kate didn't want to feel empathy, but she did. He described the desolation of his youth in a matter-of-fact tone, but the reality was—he had suffered. Suffered just like her, yet more slowly, an agony of loneliness and lovelessness that leaked over all of his childhood and into his whole life.

"She said . . . she said, 'Teague, you god-damned little bastard, you're a stupid half-breed gringo, and if you get knifed, no one will care. I sure as hell won't.' But that . . . but that kid—" He stopped, breathing hard.

Kate had wanted to see him in pain. Now she had her wish. Each word seemed to stab at his heart. His breathing faltered.

"It's all right." Kate hugged him lightly, taking care not to hurt his broken ribs. "She didn't mean it."

"What?" He stared at her as if he'd forgotten she sat on his lap.

"Your mother didn't mean what she said about not caring if you got killed."

"She meant it. The irony was, *she* died that day. We had a gang war. I was one of the big shots. She didn't want me to . . . she didn't want me to go, but I knew best. And when it was all over, she'd gone into the streets and been shot by a stray bullet. And worse"—he took a long, harsh breath—"worse . . ." He stared at Kate as if he wanted to speak, but the words wouldn't come.

Kate held her breath, waiting for the confidence that proved that, even if he didn't love her, he trusted her.

At last, he shook his head and sagged against the back of the chair.

"Okay." Kate battled disappointment. "First of all, you didn't kill her. I suppose it feels that way, since she came to the war to get you."

He snorted. "No, Kate. Not me."

"Who then?"

He shrugged and turned his head away.

Kate made a resolution. When this situation was over, she was going to abandon her principles and investigate Teague. Whatever secret he hid was destroying him—and them. "But as for that stuff she said to you about being in the gutter—she's wrong." Kate didn't have a doubt about that. "You're smart and you're ambitious and you're talented. You're on your way to the top, and nothing is going to stop you."

"Thank you." He sat up straighter. "I think that most of the time, then I hear her voice in my head and remember the sounds of that day and . . . that's why I envy you, and that makes this whole thing worse. Your mother is everything I ever dreamed a mother could be. She bakes, she sews, she's funny, she . . . loves you. So much. It's like . . . a Kodak commercial, she loves you so much."

Kate realized where he was going with this, but she couldn't see a way out.

"I swore to her I'd keep you safe. You have to let me try, if not for you or me, then for her. She's a good woman, and she deserves better than her kid in a coffin."

For a man who hadn't had a mother to teach him, he was awfully good at wielding guilt. "Yes, and I can't stand waiting for trouble. It reminds me of those days of being helpless, not knowing what was going to happen to Dad, not being able to do anything to help."

She wasn't bad at wielding guilt, either.

With all seriousness, he considered her. "I can understand that. All right. Let's compromise. If you give me three days to figure out the lay of the land with Oberlin, I won't interfere with your work."

She could hardly believe it. Her mom said you could teach a man, but you couldn't teach him much. Teague had proved her mother wrong. He understood her concerns; he was willing to negotiate. "You won't follow me all the time?"

"As long as you'll promise to check in every couple of hours."

"Every four hours. And you won't send someone to follow me either?"

"You're awfully suspicious."

She crossed her arms over her chest.

"I won't follow you, have anyone else follow you, as long as you tell me where you're going and—"

"Check in every four hours," she finished for him. "You'll trust me even if I have to deal with Oberlin, and you'll keep me informed of any progress you make."

She could see by his expression that he didn't want to give her that. But they had survived their first fight. It had been a fight that revealed too much too soon, and showed feelings so tender she ached for herself, and ached for him. She slid out of his lap. "Come on. You can do this. I can't live in a prison of safety."

He closed his eyes. He seemed to be searching for the right words, for the right emotion. She could see his struggle. "I would keep you in a prison if I could. I'd do anything to keep you safe."

His eyes popped open. They were dark, but not bleak. Not empty.

Warm, alive, intense.

"But at some point," he said, "I'm going to have to let you go."

It was, she thought, a classic and graceful surrender. "I'm an adult. I've lived through more in twenty-four years than most women live through in a hundred."

"I'm going to do my best to make sure you don't live through more experiences that make you feel a hundred years old." He stood, too. "I've got bruises all over, cracked ribs, my face is still swelling, and my lips feel like hamburger." He sighed wistfully. "But I'll be good as new in a couple of weeks."

"So." She offered her hand. "Do you want to go upstairs and let me tend your wounds?"

He put his hand in hers and let her lead him. "Please."

Gabriel had been the Prescott family's foster child, with his dark hair, green eyes, and the cheekbones of a Mayan statue. He had been an orphan all his life, and as a child he'd learned to be wary of affection. During his early years, affection had been a trick to make him behave, or a precursor to a slap. So when he was eleven, and the Prescotts took him in, he had spent the first year wary and standoffish. He hadn't made trouble, but neither had he joined in the family celebrations or the group hugs.

He'd gone to church because Mr. Prescott was the minister. He'd helped in the parish because Mrs. Prescott was the minister's wife. He'd been polite to the oldest girl, Hope, because she was so good at everything—playing sports, creating art, being responsible and perky—that if he was rude to her, she'd just try harder to win him over. He couldn't bear that.

He'd gone to school and made good grades because the family had enough trouble with Pepper, who hated being the preacher's middle kid, and they didn't need any more.

He'd helped with the baby, Caitlin, because . . . well, because he couldn't help it. He liked babies, always had, and with her dark wisp of hair and her blue eyes, she was a cutie.

She looked like her mother's baby pictures.

Eventually, the Prescotts wore him down.

From his first day, Pepper seemed to think he was a rebel like her, and she had run to him with her problems. He found himself explaining her outrageous behavior to her parents, and, as often as not, he got her free from time-outs.

When he'd started school in Hobart, some of the boys picked on him. Hope had interfered, and what would have been a nice, quiet, new-kid trouncing had grown into a raucous fight involving a furious Hope, who belabored their prejudice and unchristian behavior. Despite a visit to the principal's office to get Hope and Gabriel out of trouble, the Prescotts pronounced themselves pleased with their children—and they meant Gabriel, too.

Mother Prescott hugged him every night before he went to bed and every morning before he went to school. Father Prescott dragged him out into the shop to learn woodworking because, he said, in a household of women men needed to have their own space. And at the age of five weeks, Caitlin smiled her first baby smile at him.

That was why, on his second Christmas with the Prescotts, he thanked his new parents by calling them Daddy and Mama.

For one moment, the Christmas celebration had grown quiet. Daddy smiled at him and nodded. Mama's eyes filled with tears, and she wrapped him in a hug. It was, for Gabriel, a seminal moment, one of two that defined him for the rest of his life.

The other was the murder of his parents and the destruction of his family.

He had almost all his siblings back now. Hope and Zack and their kids. Pepper and Dan and their kids.

But he didn't know where Caitlin was. The loss of their baby gnawed at the fabric of the family's contentment.

Right now Hope, Pepper, and Zack were flying in from Boston to join Dan and Gabriel, Jason Urbano and Griswald in Austin. The whole family and their friends were determined to see the completion of their sting operation. Everyone wanted to be present when they caught George Oberlin in their trap. They all wanted to make him confess to their parents' murders; they would force themselves to be satisfied with the information about Caitlin.

Then, with God's help, they would find her.

This was the culmination of twenty-three years of misery, heartache, and planning.

The family was balanced on a knife's edge. They would allow nothing to get in their way. No one to destroy this chance.

Which was why, when Gabriel heard his computer alarm go off, he read the blinking message and picked up the phone. "Hey, Dan, do we know anything about Ramos Security? Because someone there has been snooping around Senator George Oberlin."

Twenty

First thing in the morning, Brad called Kate into his office. "How do my eyes look?" he asked.

She looked at them, red-rimmed and bleary. "Fine?" she ventured.

"They look like two piss holes in the snow." He leaned menacingly over his desk. "Don't they?"

"Yes, sir."

"That's because that's how they feel. Do you know"—he glared at her—"what a big pain in the ass you are?"

"I have my suspicions." Was he still mad about the school-funding vote?

"No. There's no way you can know how much trouble you've put me through." Opening his desk drawer, he pulled out a half-filled bottle of bourbon. "First for the good senator, then for your damned boyfriend."

One thing at a time. "The good senator?"

"He wanted you to have this job. You might say he insisted."

"He insisted." She could scarcely wrap her mind around Brad's words. "Senator George Oberlin insisted I have this job? *This* job?"

"Hell, yes! Got a phone call one night, and just like always, I did as I was told. Oberlin has that effect on people." The biting odor of bourbon wafted across the desk as Brad filled a plastic cup.

"Why? Why did he want you to give me a job?"

"I don't know." Brad was weaving on his feet. "I'm not on the list of people permitted to ask him personal questions. I'm too far below him on the social scale. I'm on meds for—" Brad caught himself. "Oberlin doesn't confide in me."

She grew cold. "Have you had to hire other reporters for him?"

"No, this was a first." Emphatically Brad shook his head.

Brad was drunk. And maybe more than drunk. Coke? Tranquilizers? She didn't know what Brad's problem was, why he was on meds. She didn't care. He was talking; she was listening. "You didn't report on Oberlin's wife trying to stab me. Is this why? Because you have to do as you're told?"

"Aren't you clever?" Brad sneered. "A regular Einstein of the reporters' pool. But for someone who sashays around here thinking she knows everything, she sure has a lot of guys managing her from behind the scenes."

"Who else?" Heat shot through her.

"Another one of your boyfriends. I shouldn't follow instructions, but what can I do? I'm not going to get beat up for the sake of little Miss Montgomery."

"Are you talking about Teague Ramos? Teague gave you instructions?" Kate's eyes narrowed into slits. If Brad had been anything but blasted, he would have been afraid—*of her.*

But right now, he hadn't the sense God gave a garter snake. "Teague wants you assigned to something that will keep you busy and out of trouble." Brad took a good, long drink. "So I'm sending you to interview elementary-school teachers about the school-funding bill and how it will impact their jobs."

"That's a good piece." She knew she

sounded genial. Too bad she couldn't stop clenching her hands into fists.

"What trouble can you get in at a grade school?"

"You are so right. What trouble can I get into doing my job?" Teague had said he was going to trust her. He had said he wasn't going to check up on her. He had lied—although she supposed he hadn't realized Brad was mouthy when inebriated.

She was so mad, she was almost hyperventilating. "I should speak to at least three teachers."

"At least." Brad couldn't have made his indifference more clear.

"Probably one in Austin, one in New Braunfels, and one . . . somewhere rural." She hesitated. "Shall we say Hobart, Texas?"

"Sure. If there's a Hobart, Texas, then you go interview a teacher there. Don't come back until you're ready. I am, believe it or not, a busy man, and I've got more important things to do than babysit every reporter who works for me." Brad fluttered his fingers at her. " 'Bye."

She stood, betrayed and stripped of her

pride. "Hobart it is. Thanks, Brad. You've been a big help."

"How's Oberlin today?" Teague asked as he entered the main security office.

"Not as twitchy as yesterday," Gemma replied, her gaze fixed to the monitors. "Although he's starting to ask around for Kate. Look." She pointed. "He just spoke to Linda Nguyen, who about took his head off."

"That girl better be careful." Big Bob leaned back in his chair with his eyes closed. "It seems our boy is pretty good at removing heads himself."

"Or at least bashing them in." Rolf sat before the computer. He assessed Teague with a glance. "You look like hell, Teague."

"I'm okay." Teague passed off his various injuries as minor, but he knew if they hadn't rescued him, the thugs would have overwhelmed him and he'd have had internal bleeding and major broken bones . . . if he had been lucky enough to survive. Obviously Oberlin hadn't ordered his death, or he'd be in the morgue with a bullet hole in his chest. But he'd wanted to give Teague a warning, or make him suffer for poaching, or both. Or maybe mess him up enough so that Kate wouldn't love him anymore . . . that hadn't worked too well.

"Yeah, he's okay," Big Bob said. "No one cares about *him,* anyway. How's Kate?"

"She's fine, thank you."

"She fights good for a girl." Big Bob pulled on one of Gemma's curls.

Teague chuckled softly. His sweet girl Kate had rushed right into a fight, swinging her shoe and her briefcase and blasting two professional hit men. Sure, they'd obviously had instructions not to hurt her, but she'd still done damage.

"The guys who beat you up . . . they're in jail, charged with assault and battery. The police say the men don't know who hired them. All it took was a voice on the phone and a valid Visa card." Gemma looked grim. "Which, by the way, is billed to an address in Mexico."

"Figures," Teague said. Last night Kate had been more than willing to press him to the mattress and kiss him tenderly, caress each of his bruises, hold him down and have sex with the care of a woman in love.

In fact, she'd said . . . it was in the middle of that fight, in the middle of a sentence, and she seemed unaware . . . but she had said she loved him.

Well, not exactly. She had said, *I let love sweep me off my feet and out of any good sense I ever learned.*

He hadn't responded, but that didn't mean he hadn't noticed. That was why he had reclined on the bed and fought every primitive conquering instinct to let her make sweet love to him. It had been a strain, but my God, the rewards had been worth it.

"Boss?" Rolf gestured him over. "I've got something for you."

Breaking free of his reverie, Teague hustled over. "On Oberlin?"

"He is one interesting piece of shit." Rolf fixed his Nordic blue eyes on Teague. "May I point out, it took some major hacking to get this."

"May I point out, that's why I pay you the big bucks." Pulling up a chair, Teague eased himself down. Cracked ribs were a bitch.

"May I point out you may have to bust me out of jail because I had to hack into federal computers."

"Don't worry, man." Teague clapped his hand on Rolf's shoulder. "I'll be there every visiting day."

"That's all right then." Rolf pointed to his computer screen. "A woman in Houston—Gloria Cunningham—spoke to the police and the FBI about the good senator, practically accusing him of embezzlement and murder. She's from Hobart, Texas, same place Oberlin is from. The FBI got riled up. Apparently the Feds have been unhappy about a courthouse fire that happened quite a few years ago. Took out a bunch of official documents. That led them to listen to Mrs. Cunningham very seriously. Now they're investigating other matters in Hobart. Crimes that have been too easily solved by the local cops—and unexplained deaths. They sent a couple of agents out to visit Oberlin, and the agents' report was not good." Rolf turned away from the screen. "They seem to think Oberlin fits the profile of a possible serial killer."

"Yeah." Teague pushed back. *A serial killer.* Last night for the first time he'd said the words to Kate. Today the FBI concurred.

"He doesn't kill for fun, you understand, just the people who get in his way," Rolf said. "With a face like you're wearing, I'd say you're in his way."

"I know," Teague said. "I don't want to get out of his way, though. If I did, there'd be nothing between him and Kate." And she thought she . . . she said she loved Teague. Not that he wouldn't protect anyone with equal fervor, but something special had happened when she'd said that.

Love.

First Big Bob and the other guys had said she had him hog-tied. Then her words: *I let love sweep me off my feet and out of any good sense I ever learned.*

If Teague were smart, he'd put that comment out of his mind and never think of it again. If he was the ruthless jerk he used to be, he'd exploit her affection until she'd given him everything he wanted, then he'd ease her out of his life.

But he had these stirrings . . . emotional stirrings . . . he couldn't identify them, but from what people had said and what he'd seen in the movies, he was afraid the emotional stirrings might be—

"Where is she?" Gemma asked.

"Someplace safe." He hoped. He hoped Brad managed to follow directions and keep her busy today.

Really, Teague had done Kate a favor by getting her out of the capitol building. The cold front had blown through. It was a beau-

tiful autumn day. There had to be news stories all over Austin that she could cover.
Plus, she'd be safe. Teague really needed
for her to be safe.

She loved him. Fool that she was, she
loved him. And he—

"What are you going to do with this?" Rolf
indicated the FBI report.

"Go to them with the information I have,"
Teague said. "Get protection for Kate."

"And yourself," Big Bob added.

"And me. I hesitated to turn this over to
the Austin police. Oberlin's got too much
power. But if the FBI's already investigating him, they'll take my input seriously."
Teague's cell phone rang. "We'll get this situation cleared up before Kate does something stupid."

"Yeah, like sleep with you," Gemma said.

Pulling the phone out of his pocket, he
glanced at the number.

Mrs. Montgomery. Kate's mother.

Apprehension flew through his mind. Was
she going to tell him that he was right, that
he wasn't worthy to touch her daughter?
Was she going to demand to know the
truth, the whole truth, about his background?

Did she have information that would help him discover the truth about Oberlin's obsession with Kate?

He flipped the phone open.

Mrs. Montgomery's rich, sweet, Texas-flavored voice greeted him. "Teague, how good to talk to you again."

He knew she hadn't called him to exchange pleasantries. "Are you all right?" Oberlin hadn't sent someone to hurt *her,* had he? "Are you alone?"

"Yes. Yes, I'm fine. No one's here." Her voice changed, became strained. "Can you come over? Now?"

"I'm on my way." Briefly, he told his crew, then headed out the door.

He met Juanita coming in. Her mechanical wheelchair whirred, but her greeting died on her lips when he cupped her chin and looked down into her brown eyes.

He had told Kate he believed in Fate. Here was the evidence of its existence. Juanita was here, right now, the living reminder of what could happen when he listened to his own reckless soul.

"What's wrong, *querido?*" she whispered.

"Nothing." He rubbed his thumb across her cheek. "Yet."

As he drove, unease plagued him.

Kate hadn't called and checked in.

It wasn't time yet. She wouldn't call before noon, but the more he thought about it, the more he worried about fixing her schedule with Brad. If Kate found out, she could possibly . . . would *definitely* be pissed.

She might be mad enough to do something foolish.

Goddamn it, Teague, you little bastard, you can't take that kid to a gang fight. Don't be so goddamned stupid. You're a goddamned stupid half-breed gringo and if you get knifed, no one will care. I sure as hell won't. But that kid is only fourteen. If something happens to her, her father will kill you. Look what he did to me. He's a lousy brother and a lousy father, but he doesn't let anyone hurt me and if someone hurts that kid, it's going to be him. You'd better not take her! You'd better not!

Damn it, Madre, if she wants to tag along, she can. She'll be okay. I won't let anything happen to her.

Once more, Teague might have done something with the best of intentions . . . and ruined another life.

The Mrs. Montgomery who let him in was

not the same Mrs. Montgomery he had met previously. She wore brown slacks with a blue silk shirt that tied in a bow at the neck. Her upsweep of brunette hair looked regal. She didn't flinch at the sight of his face. She gestured toward the living room as he entered. "Come on in. Can I get you something to drink?" She said the right things, but her face looked drawn.

She wasn't simply Kate's mother anymore, she was a frightened woman, and he responded as he always responded to a woman in need. Taking her hand, he led her to the couch. "Let's sit down and you can tell me what you're worried about."

She sat with him, her stricken eyes fixed on him. On his bruises and his stitches. "Are you . . . may I ask what happened to you?"

"I ran into a few guys who didn't like my face." It hurt to smile, but he gave it a try. "Your daughter took one of them out with the heel of her shoe."

"Oh, dear." Mrs. Montgomery didn't smile back. "Is this because . . . do you think this is related to the matter you discussed with me before?"

"I would almost guarantee it is. Do you

know something that will help us figure out what's happening?"

"I know you thought I knew something about the adoption that I didn't tell you, but it's not true. Or wasn't. Her gaze shifted away from his. "All those years ago, almost as soon as we signed the papers, Skeeter said something funny was going on. I . . . I guess I knew he was right, but Kate was my baby. Caitlin. We changed her name, but that was what her family named her. Caitlin. I don't think that was a bad change, do you?"

"Not at all. She probably would have picked Kate as a nickname, anyway," he said in a soothing tone.

"That's what I thought." A little of the color came back into Mrs. Montgomery's face. "From the first moment I saw her picture, I wanted her. When I held her . . . I loved her so much, and she needed me. She was so unhappy. Do you know the first thing she said to me was 'Mama'?"

"I'll bet all babies love you."

"Not like Kate. She was special—and I was afraid. Afraid to come back and find out Skeeter was right. That something funny was going on. That's why we stayed away from the States for two years. Finally, my grandmother turned one hundred, and we had to come back for the big celebration. And Skeeter . . . I knew Skeeter was going to insist we go back to the adoption agency, and he did." She squirmed under Teague's gaze. "It was gone. I'm not lying. Gone! No trace of it existed. Skeeter checked the records—the adoption agency had never been there."

Teague's watchfulness became bone-cracking tension. "What did you do?"

"We checked . . . we checked to see that Kate's adoption had been filed correctly with the state."

"And it had been."

"Yes. I begged Skeeter, *begged* him not to look further. He loved Kate, too, you know, and he had a job overseas. We left. We never looked for him again."

"Him?" Teague hated this whole story. He just knew it was going to have a bad ending.

"The man—the minister—who gave her to us. Pastor Wright. Blond man, very tall and handsome." Mrs. Montgomery lifted her tear-filled brown eyes to Teague. "I was watching television this afternoon, and I saw Senator Oberlin interviewed about, um, school funding. He looks like . . . he looks like Pastor Wright, the man who ran the church adoption." She swallowed. "He *is* the man who ran the church adoption."

Teague forgot his company manners. "Shit."

"Yes." She started to cry. "Senator George Oberlin gave us Kate."

Teague took out his cell phone and checked the time. Why hadn't Kate called? It wasn't noon, but . . . Brad had screwed this up, hadn't he?

As he dialed Kate's number, Mrs. Montgomery asked, "This thing with Senator Oberlin pretending to be a minister is bad, isn't it?"

"I won't lie and say I like it." *Teague hated it.* "The only time a man can masquerade as someone else is at a Halloween party, and in Oberlin's case, it would be Count Dracula."

Mrs. Montgomery's face crumpled. "This is my fault. I knew there was a possibility Kate was kidnapped from her real parents, and I didn't do anything about it."

He listened to Kate's cell phone ring. She didn't pick up.

He cut the connection. Taking Mrs. Montgomery's hand, he pressed it in his and looked earnestly into her eyes. "This is most definitely not your fault. It's the fault of the man who kidnapped her, if that's what happened. From what I can tell about Oberlin, that's the least of his sins."

A tremor shook her. "Is he . . . is he going to kill my daughter?" Clearly, her husband's brutal death had left its mark on Mrs. Montgomery, too.

"It's my job to make sure he doesn't. Mrs. Montgomery, if you'll get a jacket and come with me, we're going to the FBI to tell them your story. Then I'll tell them what I know and suspect. We're going to put Oberlin in jail—and hopefully, in hell."

Hurrying to the coat closet, she pulled out a brown jacket that matched her pants and picked up a purse that matched the whole ensemble. "This whole ordeal is God's punishment on me for not trying to do the right thing."

"Mrs. Montgomery, unless you have a connection I don't know about, I'd say we can safely assume you don't know what God's intention is." He helped her into her coat and held the door. "Maybe you've been put here to right a great wrong."

"Before I thought you were a nice young man. Now I know you are." She walked out into the sunshine with him. "Call me Marilyn."

"Thank you, Marilyn. I will." They headed for his car, and, as they walked, he dialed Kate's cell phone again. When she didn't pick up, he told her voice mail, "Call me. Kate. I've got news. We're getting somewhere in our investigation."

He hung up, pocketed the phone, and wished he knew why she hadn't answered. Was she doing an interview? Was she in an elevator or a basement where service didn't reach?

Had Oberlin kidnapped and killed her?

His hands clenched into fists. Pulling the phone from his pocket, he dialed his people at the capitol. "Gemma? Is Kate there anywhere? No? How about Oberlin?" Gemma assured him that Kate was nowhere in sight and that Oberlin was wandering the corridors looking for something—Kate, probably.

So right now she was safe, at least from Oberlin.

Knowing that Oberlin had been the one who had given Kate to the Montgomerys, Teague could safely assume Oberlin had known her natural mother. Had he killed her mother? That must be what Evelyn Oberlin had meant when she said he was going to kill Kate *again.*

Teague concentrated, trying to understand the crooked passages and rotten places that constituted Oberlin's mind. He couldn't, and the sound of his name, spoken in a tone of surprise and delight, caught him by surprise.

"Teague? Teague Ramos?"

Two guys walked toward him on the sidewalk. The one who had spoken, the blond, looked familiar. Not in his face, but in the way he walked, the clipped way he spoke. Military or former military, Teague decided, someone he'd met along the way. But he couldn't remember the guy's name, and it seemed inauspicious that he appeared now when Teague was already battered from yesterday's attack. "Yes?"

"I thought I recognized you." The guy put out his hand to shake.

"Do I know you?" Teague moved between Marilyn and the men.

"No, but we need to talk." The other guy, the one with dark hair and green eyes, sounded very serious and very intense. "We have a mutual acquaintance."

"And that would be?" Teague asked coolly.

"George Oberlin." The first guy took his hand back, but he stood way too close for Teague's comfort.

Marilyn piped up, "Unless you're an FBI agent, we don't have time to talk to you. We're going there right now to have him arrested."

Oh, shit. Teague brought his hands up to fight.

"We can't allow you to do that."

The first guy grabbed Teague around the ribs.

Through the haze of instant, shocking agony, Teague grabbed his wrist and twisted.

The second guy stuck a needle in Teague's neck.

Teague fell unconscious to the sound of Marilyn Montgomery's screams.

Today was the best day of George's life.

Today he was waiting for the phone call that announced Givens Industries had broken apart and sunk as deep as the *Titanic* and that he, Senator George Oberlin, owned competitors' stock now worth billions.

Today he would make his wealth, his power, and his intentions clear to Kate, and at last, after years of disappointment and bitterness, she would be his.

And today, in celebration of all his many accomplishments, he wanted to feast his eyes on Teague Ramos. The men he'd hired were in jail, but they didn't know who had employed them. And according to the hospital, Ramos had been battered. Not as badly as George had ordered, but enough that George wanted to catch a glimpse of the damage. George was a man who liked to see what he'd paid for.

He checked the usual places: the rotunda, the supreme court building, the east corridor.

He asked his usual sources: the tour guide, the page, Mr. Duarte. No one had seen Ramos.

Had the bastard taken the day off? Simply because of a few cracked ribs and some swollen features? Ridiculous! The Texas state government paid good money for Ramos to do a job, and do it he would, even if George had to make a formal complaint.

Then a dreadful thought struck George. He hadn't seen Kate today. Had she experienced misplaced compassion and stayed at Ramos's home to care for him?

"Oh, no." George dialed the television station. "Oh, no. You're not going to get away with that."

The operator at KTTV picked up, and George announced, "This is Senator Oberlin. I need Brad Hasselbeck."

"Yes, Senator. Hold, please."

When Brad picked up, George knew at once Brad had gone off his medication. He sounded manic.

In a voice too quick and too cheerful, he said, "Senator! Kate Montgomery's boyfriend! I suppose you've called about Miss Montgomery, but you're too late! I sent her out on a job!"

"I am not her boyfriend, and you will stop making such an inappropriate accusation." Oberlin felt a rush of heat to his cheeks. Just what he needed. A station manager who babbled that Oberlin loved Kate. To ensure Brad's complete comprehension, George added, "Shut up, Hasselbeck."

"Sure, Senator. What do you want to talk about?" Brad sounded as if he'd indulged in a few drinks, too. Great.

"Where is Kate Montgomery?"

"Shhh," Brad hissed in mock alarm. "Don't start rumors by acting concerned! You're not her boyfriend!"

"You idiot!" George snapped.

"Yes, I'll have to agree with you there. I am an idiot. I hired her because you told me to, and now I'm going to lose my job because I overpaid for a reporter who doesn't do her job. So I am definitely an idiot. But not as big an idiot as a distinguished older senator who chases after some young beauty who doesn't give a crap about him." Brad chortled.

"What do you mean?" George whispered. He was George Oberlin, a senator in the Texas legislature. He was going to be a U.S. senator. He was going to be president!

Brad's hilarity grew more raucous. "There's no fool like an old fool. Why would Kate care about you with your dull parties and your wrinkled body? She's got Teague Ramos! Teague Ramos!"

"She hasn't got him. She doesn't want him," George said scornfully.

"Everybody knows she's sleeping with Teague!"

"That's not true." George was an important man. Kate wouldn't betray him with a Mexican. With a nobody.

"What? That everybody knows or that they're doing the wild thing together?" Brad lowered his voice and crooned, "I'll bet she laughs at you every day. I'll bet she and Teague screw their brains out every night, and together they laugh at you for daring to imagine she would prefer saggy old you."

"Shut up."

"The gossip is that they're in love." Brad guffawed again. "They can't take their eyes off each other."

Yes. He'd seen them look at each other. At his party, he'd thought . . . but then he'd discovered Teague was her bodyguard. Just her bodyguard.

He hadn't seen them together at all after Teague had apprehended Evelyn, so George had assumed . . .

"They're humping like rabbits anywhere they can. And laughing at you!" Brad sounded absolutely satisfied.

So Kate had been lying to him. At first he wanted to cry. Then . . . then the burn started. He hadn't felt it for twenty-three years.

"Where is she?" George ground out the words.

"Where's Kate, you ask? Teague Ramos

called first thing this morning and wanted her kept busy and out of the capitol complex, so I sent her off to interview schoolteachers!"

"I want to know exactly where she is. Her exact location." George's chest hurt from the heat of his fury. At Ramos. At Brad. At Lana. At her daughter, for doing the same thing Lana had done—loving the wrong man.

Inured to George's wrath, Brad said, "She's going to interview a teacher in Austin. Then she's off to New Braunfels and someplace rural!"

"Someplace rural?" George couldn't believe she would dare. "Where?"

"Someplace I'd never heard of before, I can tell you that! Um"—George could hear Brad snapping his fingers—"Hogert? Heggler?"

"Hobart?" This was as it should be—a clear sign he would triumph again.

"That's it! Hobart, Texas! Miss Montgomery is in—"

George didn't wait to hear the end of the sentence. He cut the connection and headed for his car.

Twenty-one

"Ma'am, may I see your proof of insurance and driver's license?"

"Yes, Officer." Glumly, Kate dug around in her purse and her glove compartment until she came up with the two items requested. She passed them out her open window.

Cars whipped past on the highway going south through the Hill Country. The drivers looked curiously at the black-and-white Texas state patrol car with its red and blue flashing lights parked on the side of the road behind the BMW sports car.

Kate hated being in trouble. She felt as if everyone recognized her. She wanted to sink through the seat.

No, what she really wanted to do was kick Teague right in his glib promises.

"Let me run these, please. I'll be back in a minute." The officer, a tall, middle-aged woman with a somber mien, seemed uninterested in Kate's red-faced embarrassment or that her car was clean, that she was nicely dressed, and that she was having a good hair day.

In fact, when the officer came back, she seemed even more stern than before. She passed the license and the insurance card back and asked, "Ma'am, do you know how fast you were going?"

Kate knew *exactly* how fast she was going. She knew exactly why, too. Because that rat she loved had lied to her. He didn't trust her. So in a rage, she had put her foot to the floor and driven as fast as she could toward Hobart. "Ninety," Kate said. "I was doing ninety."

"Actually, ninety-one." The officer pulled out her pad and started writing. "Do you know what the speed limit is?"

"Sixty-five."

"That's right. Ma'am, this is a serious infraction." The officer tore the ticket off. "Luckily, this is your first violation."

Kate's cell phone rang. She glanced at it and saw the Caller ID. Rage bubbled inside her. *Teague.*

She *so* didn't have time for him right now. It was his fault she had a ticket. His fault she wasn't getting to Hobart by noon. And she was hungry, damn it.

She turned off her phone, tossed it in the cup holder, and looked back at the officer. "I've never done anything like this before."

"I'm glad to hear that. Ninety-one is not a safe speed on this highway." The officer handed the ticket to Kate. "Keep your speed down, please. I'd hate to pick you up again."

Kate waited until the officer had walked back to her car before mimicking, "I'd hate to pick you up again."

It was Teague's fault she had a ticket and Teague's fault she was making fun of an officer of the law. That man had turned Kate into a spiteful lawbreaker.

She started her car, then circumspectly eased back onto the road.

The patrol car eased on behind her.

Kate got her speed up to sixty-five.

The officer got her speed to sixty-five.

Kate set her cruise control and grimly continued toward Hobart. She didn't lose the officer until she was past New Braunfels. If Kate could make it back before school closed, she could get the interview with a schoolteacher later today.

This morning, she had polished off the meeting with the elementary teacher in

Austin in about fifteen minutes. How long did it take for some poor, underpaid educator to say she felt the children of the state had been robbed?

This wasn't a story. This was a farce. A farce manufactured by Teague Ramos, a big fat liar in need of much lesson learning.

Kate glanced at her cell phone. Teague could stew a while longer, but . . . Kate put on her headset and dialed her mother's house.

The phone rang. No one answered. Idly, Kate wondered if she should call Aunt Carol—Mom was probably over there telling the decorator how to hang the drapes—but when Aunt Carol got her on the phone, Kate could never get off.

And Kate was only fifteen minutes from Hobart.

At least if her mom was out of the house, Teague couldn't talk to her, ask her where Kate had gone, and scare her half to death.

She would call her mother again after lunch.

And although it went against the grain, she supposed she'd call Teague, too. She didn't doubt he was worried about her. But she cared about that as much as he cared about keeping his promises.

At twelve-thirty P.M. she drove her BMW past the city limits sign—HOBART, HOME OF FIGHTING FARMERS, POPULATION 4,802.

Kate marveled at how exactly Hobart fit her idea of a small Texas farming town. Just off the highway, Wal-Mart pulled in a steady stream of customers. A Dairy Queen and a Subway sat across the street. One of Hobart's four stoplights was located at that intersection. The downtown was six blocks long and two blocks wide. There was a furniture store, five bars, three restaurants, a pool hall, and a karate studio. The buildings downtown looked shabby: thirties, forties, and fifties architecture in need of sandblasting. At one end of Main Street sat a new courthouse and town hall; that complex looked good. Opposite was the city park with red and yellow plastic playground equipment and an old mildewed pool, fenced off and empty.

Kate drove up and down Main twice, studying the lay of the land before deciding on RoeAnn's Diner. It looked clean, it was busy; the big windows looked out onto the street, and the painting on the window showed a giant milk shake.

Usually she didn't indulge in milk shakes, giant or otherwise, but simply driving into Hobart put her in a better mood. When she thought about Teague and the way he'd tried to manipulate her, she was still livid. But underneath the fury lurked a sense of satisfaction; she had taken control of the situation.

When she remembered Teague's swollen face and his bruised ribs, she felt sick. Someone *had* to find out what was behind Oberlin's behavior. Someone had to determine why he'd never been caught. And someone had to stop him before he killed her, or Teague, or both of them.

Teague could stop him, but first, Kate would give him all the information he needed.

She attracted quite a bit of attention while she maneuvered her car into a parallel parking spot. Apparently BMWs were rare in Hobart.

She attracted as much attention when she stepped out, and she was glad she'd dressed modestly in black slacks, a black sweater, and a forest-green jacket. As a matter of fact, she'd dressed for possible combat—yesterday had taught her the disadvantages of fighting in a skirt. And she wore comfortable flats—the soles of her feet were still sore, and, until Oberlin had been arrested, she wanted to be able to flee.

Inside, the RoeAnn had the look of a fifties diner, with red vinyl and chrome chairs and matching tables, and a long bar with red vinyl and chrome stools. A jukebox flashing with fluorescent pink and green lights played a medley of Elvis songs. Best of all, the place looked clean and smelled great, like hamburgers and homemade pie. Almost every table was full, and every head turned to survey her.

She smiled; she needed to talk to people here, and people naturally warmed to someone who smiled.

A few of the younger people smiled back. Some of the older ones looked shocked and glanced away. One waitress stared at her, wide-eyed, and when Kate said, "Can I sit anywhere?" she broke and ran toward the back.

Kate thought the restaurant must employ the mentally challenged, which was a good thing unless you were a stranger and wanted to eat lunch.

But with her pencil, the other waitress indicated a booth.

Kate nodded and slid in.

Sitting there, she considered the situation with Teague. How he had said he wouldn't interfere with her reporting. How angry she was at him for lying . . . How she had promised to check in with him.

It had been more than four hours since she'd left him. He'd tried to call her once, and she'd turned off her phone. Sadly, she hoped he was worried about her. She wanted him to learn a lesson. But she knew she was being harsh; she was being stalked by a murderer.

George Oberlin lurked in Austin, waiting to touch her, to say horrible words that insinuated that she would trade her soul for his money, his influence. He scared her for more than his murderous tendencies. He scared her because he seemed to think he was a typical man.

Teague had every reason to be frantic with her silence. So, grudgingly, Kate pulled out her cell phone and called him.

He didn't answer, and his message cut in

and out. She glanced at the display. The signal here was weak; this town was a hole where cell waves sank without a trace. But she left a message anyway: that way he couldn't gripe at her for not keeping her word. "Teague, it's Kate. I'm in Hobart. I'm doing my research. I'm fine. I'll be back in Austin tonight." Taking a breath, she said, "I know what you said to Brad. Don't ever try to control me again, or I swear to God, I'll leave you and never look back."

She hung up, stared at the phone in her hand, and realized the shoe was actually on the other foot. She had hoped Teague would be worried about her. But now she was worried about Teague.

She dialed Teague again. He still didn't pick up; when she heard his message, she said, "Call me back and tell me you're okay. I'm, um, concerned."

The skinniest little old lady in the world sat facing her at a table across the restaurant. Her stooped shoulders and white hair showed the burden of her age, her ebony-skinned face sagged, but she smiled cheerfully at Kate.

Kate smiled back.

The old woman's companion turned to glance at Kate, then shook her head.

Kate glanced at the menu and figured she'd better stick with something basic to go with her milk shake.

The waitress who'd pointed out this booth to her and wore a name tag that said CATHY, stopped by and asked, "What can I get you?"

"A French dip sandwich with fries and a chocolate shake."

"That shake in the window gets 'em every time." Cathy grinned as she scribbled down the order. "It's made with Bluebell ice cream, you know."

"I should just plaster it to my thighs," Kate told her. "That's where it's going to end up anyway."

"It's more fun going in the top." Cathy winked.

The old lady still smiled at Kate, and, when Kate caught her eye, she waved.

Kate waved back.

The old woman's smile grew.

The waitress glanced over. "That's Mrs. Parker. Sweet thing, but she's slipped a few gears, if you know what I mean. Her daughter was living in California. She moved back to take care of Mrs. Parker at home, but Maureen is no spring chicken herself. I don't know what they're going to do." Cathy shook her head. "It's a shame when the mind goes first."

"She seems happy," Kate said.

"She was my second-grade teacher. It's . . . hard when she doesn't recognize me." Cathy cocked her head and studied Kate. "You look familiar, yourself."

Kate saw Mrs. Parker get to her feet and reach for her walker. "Does KTTV out of Austin reach this far?" Kate asked. "I'm a reporter there."

"No, most of our stations are out of San Antone, but maybe that's it. Last year we went to Austin for our anniversary." Before Kate could explain she hadn't been there last year, Cathy went to pick up an order and to yell at the other waitress for malingering.

With a helpless, apologetic glance at Kate, Maureen helped her mother make a slow progress across the floor. They reached Kate's table, and the daughter said, "Mama's a little confused today. She thinks she knows you."

"I do know her." The old lady sank down in

the booth and reached across the table. Taking Kate's hands in her fragile, crippled fingers, she asked, "Where have you been keeping yourself? I've missed you."

"I'm glad to see you, too." Mrs. Parker had made a harmless mistake, and Kate didn't try to correct her.

"How are the children? Last time I saw Hope, she had gotten so big! Why, I remember when she was just a baby and the sweetest thing I ever laid eyes on. And driven! Not like that rascal Pepper."

Kate played along. "No, not like Pepper at all."

"I warned you about naming a child Pepper, didn't I? That little girl is as smart as a whip, but she'd rather run and chatter with her friends than do math. She's a trial, that one." Mrs. Parker laughed a long, clear laugh. "I can't quite remember. How old are the girls now?"

Kate didn't know how to answer. As she dawdled, Mrs. Parker's merriment faded. Tears filled her eyes.

"Who would have thought those children would disappear like that? One minute they were here, the next minute they were gone, and everything in Hobart changed."

"Oh, Mama." Maureen handed her mother a handkerchief.

Except for the whir of the milk shake machine, the restaurant was unusually quiet.

Kate glanced around. Everyone in the restaurant observed them.

"Even the foster boy vanished, and you had really gentled him." A tear dropped off Mrs. Parker's wrinkled cheek.

"But the girls are fine." Gently, Kate squeezed Mrs. Parker's fingers.

"Are they? Well, good. Good. I was worried about them, I can tell you." Mrs. Parker dabbed her eyes.

The other waitress—the odd, frightened one—ventured out of the kitchen and stood behind the counter, filling coffee cups and staring at Kate as if she'd grown a second head. Kate began to feel as if she'd fallen into the *Twilight Zone.*

"You had a baby, too. What was that child's name? Caitlin. Caitlin Prescott. Such a pretty child. I always said she would grow up to look like you." Mrs. Parker scrutinized Kate. "My goodness, I don't know how you do it, but you are looking younger every day. You haven't gone off and had one of those extreme makeovers, have you? So foolish to meddle with God's work. But no, you're the minister's wife. You wouldn't do that."

"Mama, here comes Cathy with this lady's order." Maureen touched her mother's shoulder. "We'd better go back to our table and let her eat."

"Of course." With the help of her walker, Mrs. Parker hefted herself to her feet. "Don't be such a stranger! I get lonely since I've quit work. Come for a visit. I'll make you a pear pie. You know, Lana, you've always loved my pear pie."

Lana.

"Thank you," Kate faltered. "It was wonderful to see you, too."

Lana. Evelyn Oberlin had looked into space, called Lana's name, said she was sorry. . . .

As the mother and daughter walked away, Kate wiped her suddenly sweaty palms on her napkin.

Mrs. Parker had given details, names. She had insisted Kate was Lana, a minister's wife . . . and she had suffered that moment of sadness.

What was it she said? *Who would have thought those children would disappear . . .*

Cathy slid a huge platter with the French

dip and the fries onto the table, then returned with a glassful of milk shake and the rest in the metal shake container. "It's as good as it looks," she advised, and whipped off to pour coffee at the next table.

Who would have thought those children would disappear . . .

Kate stared at the food. She glanced around the diner. The people now hunched over their plates and examined her out of the corners of their eyes.

Who would have thought those children would disappear . . .

Dear God. Kate's whole life had changed today. This minute. Now.

She picked up her phone and dialed Teague. "Damn it!" she whispered when he didn't answer. The signal still cut out, so she left the message three times. "I found my family. I found my family. I found my family. Come to Hobart, Teague. I think he killed them all."

Someone stepped up to the table. "He didn't kill them all."

Kate glanced up.

A woman of maybe forty stood there. She had an hourglass figure with a little too much sand in the bottom, hair dyed flame red, and wore a Hawaiian shirt, pink shorts, and running shoes without socks.

"He didn't?" Should Kate get in her car and drive away as fast as she could, or stay to find out who she was and what had happened?

How could she walk away from her past when she'd found it?

"I'm Melissa Cunningham." The woman smiled and stuck out her hand. "I was wondering when one of you all would come back."

Kate shook hands. "So you recognize me?"

"Of course I do." Melissa leaned across the table and looked into Kate's eyes. "You're one of the minister's kids. You're Lana Prescott's baby daughter."

Twenty-two

As he drove toward Hobart, the phone rang in George's car. He glanced at the number.

Jason Urbano.

Today, George had his revenge, his money . . . and when he got to Hobart, he would have his woman. One way or another, he would have Kate.

With absolute composure, he opened the connection. "It's about time."

"Senator Oberlin?" It was a woman's voice. It contained the faintest hint of Texas in its accent.

George frowned. Urbano should not have had his secretary call. "Yes?"

"This is Hope Givens."

Hope Givens? George stared at the highway as it wound through the Hill Country. The blood buzzed in his head.

"Hope Prescott Givens," she added helpfully.

Had Urbano failed him? Had Urbano *screwed* him?

"Senator, are you there?" She sounded exactly as she had twenty-three years ago—perky, composed, very much the minister's daughter.

Well, she'd sounded that way most of the time. Except when she'd found out that her parents were thieves, that no one wanted her and her siblings. *Then* she had shouted and cried. Poor, stupid, pathetic child.

"I'm here." That poor child had grown up to be the bane of his existence.

Not like his sweet Kate. Kate, who was sticking her nose where it did not belong.

"Good. I wouldn't want to lose you now." Hope managed to make simple words sound like intimidation.

She was threatening him, Senator George Oberlin. "Why are you calling me?"

"Why am *I* contacting you instead of Jason Urbano, do you mean?"

"What are you talking about?" George clutched the wheel.

"I mean, you were expecting a call from Jason telling you that Givens Industries had collapsed, that your investment in our competitors resulted in a fortune, and that I would never bother you again."

George heard his own breath. How did she know? Urbano had told her. He *must* have told her.

"Just in case you're making plans to release the information you've collected about Jason, I wouldn't. It's all phony, and it'll make you look like a fool." In a reflective tone, she added, "A bigger fool."

Comprehension struck George like a well-wielded baseball bat. He didn't even have to listen to know what she was going to say next. But he did. He listened very closely. He needed to know how many people would suffer his revenge.

"More than a year ago, my husband and I made a plan. We decided that if we couldn't convince you to tell us what had happened to my sister Caitlin, we would motivate you to cooperate by"—she pretended to think—"what's the word?"

George heard a man's crisp Boston voice on the line. "Blackmail."

"Yes, that's it. We would blackmail you into cooperating with us. So we set up a sting operation that involved Griswald—you know him as Freddy."

"Present." Freddy's crisp British accent. "And Jason Urbano."

"Hello, Senator." Urbano sounded so smug. So superior.

"Also, Gabriel is a part of this—remember Gabriel, Senator? My foster brother?" Hope taunted Oberlin with his failure. "The muscle in our group is Dan Graham, my brother-in-law."

"Brother-in-law?" George couldn't believe what Hope was saying.

"My sister's husband." Kate spelled it out so he couldn't be mistaken.

"Yes, it's true, I'm here, too." Another woman spoke in a firm, no-nonsense tone, one that reminded him so much of Lana a cold shiver slid down his spine. "Do you remember me? I'm the middle daughter. I'm Pepper."

"Quite the family reunion." He imagined them all standing there around a speaker phone, gloating. Then a horrific thought struck him. "Where are you?"

"We all came to Austin to be close to you," Hope said.

"Not so very close to me." Thank God, they weren't in Hobart. Even when they figured out where he had gone, he was two hours ahead of them. Two hours closer to Kate. "Why are you calling me?"

"You're an intelligent man, Senator. You know why we're calling you." Pepper's voice again, still with that stern, authoritative tone that sounded so much like Lana directing the Sunday School.

"It's not true that Givens Industries is going to fall, but it *is* true that we have sufficient taped evidence of your intention to commit industrial sabotage." Hope paused. "We can ruin you."

As George realized the magnitude of the sting, he swerved onto the shoulder of the road. The right wheels hit gravel. But he managed to correct before he spun out. He was a good driver. He *was* in control. "Tapes can be falsified."

"True. But your large investment in competitors' stocks proves your intention to destroy the corporation and defraud the stockholders." The nasty little bitch added, "I believe you overextended your credit, also. You can sell your investments, of course, but I don't think you're going to recoup your outlay. You see, we know how to play the market ourselves. The price you paid for the stocks is not what you're going to recover."

All these years. George had trapped police officials. He'd blackmailed other legislators. Now he was being jerked around, and by a simple minister's daughter.

"Are you there, Senator?" Hope asked.

"Yes." Yes, he was here, and he was going to make Hope sorry. He was going to make them all sorry. "What do you want?" As if he didn't know.

In a soothing tone, she said, "I'm not asking you to admit your guilt in the stolen church treasury. I'm not asking that you accept responsibility for my parents' deaths. But I want to know what you did with Caitlin. Senator, tell me what you did with my sister."

"Hope Prescott Givens, I know exactly where your sister is."

He heard a sharp intake of breath from more than one person.

"Did you kill her?" she asked.

"When she was a baby? Don't be ridiculous. She's alive. I haven't killed her." A red tide of fury rose from his gut and washed over him. "Yet."

"No. Wait! Senator!"

With a little smug satisfaction of his own, he pressed the end call button, stepped on the gas, and sped toward Hobart.

Teague came awake to shouting and jostling, doors slamming . . . he was in a stopped vehicle. His head hurt, his ribs hurt, his face hurt. He felt like hell.

Some guys had grabbed him, stuck a needle in his neck, and—

"Marilyn!"

He sat up so fast nausea hit him in a rush.

"Lie down." It was a man's voice. He sounded more than a little harassed as he pressed Teague down onto his back. "Or you'll toss your cookies for sure."

"Where the hell am I?" Teague pressed his hands to his face. "What have you done with Mrs. Montgomery?"

"I'm right here, dear." Her warm, kind voice spoke above his head. "They're going to drop us off at the FBI."

"You are kidding." He looked around. He rested on the carpeted floor of an industrial-sized van. Benches lined the walls on either side. The windows were darkly tinted. Two women he had never seen before sat on one side. Nice-looking women—a brunette with highlights, and one with hair as black as Teague's. They clutched each other's hands, they watched him, but they weren't really seeing him. They both had an unfocused, strained look in their eyes.

Marilyn Montgomery sat on the opposite bench, looking anxious but composed. "They've all been very nice, but now they're in a hurry to go to the airport."

"This doesn't make any sense," Teague said. "Why are they dropping us off at the FBI? Why did they take us in the first place? *Who are they?*"

"We took you because you're investigating Senator George Oberlin, and the lady said you were going to the FBI about him." The military man who'd stuck the needle in Teague stood, feet braced, holding on to a strap and looking at ease. But tough. Flinty-eyed. "And we're the people who have been after Oberlin for way too long to have you tip him off now."

"But?" Teague looked up at him.

"He's not cooperating," the guy said briefly. "He's crazy."

"No." Teague drew the word out, injecting disbelief into his tone. "Ya think?"

"I'm Dan Graham." Dan extended his hand. "Sorry about the needle."

Teague considered the hand. But he figured Dan was telling the truth. If these people had been planning to kill Marilyn and him, they would have done it already. He shook hands. "Teague Ramos."

Dan inspected Teague's face. "Somebody worked you over good."

"Yeah, one day I walk down the street, and people beat me up. The next day, they stick a needle in my neck to knock me out." With heavy sarcasm, Teague said, "I can't *wait* to see what tomorrow brings."

The engine started, the van moved forward.

Teague looked toward the front.

The driver was a total stranger . . . but maybe not. Teague thought he'd seen him somewhere. In the movies? The newspapers? The guy riding shotgun was the bastard who had grabbed Teague and held him for the injection. Teague was pleased to see he now had an Ace bandage wrapped around his wrist. Apparently, Teague had done a little damage before he'd blacked out.

No matter. In Teague's current condition,

with his cracked ribs, his battered face and a crushing headache, he wouldn't care to take him on. Take on any of them. The three men exuded that air of competence that warned other men to step carefully.

The women weren't like the guys. They exuded intelligence, beauty, charm, but not toughness. They were the kind of women men lost their heads over. Women who domesticated the world. Women . . . like Kate.

Slowly, testing his balance, Teague sat up. These women didn't really look like Kate, but they had the same air about them. Women in command. Women . . . he fished out his phone.

The red message light blinked.

Dan's hand clamped over his. "What are you doing?"

"I'm supposed to be guarding Kate Montgomery from Oberlin. I'll talk to her and make sure she's all right." He challenged Dan with his gaze.

"I'm sure she's all right. Oberlin's got other matters on his mind right now," Dan said.

"Then it doesn't matter if I call her." Teague saw the glance Dan exchanged with one of the women, intimate and worried.

Teague challenged him. "Would you leave the matter to chance with your woman?"

Dan released his hand. "Call her. If she's near Oberlin, tell her to get away. He just discovered how much trouble he's in."

Teague dialed her cell. It rang.

Marilyn sat forward and intently watched him. "Come on, Kate," she said.

Kate's voice mail picked up.

"I didn't get her, but that's all right," he soothed. "I've got a message. She promised to check in. I'm sure it's from her." He pressed the button to connect with his voice mail.

"Do you know why Oberlin is stalking your Kate?" the dark-haired woman asked.

The automated voice went through its perambulations. "You have four new messages. The first new message . . ."

Big Bob's voice boomed in Teague's ear. "Hey, boss, thought you would want to know Oberlin left for lunch early."

"Oberlin left for lunch early." Which was interesting, but Teague wanted to hear from Kate.

"Kate looks like someone he knew." Marilyn didn't take her gaze off Teague. "Someone he . . . well, we think he killed this other woman."

"Killed . . . if he kills . . ." A sob escaped the brunette. "The last time I saw her, she was just a baby and now—"

The other woman wrapped her arms around her and rocked. "It's okay, Hope. We can't give up now."

"Has he killed someone you know?" Marilyn looked from one to the other.

"Not yet." The driver spoke in a crisp Boston accent. "Not if we have anything to say about it. And we do."

The second new message: Kate's voice spoke in Teague's ear. Teague gave Marilyn a thumbs-up. He relaxed a little, until he heard, "Teague, it's Ka—"—her voice cut out, then in—". . . in Hobart."

Teague shuddered. "Hobart?" he said out loud.

Both women started. Together they exclaimed, "Hobart!"

The guy in the front whipped his head around. "What about Hobart?"

Teague emphatically waved them to silence.

"I'm doing my . . . fine . . . be back in Austin tonight. I know what you . . . Brad."

That son of a bitch, Brad. He must have squealed on Teague.

"Don't ever try to . . . I swear to . . . leave . . . never look back."

Teague didn't care about the ladies' delicate sensibility. "Goddamn it to hell!"

"Hobart? What about Hobart?" Dan demanded.

"Sh!" Teague glared.

The third new message . . . Kate's voice again: "Call me . . . right . . . me . . . okay . . . worried about you."

"Well . . . good. That's good. That's really good." Teague slid over to rest his back against a bench. Except why was she worried about him? Teague made a circling motion with his hand, trying to get the voice mail system to hurry up.

Then the fourth new message: "I found . . . family. I . . . my family. Come . . . Teague . . . think he killed . . . all."

Teague's heart leaped into his throat. Kate had done her damned investigation and come up with trouble. He hung up. In curt tones he said, "I have to get to Hobart. *Now.*"

Dan gripped his shoulder. *"Why* Hobart?"

"Where's Hobart?" Marilyn asked.

"South of San Antonio," Teague said. "Three hours away."

Everyone in the van shouted at him: *"Why Hobart?"*

What was wrong with these people? *He* was the one with the problem. "Kate's in Hobart. She says she found her family. She says he killed them all."

Marilyn took a horrified breath.

"Kate?" The brunette, Hope, stared at him. "Are you saying Kate is my sister Caitlin?"

Teague marveled at how quickly every difficulty could be surmounted when money was no object.

The helicopter ride from Austin to Hobart took a half hour. The exchange of information between Teague and Marilyn and Hope, Zack, Pepper, Dan, and Gabriel, died with the noise of the rotor blades, but as they landed Dan handed out weapons. Hope and Pepper each took one, as did Gabriel.

Of course. They would be Oberlin's main targets.

Zack waved Dan's offer of a Beretta 9mm

toward Teague, and Teague grimly accepted.

When he saw Kate, he planned to tell her that this kind of incident was *exactly* the reason why he hadn't wanted her to go to Hobart. Ruthlessly and without ceasing he would say, "I told you so." As the helicopter powered down and the coil of tension in his gut grew tighter, he planned some pithy replies to her defiance.

She had damned well better stay alive to listen to them.

Again he tried to call her. The call went straight to her voice mail; either her phone was off or she was out of the service area.

A luxury van met them. Zack drove, Dan rode shotgun . . . the plan was for the Prescott children to stay behind the tinted windows until they knew they were safe. Gabriel and Teague rode in the second row of seats. Hope, Pepper, and Marilyn rode in the back, and when Teague glanced behind him, he saw Marilyn wiping away tears while Hope and Pepper hugged her.

Kate had really nice sisters. She needed to meet them.

Again, he called her. This time it rang, then the signal cut out.

Wrapped in edgy silence, they drove into Hobart. Tension rose with each turn of the wheels.

Hope and Pepper looked around, but they didn't exclaim as people often did when returning to their hometown. Their pensive silence made Teague think that, for them, everything was familiar—and painful.

Zack turned onto Main Street and slowed. Dozens of people stood in the road, arms folded across their chests, talking, craning their necks to see through the crowd. More were running up. Teague could see flashing lights in front of the RoeAnn Diner. A police car and an ambulance. Behind them, they could hear the wail of sirens.

The blood pounded in Teague's brain.

Dan rolled down the window and hailed an onlooker, an upright older man with a white fringe of hair and a well-worn cowboy hat. "Excuse me! What's going on?"

"A woman was shot!"

Before the van came to a complete halt, Teague leaped out and pushed his way through the crowd. He heard murmurs as he went:

"Never happens here."

"What's the world coming to?"

And, in tones of disbelief, "Senator Oberlin? Are you sure it was Senator Oberlin?"

Teague got to the police line—a sparce line consisting of two officers in blue uniforms, shouting, "Stay back. Give her some air!"

"She's not dead." Dan stood at Teague's side.

But the ambulance crew was frantically working on the prone form on the sidewalk. Teague saw blood spatters on the concrete. He tried to lunge past the policeman, but the officer caught his arm.

In a flurry, Teague pulled out his Texas Capitol security identification. He flashed it. "Let me through."

At Teague's tone and the sight of the badge, the officer gave way.

"This is Teague Ramos, in charge of security at the Texas Capitol," Dan said. "We heard one of our senators did this."

"That's what they say." Worry lines marked the officer's broad forehead.

Vaguely, Teague heard Dan ask, "Do you know who the victim is?"

But Teague had already caught a glimpse of the still body.

It wasn't Kate. Through the immediate relief and the ongoing worry, he barely heard the policeman's answer.

"Her name's Melissa Cunningham. It seems Senator Oberlin drove into town. She had words with him. He shot her in the belly." Hastily, the officer added, "Or so some witnesses say."

Teague turned on him. "Where's Oberlin now? You have to send people after him." Teague supposed he had that look in his eyes, the one that had scared Kate, the one that had sent grown men fleeing, and he was glad. He wanted that information.

The officer stammered, "We haven't sent . . . we don't have the resources . . . Melissa's life is our first priority. . . ."

"More important than a crazy senator with a pistol?" Teague shouted.

"Young man! Don't shout at the officer. It isn't polite."

Teague wanted to shout at the stooped old woman with the walker, too. "I need to know where Oberlin went."

"He went to the cemetery. Take the old highway; it's five miles out of town." The black woman spoke precisely, and her brown eyes looked sharp and alive. "He's after the young lady who looks like Lana, and if someone doesn't do something, he's going to kill her, too."

"Mrs. Parker, that's speculation, and I'd appreciate it if you'd stop!" the officer said.

"John Jeremy Wringle, I taught you to show respect for your elders. I'd suggest you do so," Mrs. Parker replied.

Gently Teague took her arm. "How long ago?"

"Thirty minutes." She turned to the woman next to her, probably her daughter. "I taught George Oberlin in second grade, and I knew something was wrong with him then."

Teague strode toward the van. Dan walked with him. The crowd parted before them, taking no chances with these tough, stern warriors.

Teague fixed his gaze on the flashing lights now parked behind their van at the outer limits of the crowd. "I'm taking the police car. I need a diversion."

"We can give you that." Dan smiled a very unpleasant smile.

The officer stood in the open door of his car. The motor was running. He spoke into the walkie-talkie on his shoulder. He looked hassled by the questions shouted at him by the still-gathering mob—and he made no attempt to go after the guilty party.

So this was Hobart. This was Oberlin's town, and the police didn't know whether to go after him and risk their jobs, or risk another public shooting.

Teague moved into place off to the side and behind the officer.

Dan spoke to Zack in the van.

The doors opened. Hope, Pepper, and Gabriel stepped out.

"Excuse me," Hope said in a clear voice.

Heads turned.

Teague saw second glances and stunned double-takes. He moved closer to the police car.

She continued, "I understand George Oberlin committed this crime. This is not the first time he's done violence. Do you all remember the Prescott family? Do you remember what happened to us?"

"Hope!" A woman cried out. "I remember you. I remember . . . Pepper and . . . Gabriel?"

"They said Caitlin was back, but I didn't believe it." A middle-aged cowboy shook his head in wonder. "That I should live to see this day!"

Teague was in position.

"Believe." Hope turned to the officer. "I remember you, Bill Browning. You helped take my family away."

Browning gobbled like a turkey.

"Are you going to let George Oberlin kill my sister, too?" Pepper asked fiercely.

Browning started to slam the police car door and make for Hope.

Teague caught the door before it closed and slipped inside.

The officer turned.

Teague rammed the shift into reverse. He put his foot all the way to the floor. With a squeal of tires, he backed up the street. He saw Officer Browning reach for his gun. He saw Dan tackle him.

Then Teague flipped on the siren, turned the car around, and sped toward the cemetery.

Toward Kate. Toward the woman he loved.

Twenty-three

The peace of Hobart's cemetery should have been soothing.

The cool breeze touched Kate's face. Birds chirped in the ancient, bent branches of the live oak trees. The grass had been cut but not trimmed, and long tufts clung to the corners of the headstones.

Yet she stared in turmoil at the simple iron markers:

Bennett Prescott.

Lana Prescott.

Her parents.

Her birth parents.

She had been lucky. All the time she was growing up, she'd had a father and mother who loved her, who supported her. But the knowledge had haunted her; she'd been left on a church step. Daddy and Mom had put a good spin on it; Kate's birth mother hadn't been able to keep her, so she'd placed Kate someplace where she'd known she'd be safe. As Kate grew, she realized that adoption was the right way to get rid of an incon-

venient child. It seemed likely her mother
was a desperate teenager—or an unlucky
prostitute.

But Melissa Cunningham had told her that
her mother hadn't tossed her onto a church
step and walked away. Her parents had
been married, a minister and his wife.
They'd been killed in a car wreck. They'd
been accused of embezzlement, but no one
had investigated the facts. The police in Hobart had taken the word of the church trea-
surer who just happened to be . . . George
Oberlin.

Now Kate's parents were buried in the
part of the cemetery close to the parking lot,
where the poor people lay. In the next row
beneath the trees, heavy, raised headstones
were decorated with angel statues and en-
graved poems. But for her parents, the
stones were simple and said only:

Bennett Prescott.
Lana Prescott.
Nothing more.

Yet someone had placed flowers on their
graves. Bits of the blossoms remained
there, their golds and reds faded by the sun.

Melissa had made it clear that she
doubted the Prescotts' wrongdoing, and

that her mother had blamed herself for the family's disintegration and had blamed George Oberlin for their deaths.

Mrs. Parker had made it clear that Lana Prescott had been a beloved friend of hers.

Lana had been Kate's mother.

Bennett had been her father.

Somewhere out there, Kate had a family: two sisters and a foster brother, lost because *somebody* had made sure they were separated. And that somebody was . . . George Oberlin.

The reporter in her realized that this was a huge story, one that could establish her national career.

The human being in her wailed like a baby to know that one corrupt man had ruined so many lives.

Her damned cell phone didn't work.

Melissa had taken the phone numbers Kate gave her—for Teague, for Kate's mom, for the FBI, for KTTV. Melissa had promised to go home and call each one, one after the other, to get them out here. Kate was done thinking she could handle this matter on her own. By God, she was calling in the cavalry.

Turning away from the graves, she watched a beige Lincoln Town Car drive up the road and turn into the lot. It parked beside her car, the only other car at the cemetery.

George Oberlin stepped out.

Of course.

How could Kate have been so foolish as to think she could slip into Hobart undetected? Like a giant squid, he had tentacles that reached everywhere.

He started toward her. At the sight of his upright figure, his blond hair, his stately stride, her heartbeat lurched in revulsion. This jerk had killed her parents. Because of some sick obsession, he had killed her mother and her father and had taken Kate and given her away as if she were garbage.

George Oberlin was a murderer. A serial killer. A ruthless man with no morals.

Hatred burned hot in her. Was she afraid? Yes, of course. But she wanted, needed to know why and how he had obliterated her family.

Facing him as he neared, she stood at her parents' graves. He had to realize she knew the truth about herself, yet still he postured—chin up, an earnest smile on his lips—still tried to make himself look good in her eyes. Stopping before her, he allowed his gaze to drift over the grave markers. "What did that woman tell you?"

"Do you mean Melissa Cunningham?" Kate challenged him with her hostility. "She told me you killed my parents."

"Speculation. Unfounded speculation," he promptly said.

"Which you didn't deny." She slipped into her role as a reporter. "Don't you think if someone is accused of a murder that he didn't do, he would be shocked and immediately renounce the charges?"

"My dear," he said, sounding every inch a man wounded by vicious slander and her mistrust. "I thought that of course you would realize such a tale was preposterous."

"I am not your—" She took a breath. She shouldn't be out here with him. But she wanted the truth, and if she was going to obtain it, she needed to be cool. Interested. "But you killed your wife. You killed Mrs. Blackthorn. So it's safe to assume you killed my parents."

"I did what had to be done. What people forced me to do. I came up from poverty. Poverty!" Oberlin slipped into his senatorial mode. He straightened his shoulders. His voice took on the smooth tones of an orator. "My father was a truck driver. He swore. He drank. He spit. He stank. And my mother— she was so good, so sweet. He made her afraid. Every day, she was afraid he would hit her again. Or hit me again."

"Your father sounds like a monster." Inevitably, she compared Oberlin's youth to Teague's. What turned one man into a monster and the other into a guardian? "But I don't understand. What is it that gave you the excuse to kill my parents? That you had a bad father or a good mother?"

The facade of the senator slipped. A dark, dull red crept from Oberlin's collar up to cover his neck, his face, his ears. "If you will just listen"—he took a breath, the color inched down—"I can explain it all."

"Please do." She gestured at the gravemarkers.

"When I was five, my father killed my mother." Oberlin's tone remained even, but he was breathing hard. "Have you ever seen someone beaten to death? It's horrible."

"I can imagine." Unfortunately, she could imagine the scene. The photos of her father gave her all-too-vivid a reference, and left her without pity for a man who had turned his childhood tragedy into a reason to kill without conscience. "Is that how you killed *my* parents?"

His face contorted with temper. He swung toward her.

She hustled behind a standing headstone. He was broad-shouldered, with big bones. And taller than her by at least six inches.

Not as tall as Teague, but Teague's height had protected her.

Oberlin's height menaced her.

"You're not listening to me. You have a closed mind about this." Oberlin's voice rose. "I thought as a reporter you would listen to me."

His appearance was deceptive. Beneath the mask, he seethed with frustration barely held in check. She would do well to remember that. "You're right. I'm not being fair. Make me understand." Because she needed to hear how he would justify the unspeakable to the woman he had so grossly wronged. And because . . . Kate was alone out here. He could rape her. He could kill her.

"What happened to your father?" she asked.

"Nothing. The deputy who investigated

used his fists on his family, too, so my mama's death was ruled accidental. My father kept driving truck, drinking, doing drugs, bringing home women to beat . . . when I was seventeen, he died. He fell and cracked his head open."

Fell down the stairs? Kate clamped her lips tightly to prevent the question from escaping.

"When Father died, I already knew what I wanted to do. I wanted to catch deputies like the one who'd laughed with my father over my mother's bloody body and make them pay. So I married Evelyn because her family had money. I didn't love her. I swear to you, I never loved her."

Kate could scarcely contain her aversion. Did he think that made the story more palatable—her knowing he had never loved the woman he'd lived with for twenty-five years?

"But her father didn't like me. He didn't believe in me, in my vision. He was a stupid, dirty rancher who wouldn't finance me. So I had to resort to taking a little money from the church." Her incredulous disdain must have shown in her face, for Oberlin added hastily, "I was going to put it back! As soon as I was elected to the Texas State Senate, I was going to sneak the money from the treasury back. Ultimately, it would have been good for the church. I could have greatly added to their coffers."

"But?"

"I fell in love with your mother."

"What?" Kate almost staggered from the shock of his words. He had loved her mother? He dared to claim he loved her?

"How could I help it?" Kneeling beside her gravestone, he reverently touched it with his fingertips.

He wasn't posturing this time. He meant it. Grief creased his face. "She wasn't the most beautiful woman I've ever seen. She was pretty like you. But not like you. She was older than me and a little broad in the hips. After all, she'd had three children." He looked up in appeal, as if expecting Kate to understand.

"I wouldn't know." Kate breathed hard. "I've never even seen a picture of her."

"I can show you pictures. I've got your photo albums. You can see what she looked like!" He made the offer without comprehending the atrocity of stealing a family's memories. "But you'll see. It wasn't her looks that drew me. It was her . . . soul. It shone out of her like pure light. Everybody loved Lana. She was so kind. She shone with kindness, with motherliness. She was a Madonna."

"Did my father love her?" Which seemed more to the point than Oberlin's obscene adoration.

"Yes, and she loved him." Oberlin stood slowly, as if his knees hurt. "What followed was my fault. I admit it. I should never have declared my ardor. But imagine, if you will, a handsome young man who has been the object of many women's interest, but who has never loved before. I was overcome by passion, and I confessed . . . she was holding you, feeding you, and you both looked so beautiful. I told her everything. What I wanted, what I imagined, how I would make her rich, how I would worship her. And she . . . she was . . . she said she was married!"

Kate bit hard on her tongue to keep back the sarcastic retort.

"She was very kind. Kind to me like I'd seen her be kind to other people. Poor people. People who needed charity. Like I was one of *them.*" He sneered at the memory. He stared down at the headstones, and Kate realized that, for the first time, he'd forgotten her. He was caught up in a world long gone, trapped in emotions he had never left behind. "But I was strong. I pretended that it was a mistake, that I hadn't really meant it. I knew she didn't believe me, but at least I thought she would honor my trust."

Slipping her cell phone out of her pocket, Kate glanced at it. Still no signal.

And Oberlin was getting to the end of his story.

Her heartbeat tripped and trembled. She slid a few steps toward the parking lot.

Oberlin was too caught up in his memories to notice. "About a week later, the pastor called me over. I went into his woodworking shop. He was there making some stupid thing. A table for the bedroom. For Lana, he told me. And the way he told me, the tone he used, that compassionate expression on his face . . . I knew she'd betrayed me. She'd told him that I loved her." His voice rose. "She'd laughed at me behind my back."

"If she was as kind as you say, she didn't laugh at you!" Kate grew hot and indignant on behalf of a mother she couldn't remember.

"Then why did she tell him?" Oberlin swung toward her.

"Because he was her husband. If they were anything like my parents, my adopted parents, they didn't keep things from each other! That's the way it is when people love."

"It was a secret." He stalked toward her. "It was *our* secret!"

"Apparently not," Kate snapped, then wished she could call back the words.

But Oberlin's craziness sounded too much like stupidity for her to have patience. She wanted to slap him and to tell him to get some sense.

But she reminded herself that a killer like Oberlin was beyond reason, so she backed up. She fingered the keys in her pocket. House key. Mailbox key. Car key. She pressed the button to open the Beemer.

The headlights flashed. It was unlocked.

Oberlin kept pacing toward her, his gait stiff-legged and resentful. "Pastor Prescott told me he'd found my changes to the accounting books. He told me I had to return the money right away. I tried to explain my plan, that when I was a senator, the church would be rich, but he wouldn't listen to reason. He was going to steal my livelihood."

"Your livelihood?" She couldn't comprehend Oberlin's audacity. "It sounds like you didn't *have* a livelihood."

"You sound like *him.* You sound like your father!" Oberlin held his hands out as if he was desperately grasping for reason, only to find it slipping away. "I couldn't be a senator without that money. I hated being invisible, hated my father-in-law sneering at me. I needed to be a senator, and Bennett Prescott would not let me!"

Kate stopped slinking away. "So you killed him."

"I picked up his stupid piece of wood and knocked him across the head."

For one second, Kate shut her eyes. Oberlin had killed a man—had killed the father of four children, a minister and a good man, *her father*—because he wouldn't allow Oberlin to steal money from the church treasury.

When Oberlin spoke again, he stood two feet away. "You understand. It was necessary."

Opening her eyes, she stared at him.

He appeared noble and important and

sorrowful, like some politician forced to agree to a prisoner's execution.

"And my mother?" Kate's lips felt stiff.

"I still feel grief about that. She came in. I wasn't expecting her."

"No. I don't imagine you were." Somehow, the cool breeze had turned corrosive. It lashed at Kate's skin. It hurt her lungs.

"But she knew I was out there, so it turned out for the best." A murderer's logic.

"Did you hit her with the same piece of wood? The present my father was making for her birthday?"

"She didn't know . . . she thought he fell. . . . She was kneeling beside him . . . but she turned at the last moment and saw me and I—"

"For pity's sake!" Kate put out her hand to stop him. She couldn't stomach anymore.

Oberlin grabbed her fingers. "Kate, you understand. It was necessary."

Desperately she tried to extract her hand.

"It was all necessary." He held tight, un-caring that he ground her knuckles together, that the joints strained and bruised. "When I saw you, when I recognized you, I realized I'd been given a second chance. That you had been sent for me."

"No, I *haven't.*" She twisted her fingers free. Thrusting her hand into her pocket, she pulled out her phone and opened it as if to make a call.

"No!" Grabbing the phone out of her hand, he smashed it against a standing headstone.

She recoiled. Her mouth grew dry and her mind froze.

She was here with him. She was alone. And she had denied him. *She had said no.*

"You can't do that." Blood vessels burst and crimson crept into the whites of his eyes. "You can't call *him.*"

From far away, she heard a siren. Finally. Thank God. *Finally* someone was coming.

Her brain started working again. She had keys in her pocket. Keys could be a weapon.

Before she could reach for them, Oberlin grabbed her wrist. "Did you betray me with *him?* Did you?"

"I didn't betray you." She stood still and stared into his eyes. "I am not yours."

"That cheap womanizer. Ramos is nothing but the son of a whore."

She jerked as his words hit home.

Oberlin saw her reaction, pressed his advantage. "You didn't know that, did you? He didn't tell you that. God knows who his father was. One of a thousand. One of a million."

The sirens were louder.

"You're hurting me," she said.

Oberlin looked at her wrist gripped tightly in his hand. With an expression of surprise and horror, he released her. "I'm sorry. I shouldn't have . . . but you have to listen to me. You're meant for me, not him. You'll be the jewel on my arm."

"I have my own jewels and my own arms." She fell back, rubbing her wrist. Slowly she dipped her hand into her pocket. She slipped one key between each finger, then clenched her fist around the key ring. In a polite tone, she added, "But thank you."

"You think you're in love with Ramos, but you can't be. He's a liar." Oberlin's chest heaved as he followed her, palm outstretched. "He tells girls he's a magnificent lover, but he's not."

She didn't mean to. It was a stupid thing to do. But she was nervous. She knew the truth. So she laughed.

Oberlin's control exploded into shards of insanity. "Bitch." He slapped her, a fast, backhanded blow that whipped her head around and brought tears to her eyes.

He lifted his palm to slap her again.

She blocked his hand with one upraised arm. Brought the other out of her pocket and stabbed at his face. The keys ripped into his cheek in two long scratches. He jolted backward. His fingers flew to his face. Came back bloody.

A police car came screaming into the parking lot, lights flashing, siren roaring.

Oberlin started for her again.

She ran toward the parking lot.

Before she had gone three steps, he caught her by the shoulder.

Turning on him, she slashed at him again, but he held her off with the length of his arm. "Don't touch me," she shouted. "Don't you ever touch me! I won't let you kill me like you killed *my mother.*"

The police car's horn blasted. The driver whipped around like a maniac, took aim— and jumped the curb. He drove right at them, over the well-tended grass, over the flat gravestones.

Oberlin glanced over, but instead of panic she saw deadly satisfaction. "It's him," Oberlin said.

Teague. She saw him, too. Teague was driving—straight at them.

Reaching into his breast pocket, Oberlin pulled out a gun. Feet braced, he aimed at the windshield.

With a banshee shriek, she leaped at him.

He fell sideways.

The shot shattered the glass. The car careened wildly. Skidded in a circle, grass flying. Smashed into a standing headstone and came to a halt.

Kate ran to the driver's side and jerked open the door. Teague slumped sideways onto the seat, blood pouring from his scalp.

"Teague!" She leaned into the car.

The sirens still screamed. The lights still flashed. From the parking lot she heard more brakes squeal. Heard people shout.

She didn't care. "Teague. Teague, please."

In an awkward motion, he flung his arm up, knocking her away.

She staggered backward.

He launched himself out of the car with sudden, gawky motions.

He was alive.

She was glad.

He was wounded.

She was terrified.

George Oberlin stood laughing, his pistol pointed at Teague.

Men and women raced across the grass, yelling, but they wouldn't get there in time.

Teague moved into the open, away from the car. Turning his head, he looked at her. Blood smeared his pallid face. His eyes looked swollen. Sliding his jacket back, he pulled out a pistol. He lifted the pistol, squinted at Oberlin.

He couldn't aim.

She knew it. Oberlin knew it.

He offered himself as a decoy to draw Oberlin's fire.

She glanced at the senator. He set his feet again. Prepared to shoot.

Teague was going to die.

In the police car. A shotgun. Leaning in, she pulled it off the rack. She pumped it.

Oberlin followed Teague with the barrel of his pistol. She saw his eyes narrow.

She lifted the rifle to her shoulder.

Out of the corner of his eye, Oberlin glimpsed the motion.

His head turned. His mouth opened. He screamed, "No, Lana!"

Kate fired.

Twenty-four

George didn't see how Kate's shot could have missed—but it did. He was still standing, staring at Kate.

The whole terrible group of Prescotts and their mates ran up, helter-skelter, their pistols out.

Silly Kate. She didn't know how to fire a shotgun. How stupid of her to think she did. To think she could kill him. He smiled. He was going to kill them all. Wipe every Prescott off the face of the earth.

He raised his own gun . . . but he wasn't holding it. He looked at his hand. It was empty. In his fright, had he dropped the weapon?

Moreover, the Prescotts weren't staring at him, they were staring at the ground near his feet. Hope—he recognized Hope—had her hand over her mouth. Pepper—he recognized Pepper, too—looked sick.

Only Kate stood with her chin up. "I'm a reporter. I've seen such sights before," she murmured, "but I've never been glad before."

"Kate." Ramos stood still, swaying, his arms extended.

She went to him.

He hugged her, his head on top of hers.

What sights? What did she mean?

George looked down on the ground to see what they were talking about.

A man's body lay there. A bloody wound split his chest. A gun, George's gun, lay inches from his splayed fingers. Crimson spattered his outflung arms, his belly, his chin . . .

"What . . . ?" George pointed a shaking finger. "What . . . ?" His own *face* was on that body. His body rested on the green grass. Rested there as if he were . . . dead.

Dead! No, that was impossible.

He pointed at the body. "Who's that?" He looked up at the Prescotts.

They didn't answer him. They acted as if they didn't hear him. They gathered around Teague and Kate. They acted as if they had been reunited after years of toil and grief.

As if George wasn't still there and dangerous.

"Who's that?" He spoke louder, and he used his senator-addressing-the-press voice.

Then he realized that two people had joined the Prescott children.

He stared so intently he could almost see through them. He shuddered, a bone-splitting shudder, when he recognized them. He hadn't seen them for twenty-three years, but there was no mistaking them.

Bennett and Lana Prescott, and they looked . . . they looked *alive.*

They were dressed casually, as they had always dressed, and both observed him, their eyes as intelligent and perceptive as those days when he'd been younger and not quite so . . . he cut off the thought. He wasn't *evil.* That was an old-fashioned concept, like heaven and hell and sin and redemption. If he believed in that stuff, he'd have to believe that, when he died, he was going to burn in hell. That was nonsense. Ridiculous nonsense used to pull money out of a man's wallet and put it in a church's coffer.

Why were they here?

"Who is that?" George still pointed at the body.

But the Prescott children paid no attention.

"Who do you think it is, George?" Lana's voice sounded the same as it always had: clear, calm, warmed by a hint of Texas accent.

"It looks like me," he said. "But it can't be. I'm here."

"You *are* here," Bennett said, "in the one place you never wanted to be."

"You talk like a preacher," George sneered.

"Where do *you* think you are, George?" Bennett's voice wasn't as kind as Lana's. Bennett sounded harsh, as if he hadn't forgiven George's transgressions.

Damned parsons were all the same. They couldn't practice what they preached.

"Look around you, George," Lana invited. "Our children can't see you. They're turning away. They're hugging each other." She smiled to see them so intertwined. "They're hugging their husbands, their loved ones. Listen, George. Listen to what they're saying."

He didn't want to, but he had to. It was as if he could hear nothing else.

"I can't believe . . . it's finally over. I can't believe . . ." Hope put her head on Zack's chest and cried.

The others gathered around her.

"All those years." Pepper's voice shook. Dan held her, her back to his front, his arm crooked around her chest while she stroked

Hope's hair. "All those years I thought Daddy and Mama had abandoned us. All those years I hated them, and they . . ."

"If Daddy and Mama"—Kate cleared her throat, as if the names unsettled her—"if they were the good people you say, they would forgive you for anything you thought. They would understand."

George looked at Bennett and Lana, and they were nodding. Their eyes shone as they watched their children, and their hands stroked the aura of love around them, strengthening it, making it pulse with gold.

And Kate . . . Kate stood there in the center of the family. Those damned Prescotts. Every one of them smiled at her, hugged her, exclaimed over her. Kate looked awkward and uncomfortable, as if she didn't know how to deal with these strangers.

She would be happier with him. With George. Kate was *his.*

Bennett seemed to read his mind. "Not yours, George."

Almost his. Like Lana. Almost his. Kate would have been his, except for that bastard Ramos. She had her arm wrapped around him. She murmured loving words as she tried to look at his wound. She didn't seem to suffer any guilt at all about committing murder.

George's own murder.

"I can't be dead," George said loudly, as if saying it would make it true. "It's not possible."

"Look around, George." Evelyn's voice spoke from behind him.

Spinning around, he faced his wife.

She didn't look nearly as peaceful as Bennett and Lana Prescott. Her eyes were fierce and cold, and she wrung her hands over and over, as if nothing could ease her distress. She had bruises on her legs and her arms from falling down the stairs. A bloody cut opened her cheek, and her head sat oddly on her body.

Broken neck.

"I've been waiting for you, George." She waved at her grave with the double tombstone he had so lovingly had inscribed:

Dutiful daughter
Beloved wife
Dear companion

The other half of the stone was blank, awaiting another name.

"You bought the grave beside me. You had a politically correct tombstone placed between the graves. But you didn't plan on using it. You thought you'd be laid to rest beside your *new* wife. But your body will be here with me."

The grave was open. *His* grave was open. It looked as if someone had laid a coffin-sized rectangle over the green grass, a rectangle of black that blotted out all color, all light.

"Go and look, George," Evelyn commanded.

Her head had tilted sideways like a flower on a broken stem. The skin over her bruises peeled back. Still she stared at him, her eyes unforgiving, while she wrung her hands. *"Look,* George!"

George glanced at the Prescotts. Ramos had fallen. The Prescotts gathered around him, giving first aid. But George couldn't quite hear them. They seemed distant somehow, as if they'd moved away from him.

That man's body seemed to lie farther away, too. It seemed smaller. A fly had landed on the open wound and . . .

George flinched and turned his head away.

The grave was still open, a shaft of the blackest black he'd ever viewed. It was impossible, of course, but it appeared to lead down to . . . nothing.

He took a step toward it.

He turned back. Odd. He could still see Bennett and Lana perfectly well. Lana gazed at him. Tears shimmered in her eyes, and she looked as if she were sorry for him. Sorry for George Oberlin, senior senator and one of the wealthiest men in Texas!

Bennett looked grave and stern, like a minister of the Almighty who actually *believed* in God, actually *believed* in His commandments, actually *believed* in eternal damnation—and expected to see it done. Now.

"Go and look, George." Evelyn paced toward him. The wound on her cheek had broken open. She looked gruesome. And dead. And vengeful. "Look into your grave."

He didn't want to, but he didn't want her close to him, either. He didn't want her to know he was afraid, and for some reason, he had to know why that black rectangle was there.

He walked closer to that still, waiting darkness. Got within a foot. Stopped.

"Look!" Evelyn said.

He edged closer.

There was nothing down there. It was just . . . black. It didn't smell, it gave off neither heat nor cold, and when he leaned over, he could see . . . nothing. It was like looking into the depths of the universe where no star flickered in companionship, no sun gave warmth and brought forth life. It was a void. A blank.

Nothing.

"Justice is always done, George." Evelyn's voice spoke right in his ear.

He spun to look at her.

She looked healed and content. How was that possible?

He wanted to slap her. "I killed you. I killed them. I cheated and I lied. I blackmailed the highest men in the land. Justice?" He laughed, and for a wonderful moment he felt like himself again. Like George Oberlin, the most powerful man in Texas. "There's no justice in this world."

"You're not in that world." Evelyn sounded happy. Too happy.

Something grabbed his foot.

He looked down. A slice of the blackness had wrapped itself around his ankle, obliterating it.

He tried to leap away. He couldn't move.

"Sometimes justice takes a little time," Evelyn said.

Fingers of blackness crept up his leg. Like snakes they writhed.

"No!" He tried to shake them off.

They were inexorable, slithering, splitting apart, reforming . . .

He couldn't see his knee anymore. He couldn't feel his thigh. Parts of him . . . weren't there.

And at last he understood. The blackness was obliterating him. *Him,* George Oberlin. He was dead. It didn't matter that he had power, that he had money.

He was dead.

That *was* his body. This *was* his grave. He had faced some of the people he had killed. Now the darkness would take him.

He screamed.

The darkness gave a yank.

He flayed his arms. He toppled. He screamed again. The ground came up to meet his face. He clawed at the grass, but he couldn't feel it.

He opened his mouth to scream again, but he didn't have a mouth, and it wouldn't matter if he did. There was no sound. Everything was gone. All light, all language. Every dream, every thought. Every sense . . . evaporated.

Himself. His soul. Banished.

George Oberlin faded into eternal night.

Twenty-five

Teague came awake to the shriek of the ambulance and a single thought.

Was she okay? Was Kate okay?

He had a vague recollection of seeing Oberlin with a gun, of seeing Kate shoot him, of staggering around a graveyard with people. . . .

Kate's family.

Was she okay?

The strain of trying to remember made his brain feel as if it were bursting. Each rut in the road rattled his bones; some guy in blue fatigues stuck a needle in his arm.

Teague exploded into action. "You aren't going to drug me, you bastard. Let me go, I've got to save her!" Before she got shot. Before he had to face the results of his incompetence. His stupidity. For years and years . . . all those years, and this time it would be worse. So much worse.

"Teague, stop it right now!" A face appeared over the top of him.

"Kate?" It was Kate. She was beautiful. She looked healthy.

She looked stern. "You're hurt, and they're trying to help you. We're going to transfer to the helicopter to go to San Antonio, but you've got to calm down."

A needle pricked his arm. He could still feel the pain, but as if it was someone else's. The most wonderful sense of well-being lifted him. "Kate, I love you."

"Sh." She place her cool hand on his hot cheek. "Not too long now."

He did love her. What a fool he had been not to realize it sooner. What else should he tell her? Oh. He knew. "Will you marry me?"

Her lips moved, but now, although he heard the words, he couldn't comprehend what she said. Yet he did comprehend one thing. She had only just found her family, yet she had remained with him. She was coming to the hospital with him.

He relaxed against the stretcher. He let the paramedics torture him with needles and bandages.

Because he'd saved Kate. She was alive and unharmed.

For once in his life, he had stopped the bullet and saved the woman he loved.

Kate stood alone in the hospital waiting room, rubbing her arms and wishing somebody, anybody would come out of that door and tell her Teague was going to be all right. She knew he was alive. But she'd never seen so much blood.

Wooziness struck her, and she staggered to the drinking fountain. She bent down, put her face in the stream of water, and hoped none of the other people in the waiting room had noticed.

As the faintness subsided, Kate stood. Leaning her hand against the wall, she stared at her feet.

Teague had been irrational in the ambulance, trying to hit the paramedics and shouting. She'd calmed him down enough for them to give him his medication, but dear God. So much blood. And then . . .

She wanted her mother.

Kate rubbed her forehead hard.

She wanted her mother, and she was going to get her whole family. They'd been nice at the cemetery, introducing themselves, petting her as if she were a long-lost dog. But Kate didn't know them. Hope and Pepper, Dan and Zack, Gabriel . . .

Who were they really? She didn't remember any of them. They couldn't comfort her right now any more than the strangers who sat in the waiting room or the cowed volunteer who manned the sign-in desk or the callous nurse who ran the ER like a drill sergeant. Kate wanted her mother.

"Darling!" The beloved, familiar voice spoke from the doorway. "We came as fast as we can."

Kate jerked her head up. "Mom!"

Her mother hurried into the waiting room and took Kate into her arms. "How is he? Is it bad?"

"I don't know." Kate let her head drop onto her mother's shoulder. "Oh, M-Mom." Kate's first sob broke forth. "I'm afraid he's going to d-die from saving me."

Gentle hands clasped Kate, clasped her mom, led them both to a couch.

"The bullet sliced through his scalp," a man's voice said. "It's probably not serious."

Kate lifted her head.

Everyone was here. Her whole family. Surrounding her and her mom.

She looked at the man who had spoken. Dark eyes, blond hair, tanned, tough-looking. He was related to her.

Right now, she couldn't remember his name.

"That's Dan, my husband. He's a rancher and a former terrorist hunter." Kate's sister seemed to recognize Kate's confusion. *Pepper* recognized Kate's confusion. Black, curly hair, green eyes, a face that should, in years past, have led Kate into mischief.

"Probably?" Kate choked.

"Dan's not a doctor, but he's seen a lot of wounds," Hope spoke. Kate's other sister. Brown hair, blue eyes, a face that made Kate feel as if she'd come home.

"He was . . . was fighting them." Tears welled in Kate's eyes. Impatiently, she brushed them away. She couldn't see, and she needed to see, to hear, to be alert in case the doctor came out to report on Teague. "The paramedics. He was fighting them. I got him calmed d-down. Th-they gave him a painkiller, and all of a s-sudden, his eyes rolled back in his head and he was uncon . . . unconscious."

Mom kept her arm around Kate's shoulder.

"I've seen a lot of bullet wounds, had a few, too, and being unconscious is not necessarily a bad thing," Dan said.

"The paramedics thought it was. They jumped on him, started oxygen and . . . I don't know what they were doing." Kate took a long, wobbly breath.

Hope turned to her husband. "Zack, can you find out what's going on?"

Zack—black hair streaked with silver, dark eyes, distinguished-looking—nodded, patted Kate's shoulder, and strode toward the desk where Godzilla the Monster Nurse reigned with contempt and disinterest.

"Don't worry, Caitlin, people tell Zack what he wants to know." Gabriel spoke. Kate's foster brother. Dark hair, green eyes. Handsome.

"She wouldn't talk to me." Kate's voice still wobbled abominably, and she never took her gaze off Zack. "She wouldn't tell me anything."

Zack spoke to Godzilla, and when she answered scornfully, he put his hands flat on the desk, leaned over, and spoke again.

Godzilla straightened. Without removing

her gaze from Zack, she picked up the phone and made a call. She took notes, then handed them to Zack, explained them, and watched as he strode back to the waiting family.

"How did he do that?" Kate whispered.

"You should have seen him calling in a helicopter for us so we could follow you here." Marilyn sounded awed. "He has a way of addressing people that makes them want to help him."

"It's the result of having way too much money all his life," Hope said.

Zack walked up. "The bullet creased Teague's skull. He's in shock. He has a concussion. That's why he's unconscious."

"Is he going to be all right?" Kate asked.

"She wouldn't say a word about that. She said she's not allowed. But she sort of nodded, so I assume the prognosis is good. Or at least not bad." Zack nodded, too, in satisfaction.

The relief was so strong, Kate closed her eyes and put her head back on her mother's shoulder.

"Thank God!" Hope made the words more than an exclamation. They were a prayer.

"Yes, thank God." Kate's mother rubbed

Kate's back in that momlike manner that comforted her so much.

"Teague's in ICU," Zack said. "Kate, you can see him. The doctor's coming to walk you down and fill you in."

Kate stood at once.

Her mom remained sitting, her hand still in Kate's.

"That nurse told me only relatives could see Teague." Kate kept her gaze on the door. "I told her there weren't any relatives. She said she guessed he wouldn't have visitors then."

Everyone looked toward the nurse in horror.

Not a muscle moved on Zack's face. "I convinced her otherwise."

At that moment, Kate realized how protectively the family hovered around her. *Her* family. Until four hours ago, Kate hadn't heard their names since she was ten months old. Now they were here. They were anxious—about Kate. About their little sister.

It was odd and wonderful and . . . just odd.

But she didn't have time to think about it, because a tired-looking woman in a white coat stepped into the room. "Miss Mont-gomery?"

Kate hurried toward her.

"Hi, I'm Dr. Kahn." The doctor shook Kate's hand. "You can see Mr. Ramos, but I warn you, he's very still and very pale."

On the way to ICU, Dr. Kahn assured Kate the bullet had barely touched Teague's skull, but any contact between a bullet and the head made her unhappy. Still, she thought he would recover with no problem except for some crushing headaches. She warned Kate that the bruising from the acci-dent and the bullet looked worse than it was. She led Kate to the bed, where Teague was connected to tubes, monitors, and printers that spat forth unintelligible gibber-ish, and admonished, "Ten minutes only."

His stillness hit Kate like a blow. She was used to seeing him vital, responsive, and so alive that a current of awareness always arced between them. Now he was pale, his purpling bruises showing beneath the white bandages that wrapped his skull. "Oh, Teague," she whispered. Carefully she took his hand. It lay limp in hers. "Teague, listen. I love you. I want you to be awake so I can tell you. Teague, I love you."

He squeezed her fingers. Just the slightest pressure.

And one of his monitors went off.

Dr. Kahn and a nurse hurried toward the bed. Dr. Kahn looked at the readout, then lifted Teague's eyelids, and shone her flashlight in his pupils. She smiled. "Well. Good."

"Is he conscious?" Kate asked.

"No, but he won't be unconscious forever."

The satisfaction in Dr. Kahn's voice made Kate straighten. "Was there a chance of that?"

"We're talking modern medicine and the human brain. There's always a chance for anything." Dr. Kahn put her flashlight away. "Five minutes, and keep talking to him."

When Kate walked back into the waiting room, the family, her family, assaulted her with questions. "How did he look?" "What did the doctor say?" "Do you feel better now?"

Kate told them the whole story, and when she was finished, her family indulged in a discreet celebration that made Godzilla say, in chilling tones, "Other families are here, and their less fortunate circumstances should be considered."

"She's right." Gabriel herded them toward the door. "Come on. I scouted out this floor. There's a patio this way for patient and visitor use."

Godzilla's glare made them feel like guilty schoolchildren.

As they escaped, Pepper gave a muffled snort. Hope snickered. Soon the whole group shook with guilty, suppressed laughter as they made their way toward the glass doors that led outside onto a roof garden. There dim lights shone on the few hardy potted plants that struggled for life against the chill wind.

Dan and Gabriel held the doors while Kate and her sisters stepped outside. Then their hilarity burst forth. They giggled together, saying things like, "Did you see her?" "I thought she was going to breathe fire."

They hiccuped to a halt. Their gazes met. *Family.* The truth began to sink into Kate. These were her sisters. She had a *family.*

"She looks so much like Mama," Pepper said in an awed voice.

"We would have found her eventually." With shaking fingers, Hope pushed Kate's hair away from her face. "She would have become a national reporter and when we saw her, we would have known."

"Thank you for . . ." Kate hardly knew what to say. They remembered her. She didn't remember them, and she didn't know how to deal with the obviously wrenching emotions her sisters experienced. Feeling awkward and out of kilter, she said, "Thank you for looking for me. For never giving up. When I think of all the years you spent, I can't believe it. You were so strong."

"You were our baby. We had to find you," Hope said.

Kate glanced at the three guys. They still hadn't come out. They were still bunched together holding the doors, and they looked uncomfortable and unhappy—men caught between two conflicting currents of emotion and uncomfortable with them both.

"Where's Mom? Where's my mother?" Kate looked inside, and there stood her mother, watching Kate with her sisters and wiping silent tears off her cheeks.

"Mom?" Kate started back inside.

"Oh, no!" Hope said. "We forgot about your mother."

"We're shits, all happy to see each other

while we neglect her." Pepper sounded disgusted.

Kate threw her arms around her mom's
neck. "What's wrong? Why are you crying?"

"I feel so h-horrible." Mom could scarcely
speak. "All these y-years, I d-deprived you
of this wonderful f-family and them of y-you.
It's all m-my fault."

Hope followed and elbowed Kate aside.
"Your fault? All these years, we've been so
afraid for Caitlin. We were afraid she was
mistreated. We were afraid she'd been sold
into slavery." Hope choked up. She shook
her head as she unsuccessfully tried to
speak again.

Pepper picked up where Hope left off.
"We were afraid she was dead. Now we discover this beautiful, wonderful woman is our
sister, and she's had a happy life, and we're
so happy and so relieved. So yes, it's your
fault she grew up happy, and we love you
for it. You're part of our family now."

Kate wanted to kiss them both. Mom was
still crying, but she was smiling, too. She
opened her arms. "I'd be honored to be part
of your family."

Kate didn't know how to be a sister. Not to
anyone—not to these women, not to those

men. But at the moment Hope and Pepper embraced Mom, Kate embraced the family.

The Prescotts were once again a family.

Six days later, Teague watched Kate walk into his hospital room. At the sight of him in his leather jacket and his jeans and running shoes, her eyes widened. Her smile blossomed. She seemed so damned happy to see him.

Well. He could cure that.

She wore blue jeans, a long-sleeved white T-shirt, and a hideous brown, blue, and orange thigh-length knit cardigan that he wouldn't have given to the poor.

She looked . . . beautiful.

His breath caught, and the headache that nagged at his brain—and that he always denied having—worsened.

"You're dressed!" she said.

"And ready to go." He picked up his suitcase and headed toward the door. "More than ready to go."

"You can't just walk out of here." She caught his arm. "The nurse will bring a wheelchair."

Her touch seared him like a lightning bolt.

Didn't she know . . . ? Didn't she realize . . . ? Every time she brushed her lips
against his, every time she slid her arm beneath his shoulders, he burned with need.

During the last week, he'd carefully
wrapped himself in indifference. Emptiness
would work as an anesthesia against the
pain that he knew would come . . . when he
told her the truth.

But every time she touched him, the elec-
tricity blasted away the darkness, illuminating the dark corners of his soul and bringing
him to unwilling life.

He steeled himself to sound indifferent. "I
don't need a wheelchair."

She sounded patient and amused when
she replied, "The hospital doesn't care if
you need a wheelchair. They don't want you
to fall down on the way out and sue them."

Great. She'd started humoring him. She
probably didn't feel the strain of not making
love for a week. She certainly seemed to be
handling the advent of her family well.

Better than he was. All the Prescotts had
come to visit him once a day, and they
had enfolded him in their affections. He
had saved their sister's life. They loved him
without reservation.

When they weren't here, Kate talked about them. She filled him in on all their idiosyncrasies, where they went, and what they ate. She confessed her mixed feelings about inheriting such a close-knit family—God knows he related to that. She told him how strange she felt when she realized she had killed another human being—although Oberlin had scarcely fit the description.

He told her how he had handled the amazing mix of emotions he'd experienced when he'd killed in the service. When he was done, she nodded and told him that Dan had said the same things.

Kate didn't need him anymore. Oberlin had been right about one thing: Teague didn't fit in her life.

"I don't want a wheelchair," he said stubbornly.

"You tell her." Kate widened her eyes in mock horror. "Godzilla's on duty."

"Shit." The crease in his skull ached. He pressed his fingers into his forehead.

The door bumped open, revealing a wheelchair with Godzilla the Monster Nurse at the helm.

Kate rubbed his arm, then stepped away to let Godzilla manage him into the chair.

Before he knew it, he was traveling through the hospital corridors like an old man so enfeebled he couldn't even walk a block. The passing nurses bid him cheery farewells, and two of them smiled in a way that reminded him he was not an enfeebled old man but valuable dating material.

Kate noticed, too, because she moved closer and put her hand on his shoulder.

And the lightning flashed through him again.

He shouldn't have made love to her in a storm. The charge still lingered in the air, igniting his desire and scrambling his thoughts.

He'd lost his mind . . . and his heart.

Near the entrance to the hospital, Kate took his suitcase and left him to bring her car around. He waited grimly, Godzilla breathing down his neck, but she couldn't stop him when Kate drove up. He stood and got in the car on his own. Godzilla slammed the door as if she were glad to be rid of him.

"Let's get out of here." He glanced over at Kate.

She put the car in gear and drove off, and she was grinning. She had the nerve to look happy.

"What?" he snapped.

"A week ago, I thought you were dead." She actually sounded happy, too. "Now I'm taking you home."

"No, you're not. We're going to visit . . . someone." Bleakly he took Fate by the neck and twisted. "Turn left here."

Kate raised her eyebrows, but did as she was told. "Do I get to know who we're going to visit?"

"Juanita."

"Juanita from Ramos Security?"

"Yes." He took a breath. "Her name is Juanita Ramos."

Kate stiffened. "She's your . . . ?"

"Cousin. Juanita is my cousin."

"Good." Kate relaxed again, handling the powerful little car with ease. "Any reason why we're visiting her now when you should be going home to rest? I mean, I can chat with your relatives later."

"No. There is no later." He couldn't delay. He'd been dreading this moment ever since he woke in ICU and realized that for the first time in his life, he loved someone with all the fervor and fire of his Latin soul. Love . . . love required the truth. No woman could love him once she *knew.* Certainly not Kate with her Protestant morality and her upright character.

Of course, she would feel sorry for him. Be kind to him . . . and the thought of her kindness made him grind his teeth.

Kate pulled up to Juanita's apartment building and parked in a visitor's parking space.

The place was shabby, in need of paint, and Teague found himself explaining, "She won't let me help her. She insists on living on her wages, and her condition is expensive. . . ." He trailed off. He shouldn't be trying to whitewash himself. "Come on."

They got out. Kate met him in front of the car. He indicated the way, but she didn't seem to understand he wanted her to walk ahead. Instead she slid her hand into his. "Is she expecting us?"

"Yes." Tension held him in its grip.

"Are there more in your family?"

"No one that I claim."

"Then this is sort of like meeting your parents, isn't it?" Her grip tightened.

He wanted to shake free of Kate's hand. He wanted to kiss her fingers. He wanted to be absorbed into her bloodstream, see with her, hear with her, breathe with her. He was dying a slow, agonizing death, and she didn't even seem aware of his pain.

"No." He stopped before Juanita's door. He knocked. "No. Not at all like that."

The look Kate shot him told him she wasn't as unaware as she would like him to think. She knew something was going on. . . . Well, of course she did. He hadn't voluntarily touched her since he awoke six days ago. And he wished he could kiss her one last time.

She seemed to know what he was thinking, and she was willing. She leaned against him, her body pliant. She turned her face up. She closed her eyes.

His resistance was no match for her surrender.

Juanita answered the door. "Oops!" Her brown eyes twinkled. "Want me to go away again?"

"No." Harshly he shook off Kate's enchantment.

As if she were hurt, Kate looked down and bit her lip. But better a little pain now than the slow grinding disillusionment of years.

Juanita moved her wheelchair out of the way. "Come in! I've been expecting you." At home, she usually wore a loose-fitting dress and slippers to keep her feet warm. Today she was dressed like the hostess at a party, with a red shirt that made her dark hair glow, a flowered skirt that looked appropriate for a fiesta, and flats that looked fashionably comfy.

"Something smells good." Kate followed Juanita through the tiny apartment toward the dining room.

"I knew Teague would be hungry after eating that awful hospital food—unfortunately I know my way around the hospital—so I fixed shrimp enchiladas and charro beans."

Teague couldn't believe the round laden table with its celebratory tablecloth, the loaded casserole, the Crock-Pot, and the shining silverware.

"And look—" Juanita lifted a cloth napkin to show them a pile of tortillas.

"Did you make them yourself?" Kate asked.

"No, but I bought them at the Tortilla Stand." Juanita grinned. "Margarita?"

"Only one. Teague's not allowed to drive." Kate grinned back.

"I'll bet he hates that." Juanita moved efficiently through her kitchen, putting the finishing touches on the salad. "Teague, would you pour while I get the plates?"

"I can drive." Teague could scarcely contain his irritation as he poured Kate a margarita from the frosted pitcher. This meeting was not going as he had planned. He'd envisioned a hurried visit to show Kate the reality of Juanita's condition, then a quick conversation and a speedy dismissal, followed by years of desolation.

Yet Kate had said she was meeting his relatives, and she'd acted as if it meant something. Juanita was behaving the same way. What was it with women? Why did they have to make everything an event? Why did they have to make unwarranted assumptions?

What was he going to do without Kate?

He knew the answer. He'd seen hell a few times in his life. He walked through hell more than once. He recognized hell in the darkness, the barrenness of light, of emotion, of being. And when Kate was gone, he would live in hell.

"Your home is lovely." Kate sipped her drink. "Did you decorate it yourself?"

"Thank you, I did! I knew I wanted a little sense of home—Teague probably told you I was raised in the same border town as he was—"

"No. He just today told me you were his cousin." Kate's voice was matter-of-fact as she tattled on him. "I thought he was a complete and total orphan."

"He doesn't tell people we're related." Juanita's voice was equally matter-of-fact. "He has a thing about nepotism, and of course I can't get a job just anywhere. I have to work for him or take a lower-paying job."

Teague hated that it was true. "Juanita's the best security person we have. Her reports have resulted in more than a dozen arrests in the past year."

"I owe the state of Texas a lot," Juanita said. "The Shriners Hospital in Houston operated on me for free. That's why I'm able to get around as well as I do. So it's kind of great being able to say I protect the capitol."

"I used to have a job at the capitol, too." Kate dipped a chip in the beans. "This is wonderful. You'll have to give me the recipe."

"What do you mean, you *used* to have a

job at the capitol?" Teague knew he wasn't going to like the answer.

"I got fired." Kate's mouth looked a little puckered. "Brad seemed to think I'd been nothing but a waste of money since I got to the station."

"That son of a bitch!" Teague couldn't believe it. "Doesn't he realize what you've gone through?"

"He doesn't care. He didn't want to hire me in the first place, and he doesn't have to keep me now." Kate looked remarkably unconcerned.

But Teague knew better. She loved her job. "I'll talk to him."

"No, you will not. I've already had one person fixing my employment." Kate's eyes flashed. "I'm not having another one."

"I think we'd better eat." Juanita placed little bowls of sour cream and *pico de gallo* on the table, and a small smile creased her thin cheeks.

When Teague and Kate had seated themselves, Juanita rolled into her place and took each of their hands. "At every meal, I always thank God for another day of life. Today I thank God for your lives, too."

Twenty-six

By the time Teague and Kate left Juanita's apartment two hours later, Kate had been regaled with Juanita's humorous version of Teague's teenage years. She hadn't told Kate everything—she hadn't told Kate the big thing—but she had painted a picture of a swaggering tough who stood down gangs to protect his little cousin in the school yard and then whimpered over a haircut.

Teague watched as Kate laughed at all the right places, and the sound of her merriment felt like knives in his gut.

But she was thoughtful and silent as they made their way to her car. She probably made some assumptions. Probably the right ones. The next hour would be difficult, but he'd been through worse hours, and when it was over—well, it would be over.

He watched the scenery swing by, and said, "You've taken a wrong turn, Kate."

"I'm not taking you home." She took another turn.

"I don't want to go to your house."

"I'm not going to my house, either." She had a determined jut to her chin. An ominous jut.

He waited, but she didn't continue. "Where are we going?" he asked.

"To the park on Town Lake."

Which was a pretty park and a pretty lake, but he wanted to get this confrontation over with, not have a picnic. "Why are we going there?"

"It's wonderful this time of year." That was no answer, but she didn't volunteer anything more.

She pulled into the almost empty parking lot. The grass was still green—of course, it was Texas and barely November—but some of the leaves had turned color. Through the branches, the lake was smooth and blue. A couple huddled together on a picnic table. No one else was in sight.

Kate turned to Teague. "Shall we walk?"

"Sure." His head still hurt, but he figured the pain would be relieved as soon as he finally told her what he had to tell her. "We've got to talk, anyway."

"I know." She opened her door. "So let's walk."

Ah. That was why she'd come here. She wanted to talk, too, and on neutral ground.

They strolled side by side across the lawn toward the lake's edge, but this time she didn't reach out and take his hand. This time, she didn't touch him at all.

The day was chilly, probably fifty-five degrees, and even with his leather jacket on he was cold. He told himself it was because he'd just left the hospital. Actually, it was the distance between them. A distance he'd better get used to.

Not far from the water, she sat on the grass, turned up her collar, tucked her hands in the pockets of her sweater. The silence between them became uncomfortable, then deadly, and Kate made no effort to lift it. If someone was going to start the conversation, it had to be him.

He was glad he was standing over her. He could impose the truth on her. She needed to know.

"It's my fault Juanita's in that wheelchair." There. The truth had come out too bluntly, but at least he'd said it.

"I'd sort of figured that out." Kate tucked her face further into the collar of her sweat. And waited.

"Juanita . . . when Juanita talks about me, I sound so innocent. I wasn't." God bless Juanita. She loved him and made him out to be better than he was. "I ran with a gang. Was one of the leaders. Played out my life on the streets. Drank and did drugs. Would have died in the gutter, just like my mother predicted, except . . ."

"You got a wake-up call." Kate looked across the lake.

"Sure. You can call it that. My mother . . . I'll never forget what my mother said that morning." The words, the ones he never could speak aloud before, spewed forth dipped in the vitriol of the past. *"Teague, you little bastard, don't be so goddamned stupid. You're a goddamned stupid half-breed gringo and if you get knifed, no one will care. I sure as hell won't. But that kid is only fourteen. You can't take her to a gang fight. Her father's the meanest son of a bitch I ever met, and I've met a few. If something happens to his kid, he'll kill you. Besides, she's smart. She's a nice kid. Not like you."*

"Your mother must have been a pleasure." Kate didn't meet his eyes.

The dark emptiness now encroached

without any encouragement. "A lousy mother is no excuse for what I did."

"No, you're right." Kate accepted that all too easily. "So you took Juanita to the gang fight."

"From the time she was little, she tagged around after me. She worshiped me, and I took care of her. It made me feel strong. Benevolent." Bitterly he said, "What a joke."

"She still seems to like you. If I didn't know better, I'd say she was selling me on you today."

Juanita *had* been selling him to Kate. "She wants me to marry."

"Of course she does. And why not?"

"I . . ." *I haven't met the right woman.* But he couldn't say that. He didn't believe it.

And from the sudden sparkle in Kate's eyes, she wouldn't accept that answer.

"Finish your story," she said.

"That kid is only fourteen. She'll follow you into hell . . . and she did. Juanita wanted to come see a gang war, so I *brought* her. It was time she toughened up, smelled the blood, felt the excitement of fighting with knives, of winning. We broke windows. We looted. We waged war on one another, and the police couldn't keep up with us." He still

remembered the dust rising from the streets, the shouts, the sweat.

His head throbbed harder. "Then somebody broke the rules. Someone brought a gun." The words had been so easy, words he'd rehearsed all week, a flat retelling of horrific events. But now they dried up and he was left with one memory.

The sound of that single gunshot.

He'd heard a lot of gunfire since, but even now, it rang in his ears.

He walked away from the memories and from Kate, but he couldn't stay away. He had to finish the story. He came back, and again he told himself it would all be done in about an hour. He could survive anything for an hour.

"One bullet. That bullet severed Juanita's spinal chord. She almost died." She had fallen at his feet, still conscious, and looked up at him. "I should have died."

"But you didn't." Kate seemed disconnected in a way he'd never imagined. "God or Fate or whatever you believe in decided you should stay."

"Yes. And face what I had done." Over and over again. "That night when I went home . . . I found the cops there."

"To arrest you?"

"No. To tell me my mother went out on the streets, drunk and God knows what else, screaming insults at the police—and somehow, she ended up dead." The dark and the cold enveloped him. "It was a hell of a day."

"So you killed your mother, too."

At Kate's cruel words, the last, faint shred of hope, a shred he hadn't even recognized, shriveled.

He bared his teeth. "No. No, I'm not taking credit for that. My mother was a prostitute when it suited her. If she had a windfall, she spent it as fast as she could. She was mean drunk and she was mean sober, and she didn't go out that day to rescue Juanita. She didn't want me to take Juanita out because she was scared of her brother. She went out that day . . . because she liked to live in hell, and hell was happening almost on her doorstep."

"I know." Kate's gaze flashed to meet his. "Juanita told me."

For the first time, Teague realized he'd been handled. And as Kate stood and brushed the grass off her rear, he got the feeling he was about to be handled some more. "What else did Juanita tell you?"

"After you were shot, she was worried to death about you. We talked quite a bit. She pretty much told me what you told me, but she added a few things." Kate shook back her hair, the same way she did when she was doing an interview. "She said before the accident her father used to beat her, and you stood up to him. Even when you were half his size, you attacked him, distracted him, took the blows for her."

"It made me feel important."

"To be someone's hero? Sure it did, but you suffered a lot of pain for that importance." Kate walked to the shore, picked up a stone, and skipped it across the water. "Juanita told me while she lay bleeding in the streets, you stood guard over her, protected her from the riot, rode with her in the ambulance. She said her father tried to kill you in the waiting room."

"Yeah, if someone was going to hurt her, he wanted it to be him." What a great family he'd come from.

"She said that he chased you out of town, that you went and joined the service." Kate skipped another rock. "She said when she came home from the hospital, her father left her in her bed to rot. You sneaked in when

you had leave. You took the most dangerous missions so you could have the extra
pay, and as soon as you had enough
money, you left the service, brought her to
the Shriner's Hospital for her surgeries; then
when she had recovered, you gave her a job
at Ramos Security."

"I owed her."

"Of course you did." Kate turned and
walked toward him, right at him, her eyes
fixed on his, and now he saw the determina-
tion in her. "But you paid the debt. Juanita's
not a stupid woman, and she's not some
wheelchair-bound saint who sees only
the best in you." Kate lashed at him. "She
knows what happened. She knows what
you owed. She told me you'd more than
paid the debt. And she loves you. Do you
value her love so little that you believe
you're worth nothing?"

"You don't understand. It's not that simple." But it took all his strength of will not to
back away from Kate's advance.

"Yes. It is. You did a horrible, stupid thing.
So did everyone in those gangs that day. But
I doubt any of them have paid as dearly as
you have." Before he could answer, she continued, "I've done horrible, stupid things, too.

I got a ticket for driving too fast—but I didn't drive off the road or cause an accident."

"That's hardly the same thing."

"It could have been worse, but I was *lucky.* And I'm a smart woman, but that day I got mad at you for lying to me, so I went to Hobart thinking I could do a simple investigation. Look what happened. I got you and Melissa Cunningham shot, and I came this close"—Kate held out her fingers a centimeter apart—"to being killed myself. What do I owe Melissa? What do I owe you?"

"Nothing." He didn't want Kate to think she owed him. "It's not like that."

"Well, too bad, because I'm going to name my firstborn daughter after Melissa, and I'm going to love you for the rest of my days." Kate's voice grew choked. She shook with suppressed tears. "And there's not a thing you can do about it, Teague Ramos, so don't you ever try to stop me."

He stared at her. At those bright blue eyes, shining with tears of sincerity. At the soft skin, the long throat, and her lips, trembling under the force of her emotions. At the force of her love.

Inside him, something broke. The darkness that had haunted him all his life crumpled into ruin and slid away.

He felt free, lighter and buoyed by love. Kate's love.

In a voice hoarse with devotion, he said, "You don't owe me anything, but if you want to give me something, there's only one thing I would ever want . . . and that is your love."

"Well, good." She fumbled in her pocket, pulled out a Kleenex, and noisily blew her nose.

"Yeah. Good." He had a stupid grin on his face. "This last week has been hell."

"I know." She wiped at her cheeks. "A guy shouldn't propose and then pass out."

"Huh?" Was she serious? She had looked serious. "When . . . ?" Recollection fell on him like a piano out of the sky. He remembered. The pain, the panic, the joy he felt at the sound of her voice. "In the ambulance. I proposed and I said . . ." Oh, God. He'd said he loved her. He had proposed!

He could never remember being so discomfited. He turned away from her, stared out at the lake, raked his fingers through his hair. "Listen, I was out of my mind."

"So the only time you'll tell me you love

me is if you're shot?" She slid her hands up his arms to his shoulders.

And that damnable lightning streaked through him again. "I don't mean that."

"Good. While I'm willing to shoot you to hear that you love me, I might miss one day and really hurt you."

He laughed. He turned into her embrace and looked down at her face. Kate held power in herself. Strength in her smile. Like her mother, she had the ability to command the light, and she brought the light into him. So, completely conscious and quite aware of his words, he knelt before her. "I love you, Kate Montgomery. I'm the wrong guy for you. You deserve something more than a man so damned by his past he'll never be free of the demons." He took her hand. Gently, he rubbed her knuckles. "But Kate, you'll never find anyone who loves you more than I do."

"That's all I ask."

"Will you marry me?"

"Yes, Teague Ramos." She slid her hands through his hair. "I would be honored."

Melissa Cunningham leaned close to Hope and in a stage whisper asked, "Do you suppose Caitlin and her man ran out for a quickie?"

"No, Melissa. They didn't run out for a quickie."

"It's been a half hour and no sign of them yet." Melissa looked around the church, listened to the rustles and the whispers as the congregation got restless, and added, "That quartet you hired must be getting tired. They're going to want more money."

Hope reflected that having all her dreams come true carried a heavy fine—she was eternally indebted to Melissa Cunningham for defying George Oberlin, taking a bullet on behalf of the Prescott family, and delaying Oberlin long enough so that Teague was able to rescue Kate.

Unfortunately, Melissa and Hope were the same age, so now Melissa considered herself Hope's best friend. She sat beside Hope in the church and made what she thought were humorous comments while the rest of the family smothered appalled laughter.

"You know, when we were teenagers, I never liked you," Melissa said reflectively. "It always seemed you were better than me at everything you did. But you've changed."

Seated at Hope's side, Zack shook with hilarity.

Pepper craned her neck around him and mockingly widened her eyes.

Hope was glad Gabriel stood with Marilyn at the back of the church, waiting to walk Caitlin down the aisle—if she ever came down the aisle—or Hope would never hear the end of this.

After all, Hope, Pepper, and Gabriel were thrilled to be reunited, but they *were* siblings.

"I would've thought Caitlin would ask her sisters to be her bridesmaids." Melissa had worn purple and red to the wedding with gray running shoes and no socks. An interesting choice.

"Kate has a lot of friends she's known for years. She asked them to be bridesmaids. She needed someone to sit in the front row and be her family." And, to tell the truth, Hope and Pepper had asked to sit during the ceremony.

All these years, they had both strained and struggled toward one moment, the moment when the whole family was together again, healthy and whole. Now they'd achieved that goal, and this was the official celebration of their triumph.

But where was the bride?

The Prescott family was back in Hobart, in Daddy's own church. The redbrick building held no more than three hundred people. It was full. The entire Givens family was here, as were the extended Graham clan and Pepper's best friend Rita and her family. Griswald stood at the back directing the entire wedding, and what he must think of Caitlin's nonappearance, Hope couldn't imagine.

But when this was all over, she bet he would tell her.

The Montgomerys were here, and Marilyn's family, which included, as far as Hope could tell, half of Texas. Jason Urbano, his wife, and his children sat right behind the Givens family.

Whatever empty space existed in the pews, the town filled.

Not all the town, of course. The police—or rather, former police—weren't here. The county judge had been ousted in a recall election, and he chose to stay away.

But the majority of Hobart, the ones who had had nothing to do with Oberlin's crimes—they were here if they'd been able to finagle an invitation, and if they hadn't, they waited at the reception.

Last week, after Hope and Pepper arrived in Hobart to finish the preparations for the wedding, they'd been stopped time and again while people expressed their pleasure at having them back. And if sometimes people's gazes skittered away, that was all right. They hadn't done anything to save the Prescott family, but Hope understood that they had been trying to live their lives and not get run over by the lethal tank that was George Oberlin.

As Hope's eight-year-old daughter, Lana, had said, "Ding-dong, the witch is dead."

And as Pepper's six-year-old son, Russell, had said, "Witches are girls, stupid."

So Lana had knocked him flat.

The family kept those two cousins separated as much as possible. Zack said it saved on emergency room visits.

"Even if Kate doesn't marry that guy, the church looks beautiful." Melissa gazed around with pride.

"She will, and yes, it does." Hope had given Melissa the task of refurbishing the aging church, and she'd done a marvelous job. The fresh white paint gleamed, the stained-glass windows shone, the altar sported a snowy-white altar cloth embroidered by Melissa herself with colors so delicate Hope wondered if Melissa hid a different side.

Hope slid a sideways glance at Melissa as she spit on her handkerchief and scrubbed at a spot on her dress.

No. Melissa had not a subtle bone in her body.

"I'm hearing something at the back." Melissa craned her neck around. "Yep, there's Teague's cousin coming now. Wonder what she's got to say."

Juanita rolled down the aisle and stopped by the Prescotts. Hope and Pepper—and Melissa—leaned forward to hear the explanation. "I had to do some work on Kate's dress. Move her bustle up to cover the open buttons."

"What?" Hope blinked in surprise. "What are you saying? The dress fit two weeks ago."

"She's had a little swelling around the waist since then." Juanita smiled at their open-mouthed astonishment.

"Glory be, she's pregnant!" Melissa said.

Hope and Pepper turned on her. "Sh!"

Tittering swept the church.

"She's four months along," Juanita said.

"But her size shouldn't have changed that much in two weeks," Pepper protested.

"That happened to my aunt," Melissa said. "She had twins." She had their full attention and would have said more, but at that moment the quartet played the opening strains of the processional.

Juanita rolled into place on the groom's side of the church.

"Look at that!" Melissa exclaimed. "We have a bride. This wedding's going to take place after all!"

The small door behind the altar opened, and Teague filed out, followed by six groomsmen. A grinning Big Bob towered over them all.

Catching Hope's eye, Teague nodded. Then he trained his gaze at the back of the church.

He looked so handsome, and he loved Caitlin so much.

Hope's throat started to close with emotion.

Oh, no. Not already.

The bridesmaids, dressed in pink satin

gowns, came down the aisle two by two, followed by Pepper's three-year-old twins, Courtney and Matthew.

They were so cute in their miniature outfits. And except for a small incident halfway down the aisle, when Matthew wanted to drop rose petals and Courtney shouted, "No! You have the ring!" they performed very well.

Hope felt the tears gather in her eyes.

Then the organist played the first bars of the "Wedding March," and Caitlin stepped into view. Marilyn stood on one side, a vibrant woman who had raised Hope's baby sister to be a confident person. Gabriel stood on her other side, an amazing man who had overcome all obstacles to rejoin their family.

And Caitlin. She wore a simple, white, off-the-shoulder gown that had a beaded bodice and a small train. They had pinned Hope's veil into her dark hair.

Pepper had worn it, too.

So, Lana declared, would she.

An upsweep bared Caitlin's long neck. She wore diamond studs in her ears. Like every bride, she looked beautiful.

But it was the way she looked at Teague

that made Hope burst into tears. Caitlin looked at Teague as if he were the only man in the world who could make her happy. Hope recognized that look. It was the look Pepper got when she looked at Dan. And Hope knew it was the same look she wore when she looked at Zack.

The congregation stood as the bride started down the aisle.

Hope found Zack's handkerchief thrust into her hand.

Pepper traded places with him, and she was crying, too. In a whisper, she said, "I wish Daddy and Mama were here to see this."

Hope nodded fiercely.

With cheerful certainty, Melissa said, "Oh, dear girls, they're here. Don't you worry, they're here."

CHRISTINA DODD's novels appear regularly on the bestseller lists of *The New York Times, USA Today,* and *Publishers Weekly.* She is the author of twenty-seven novels, including *Some Enchanted Evening, One Kiss from You, Scandalous Again,* and *My favorite Bride,* as well as two previous bestsellers featuring the Prescott sisters: *Almost Like Being in Love* and *Just the Way You Are.* Dodd also coauthored *Once Upon a Pillow,* a sparkling romantic saga published by Pocket Books. She has won numerous awards, including the prestigious Romance Writers of America's Golden Heart and RITA Awards. She lives in Washington State. For updates and to sign up for her newsletter, visit her website at christinadodd.com.